Also by Martin Sylvester:

A LETHAL VINTAGE

A

DANGEROUS
AGE

A DANGEROUS AGE

MARTIN SYLVESTER

WITHDRAWN

VILLARD BOOKS · NEW YORK · 1988

Grateful acknowledgment is made to Routledge and Kegan Paul Ltd. for permission to
reprint excerpts from *Clausewitz on War*, edited by Amos Rapoport, 1968. Reprinted by
permission.

Library of Congress Cataloging-in-Publication Data

Sylvester, Martin.
A dangerous age.
I. Title.
PR6069.Y43D3   1988   823'.914   88-14251
ISBN 0-394-56790-0

Book Design by The Sarabande Press

Manufactured in the United States of America
9 8 7 6 5 4 3 2
First American Edition

A DANGEROUS AGE

THE PROVINCE
OF CHANCE

War is the province of chance. In no sphere of human activity is such a margin to be left for this intruder, because none is so much in constant contact with him on all sides. He increases the uncertainty of every circumstance, and deranges the course of events.

—Clausewitz

What can go wrong, will go wrong.

—Murphy (attrib.)

The second bullet smacked the granite wall eighteen inches from my left ear, sending up a little cloud of gray powdered stone. A faint smell of dissipated heat—kinetic energy—lingered on the air for an instant, and was gone. They say you don't hear the shot that kills you: curious, then, that I heard no report following the shot that missed; no distant crack; nothing. We seemed to be on our own, me and the bullet.

A long scar suddenly appeared on a mossy stone beside my head, and a ricochet screamed off up the hill. Again, no report. All around me spread Dartmoor, craggy, boggy, and unmoved. There's nothing makes you feel so alone as empty landscape, in my opinion. But this loneliness was an illusion. Somewhere out there was man, the killer ape, misusing his ingenuity again. Why? *Why?*

I enjoy a conundrum, and looked forward to getting to grips with this one. In the meantime it seemed a good idea to get moving. The bullets were arriving singly, which indicated that a rifle, rather than an automatic weapon, was being used; also, to miss me by eighteen inches when I had been a sitting target must have meant that the rifleman was working at long range, or was a rotten shot, either of which gave me some comfort. So if I stood up and ran, my chances seemed good. While thinking this, I was doing it.

Sergeant MacWhirter, whose loud-hailer had blasted me and sixty-nine fellow recruits round his muddy assault course during my national service days, would have been proud of me (though not admitted it). I sprinted, slowed suddenly, jinked, sprinted again, and finally made it through a gap in the wall, jumping the remains of a gate and feeling relieved it wasn't a full height five-barred job— I don't know if I could have cleared that without a scramble. If the unseen rifleman tried another shot, I saw and heard nothing. I hoped he was as impressed with my display of infantry basic field craft as I was myself—I would never have guessed that it was all still there, those automatic reactions, ready for use at a second's notice. And effective—I felt sure I had given him an impossible task. The first time, in fact, that my training had been put to the test. And probably, I thought, the last—but I was wrong about that.

As soon as I was through the gap in the wall, I was seized by a sudden fright that there might be another rifleman waiting for me to do just that. No reason—but being shot at, I can now say from experience, brings on an instant persecution complex; the whole world is out to get you. I dived for cover between the wall and a boulder that lay some six feet out into the field—it wasn't nearly as big as I would have liked, but gave some protection from the opposite direction. Panting, heart thumping, but temporarily safe, I assessed the situation. If I kept absolutely still I would be almost invisible, just part of the landscape. It was a good thing I hadn't got the dog with me.

Well, of course, I hadn't been more than a few seconds behind the shelter of the wall before reality began to reassert itself. Nobody could be trying to shoot me, not really. I'd surely overreacted to something that must have a perfectly simple, obvious explanation. My life had been entirely conventional, and although in business you can't avoid the occasional antagonism, some friction as paths or personalities diverge, I could think of nothing that would remotely justify a hole in the head. Put like that, and there was no other way I could think of putting it, the bullets meant only one thing—that someone was amusing himself at my expense. Possession of a firearm does peculiar things to people, can release submerged aggressions, power fantasies, like kids going *bang*, you're dead. Looking down the sights, imagining what would happen if the trigger were pulled. Power from the barrel of a gun. Only, sometimes, imagining isn't enough. The next stage is to fire a shot or two, close enough to make the victim jump. Or run, like me. See the funny man sprint away in panic, jump the old gate, hide behind the wall. Into the mud, ha ha! That's it, of course. Well, he certainly got his money's worth from me, this homicidal humorist.

That must be it. So, first I'll shout, "All right! That's enough—game's over! I'm coming out now."

He must have heard that. So now, I'll get up and go home. I'll have something to say if I catch sight of him as I go. And, of course, to the police. People like that shouldn't be able to get hold of rifles.

So, I'll stand up. Why not?

Now.

Or, perhaps, just to be on the safe side, I'll prop my hat on some bracken stalks and lift it slowly above the wall. As we're playing games . . .

Christ!

An invisible force plucks at the hat. I lower it, note the tiny punctures in front and back. My hand shakes. Needles jab my spine. Not a game. That could have been my head.

I crouch against the wall, thoughts whirling. This shouldn't be happening—but it is. I have to keep calm, work it out.

Right then, a quick recap.

I'd left the house late in the afternoon, after a massive Sunday lunch, with just time to walk up to Grig Tor and back onto the road before dark, about two miles each way. I like to get out onto the moors, nothing too energetic, but it's a way of coping with the lengthy

lunches that Claudine insists on: the French are religious about
lunch, especially on Sunday with as many relations as can be gathered up. That Sunday we had both Claudine's parents over from
Bordeaux, my brother Ralph and his wife—they live about ten miles
away—and five assorted children. That's a small party by French
standards, but Claudine was in her element, and there was a lot of
hugging and kissing and general hubbub, followed by Le Déjeuner.
I can't resist the recitation—these words revive the taste of that
particular Sunday; they should be *sung* but cold print will have to
do. Listen!—*crudités*, followed by fish soufflé with cru classé Graves
(Malartic-Lagravière); *Rognons de Boeuf au Madère* with Pomerol; Brie
with Château d'Angludet '70, and finally Tante Marie plum pudding
with sweet champagne.

The three Bordeaux wines were in honor of Claudine's parents,
for whom the rest of France doesn't exist. "*Doucement, doucement!*"
they shouted happily each time I refilled their glasses, which was
often. After three hours of this, a walk seemed a good idea to me,
though the French showed no sign of strain, and it clearly didn't
appeal to them. Anyway. Claudine would have had to change into
her walking outfit—the ultimate in tweedy chic—and the whole plan
would have been delayed, so I wasn't sorry. My brother couldn't
come as he had to get back to his farm. The children managed to
disappear at the first suggestion of a walk. So I was on my own.
Even the dog refused to leave the aroma of rognons that hung about
the kitchen, and watched from the back door, yellow eyes guilty,
as I set off alone down the drive.

My house is just off the edge of Dartmoor, tucked away in one
of the little valleys that provide shelter from the frequent wind and
driving rain. In contrast to the bleak uplands, we are surrounded
by woods and neat green fields. After a mile you leave this comfortable domesticity; the road stops at a last outpost of stone cottages,
and a concrete track leads steeply up past old tin-mine workings, to
the moor itself. Now you are in real Baskerville country, where in
the twilight every hummock becomes a hound. At last even the
concrete road peters out by the last of the mine huts, now no more
than a pile of weedy granite blocks, and a track—or stream bed,
depending on the time of year—leads to the open moor.

It's a steep climb to Grig Tor, and I spent some minutes up there, getting my breath back. On a clear day you can see right across to Teignmouth, and watch tankers steaming across a triangle of blue sea. Today, it wasn't like that; lowering clouds were blotting out the sky, and there was no chance of distant views or dramatic sunsets. I wandered over the Tor, a knob of solidified granite porridge pushed up in the subterranean simmering that formed this landscape a few million years ago. Then I started on the way down. Sheep moved away automatically as I came near, stopping as soon as they'd re-established their safe distance—about thirty yards. When I come with the dog they like a hundred yards at least, and I don't blame them: stray dogs get on to the moor from time to time and massacre them—at several places along the track I passed what looked like a pile of old mattress stuffing but for a sheep's skull, grayish white like the granite, still attached at one end. Dartmoor itself is the same: bare bone of the granite core showing through a tattered skin of bracken. You can't go up there without being reminded of the more depressing eternal verities.

Which brings me back to the bullet. I say *the* bullet, as it was the second one that sent me running for cover; the first went past without hitting anything, sounding like an express bee. I happened to be following the line of one of the dry-stone walls built to divide grazing rights; instinctively I ducked down beside it. Some pickled poacher, I thought. Then I remembered there are no rabbits this far up, and nothing else to shoot at, only sheep and ponies. Curious! I thought. Then the second bullet struck the wall by my head, and I stopped thinking and ran.

Now you know all that I knew, as I crouched behind the wall. Nothing in all that to explain what was going on, I thought; nothing to explain these holes in my hat. I looked at them more closely. Small holes. Not easy to tell the size of a bullet from the hole it makes in soft material, but these looked like .22 bullet holes. And that could explain a part of the mystery—why I had not heard the shots. I know something about firearms from having spent time in the country as a boy, and from the army. You can fit a silencer to a rifle, and it will muffle the explosion as the bullet leaves the barrel, but it can't prevent the crack that bullets, like airplanes, make as they pass the speed of sound. I had heard no crack. Therefore the bullet was subsonic, low velocity. But rifles are normally high velocity in order to keep a flat trajectory and make aiming easier. Except for the little .22 for which you can buy subsonic ammunition. Therefore I was being shot at by a .22, fitted with silencer.

My first feeling, on reaching this conclusion, was a sort of indignation. Being shot by a .22 is like being run over by a moped—it can be fatal, but if you've got to go, a Ferrari would be more dramatic and a Rolls more dignified. But then, on second thought, I didn't want to go. In that case, a .22 had some advantages for me—limited range, say a hundred yards for a head shot; limited effect if he hit me anywhere else; limited velocity, making a shot at a running target difficult.

Probable success if we run for it, then, came the suggestion.

Who said that?

It was my Left Brain, of course. In case you don't know it, the theory is that the two halves of your brain operate in different ways: Left Brain is the logical cleversticks side, good with words, and Right Brain is instinct. Ask a tennis player to explain his winning service, and his Left Brain will try to put it into words for you; after that, his Right Brain, which actually controlled the shot instinctively, will be unable to do it again because Left Brain is jamming the switchboard with theory.

Should I run for it?

Probable success . . .

No! Right Brain had joined forces with my stomach. They didn't like it. All instinct against the organism being put at risk at this stage. Collect further information first. Postpone decision.

Motion carried.

Dartmoor stone walls are built of granite boulders laid without mortar; from a distance, seen against the sky, they look more like a strip of lace than a wall due to the many gaps between the boulders. Moving from one gap to another, I could see most of the downhill slope on the other side of the wall. In particular, I could see most of the area from which the bullets, judging by the direction of impact, must have come. I waited, and watched. Meanwhile, the light was going fast. Like the sheep, I needed a safety zone—a hundred yards was minimum. After dark I would not be able to maintain this. I had to do something very soon.

After ten minutes of peering through the wall, I saw some sheep moving uneasily away from a hawthorn bush near the track, about a hundred and fifty yards down the hill. Several of them stopped and turned, looking back toward the bush, then got on with their grazing. It seemed just the place a man would choose to wait in ambush, covering the track. Not a very clever move at this stage, though, as he knew I was alerted.

After running for cover, I would hardly get up and stroll down that track. Perhaps he hoped I would think he was gone. Or perhaps he thought I would risk it after dark when, from his position, I would be in silhouette against the skyline. Perhaps he just couldn't think of anything else to do. Left Brain ran these thoughts through the computer and came up with no conclusion. Right Brain was still quivering with fright. Meanwhile my glasses kept steaming up. It got noticeably darker.

I decided to make off up the hill, keeping behind the wall as far as possible, and then running for the brow and safety. This had two snags, apart from the obvious one of being hit by a lucky shot as I ran out of cover. The first was that it left me with a very long way home; I would have to go over the moor for four miles until the next road, and then get a lift. But much worse than that was the thought that this might be only a temporary escape. I would have no idea who the rifleman was, or why he was after me. This left me defenseless against another attack, which could follow anywhere at any time. But now I had no alternative; darkness was closing in, and the rifleman would close in with it unless I retreated at once.

A sound from behind sent me spinning, nerves on full alert, muscles tensed for a desperate sprint from danger. Up the track, emerging over the brow, six or seven figures appeared, clad in red and yellow fluorescent anoraks, the recommended wear for moor walkers. It could be a trap, but I didn't think so: even assassins have to do the thing economically, and to send so many would be a waste of manpower. I began to laugh: it must have been like this in the arena when the swordfighters had finished with each other and the clowns came on. Now I had only to wait until they got near enough and I could join them on the track, keeping them between me and the thorn bush. The hidden rifleman had used a silenced weapon to avoid attracting attention; he wasn't likely to change his policy and attempt mass murder of all seven or eight of us—especially with a .22.

I went past the gap in the wall at a run, keeping low, and kept going until I reached the track, timing it so that the walkers arrived simultaneously. They saw me while I was still some yards away, and heads turned: nothing was said until I bobbed up among them. It seemed best to get in first. Breathlessness added drama to my voice.

"Did you see it?"

There had to be chorus of, "See what?" It could be difficult to do this sort of thing in cold blood, but believe me, it's dead easy to be convincing if you think your life depends on it.

I followed up with, "Down the hill there. It's been sheep worrying. A huge dog, or maybe something escaped from a zoo. Must get down and telephone. Been trouble for several weeks, but this could be it."

General conviction showed, but I had to get them down the track with me.

"Got a car down there?" They had to have transport waiting this late in the evening.

It was a minibus, they confirmed. The idea of assisting in the capture of a Beast of Dartmoor appealed to them, and we pounded down the track together. I made sure I was on the far side of the track as we passed the thorn bush. As we hurtled along I managed to check that none of them was local, although that wouldn't have been difficult to handle as there's usually a dog scare going on. Even my stay-at-home comfort-loving soppy specimen has had an official visit from the police to have her alibi checked. Nothing showed under the thorn bush, but I hadn't expected it to: he had had plenty of time to tuck himself away.

Once well past the thorn bush, I put the second part of my plan into operation.

"See anything?" No, they said, still nothing. We halted, bunched on the track, peering about us. I glanced back. Yes, the thorn bush was safely out of sight.

"Look," I said, "I think I'd better stay and watch for a while—I could have been mistaken. You go on down."

"I'll give the police a ring when we pass a box," their leader offered.

I knew at once I didn't want that. Why not? Whatever the reason, I didn't hesitate.

"Thanks," I said, "but don't bother. In case it turns out to be some quite ordinary animal. I'd rather make sure first."

"Your decision," he said, sounding reluctant. On his own I'd never have got rid of him—but he had his group to consider. "We'll be off, then. If you're sure."

"I'm sure. Thanks again."

Fraud or hero, they would never know. The walkers disappeared down the track, fluorescent jackets bobbing like Chinese lanterns in the dusk.

Now I was on my own again, and hopefully between the rifleman and his way home. I suppose assassins have homes, just like the rest of us? Hopefully? I must be a bloody lunatic—I could have been miles away by now. I reminded myself it was to prevent next time: *Homo sapiens* is meant to be distinguished from other animals by his ability to endure present pains in order to secure future satisfactions. I hoped the pains wouldn't be too bad.

I took up a position at the top of the concrete road, behind the ruins of the mining hut. This put me very close to the road, but completely invisible to anyone coming down the track. Surely he must come this way; it was the only way off the moor for miles. I could either leap on him, or follow: following could go wrong easily if he heard me, stopped in the dark, and let me catch up. If he had a torch, and I followed, he could spotlight me for a shot that couldn't miss. A torch! Jesus, if he had *that* I was in trouble anyway. He could come down the track searching all the way. Only an idiot would pass my hiding place without standing well back and shining his torch behind it first. Even if he passed close and I was able to make my leap, what made me think I could overcome him? I'm quite large, about six feet two and fourteen stone (at *least* fourteen stone after one of Claudine's lunches), but I won't see forty again and I'm not a keep-fit type. Please God, don't let him have a torch! I've made a monumental boob, and I'm truly sorry. Please do this for me, just this once. Don't let him have a torch!

Seconds later, I got the answer to my prayer. It was No. He did have a torch.

The beam sprang out suddenly, lighting up the bracken halfway to the Tor; so powerful that the white blobs of sheep shone whiter than white. It wobbled about, several hundred yards up the track: I couldn't see the source, but it must have been about the position of the thorn bush. I guessed from the way the beam wavered that he was climbing from the thorn bush back on to the track in my direction. Then it bounced rhythmically as he walked toward me.

I kept behind the ruined hut. I longed to look out, to get some clue that would help to assess my adversary, but my only hope was to stay concealed until he passed my hiding place. My knees began to shake. At times like this, all sorts of irrelevant things flit through the mind. I started thinking of the four cases of 1961 Château Palmer I'd picked up at a bargain price at a recent auction: almost nobody there.

Did I mention that I am a wine merchant? That's how I met Claudine. She was going into Dubuisson Frères, one of the many Bordeaux merchants still operating from the Quai des Chartrons. I noticed this jean-clad *derrière* flick across the pavement and through the swing doors, how could I not, mine weren't the only eyes swiveling after it. You're meant to notice; they like to be appreciated. Contrary to the general impression, French girls have big bums and short legs, but they learn to walk so well that by the age of fourteen they all manage to give the impression of long legs and neat behinds: the clothes help of course. All this is said to encourage male chauvinism; well, possibly, to some extent, after all a Frenchman—Nicolas Chauvin—invented it, well, the political sort, that is, but I don't think it's as simple as that; given these instincts, and bearing in mind that you can't dam a river without an overflow, and all Freud said about it—the French didn't have or *need* a Freud of course—it could be just a civilized way of turning sex into an art form; after all, looking isn't the same as touching, though when I arrived to see Monsieur Dubuisson there she was in Papa's office and so I did get to touch in the end. And the flashlight is just coming level with my place of concealment, my place of concealment, of concealment.

Now!

I have to admit it was an anticlimax. In the first place he obviously didn't suspect that I might be lurking in wait for him, and marched straight past the ruined hut only a yard away, flashlight pointing straight ahead. I simply stepped out behind him and put my left arm around his throat and grabbed his rifle, slung on his right shoulder, with my right hand. Secondly, he was some ten inches shorter than me, and weedy withal. He gave a strangled cry—that's what it's often called, but this one was genuine as I had a tight grip; I suppose he thought I was about to do unto others as I had been done to, or nearly. He dropped the torch which lay on the track, still blazing away: I've never been able to find a torch that went on working after being dropped, but this one did. I could see very little, but felt that he had long greasy hair and was wearing a leather jacket; it smelled of engine oil and old cars. There was only a brief struggle, which soon subsided; he must have been aware that I towered over him. I felt secure enough to start to ease the rifle, which was in a canvas case, off his shoulder.

This was a mistake. As soon as his right arm was free, he drove his elbow back into my stomach, scoring a direct hit on Le Déjeuner. I had a sudden taste of plum pudding and sweet champagne at the back of my throat—a sort of gastronomic déjà vu. Breaking away, he was suddenly gone, up the track; I managed to keep hold of the rifle. The faithful flashlight still shone brightly in the opposite direction.

Wearily, I picked it up and, while recovering my breath, slid the rifle out of its case. Anschutz .22 target model, bolt action, extended ten-shot magazine, silencer, telescopic sight—all gleaming and in perfect condition. How could he have missed with this? Perhaps the sight wasn't zeroed correctly—they seldom are. I glanced in the magazine: low-velocity hollow-point sporting ammo, the sort that spread on impact. Nasty.

I snapped the magazine back, and worked the bolt to make sure the thing was loaded. Then I started back up the track. I didn't have a plan, but it didn't seem time to go yet.

Then there was a shout, or screech, from some distance away, to the left of the track.

Left Brain thought it might be a trap. Right Brain felt it wasn't. I picked my way slowly in the direction of the screech, gripping the rifle in my right hand, finger on the trigger, and shining the torch all around with my left. I heard nothing more: saw nothing until, after several hundred yards of cautious progress, I saw a white blob reflected in the flashlight beam, low down, not moving. I edged closer.

I hadn't seen his face before. Now it looked at me, expressionless, from an odd position only a couple of feet above ground level. With the long hair, I was reminded of a bust of some nineteenth-century composer or philosopher. Except that they're armless. His arms were stretched straight out to each side, resting on the ground. Below that his body had ceased to exist. I took a step further, and stepped back hurriedly: my foot had registered the faint quiver of bog surface. I shone the torch around: it was obvious now, an area of bright green some twenty yards across which nobody could miss by daylight. Featherbeds, they're called locally. I could see the broken surface where his impetus had carried him into the middle of it.

I turned the torch back to him.

"I'm goin' down, squire."

The accent was London: basic Cockney with transatlantic overtones. The remark was uncomplaining, dispassionate, in the best British tradition of, "Good God, sir! I've lost me leg!" The Iron Duke had made the only possible reply.

"I'm afraid you are."

He was too far in for me to have any hope of reaching him. Dartmoor trees are little, stunted things, with no long branches. He was sinking too fast for me to fetch help. He was already a dead man. I had to be realistic.

"Who are you? Who sent you?"

His small ratty eyes stared at me over the surface of the bog. A bitter expression, half humor, half defiance, twisted his face, glaringly white in the torchlight.

"Who am I, squire? Who am I?" He paused, savoring possible replies. Whatever it was, I knew I wasn't going to like it. Finally it came.

"Let's jus' say, I'm the Man from the Ministry." He followed this with an evil chuckle; then the boggy water touched him under the chin, and he gasped, "And there's plenty more where I come from."

There was a short silence while we looked at each other. Then he said, "Do us a favor, squire?"

"If I can."

"Turn the fuckin' light aht."

I switched off the torch. The noises were, if anything, worse than the sight. Eventually I thought I heard him say something else, and switched on. There was nothing there except a small patch of black water, with the bright green bog surface already sliding back into place. On an impulse, I lifted the rifle and threw it in after him. Just as I let go, I remembered it would have had a number that might be traceable, but it was too late. The weapon landed in the bog, butt first, and stuck half out of the water, Excalibur-like; then whatever it was caught on gave way and it sank out of sight.

I waited in the dark for several minutes, as people loiter after a funeral, waiting for life to reassert itself. Finally I started to shiver. It was time to go home.

ACT OF
DECISION

Who could advise, or resolve upon a great battle, without feeling his mind more or less wrought up, or perplexed by, the danger and responsibility which such a great act of decision carries in itself?

—Clausewitz

I hadn't been wearing my watch, so I was amazed to see by the kitchen clock that it wasn't yet half-past eight, and that the whole life-and-death drama I'd just undergone had delayed my return by little more than half an hour. I stepped out of the dark into the brightness of the kitchen feeling like some mythological adventurer returning from the Underworld—but nobody took any notice. Claudine and her Maman were hard at work preparing a little snack of three or four courses in case anyone was in danger of starvation, and everything was utterly normal. Such is the power of environment that I immediately started to feel normal as well. Nobody said anything about a telephone call from the walkers, and I didn't ask: if they hadn't telephoned, I would be left with an open situation in which I could think about what to do next. I hadn't decided yet if I wanted to be mentioned in dispatches, that's to say the *Western Morning News*. In any case, how would I break the news, actually? "Listen Claudine, I've just escaped being murdered on the moor and left a man dead in a bog." In a Buñuel film you might get away with it, but not in real life. And certainly not in front of

Maman. Better to tell Claudine later, and not wreck the evening to
no purpose. Preserve the sangfroid. And give myself time to think.
Meanwhile it was easy to say nothing.

I went in through the back door, kicking off my short walking
wellies in the lobby and went through to the kitchen with my shoes
in my hand. Claudine immediately got down to essentials. "Your
trousairs!" she cried. Mud had worked its way over my wellies. Not
much by English standards, but any is too much for Claudine. She
won't understand that the whole point of tweed is camouflage for
mud splashes: the English know that it dusts off eventually leaving
your trousairs as good as new, but the French take them immediately
to the dry cleaners where they have a shocked mutter about *taches*.
A *tache* is to the bourgeoisie what a blot is to the escutcheon.

Claudine snatched a clothes brush from the cupboard and fell on
her knees at my feet; she brushed vigorously with little explosions
of "*Ça alors!*" Soon I was restored to an acceptable appearance, and
cooking could be resumed. The central feature, described as a "leetle
piece of feesh," looked like turbot to me. I wandered off to get some
wine from the cellar at the other end of the house, closing the shutters
as I went. They're solid wood and fold across the inside of the
windows, with a steel bar to hold them shut. They wouldn't stop
a bullet, but anyone outside would be prevented from seeing in, or
taking aim. I wasn't expecting a siege, but I felt much more comfortable once I had them all secured.

It's a Victorian house, one of a number built by successful trades-
men in the mid-nineteenth century, after the West Country had been
opened up by the coming of the railway. The rooms are not well
proportioned, and the ceilings are too high, but there are eight bedrooms and the house manages to swallow up a dozen of us without
strain; it's like having a private hotel, and we appreciate the space,
as our London flat, which is over the shop in Kensington Church
Street, and which is where we have to spend most of our time, is
very small. I took over the house, along with the wine-importing
business, when my father died, selling my own house to pay the
death duties; since then, rates and heating bills have shot up, but
we have made some economies and hope to be able to keep it going.
Switching from oil to burning wood on open fires and in stoves has

helped. There was a fire blazing in the hall as I passed through: we use the hall as a dining room and the long refectory table was already set—a black table, with plain red plates and tall red candles. Firelight glinted off the glasses. It's the sort of hotel you'd be glad to discover.

My father converted the old coach house into a billiard room and made a door through from the hall. The green baize of the billiard table is badly faded, and as I went in I noticed one or two moldy patches starting: I ought to leave an electric heater in here all the time. But the side cushions are sound. Claudine's father was attempting a snooker. I waited. He missed. Julian came on, potted a red, the blue, another red, then the black. He missed the next red, probably on purpose. He's a thoughtful lad, and Claudine's father wouldn't lose by too much.

Julian is twenty-two, and an architectural student. He's also heavily into mysticism—Gurdjieff, Ouspensky, and so on. He spends a lot of time teaching me to think positively: turning a setback into an opportunity. I haven't had a lot of experience of setbacks, really; things have gone pretty smoothly on the whole. Except of course when Julian's mother was killed. We'd only been married three years, and Julian was still a toddler: she had been to see her sister and had driven most of the way back when the car went right over a roundabout and into a lamp standard; she died in hospital three days later. Luckily she'd put Julian in the back: he was bruised and silent with shock, but otherwise unhurt. The cause of the accident was a power workers' dispute—all the streetlights and road signs were out. She must have arrived at this familiar roundabout but not recognized it until too late. Ever since, I've felt like hurling a brick when a bland union official comes on television to say how much his members regret the inconvenience they're causing. Some of the effects go beyond inconvenience. And he visibly doesn't regret it. There must be a better way to fix wage levels.

Down in the cellar, I was surrounded by rows of familiar bottles, all begging to be chosen. Meursault, I decided. Come to me, my beauty. There's something about your fat, slope-shouldered burgundy bottle that I find irresistible: it's big, generous, like the wine inside. Not that I'm against claret, but you have to be in a suitably dry, tannic, donnish mood to get the best out of it. The family firm began, in fact, when my grandfather got his foot in the door of some Oxford colleges, in the days when undergraduates drank claret instead of synthetic lager. Now the claret doesn't get beyond the top table. I still have to go, in Grandfather's footsteps, to have dinner with bursars and listen to dons fencing. "Oh really!" each combatant says in turn, "Oh really. Do you? Does he? Did he really? Oh, *really?* How *in*teresting." It goes on and on until one of them slips up—a factual error perhaps, or a minute lapse of memory. Then a pause before the death thrust. "But, forgive me, I thought it was . . ." There's claret in their veins.

The cellar ceiling is just too low for me to stand upright. It's amazing how painful it is to stand stooped for more than a minute or two, so I have an old barrel to sit on when I have things to think about. As now.

Well, of course I must go to the police, I told myself. No question. They'll get that poor sod out of the bog, identify him, and sort it all out. Hand it over to the experts, and forget it. Well, not the episode, but the problem. I wasn't likely to forget that white face with the bog up to its chin. So that's it. I'd better ring the police now.

And yet . . . and yet . . .

I would have one or two things to explain away. What I'd told the walkers, for instance. And what happened, precisely, after the walkers had gone off down the hill. The police wouldn't think I pushed him in; no reason. Although I had in a sense chased him in. Well, hardly, because he could have run in any direction. With three hundred and sixty degrees to choose from, he had navigated along the one degree that led to destruction. Accidentally. They would understand that. Of course.

Except for one thing.

Why had I thrown the rifle in after him?

Well, there was a simple explanation. In case he could use it to keep himself afloat, I would tell them. There was nothing else at hand. I did the only thing possible. You can imagine my desperation to help in this terrible situation: the poor chap was sinking fast, I had to do something, my frustration, my God, it was awful. Yes, yes, it must have been awful. I can tell you it *was*! Yes, we understand, of course we do. Any normal person would feel the same.

That's it.

I hadn't felt like that, like a normal person. Sorry for him, yes, but also conscious of taking advantage, of using the situation to get the information I wanted. That's why I stood there, instead of running somewhere, anywhere, to look for help. I would have failed, probably. But I should have *tried*. There might have been something, an old gate, bit of fence wire, that would have helped to get him out. But I stood there, hoping the bog would squeeze information out of him. And he wouldn't be squeezed: he taunted me instead. "I'm the Man from the Ministry." What the hell did that mean? He taunted me, because he knew I wasn't trying to help, not really. That's why, at the end, he wanted to die alone. There's no sympathy possible between us bastards. So it was. "Turn the fucking light out." That was all I did for him.

Proof: I threw the rifle in *afterward*.

All right. Let's face it. I'd already wanted, at the moment I let go of the rifle, to keep this to myself. Why? Because I'd bloody well enjoyed myself, that's why. I had come out on top in a skirmish where most of the advantage—surprise, weapon—started with the other side. Adrenalin had zoomed. I felt ten years younger.

It had been exciting, and I had to admit that there was something in me that responded to that sort of game, to taking that kind of risk. But not to killing anybody: the game should have ended with his capture. He killed himself, in effect, by assuming that my intentions were as murderous as his own: that drove him to run off blindly, into the bog. He chose the game, and lost it in his own way.

Now I was hooked. I had some kind of private war on my hands and, for the time being at least, I felt safer conducting it myself, in my own way. Suppose I went to the police—would it help me, at this stage? There was so little information for them to work on.

I could imagine the interview.

This man in the bog, sir, how did it happen? It was panic, you see, Inspector. He ran off in a panic. And why did he do that, sir. Because he'd been trying to shoot me, but I caught him. Then he escaped and ran off. Into the bog. And why do you think he was trying to shoot you, sir. Well, I don't know but he was. I see, sir. With a .22 sporting rifle—not a very usual murder weapon, sir. No, that's why it was so cunning, you see. Yes, I see, sir. And I wanted to catch him, to find out who he was, where he had come from, he said there were more where he came from. Indeed, sir, indeed . . . would you say, sir, that you have a feeling of being persecuted, personal difficulties, money worries, perhaps?

Yes, it could easily go like that. The whole thing was so improbable, the police were bound to try to turn it into more everyday terms. And while they did so, another attempt could be planned and then made.

Then there would be the publicity—the *Western Morning News*, certainly. Followed, quite likely, by some of the nationals: Dartmoor bogs are a part of the national consciousness, along with the Loch Ness monster. All this would do my sort of business no good at all.

I felt I had an advantage now, as only I knew what had happened. I could work out a strategy; keep the other side guessing until I found out who they were. *Then* I could bring in the police.

Claudine's father was at the top of the cellar stairs. *"Qu'est-ce que tu fais là-bas*, William? You are talking with your wines? The Bordeaux, certainly, they have something to say, but the others . . . *ce n'est pas la peine! Mais Claudine dit, 'A table!'* "

He never misses a chance to plug his region. Too bad, he's got to have some burgundy this evening. I climbed up the steps and switched out the cellar light.

Up in the hall, the fire was going well, and Claudine, her parents, and Julian were just installing themselves at the table. The girls were still missing. Distant drums could be heard from above—a monotonous disco beat. The girls are nine and eleven, and growing up fast; they seem entirely French in spite of having me for a father: fine-boned, olive-skinned, and full of chatter. Claudine frowned, and let fly with one of her two-tone klaxon calls, guaranteed at up to a mile and a half—two *kilomètres*, that is. *"Ni-chole! Syl-vie! Venez manger!"*

The drums were cut off. The girls came clattering down the stairs and joined us at the table. I realized I was hungry—lunch seemed a long time ago. Onion soup with croutons took the edge off. Then it was turbot time. It smelled delicious: Claudine had cooked it au gratin with butter, shallots, parsley, bread crumbs, white wine, and a touch of black pepper. I opened the Meursault. I don't believe in opening good wine long before drinking—nothing useful is achieved by exposing a square centimeter of wine in the neck of the bottle to the air. To get the flavor going, just swirl it round the glass. *A mon avis.*

Whoever invented the telephone was a sadist. It rang just as the first forkful of turbot was going in. There was a sudden silence as the usual battle of wills took place between the family—not for *me*, we all persuaded ourselves. Finally, Julian shamed us all by getting up: he was the one it was least likely to be for, but he can't bear unresolved situations. The rest of us sat eating and looking guilty. He was back in no time.

"It's for you, Dad."

Oh shit. "Thanks, Jules," I muttered, putting down the eating irons with a deep feeling of resentment. Who the hell, who knows us, would ring up in the middle of a mealtime? Julian added, "It's the police."

This didn't cause a stir. On Dartmoor, most police work is to do with stray dogs, gun licenses, tractor accidents, everyday events during which you get to know the police quite well. They're in the pub with their hats off, looking just like everyone else. Almost. But, after today's events, it would be stretching coincidence to the limit for this to be a routine call. I reached the telephone in the study feeling tense and wary.

"Hello?"

"Is that you, Mr. Warner?" It was Bob something, the sergeant at Moretonhampstead. I can never remember his other name.

"Yes, hello, Bob."

"We're sorry to disturb you at this time of night." It's that royal "we" that makes talking to the police an uncomfortable experience. You're you, but he is The Force. It reminds you that this is an official conversation. Still, he sounded friendly enough.

"We understand there's been trouble on the moor today."

Well, the decision's out of my hands, then. The police Know All. I was just going to ring you, I'll say, just been getting my breath back. He won't like it, but there's nothing he can do except be disapproving. Here goes.

I said it.

"Oh, that's no problem, Mr. Warner. We got your message. Thought you might have some more information for us, that's all."

Message? What message? Suddenly it was obvious. The walkers. I had a sudden picture of their leader—tall, thin, glasses, little beard, big boots. I'd told him not to bother the police, but he hadn't been able to resist it: self-important.

Bob said, "We'd like a description of what you saw."

Theory confirmed. I said it had looked about the size of a large dog, probably *was* a large dog, darkish, couldn't see much, running fast, and the light was going.

"Ah." There was a pause. Then Bob said, "You can't be sure if it was a dog or not?"

I felt a little careless, euphoric even. My mystery was safe. Why not be generous? He sounded hopeful that it might *not* be a dog. What else did he have in mind? Just a break from routine, probably. We live on dreams. I could help him with his.

"Well, there was something unusual about it. The way it moved, I think." I spoke slowly, my tone dark.

I was right. Bob sounded brighter at once. "Is that so?" I felt pleased at presenting him with a touch of drama. Until he said, "I was told it might be something escaped from a zoo?"

At once I came down to earth, feeling I'd overdone it. This could get out of hand. I was wasting his time, giving him shadows to chase.

"I don't think so now," I told him flatly. "Not slinky enough." But, as he thanked me and rang off, he sounded as though he'd decided to know best. I had a strong suspicion that another Beast of Dartmoor legend had begun.

Claudine had put my plate by the fire to keep warm, and I hadn't dropped far behind. The French talk so much that their meals always progress slowly. Ten o'clock came and went. Finally the pace slowed. We sent the girls up, and the rest of us carried the dishes out to the washing-up machine. Too late for more snooker. Bedtime was declared.

In bed, I lay and thought about things. No, I didn't reach for and light up a Gauloise—that's the exception that proves the rule of my francophilia, otherwise almost unbreached. In fact, I don't smoke at all. Claudine lay beside me, her streamlined nipples poised prettily above the top of the pink sheet. She was reading—draft accounts for the last financial year had just arrived from the accountants. The slim folder was propped on her smooth, flat stomach: her dark eyes darted from column to column, assessing our current fortune, if any. I finished my thinking; Claudine read on.

"*Appuyer sur le bouton*" say the instructions in French telephone boxes. "Then you will be connected, or your *monnaie* will be returned." (They lie, of course—you normally end up with neither connection nor *monnaie*.) Still, that's what should happen in principle, *en principe*. I followed instructions, using my forefinger and a slightly circular motion for added effect.

"*Mon amour*," Claudine murmured absently.

I reckoned that my *monnaie* had been returned. It never used to be like that. Thank God we only have annual accounts. I turned out my light.

The viewpoint was from deep down. I was looking into a triangular chasm, an underground sea, filled with green slime, translucent, fluorescent. He floated upright near the bottom, arms still outstretched, black jacket floating open, black hair floating upward from his white face. His eyes were black bullet holes, aimed in my direction. Around him, tangled in the depths, were old iron bedsteads, beer cans, car tires, farmers' flotsam. I couldn't see his mouth move, but I heard his Cheapside voice. More where I come from. Others were joining him, dim at first, then clearer as they formed, like crystals, from the slime. Soon there was a whole army of them, all floating upright like him, all with arms outstretched. I wanted not to look, but there was no way. It's your game, I said, I didn't choose . . . I knew they couldn't hear, even when I shouted at them . . .

I woke up sweating. That's not a figure of speech. It was dark except for a little light from the window. Claudine lay with her back to me, breathing lightly. I moved closer and slipped my arm round her; I felt the comfortable weight of her buttocks against my thighs.

After a while I needed more than that. She stirred as I started to make love to her, and tilted her buttocks to accommodate me. Soon she caught her breath and pushed harder against me. *"Oooh, ah, chéri,"* she whispered. We relaxed together.

I don't suffer from afterward *tristesse*—it works the other way for me. Things felt pretty good.

Some minutes passed. Then Claudine murmured, *"Chéri?"*

"Still here." Things *were* pretty good. I thought I might just about manage it, maybe another minute or two. *"A votre service, madame,"* I breathed in her ear.

Claudine said, "They are not good, William, the figures. The expenses they are up, and the sales they are down. There is more competition. We must make changes."

Up and down. I knew the feeling. Oh well.

"Tomorrow darling, tomorrow," I said. "We'll get together in the office with Maggie, and plan a strategy." We were going back to London tomorrow.

Tomorrow was going to be a day for strategies, one way and another.

A LITTLE
KNOWLEDGE

By the word 'information' we denote all the knowledge that we have of the enemy and his country; therefore, in fact, the foundation of all our actions.

—*Clausewitz*

Some mornings my mind seems to have gone off on vacation, leaving behind an uninhabited and foggy void. Vague feelings of guilt float in and out: what did I do last night to deserve this? Was there an excess of wine? Or women? Or am I getting a cold? Then I think, perhaps it's not my fault at all, but just my stars in decline, my planets in opposition. Unwise to make decisions today. I should stay in my burrow, *hors de combat*, letting the world revolve unaided: otherwise, if I put a hand on it the machinery will grind me up.

That was the message, that Monday morning. I'm a simple pagan in these matters, and I've learned to trust my messages: I know that Nature can get along without me, and I know I'd better not get in the way if the word comes down that I'm not wanted. It was the system in China for thousands of years, and if the horoscope said no deals today, everybody understood and deals there weren't. For us, in our late-industrial society, it's clock in and clock off, no excuses, just get on with it. Claudine is late industrial all right. Combines it with early warning.

"It's 'alf-past seven, *chéri*."

Ugh.

"I've a feeling it's dangerous for me to get up, today," I warned her.

"It will be dangerous if you don't," she threatened.

"No, listen. Some days just don't feel right. It's a mistake to take them on. Why don't we stay here today, and go back to London tomorrow." It wasn't really a question—I knew the reasons. Claudine listed them: schools, work, meetings, accounts. She sounded like a churchyard bell; it tolled for me. Why wasn't I born Chinese?

I hauled myself out of bed. Through the window, the outside world was gray and uncertain; mist drifted between the huge Victorian specimen trees that surround our house; firs and copper beeches, overgrown to a threatening enormity. From their tops, hiding in the mist, the concealed croaking of invisible jackdaws.

In the kitchen, breakfast was in session at the big pine table. It was subdued, functional: we were off to London and the French were going back to Bordeaux; everybody drank coffee in silence while they planned the day ahead. I had a thought, and, after my first cup of coffee, slipped away to make an unobtrusive visit to the attic, from which I collected my father's deed box. Before I brought it down I brushed off the dust and bat droppings, and checked the contents; they were just as I had remembered. I took it down and put it straight into the car under the other luggage, to avoid questions. I tucked the torch in there as well. Then I went back inside for my second cup of coffee.

On the road, the mist soon cleared, shredded by the morning sun. We parted from Claudine's family by the Exeter roundabout, where they headed for Weymouth and the car ferry, hooting and waving their farewells. Then we were on our own, just Claudine and me and the three children (the dog stays at the neighboring farm): the big silver Citroën rolled up the motorway like a Boeing on endless takeoff, and by noon we were plunged into London traffic; off the flyover, up Kensington High Street, and then left into Kensington Church Street. I pulled up beside the shop. Back to base.

WILLIAM WARNER WINES, it says in white packing-case stencil letters on the black blinds. Very mellifluous, I opine. The colors used
to be gold on red in my father's time, but I decided on a new image
when I took over and took advice from a graphics consultant: now
the scheme is black and white and the only color is that of the wines.
The shop front is Victorian, with lots of black painted molding and
brass handles on the doors. Inside, it's deliberately old-fashioned in
flavor, with a sanded pine-boarded floor and black-stained wooden
shelves against white walls. None of your standard supermarket
shelving and tatty carpet squares here. And not only did we get the
upmarket effect we wanted, but our refurbishment cost less than a
standard shopfitting job. *Much* less. Everybody happy, including the
woodworm.

Maggie had seen us arrive, and was making telephone gestures at
me, so I went into the office, leaving the others to unload the car.

"The VAT people want to have a word with you, Mr. William,"
Maggie said.

There you are, you see! I *knew* I shouldn't have participated in
today.

"Thanks, Maggie," I said, "and hello. What do they want?"

"It's Mr. Winkelmann again," Maggie whispered, holding the
phone. Her face said all that she was unable to say aloud. Winkelmann! It couldn't be worse. He's the Dracula of Customs and Excise.
His bite has meant death to many a small business. Some day I'm
gonna *stake* him; meanwhile I've gotta smile, smile, *smile*.

"Mr. Winkelmann? Good morning!"

"Good *afternoon*, Mr. Warner." So it was. Well, not a chargeable
error; there's no VAT on good mornings—yet. His graveyard voice
again. "We're not entirely satisfied with the findings of our inspection. There are inconsistencies in the book figures for stock compared
with sales, particularly with regard to the trade averages, which we
apply as a guideline."

"Oh?" What else could I say?

"I would like to make a further inspection to verify the figures to
our satisfaction. You may, in the interim, wish to consider whether
there are any factors that might affect the stock figure given to us.
At your convenience."

He didn't mean it, of course. Next year, sometime, never would
suit me fine. But I agreed to make it Thursday. Better get it over
with.

"I'll need all the books made up for Thursday, Maggie," I told
her. "And just pop down to Harrods for a sharp stake."

Maggie, who really runs the business, having joined it as a short-
hand-typist during my father's time, when there were more staff,
and worked her way up over thirty years, feels just as I do about
the load of bureaucracy that we now have to carry, threatening to
push our gunwales below water level and sink us with all hands.
"I'll get one," she said, her eyes fierce behind her glasses, "and I'll
sharpen it myself."

By midafternoon, I'd got through all the pressing work that couldn't
wait. I went into my inner office and closed the door, shutting out
the rattle of our part-time typist and the burping of the computer
as it brought up invoices. Carpet I've got, and paneled walls in
blackened oak, bought from a demolition site. In a word, inner sanc-
tum: when you're selling wine, paneling is better than persuasion.
I bring customers in here when the deal is three-quarters done, but
needs a final push: a glass of wine to taste and the paneling to speak
for me, and all I have to do is provide the dotted line for them to
sign on.

The torch was there, waiting on my desk where I'd put it. Squat,
black, molded, with a big square battery and separate handgrip over
the top. I picked it up. The business end had a thick plastic lens
held in place by a screw ring, evidently waterproof. The bulb was
tungsten-halogen, as in a car headlamp: that explained the brilliance
of the beam. I could see the scene again—the beam boring into the
darkness of the moor; the sheep lighting up like motorway markers.
I'd never seen a torch so powerful. It had to be for some special
purpose; the cost of such quality comes high, and I couldn't imagine
that such a thing would sell in the normal high street motorists'
accessory shop.

Waterproof. Extra powerful. Shockproof too, as I knew. So?

A diver's torch, perhaps. I pondered this, turning it over, inspecting every detail for clues.

Then I came on the number underneath. It was molded into the case. MoD 73650017/B/76. Then a name, probably the manufacturer. But it was the first part that caught my attention: MoD. Ministry of Defense.

The Man from the Ministry. *This* Ministry?

Rubbish! He was having me on, wanting to hit me in the only way left to him—psychologically; a humorist even at that late stage in his career. I didn't believe a word of it.

Still, it was the only clue I had, and the greatest detective there never was would have known what to do next. "When you have eliminated the impossible, Watson, whatever remains, however improbable, must be the truth."

I decided to get straight on with it. The name after the number was Walsall Electrics. No address, but, as everybody knows, Walsall is a bit of Birmingham, and it could be as simple as that. I got on to Directory Inquiries.

I asked for the number of Walsall Electrics. They gave it to me.

Now what?

I thought for a minute or two, then dialed the number.

"Walsall, good afternoon," said a gummy female voice.

"Sales, please."

"Car components or other?"

"Other."

"Putting you through."

A short pause, and then a gummy male voice.

"Sales, can I help you?"

I drew a deep breath, launched into my act.

"Ah, good afternoon to you. MoD here. We'd like a . . ."

"Come again?"

"Ministry of Defense," I said in a stuffy tone.

"Oh. Oh yes. Sorry, I didn't . . ."

"We'd like your estimate for a further supply of torches, hand, part number 73650017/B/76. Would you put me on to whoever deals with these?"

"That's my department," he said. "Glad it's going well. Is that Mr. Williams?"

"No," I said, my brain cells rattling with the strain. "Mr. Williams has had to go back to Cardiff, family problems. It's on *my* desk now; my name is Chalmers. And you're . . . ?"

"Wilkins, Mike Wilkins. Glad to know you. You'd like an estimate for more of the torches. That's very good news. How many?"

"Oh," I said (what would be a realistic number?), "say, ten thousand."

"Ten *thousand*! That *is* good news. And I hadn't heard you'd finished testing. They'll be pleased to hear this upstairs."

Blown it! I thought. He's going to have second thoughts in a minute and start checking. I'll have to bulldoze.

"Well, we're only asking for an estimate, you know," I said severely. "Don't count your chickens. And the price has got to be right."

"Oh yes," he said, "but *ten thousand*. That's a lot of torches." He paused, and I wondered what was coming next—the noise of thinking was deafening. There was some going on at my end, too. His voice when he spoke again was subdued, cautious.

"I hope you won't mind my saying, if we quote for ten thousand, that'll be based on *supplying* ten thousand. If you only end up ordering *one* thousand, we'll have to requote. Thought I'd better say, as some people—not you, I'm sure—some people do that trying to catch us, trying to be clever. You know what I mean?"

"Perfectly understandable."

"No offense?"

"Not at all. But remind me—I haven't got the file in front of me—how many did we have last time?"

"Torches? Well," he said, "well. That's why it seems a bit odd to me. Surely Williams must have told you before he left?"

This was awkward. I didn't know what he was talking about. What should I say? I needed to know how many torches had been produced, and where they had been distributed. It was the moment of truth, and he was stalling.

Maggie is a marvel. There was a tap at the door, and in she came, bearing a tray with my tea and a plate of shortcake.

"Hold on a moment," I said into the telephone, "tea's just arrived."
And then, away from the phone, "Thank you, Tracy, just put it
there." Maggie looked startled at her rechristening, and was going
to say something about it, but I waved her to silence. I tinkled the
teaspoon in the saucer, holding the telephone near it; at the other
end, I hoped, he would be getting a tone poem of quintessential
government office; there had also been typewriter noises off when
Maggie had opened the door. I slurped some tea, gave a theatrical
sigh of satisfaction. Was he convinced?

"You certainly enjoy your tea," he said, sounding amused, "I'll
say that!"

A bit over the top, speaking to a man in my position—a man who
was *supposed* to be in my position. But I could make use of it to bring
him to heel. I put on my stuffy voice again.

"Mr. Wilkins. How many torches did we have last time?"

"Yes, I'm sorry," he said, immediately. "I didn't mean . . . yes.
It was ten, wasn't it."

"Ten?"

"Yes. Prototypes. For testing."

"And where were they sent to?"

"You don't seem to know much about it."

"*Please* don't waste my time, Mr. Wilkins."

"Well, they were sent out by Protoplastics. They supply most of
our high-quality injection molding, and we had to be sure about the
gas seals. We sent them the electrical bits, and they assembled, and
sent them on direct, to save time. You—Mr. Williams, that is—
told us the testing was going to be done at Porton Down."

Jackpot! Facts were pouring out of him now, like coins from a
fruit machine, even if I couldn't believe what I was hearing. Porton
Down! That's near Salisbury. I knew because I'd been on a course
there during national service; the course was called Familiarization
with Nuclear and Biological Warfare. To know all is to forgive all,
Mme. de Staël is reported to have said about people. She wouldn't
have said the same about nuclear and biological warfare, especially
after seeing the films and being shut into gas chambers to sample
the products. We finished the course thoughtful but hardly "famil-
iarized"; it was a relief to get back to our tanks and machine guns,

the simple fireworks of conventional war; things that went whizz and bang but could sometimes be avoided if you ducked.

I'd been there. That was a connection, between me and the torch and the late torchbearer. Could this be . . . *but hold on*. Think about it later. Get the facts now; he's thoroughly broken in and will tell me anything if I keep the pressure on. What's this firm, Protoplastics?

I told him I'd need to change the part number molded into the torch body and would instruct Protoplastics myself, but Williams hadn't left the address. In a moment, I had the address and telephone number.

"Where shall we send the estimate?"

"Same as last time," I told him, and rang off.

Now I sat back, sipped my tea, and began to assemble the facts. The torch had been ordered approximately six months ago by the Ministry of Defense from Walsall Electrics, who in turn ordered the body moldings from their subcontractors, Protoplastics, whose factory was in Stanmore, North London. I had been expecting a London connection to turn up, and here it was: I could still hear the incongruity of that London voice as it came to me over the bog. Only ten torches had been produced, fitted with anticorrosive gas seals, and they'd been sent to the research establishment at Porton Down for testing.

Those were the facts. Now I indulged in a little speculation. What if . . . ? Suppose I had learned something while on that course at Porton Down, which I shouldn't have learned? A little knowledge . . . which was dangerous to someone. But that course was twenty years ago! Suppose circumstances had changed in some way . . . this knowledge didn't matter then, but now it does. It would have to be exclusive to me, or to a very few others—impractical to find and silence all the members of my course; about twenty junior single pippers all from different regiments. So what did I know? Or, what did they *think* I knew? Surely there must be some more likely explanation?

Maggie came in, ostensibly for my teacup.

"What was all that about?" she asked. "Why *Tracy*?"

"Maggie," I said, "I apologize. I just wanted to give the impression of a big office, and in big offices they have Tracys."

She frowned; there was still something on her mind.

"You used to worry your father, you know. All that playacting."

"Oh come on, Maggie."

"You did. And this business won't run itself. It's not doing as well as it was."

"You've been talking to Claudine."

"Well, I *have*. She's got a head for business. She said if a business isn't going up, it's going down. It won't stand still, you know. I just hope you're taking it seriously enough, if you don't mind my saying so."

"And all this because of a jokey remark . . ." I said.

"Of course not. It's how you *look*. I know that look. It worries *me*, I can tell you." She was standing back now, holding the tea tray with both hands, the cup rattling slightly on the saucer. I got up and took her by the shoulders.

"Stop it, Maggie." She didn't look at me. "You'll be saying next, 'Where will it all end?' or 'Life is a serious business'—things like that. Stop worrying. We'll have a meeting tomorrow, plan what to do. Ten o'clock here in my office. You, me and Claudine. OK?"

She nodded. I let her go. The door swung to after her.

Well, where *would* it all end?

Good question.

The evening arrived before I was ready for it, and caught me with my pants down—psychological pants, that is. Before my telephone call to Wilkins, the episode on the moor—the white face spotlit in the darkness, the film like action sequences, the bog, all that—had seemed a kind of dream. I *had* dreamed it, as well. The torch, though tangible, was a leftover from that dream; it had the quality that attaches to unexplained objects; this made it a symbol of mystery. After the telephone call, I knew that this mystery was "Made in Birmingham." Down-to-earth, in a pedal-driven flying saucer. Wilkins had guided me in to land.

So far, so good. The mystery had been devalued, and that was healthy. What I had left was a real-life puzzle, and I could get to grips with that. My difficulty was that my other real life, my household role, was being nudged out of place. Maggie had noticed that at once. I had already become semidetached. Our subconscious chooses which part of our lives is real, and which a dream: home or office, peace or war. My domestic life was starting to take on a tinge of unreality, as the focus shifted. When the girls arrived home I could hear myself, trying to be Father, sounding more like a toyshop Father Christmas. "How was school today? Ho, ho, ho." Going through the motions.

So it was a difficult evening. I put on the best performance I could during supper, and escaped downstairs to my office soon afterward. There was the torch. I took it with me as I did my round of the building, checking the locks and burglar alarms; I was glad that because of the shop we have an elaborate security system. I felt distinctly on edge when I walked down the garden to check the garage, which has access from the side road. I trod quietly, keeping on the grass, torch switched off. There's a high wall to give us privacy from the side road, but there's nothing to stop someone climbing over it. I watched the top as I walked, half expecting to see a head silhouetted by the streetlamps behind, but nothing moved. The garage was locked, but I went in and locked the Citroën as well. Julian lives in the room over the garage, which he uses as a studio, and his light was on.

I called up the stairs, "You there, Jules?"

"I'm here."

"Keep your door locked." We all complain there are more burglars than residents in our bit of London.

"Always do, Dad."

Good lad.

"Good night."

MARTIAL ARTS

The Art of War is, therefore, in its proper sense, the art of making use of the given means in fighting . . .

—*Clausewitz*

"There isn't a simple explanation, or a magic answer."

We three had met in my office at ten o'clock precisely, as arranged, to discuss what should be done to reverse the decline in our fortunes. I had no doubt, myself, what should be done, but it was (a) illegal, and (b) beyond our powers. Blow up Kensington Town Hall. Or, to achieve a similar result more humanely, send the council on permanent holiday to Sri Lanka. With the rates we pay, they could afford it. From the amount of rubbish left on the streets, the dustmen are there already.

"Well, we can't do much about the rates." Maggie must have been reading my mind. "Other overheads, that's wages, national insurance, heat, light, phone, transport, advertising, bank charges, all up on average twenty-three percent."

"And the sales are down by seven percent," Claudine said, reading from a sheet with her own writing on it—she'd been doing her homework.

We gloomed on in this way for about an hour, looking at ideas for cutting overheads. We do this every year; last year we decided to replace all the hundred-watt display bulbs with sixties to save on electricity. Then the rates went up. Still, we have wonderful com-

munity services: anyone who's hard up can go to free karate classes
and become a mugger.

We finished, as usual, with the resolution that Maggie would go
through the overheads again; Claudine would review our list of customers to see who might be persuaded to buy more; and that I would
first check our stocks and then look for new customers. It's great
having resolutions: makes you feel something has really been
achieved. Then you realize that it hasn't, until you've done the work.

I spent the rest of the morning counting bottles in the shop and in
the cellar, ticking them off against the stock list. I'm not the best
person to do this really: it's too much like getting a compulsive reader
to check a library list; every few bottles, there's something to jog
the memory chain, and instead of counting, minutes are spent in a
daze while trains of thought go rattling happily down sidetracks.
And bottle labels are so evocative and hard to resist—as they're
meant to be. All those soldier-straight lines of vines, like an exercise
in perspective, leading the eye back to the château, half palace, half
farmhouse, with its rows of shuttered windows and Roman tiled
roof. Or the simple *vins de pays* with their landscapes and classical
bunches of grapes. And the occasional upper-crust bottle, the label
so plain you might pass it over if you didn't know what it was: no
need for the hard sell here, they've never got enough; the label carries
a tiny drawing, for instance, Latour, looking like a chess piece, dead
simple, and underneath a discreet line of lettering—Premier Grand
Cru. Outa sight, outa sight! And outa most people's price range,
too, though everyone ought to save up and buy a really good bottle
just once or twice in a while. Otherwise you'll never know what
wine really *is*.

Lunchtime, and I brought up a bottle of white Rioja to try; a
sample batch, and a new departure for us as we specialize in French
wines. But all those continental holidays are having an effect, and
Rioja is, of course, the big name in Spanish wine; usually red, with
the taste of the oak barrels it's matured in, but the white is getting
better known now. It was dryish but soft, flowery bouquet, deli-

cious. Claudine used to resist the buying of non-French wines, but she's getting over that now; we *have* to diversify, and there's a lot of good stuff coming from outside France, especially in the cheaper end of the market.

"*Pas mal.*"

"Not better than that?"

"Oh yes, I like it. *Et il se boit facilement.*"

Drinks itself easily! What a ridiculous language French can be. But she's right. In English, it slips down a treat. Should be popular.

We decided to order it, and during lunch the wine disappeared from the bottle without my being aware of pouring it out. Drank itself all up, didn't it?

After lunch my taxi came to convey me to our warehouse, with Pete at the wheel. It's my own taxi, and my solution to the London traffic problem: the Citroën is useless in traffic, and I have to spend a lot of time making the rounds of the restaurants and clubs that are our best customers and buy in bulk. We have a van for normal deliveries, but there's plenty of room for a few cases of wine in my taxi as samples and for emergencies. Pete stays to argue with traffic wardens while I go in and haggle with customers: very often the wardens pass us over as they don't notice it's a private taxi. To help the illusion I keep it as black as it was born, and have left the meter in place: we just drive round with the sign on top switched off, as though it was permanently engaged. This doesn't stop Arabs trying to get in, but when Pete's waiting for me he's learned to deal with that. "Broken dahn, guv," he shouts. "Dis camel snuffed it, you savvy?" It may not do much for international relations, but it works. And anyway, they shouldn't be so bloody pushy.

The warehouse is in Brewery Lane, down Wapping way. It's still like a scene from Oliver Twist: cobbled streets and dank brickwork. Only the clothes have changed, and you still see the Dickensian faces, the Fagins and the Artful Dodgers, now studying their chances from between the high collars of bomber jackets. You need at least one of them on your side, and that's where Pete comes in: I know he knocks off a few bottles by way of overtime, but he doesn't overdo it, and he doesn't touch the good stuff.

We rattled to a stop. Pete jumped out and unlocked the pass door into the warehouse. It's all crates of bottles now: no barrels, since we gave up doing our own bottling ten years ago. I walked down the rows, taking a general look, and then went into the office at the back. This used to be a spirits store, and is built like a fortress in solid brick with no windows; the floor is concrete with gray lino over it, and the ceiling is another slab of concrete. No roof lights, no openings anywhere except the door, and that's got a steel plate bolted to both sides. There's a small spyhole in the door—not the domestic sort that turns your best friend into Frankenstein when you look through it to see who's rung your doorbell, but a simple hole about an inch and a half in diameter, fitted with thick glass, so that you can see in *or* out. I found myself noting all these familiar details as if they were new to me. Surely I wasn't getting the bunker mentality already?

I collected the stock list from the filing cabinet in the office, and Pete helped me check off the stock. It's easier than in the shop really: everything is laid out in order, and you get through it fast as you're counting cases rather than bottles. Pete knows his job, and he has a tidy mind, which is essential in a storekeeper. There were two or three damaged cases at the back.

"Those written off?" I asked.

"Not yet—but could be," Pete said. He waited, then began to pant, putting on an eager doggy act.

"All right," I told him. "You have that one, and put the other two in the car for me."

"Oh, brilliant! I really fancy a drop o' that."

He doesn't sell it, he drinks it. Though it's not really any of my business, it's one of the things I like about him. Paternalist rubbish, of course. "Let's get back now, Pete," I said, and we got back into the taxi and took off.

Tuesday evening now, and all's well. Two days, forty-eight hours since the curtain went up. And since that dramatic opening scene, nothing. No sign, no squeak, not a sausage. Perhaps that was it: some mistake had been made, and now the forces against me have gone into reverse; been withdrawn. It wasn't likely, if that was so, that I'd get a letter. Dear Mr. Warner, do please accept sincere apologies, most embarrassing, hope you understand, deeply regret inconvenience, most fortunate no lasting harm done, please believe most sincerely? No chance of that. *Writing him off*—perhaps he got his orders mixed. It's happened before, Balaclava, wasn't it? So I won't *know* if it's all off. I'll have to assume it is, if nothing happens. If nothing happens for how long? Two weeks? A year? Will I ever be able to be *sure*?

So all is *not* well. No news is *not* good news. In military terms, I'm in a defensive role, and the other side have the initiative. If there *is* another side, and *if* the war is still on.

Tomorrow, I decided, I'm going into action. I'm not going to wait around, I'll take the initiative. Follow up the torch, see what I can find out from the Stanmore manufacturer. Protoplastics, you're my target for tomorrow. And now, just in case things get rough, I'll pay a visit to the armory.

My father's deed box, actually, which I'd collected from the attic before we left Devon. I pulled it out from under my desk in the office, and stood it on some newspaper on top of the desk. It was a monstrous old thing, originally black enameled metal, now rusty over most of its surface, and fitted with massive hinges and a lock that could have been used on the main gate at the Tower of London. All show—the key has been lost ever since I can remember. I wiped off as much grime as I could with a screw of newspaper, and opened up.

Papers, papers: wills, deeds of various properties, sundry pink-ribboned legal-looking documents, letters, reports, faded photographs. I resisted the papers—read me! *read me!*—and put them sternly aside. At the bottom of the box, like a toad in a hole, was the ugly bulk of my father's First World War Webley revolver.

I lifted it into the light. I hadn't held it since, well, I must have been about sixteen. I could remember clearly how huge, how heavy it had seemed to me then, in the dim attic light where I had been poking about among the family treasures. Since then, I had handled a lot of firearms, and grown accustomed to the feel of modern, small caliber weapons, light and well balanced. This ancient cannon was, by comparison, a dinosaur. The hole in the muzzle looked like the Mersey Tunnel. It fired a bullet almost half an inch in diameter: .45, to be exact. It weighed almost twice as much as a modern lightweight handgun. And this actual monster had preceded my father, brandished by him at distant Germans as he climbed out of his trench, over the top, to make the long walk over the mud of no-man's-land. Useless, of course, except perhaps for morale.

In that situation, you had to wave something, and it might as well be something that discharged bullets, even if there was little chance of them hitting anything. With that pistol, you could, after practice, hit an enemy at twenty paces, given time to aim it carefully. Walking over mud, you might do it at half the distance. By the time you were ten paces from a German, he would have had time to shoot you with his rifle some fifteen times over. Since I first saw this thing I've never wondered why the average life of a second lieutenant in the trenches was two weeks. He was given this to defend himself with.

Well, my father survived. And I've every intention of doing so. Maybe this pistol is lucky. It certainly *looks* frightening, and that'll be useful. Maybe they'll surrender at just the sight of it. But I'd better keep it loaded, just in case.

I looked into the deed box to see how many shots we had in the locker. It was empty. No, there was something in there, in the corner. Two. Two cartridges. The brass cases were streaked with green corrosion. They were, after all, um, about sixty years old. They looked as fearsome as the revolver: the nickel-plated bullets bulged from the cases, as big as a man's thumb. I had read about the awesome stopping power of these things: the effect is such that they throw the victim backward, as if struck by a sledgehammer. I broke the revolver open, squinted down the barrel toward the light. The spiral rifling was slightly pitted, but clear of rust. The two cartridges slipped into the six-hole cylinder, became part of it. I snapped it shut, and spun the cylinder, holding off the hammer. It whirred round, stopped with a cartridge in the firing position. Lucky

I'm not playing Russian roulette. Then I broke it open again, and the extractor pushed up the cartridges for me to take out. Well, now I'm armed. If the old cartridges still work.

And if I'm able to pull the trigger when the time comes.

I thought I saw a flash from the roof light of Julian's room over the garage. I was halfway down the garden at the time: I stopped, and watched. It happened again—a momentary glow of light, hardly noticeable, but enough to confirm that there was someone in there. It wouldn't be Julian; he would have had the lights full on, and anyway I knew that on Tuesdays he usually went to discussions at the Gurdjieff Institute, round the corner in Holland Park.

It was after eleven. Claudine and the girls had gone up to bed, and I was just completing my tour of inspection, making sure everything was locked up. I didn't have the revolver with me—it was too big to fit in my pocket, and I didn't want to prowl round the house with it in my hand in case I met one of the family. A quandary— in the time it would take me to go back for the revolver, the intruder could disappear. I very much wanted to see what he looked like, to get some clue to the mystery, maybe follow him back to his home or even, with luck, *headquarters*. I decided to press on, arming myself with whatever weapon came to hand.

A garden fork, as it turned out: still sticking in the border beside the path where some untidy gardener—me, probably—had left it, and glinting dully in the light of the streetlamp. I yanked it out of the ground and wiped the earth off on the grass of the lawn. Feeling like a revolutionary French peasant with a pitchfork about to spear a seigneur, I headed for the door to the loft-room stairs. I pushed the door gently—it was slightly ajar. It opened without a sound. Ahead was a straight flight of stairs that led to the small landing. They were plain wood, uncarpeted, and I knew that they creaked. No way of getting there unannounced. I drew a deep breath, and charged.

The loft-room door was immediately opposite the top of the stairs, and I could see a faint chink of light down one side—that, too, was ajar. I hurled myself at it and burst into the room, turning and crouching as soon as I was in, gripping the fork with both hands as in bayonet practice.

The room was in darkness except under the roof lights, which let in the hellish sodium glare of big cities at night. Black shadows and pale squares, turning the floor into a giant chessboard. It was his move.

Nothing happened.

I thought I could hear breathing.

Perhaps it was my own.

I *knew* he was there, in one of those black shadows.

But which one? Did he have a gun? And was he prepared to use it?

A full minute passed. Neither of us moved. We were like cats; frozen intensity before the spring.

Or maybe rabbits; petrified with terror. Aggression and fear are opposite sides of the same coin. And it spins, it spins . . .

I thought, if he has a gun, he'll have it ready now. He'll be waiting for me to put the light on. He'll know the light switch is by the door. He'll be aiming in that direction.

There was enough traffic noise to cover slight movement. I worked myself away from the door until I could reach Julian's desk. There's an architect's lamp on it, run from a wall socket. It was all in shadow. I reached up and very slowly tilted the metal lampshade to point away from me, down the room.

Then I crouched as low as I could and, feeling for the wall socket, switched it on and off—the briefest flash I could manage.

I was looking down the length of the room as the flash of light lit everything up, and the image stayed on my retina like a photograph. I saw the intruder, my counterpart, crouched at his end of the room. He was wearing a green sweater over blue jeans. His face was a black blob—a stocking mask. He held his weapon out in front of him—not a gun, but a large knife. He was of medium height and build.

I'm going to handle this, I thought. I switched the light on, and stood up.

His first reaction was a defensive gesture: taking a step back, he moved the knife from side to side, making sure I noticed it. No difficulty about that—it was the size of a young bayonet. I glanced quickly round the room. The top drawer of Julian's filing cabinet stood open, but nothing else was out of place. Was that it, then? Searching for papers, a document? He certainly couldn't be one of the burgling brotherhood that live off our district—they don't bother with filing cabinets. Cash, jewelery, cameras, hi-fi—that's their stock in trade.

Could try asking, of course.

"Look, I've no idea what you want or why you're here. This is my son's room, and his filing cabinet—you're unlikely to find anything to interest you in it, unless you're thinking of taking up architecture. Why don't you tell me what you're after—maybe we could do a deal?"

I paused. He said nothing, and didn't move. I supposed he was glaring at me from behind his stocking mask—I could sort of feel the heat radiating from it. Also, he seemed to be stoking up with heavy breathing like an animal about to charge.

A sense of nightmare began to weigh me down. That familiar feeling of unreality, the not knowing if you were asleep or awake. But the fork handle in my hands was real enough. So was his knife blade, which continued to weave from side to side like a snake about to strike.

I decided there was no chance of forcing any useful information out of this encounter. The important thing was to end it without injury. To reduce the risk of armed confrontation, I had to get further away from the door, and give him an escape route. I moved slowly behind Julian's desk, and along the side of the room.

As I had expected, he began to circle in the opposite direction. I kept my fork aimed at his stomach, and hoped he wouldn't try to rush me. It would have been stupid of him to risk getting impaled on those prongs: they were muddy, but sharp enough for the job.

When we'd circled far enough for him to have the door behind him, I stopped. He stopped too, staying facing me, knife at the ready. We seemed to have stuck, each in our threatening attitudes, like lead soldiers.

I felt my temper beginning to go. It was unbearably frustrating to be endlessly opposing this faceless hominoid who would neither speak nor break off and go. What's more—what would have happened if Julian had come back to this?

"You stupid burk!" I hissed at him. "I don't know who you are, or who sent you, but you're the second homicidal nutter I've had to deal with in the last three days, and I'm bloody fed up with having to defend myself against attacks that make no sense at all. Either explain yourself or piss off! I've had enough of this, and of you."

Perhaps he'd been afraid that, if he turned, I would lunge at his back. Because he gave a nod, now, with his stockinged head, and backed away, toward the door. I gave him space, and didn't follow. At last he turned, and made for the door at full speed, blundering into a bookcase and dislodging Julian's favorite glider, which was propped up there, gleaming white, T-tailed, radio controlled. It slid to the floor with a splintering crash.

I leapt forward then, cursing, and brandishing the fork. The stairs shook as the intruder flung himself down them. I heard his running feet on the path outside as he made for the side entrance. That would need securing—he must have broken the gate open. Then a car started, and roared away.

I sat down on Julian's drawing stool, and waited for the alarm bells to stop ringing all over my body. Then I crossed the floor to pick up the glider. The wings had been jerked out of position, but they were fixed with elastic to absorb shocks, and clicked back into place with no trouble. Apart from that there was only minor damage to the nose.

No casualties, in effect. And now they knew this was Julian's room, no reason for them to call again.

But, as they were interested in filing cabinets, I'd see what I could do to help.

Tomorrow.

SURPRISE
SURPRISE

The endeavor by measures generally, and especially by the distribution of forces, to surprise the enemy, which can be imagined just as well in the defensive.

—*Clausewitz*

"Ginny, darling!"

"Hel-*lo*, darling!" Ginny's voice on the phone was warm, enthusiastic. And so it should be—we have a very special relationship that's gone on for years.

"Who's that?" she asked.

Oh.

Well there's more than one darling in her life. As there is in mine. But she means it all the same. So do I.

"It's William," I said, hoping that there wasn't more than one William. There never used to be, and identity is a fragile flower. A William by any other name . . . is easier to take.

"Oh *William!* Lovely to *hear* you, darling!"

I had known, the moment I woke up that Wednesday morning, that I had become too much of a liability to the family, and must get away from the house as soon as possible. I was breaking the rules—Claudine was at home—but for the best of reasons. I would have preferred to go to Ginny's that evening, but this was difficult to arrange, and anyway Ginny said she had an article to finish. So we fixed on Thursday.

"Tell you all when I see you," I said. "Seven be OK? I'll bring the supper."

I told Claudine I was planning a short tour of our hotel clients west of London, starting tomorrow after Winkelmann's inspection of our books.

"Ah yes, wonderful!" she said, pleased at my devotion to duty. I was planning to include some hotel calls; hoping that the other side would catch up and keep on my trail, but I would also probably collect some orders. So my maneuver had something for everyone. I'll make it to general yet.

The central objective was to get together some firm information, evidence that would convince the police and enable them to round up the opposition, leaving no dangerous loose ends. I was starting work on that straightaway.

I got out the Citroën and drove myself over to the warehouse. Pete was out in the van, making deliveries, and I let myself in. The plan was simple. I was going to build a better mousetrap, and let the world beat a path to my door. Or if not better, at least bigger. And not for mice, for rats. Human rats.

The idea had been cooking in my head since the dark recesses of the night before, when I had found myself dreaming about the windowless, fortresslike construction of the office at the back of the warehouse. It was built as a spirit store, to protect the most vulnerable part of a wine merchant's stock against people breaking in. But it would work equally well in reverse, with a little modification.

I brought in my tools from the boot of the car, and set to work. It took me two hours to complete the mechanism.

Four battered green three-drawer filing cabinets now stood in a row at the back of the office, opposite the door where they would immediately be seen—these represented the cheese. The trap was baited with papers—it was papers they were after, I had learned last night. The first cabinet on the left had a hole drilled in the back, lined with a smooth plastic grommet. Through this ran a piece of twin-core flex attached to the back of the bottom drawer. The flex ran down to the skirting board at a shallow angle, concealed by the other three filing cabinets, and then ran along the skirting, loosely held by insulated staples, round the office walls until it reached the hinge side of the door, where it was attached to a small wooden wedge designed to hold the door open at right angles. The door opened outward, and I had fitted a powerful spring closer to the outside, concealing this from the casual glance by a pile of wine crates stacked against the office wall. I had fitted two new Yale spring locks to the top and bottom of the door, on the outside, but had not fitted the inside knobs.

Work completed, I fixed the two locks in the retracted position so as not to lock myself in, and looked round the room. The flex was visible where it ran along the skirting, but it looked, in its insulated staples, just like a piece of amateur wiring—to a light, perhaps. The door wedge was visible, but it was small, and it was not in a conspicuous position. Now to test it.

I am the rat. I arrive at the office door, having broken into the warehouse. I see the filing cabinets, which may contain what I am after. I start opening the drawers; I get to the bottom drawer of the first cabinet. I pull the handle, and the drawer comes partly out—not locked, evidently, but seems stiff. Perhaps a file has caught. I pull harder and . . . *what's that*? The drawer has come open, but I hear a rattle from behind me, by the door. I spin round. And the door is closing, accelerating shut. Realization, and panic! It's a trap! I leap for the door, but it's too far, closing too fast. Too late! The door has slammed shut. The locks (would) have clicked; no way to open them from inside. I'm caught!

What do I do next?

I look round the office.

Yes, well.

I telephone for help, using the telephone that is still sitting on the desk. (*Must deal with that.*)

Any other way to escape?

I couldn't see or think of one.

I left the telephone in the office, and cut the cable just outside the door, baring the ends so that they could be reconnected quickly.

There were four wires in the little cable, but each was a different color and could be easily matched when the time came.

Pete turned up just as I was finishing. I told him that I had reason to believe (that blanket policeman's phrase) that someone might try to break into the warehouse within the next day or two; that he must be careful not to upset the trap or lock himself in; and that he was on no account to tackle any intruder if he should see one, or to do anything except ring me. He was indignant.

"I'd like ter know oo'd do a thing like that," he said. "This's never bin knocked off since I've bin 'ere. It's no one from rahnd 'ere, that's for sure—must be some bleedin' foreigner." He's racially prejudiced, Pete—if you're Wapping you're all right, but the rest of the world, outside the family, are all bent geezers. It's cosy tribalism, you think, until you remember what happens when Millwall play West Ham. "I'll lay back round 'ere . . ." he started to offer.

"Thanks, but no. Definitely no. It's too dangerous, and there's no need." And I made him promise to keep out of it. It might not stick, but it was the best I could do, and at least if he couldn't be good, he'd be careful.

I had to screech back to Ken Church Street in order to have time to clean myself up before going out to lunch with Edward. He'd rung me the previous afternoon to make this date. Edward is one of my oldest friends—in fact we were at school together. He was more impressive than me, and was Head of House. That set the pattern, and he's still the same now: solid and reliable. He went straight from school into the Civil Service, wasting no time, and is now a Permanent Under Secretary—or perhaps Assistant to X in the Department of Industry. I've never sorted out the pecking order—I find that sort of thing boring beyond words—but whatever the position is, it's important. It would have to be, to interest Edward. I took the call and waited, while a succession of secretaries, a trilling of telephonists, each repeated the glad news that Mr. Edward Dundas was calling me. It was like the Hallelujah Chorus. When—will—he—speak to me—Mr. Dun-das? Inna moment! Inna moment! At last he spake.

"William? So glad I've caught you . . ." he said, or rather, boomed. Edward's voice can't be described by any other word; it's like bitterns, or Big Ben. You could put him up there if it broke down; record him for overseas broadcasts to the far-flung corners of the Empire, if we still have any, and they would never know the difference. London calling, London calling; and Edward would go *boom, boooom*. Confidence maintained.

He was inviting me to lunch, he said, because he and Tricia had *so* much enjoyed their dinner with us the previous week, but they were now, unfortunately, *so* booked up for evenings that they would not be able to ask us back for some time, several weeks even, although they would very much like . . .

"Yes, Edward," I cut in. He does go on. "I'd enjoy that. And, as a matter of fact, there's something I'd like to ask you about. Where, and when?"

"Athenian, one o'clock, tomorrow, if that would be . . ."

"Fine," I said. "And many thanks. See you there."

I was impressed. Things must be going Edward's way. Though, on second thought, the Athenian wasn't the place for the up-and-coming. But you would certainly get to be noshing with the already arrived.

I was lucky with a taxi, and got to Waterloo Place at five to one. My taxi had just left when another pulled up, and Edward descended. He paid off the driver and turned to greet me gravely. He manages to get steadily more impressive. This time I saw he had begun to affect a watch chain: gold links hung in a glistening catenary across his well-filled waistcoat. He had the height to carry it off; he was almost as tall as me, and rather more solid. Solid within and without. And now, solid gold—it had to be. I wanted to see this watch chain in action. You can't just glance at a waistcoat watch in the casual way you treat a wristwatch. There's a word for it.

"Sorry, but at least we're *both* late." I wasn't sorry, and neither of us was late: it was a plot.

Edward fell for it. He reached into his waistcoat pocket, drew out

his watch, *consulted* it. That's the word! The consultation was, of
course, satisfactory.

"Late? I think not." He smiled at me, using his uncle expression.
The watch slid back into the waistcoat pocket. He could do it without
looking, I noticed. Must have practiced in the mirror.

"Let's go in, then." Edward led the way up the huge steps toward
the monstrous classical portico. If I'd been wearing a toga, I would
have given it a hitch. We reached the revolving door. "After you,
Caesar," I said. Edward was already revolving and didn't hear. Probably a good thing. I'm really quite fond of him—one of the curiosities
of entering middle age is the realization that you have acquired some
most unlikely friends whom you continue to see just as they were
years ago—but he has absolutely no sense of humor. I can't imagine
how he managed to marry Tricia, who is small, blond, and bubbly:
she and Claudine are *très sympathiques* and are always shrieking with
laughter within minutes of our meeting, leaving me to catch up on
how Edward is rearranging the world. It must be the solid worth
that appeals to her. She probably has enough fun for both of them.

We processed across the marble-floored hall to the cloakroom,
Edward still in the lead. His thick black hair—not too long, not too
short—was starting to gray at the sides. Soon he would have distinguished gray feathers over his ears. Perfect. How does he do it?
We entered the marbled cloakroom. I stood at the stainless-steel
urinal, tinkling. There was certainly a cabinet minister on one side,
and I thought I recognized an elderly lord on the other. We all three
peed in unison, brothers under the skin. Edward, further along, was
out of synch. He isn't musical, either.

In the noble dining room, we had a small round table to ourselves.
Some fino sherry arrived, to keep us alive while we read the menu.
In the silence, the clash of metal cutlery sounded like cavalry fighting
with sabers. The waitresses, in black dresses and white aprons, were
aged ninety-five and upward. The bishops must not run the risk of
arousal. Or perhaps it was cheaper to employ pensioners. The menu
was not inspiring either. But Edward looked content: he leaned toward me in a hostly way; it was his treat.

"Have you decided?" he asked. Obviously he had. I couldn't.

"Where was it," I said to gain time, "that Lutyens made that crack about 'This piece of cod passeth all understanding'? If it was here, I think I'll have the chicken."

"Ah, Lutyens!" Edward said with approval. "The architect of Empire. More solid than Scott, less churchy than Pugin. Magnificent war memorials—the Cenotaph of course, and all those in France. And New Delhi—what a waste. The most impressive administrative center we ever had. Hardly finished before we gave it to Gandhi. Who didn't want it."

"Suited Mountbatten, though," I fed him. "Just in time for the great finale." I like to hear Edward going on about Empire. He's full of facts and anecdotes; pure nostalgia, but he can give you the atmosphere of those days. And he knows about the real people that ran it—not just the legendary superheroes like Gordon or Kitchener, but the traders and planters and second lieutenants who lived and died in those faraway places, not waving the standard as black hordes swept down upon them, but more often in bed with malaria, or an unknown wasting disease. Edward and I are members of the last generation trained to do that, to take up the white man's burden, though by the time we went to school, the Empire was already extinct. But the schools kept on, headless chickens: classics was still in, science was grubby, and computer studies not yet invented. And now—the accelerating rate of change, Alvin Toffler, and Future Shock. Don't think the news has filtered into the Athenian time capsule, yet. When it does, everything will glow white hot. Then it will implode.

"Sorry, Edward?" I missed most of that. Edward didn't seem to mind. He was happy, still rattling on about giving India back.

"I think they regret it now, in some ways at least."

"Who?"

"The Indians, of course. Well, it's chicken then, is it?"

A waitress arrived almost before Edward had raised his finger. Food was ordered: after some hesitation Edward thought we'd better have a little wine and sent for a bottle of Mouton Cadet. Well. No disrespect to the baron; it's all *right*, but it's in all the pubs and there were more interesting bottles on the list at the same price. But Edward's in charge.

"Good idea."

Soup arrived. It was . . . soupy. We both sucked up a couple of spoonfuls. Then Edward said, "Did you say there was something you wanted to ask me?"

"Yes," I said. "It's like this. I want some inside information, and you're the only chum I have who might be able to help."

Edward raised an eyebrow. "What sort of information?"

"About a company. Who runs it, what they make, that sort of thing."

"Sounds harmless. Why not ask *them*?"

"I'd rather not. Not at this stage." Edward would have a fit, I thought, if I were to tell him the whole story. I'd get a lecture on irresponsibility, that characteristic which had always distinguished us apart.

"What's the company?"

"They're called Protoplastics. In Stanmore."

Edward was concentrating on his plate, spooning up the dregs of his soup. It wasn't worth the effort, but he's tidy minded. He swallowed it down; reached for his wineglass.

"I don't recall the name," he said at last.

His manner was not encouraging, but I pressed on. "Would it be possible to get someone to look through your records, see if you've had dealings with them?"

Edward frowned. "Most irregular," he said.

"Oh come on, Edward. Where's the harm? Don't be so stuffy."

"Stuffy or not, it would be an abuse of my position," he said seriously. "And in any case, have you any idea what you're asking? The department has a whole building just for records; it could take a day or more. No, I'm afraid it's quite impossible."

I opened my mouth to argue, but was prevented by the arrival of the waitress with chicken and watery vegetables. When she'd gone, I said, "I wouldn't ask, if it wasn't important."

"What do you mean, important?"

I hesitated. "There's something very bent going on."

"Bent?"

It was like talking to a judge. "Criminal," I explained.

"Criminal!" Edward said. His jaw muscles bulged as his teeth closed on chicken. He took a swallow of wine. "Then why don't you go to the police?" He glanced across the table at me.

"Because I haven't any evidence," I said. "That's why I'm asking you."

"Ah," he said, "no evidence. Well, you don't want to go splashing accusations around then, do you? Some of these companies have very sharp lawyers—you could find yourself in a lot of trouble."

"I know that," I said, irritated. "I wasn't proposing to shout it all in public. I just thought you might be able to help me get some facts together."

"Wish I could," Edward said, "but, as I say, it's just not possible."

"Pity."

"What do you propose to do, then?"

"I don't know, yet."

"Forget it, I should." I didn't tell him why I couldn't: it would have been a waste of time. Edward was not, it seemed, in a sympathetic mood.

He changed the subject, and began to talk about his problems. As usual, the unions were negating his efforts to rebuild the Empire. As far as I could tell, Edward is in charge of some troubleshooting section, helping to get industry back on its feet. He had a lot to do with the reconstruction of British Leyland. He also tries to stir up investment for the private sector. Now he was telling me a long saga about how he'd nursed some tottering company into increasing its exports, only to have its goods held up at the docks, incurring interest charges and ill will.

I told him we had dock problems of our own. "Our shipments get locked into a warehouse when there's a dispute, and we sometimes have to wait for weeks to get them out. But my van driver can often find a way round. He chats up the pickets, and I let him hand out a few cases to help him through the gates."

Edward's distaste at this pragmatic approach was clearly visible. "One of these days," he said, "there will *have* to be a shake-up at the docks. But it's one of our more intractable problems."

"You must often wish there was a shortcut," I said.

"All we need," Edward said seriously, "is order. We have to do away with the present chaos, and replace it with *order*."

"*Jawohl*," I said, "*mein Führer*."

"No, seriously," he said, "we do need to put talented people in charge and get our production and our distribution modernized before it's too late. Both unions and management must be made to see . . ."

"Sure," I said. Boredom was setting in. Few subjects bore me as much as industrial relations, unless maybe it's education. The talk just seems to go round and round, getting nowhere.

Edward shrugged and fell silent, forking up the remains of his chicken. He followed it with the last of his wine.

"How's Tricia?" I asked.

"All right," he replied briefly. He reached for the menu. "Pudding, or cheese?"

"Cheese."

The conversation had definitely lapsed. We ate some Stilton, a fairly safe bet in places like this. It was, in fact, good. Edward didn't suggest port.

"I'd better get back, William, if you don't mind," he said. "Got a lot on my plate at present."

We walked across the dining room, and out through the reading room where two bishops were squabbling over something in *The Times*. I felt depressed: this mausoleum got on my nerves. If I ran it, I thought, what would I do to liven it up? Bishops wrestling in mud, perhaps? Slap, ugh, oof. Come on, Salisbury. Sock it to him, Winchester. And on Saturday night, Big Daddy from Canterbury. Grunt, groan, kick 'im in the chasuble.

"Very kind of you, Edward," I lied. "I enjoyed that."

Edward looked at me and nodded. His taxi was waiting, summoned by the hall porter. He stepped into it and was whirled away, back to the corridors of power. It came to me, at that precise moment, that Edward was everything I had always wanted not to be. How lucky I was!

The hall porter had followed me out. "Shall I get you a taxi, sir?"

"No thanks. I think I'll walk round to the tube."

I set off for Green Park Underground. Such was my relief at getting out of that place, I nearly did a Gene Kelly on and off the curb, but it's easy to wreck your ankle doing that.

6

INHERENT
DIFFICULTIES

There are upon the whole very few instances where anything great has resulted from such surprises; from which we may justly conclude that inherent difficulties lie in the way of their success.

—Clausewitz

The telephone rang while we were still having breakfast. It was Pete.

"Trap works a treat!" he said. He sounded entertained; I had been worried that he would think it all a bit of a laugh.

"What? There's someone in it? *Jesus,*" I admonished him, "*be careful!* Don't touch anything. I'll be right over. Stay outside the warehouse and watch, but if anyone comes, in or out, just clear off. *Don't try anything.*"

"Don't worry," he said, "I won't do nuffink. See yer." And he rang off, his voice amazingly calm. I would have guessed he'd be good in a crisis.

I told Claudine I had to get over to the warehouse at once as Pete needed me. I dashed into the office, snatched the Webley out of the deed box, broke it open, shoved the two cartridges into the cylinder, set the cylinder so that the gun would fire on the *second* trigger pull and would be safe against accidental firing, dropped it into my briefcase, ran down the path to the garage, unlocked the side door, edged round the car, threw open the up-and-over street door, unlocked the car, threw my briefcase on the passenger seat, jumped into the driving seat, jammed the key into the ignition, started up, waited bursting with impatience while the ingenious Citroën hydraulic suspension slowly pumped the car up to running position—no getaway car, this—drove out of the garage, stopped, scrambled out, slammed the garage door shut, scrambled back in, and took off with a squeal as the front tires scrabbled for grip on the tarmac. I felt exhausted already, my nerves jangling; I'd missed my second shot of coffee.

The rush-hour traffic was in full flood: I drove like a junior executive in a new company Ford, jamming the car into gaps and edging other drivers into collision courses with curbs and traffic islands. People don't expect Citroëns to be aggressive: I made up for this with ferocious acceleration in bottom gear, the engine screaming, and by making full use of the two-stage horn: a light touch brings a polite beep, but if you keep the button pressed you get a blast from two-tone air horns that sound like the accident's already happened, and stops all but the most hard-nosed drivers in their tracks.

I turned into Brewery Lane and rumbled over the cobbles to where Pete was standing by the van. There was a blue Mini Metro parked just in front. From the plates, it was a last year's model, well polished and cared for, but it had no wheels and was sitting on four piles of bricks. Must have been left overnight. Not a sensible thing to do round here.

I got out of the car with my briefcase. "Door's open," Pete said.

"Right," I said, "I'll go in and take a look. You wait here, and if anyone comes and looks like going into the warehouse, give me three blasts on the van. Then get into the van and be ready to take off in a hurry. If they approach you, take off anyway. I'll look after myself."

"You know best," Pete said, "but I think I'd better . . ."

"Later," I said, "later. I've got to get in there and get it over with."

"You're the gaffer."

I unzipped the briefcase, but didn't take the Webley out until I was inside and had shut the pass door behind me. I stood with my back to the door, gun in hand, and swept the warehouse with a careful inspection, left to right. I could see the steel-clad office door in the distance, tight shut. There were signs that some of the wine crates had been moved, but that could have been done by Pete when he made up his deliveries yesterday. I could see nothing that indicated a possible hiding place, but I walked slowly across the ends of the rows of crates, looking carefully down each one. Traps can be reversed, of course, and an ambush could have been laid to catch me as I walked up to the office door. Someone could be in wait at the far end of one of the rows of crates: it was impossible for me to check this, but I reckoned that if there was anyone there, they would choose to wait at the end of one of the rows nearest to the office door. I decided, therefore, to move across my end of the warehouse and to make my approach along the side wall farthest from the office. That way I would only have to guard my front, and I would arrive at the other end of the warehouse behind the row of crates least likely to be occupied, and which I could in that case use for cover.

I began to move across the entrance end of the warehouse, taking extreme care each time I passed a row, and making the minimum of noise. My leather-soled shoes were inaudible on the concrete floor, and any slight sounds—the soft rustle of clothes, the faint creak of my leather belt—were overlaid by the contentious clamor of distant traffic. It was deadly quiet in the warehouse. The only sound not made by me was the sporadic ping of water drops coming from the brick-walled lavatory next to the office, where an ancient iron cistern was slowly rusting its life away. My stomach began to rumble as if in sympathy; an interrupted breakfast resented. The gun was heavy and cold, drawing the heat from my hand and making my palm slippery with icy sweat.

Now I reached the side wall, and began to work my way along it. It was the most risky part of my plan. I had a solid row of crates on my left, and the warehouse wall on the right—an unplastered, rough brick wall covered with flaking whitewash, the sort of wall that gangsters end up against, the garage where the St. Valentine's Day massacre took place, the tommy guns blatting out the heavy lead slugs, the victims sagging in their double-breasted suits, sliding down the wall, their blood seeping into the hollows of the oily concrete floor. Come on Warner! Don't overwork the imagination. You're armed this time. Yes. With two sixty-year-old bullets. I can imagine *that* scene all right. Drop it, or I'll shoot. He doesn't drop it. I shoot. Click. Sod it. Click again. Then it's his turn. Bang.

Well, I won't fire it unless there's no alternative. I'll just try to frighten him to death.

If there's anyone there. And if I find out before I've frightened *myself* to death.

The end of the row of crates was coming up now. I reached it, took a short break, and then, very, very slowly, knelt on the floor and looked round it.

I hoped this would present a more unexpected target, my head being about eighteen inches off the floor. But it didn't matter anyway.

There wasn't anyone there.

I straightened up. The way was now clear for me to tackle whoever was in the office. Maybe Pete had made a mistake, or—unlikely—was pulling my leg. I crept quietly to the office door. Being careful not to touch the door, which might have moved and announced my presence before I was ready for it, I leaned forward and put my right eye to the circular spyhole.

There were two rats in the trap. One of them was about five feet nine, thin, dark, balding, and with the face of a man apart.

Who believes in conspiracy theory.

Who has measured out his life in paper clips.

Who drinks Riesling made from Boots's wine kits.

I slid the Webley back into the briefcase, unlocked the door, and went in.

"You can be very sure I shall report this!" said Winkelmann.

We had a little chat, which I won't go into. Then he left, trailed by his assistant. As soon as they'd gone, Pete came into the warehouse. He looked pleased with himself. Well, he'd tried to tell me, if not very hard.

"You should have let me know yesterday afternoon, when they arrived," I told him.

"Yer, wool, I give you a tinkle, but the phone was up the spout," he said. "Bit of luck, wonnit?"

I'd forgotten to tell him about the wire being cut.

"'E kept sayin', as a VAT inspector 'e 'ad powers. To search premises, take away papers and stuff. I said to meself, you got *powers*, mate, you fly away outer this, and left 'im to it."

"We don't have a Croix de Guerre in this organization," I said, "but I award you a bottle of Veuve Clicquot, Yellow Label. Was that their Mini Metro outside? The one that's short on wheels."

"Ah, wool," Pete said, "I offer them a lift, but they don't take no notice. Jus' walk on past."

"And the wheels? What happened to them?"

"Who knows," Pete said, "who knows."

The sun was shining on Brewery Lane as I emerged, after resetting the trap. Pigeons swooped and chortled. I pressed the button to open the sliding roof, and drove back slowly, feeling luxurious. There was a half-played tape of jazz in the player, and I switched it on. Toot, tooty-toot, tooty-toot, toot, toot. Not real jazz but the Piccadilly Hotel Band, playing "He's a Good Man to Have Around," 1929, with vocal refrain. I had to join in.

There was time for some shopping. Apart from food and more or less ordinary provisions, I bought twenty meters of strong nylon cord; a ten-inch Sabatier carbon-steel cooks' knife with riveted black handle; a box of .410 shotgun cartridges loaded with number six shot (for which I had to produce the shotgun certificate I carry in my wallet); a stick of black theatrical makeup; and, from a joke shop, two lifelike masks of Ronald Reagan. He wore a happy smile, as if welcoming kiddies to join his party. That was what I had in mind, sort of.

My last stop was in Knightsbridge, at Yves Saint Laurent. I've always worn English suits from the "right" places—a wine merchant has to watch his image—but the prices are now astronomical, and anyway I would like to move on, evolve, if I could find the right direction. I tried on one or two gray numbers. Possible, I thought; the trousers were much baggier than English trousers and made me look like Simenon, *sans pipe*. Was that a good thing? I decided to discuss it with Claudine.

I was back in time for lunch. I didn't give the whole story about Winkelmann, but said he'd got locked in the warehouse by accident last night, and would not be turning up for the inspection today. Claudine hooted with laughter and rushed off to tell Maggie. I heard them both shrieking in the office. Maggie came to put her head round the door. "Serves him right," she gasped, "the sneaky thing!" I had reset the trap before leaving, and told Pete to keep his mouth buttoned up; Winkelmann himself would be unlikely to go into detail when, or if, we saw him again; the secret was safe for the time being.

Over lunch, I told Claudine about Saint Laurent. "*Ah non!*" she expostulated. "*Non, non, NON!* You will look like a Frenchman!"

"Like Simenon!" I said. "Is that bad?"

"But of course! You are not a writer of thrillairs! You are the English *marchand de vin* who wears the English tweeds. That is certain." Would she have married me if I did *not* wear the English tweeds? That is not certain.

Lunch over, I shut myself in my office, and tried a shotgun cartridge in the revolver. A .410 shotgun is, of course, a small caliber gun used by boys and for shooting rats in barns, as opposed to the much bigger twelve bore, which is the sportsman's normal means of communication with our furry and feathered friends. I had bought these cartridges as a substitute for proper bullets, which could not be obtained legally, even if the correct type still existed, which was unlikely. The cartridge was the right diameter to fit into the cylinder: the only snag was that it was too long. I took the gun and the cartridges to Julian's room over the garage and, sitting at his workbench, cut the cartridges down to size with a Stanley knife. I left the cordite charge intact, but reduced the greased wadding—which pushes the shot along the barrel like a piston—to half its original thickness; this was to make more room for the pellets. Even so, in the shortened cartridge there was only room for some twenty pellets—far fewer than there had been, but enough to be effective at close quarters. I finished by replacing the cardboard disk that retains the pellets and crimping the top of the plastic cartridge body to keep the contents in place, adding some dabs of five-minute epoxy glue inside the rim for extra security. Once I had a production line set up, the job was easy, and in half an hour I had converted the whole box of twenty-five cartridges. Though they would have much less stopping power than the ancient bullets, I could at least be sure that they would fire: the noise alone would persuade an opponent to keep his distance, and the spread of shot would actually give me an advantage in snap shooting. What I now had, in effect, was a miniature sawn-off shotgun, with up to six shots.

I loaded the gun with four of the shot cartridges and the two bullets, and put it back in my briefcase. By spinning the cylinder, I could select either shot or a solid round for firing, and I'd set the gun to fire shot first, followed by a solid round. That way, I could be sure the thing would go off when I first pulled the trigger, and avoid the terrifying fear of a misfire that had dogged me as I stalked through the warehouse. Learning by experience, it's called, and anthropologists define civilized man by his ability to do so. To go bang rather than click. Well, that's what they say.

I spent the rest of the afternoon in my office, collecting together the bumf I needed for tomorrow's sales trip, and marking up my stock list with current prices. Burgundies were in even shorter supply than usual, and I was embarrassed to see what I was going to have to charge for even a modest Mâcon. The wine just wasn't worth it, but my hoteliers would want to have it on their lists just the same, ready for when a diner would cry expansively, "Let's have a bottle of burgundy," and if it costs a lot, well, it must be good, mustn't it?

I was glooming over this, and wondering if I dare suggest a cheaper but better alternative such as Hungarian Pinot Noir, when the telephone rang. It was Edward—not a succession of secretaries this time, but the man himself. Did it mean he'd dialed me with his own distinguished digit? I was flattered!

"Our lunch yesterday," he said. "I've thought some more about what we were talking about, and I'm afraid I was rather unhelpful."

"Don't give it another thought," I said, touched. "I quite understand your position. It was tactless of me to ask."

"No," he said, "not at all. Not at all. We've known each other for a long time, after all, and that makes a difference. Well, as I say, I've given it some more thought, and come to the conclusion that I *can* help you, on certain conditions. I *have* got my position to consider—I know you'll make allowance for that if this sounds overcautious."

This was good news! "My dear old Edward," I said, "the last thing I want to do is to land you in hot water with Them Upstairs. What do you suggest?"

"Well," he said carefully, "it's like this. If you'll let me know exactly what you think this firm—we won't mention the name—has done, I'll get someone to run a check, and see what comes up. The condition is that I won't be able to let you in on what we find, if anything. You'll have to leave it to me from then on."

My spirits fell. "That wasn't what I had in mind," I admitted.

"No. I realize that. But it just isn't on for me to hand out confidential information to someone outside the department. You must see that."

I supposed I did.

"Good," Edward said. "I hoped you'd take it like that. Now, we'd better arrange a meeting, just between ourselves, so that I can make a note of what it's all about. Tomorrow evening? There's a wine bar just round the corner from here, in Fleet Street, where one can talk. Half-past six suit you?"

"I'm just off on a sales trip," I told him. "Not sure how long it'll take, but a couple of days, at least."

"Oh. Pity. Well, I might even manage a few minutes this evening, if that would help."

I would be on my way to see Ginny then. But I didn't tell Edward that: I don't share that side of my life with him. I wouldn't, even if Tricia, his wife, was not Claudine's best friend.

But in any case, I wasn't liking his idea. I didn't want to be shut out from *my* investigation. I was too involved in it now, too embattled. I'd rather carry on by myself, without his help.

"Look, Edward, I appreciate your offer, I really do. But it would be a lot to ask of you, and now you've explained the problems, I think maybe I'd better just chug on by myself. But thanks all the same."

Silence from Edward. I could imagine him pursing his lips, frowning in disapproval. Irresponsible again, he'd be thinking. And this time he was probably right. But my mind was made up.

"Are you sure that's wise?" he said after a long pause.

"No," I said, "but it's what I'm going to do. It's no good, Edward, I just feel I have to, it's the way I am."

"Well," he said, "well. If you're sure . . ."

"I'm sure. But thanks again. And thanks for lunch, as well—it's my turn next time."

"Let me know if you change your mind," Edward said, and rang off.

Decent of the old stick to go to that trouble; I felt bad about turning him down. I thought briefly about calling him back, accepting his offer, handing the whole thing over, so that I could return to normal life. But no, I couldn't do it. Just couldn't.

He probably wouldn't have been able to find out anything anyway. He surely wouldn't have been able to spend much time on it, at the expense of his other work. I knew how busy he was.

All right, I know. Excuses, excuses. The fact is, I've got my teeth into it now, and can't give up. Might as well try to reverse a cavalry charge. Lances leveled, enemy almost in sight, just round the next corner. Cannons to left and right, a blunder maybe, but got to go on. Into the jaws of death, into the mouth of hell. Six hundred lunatics. Six hundred and one.

Now, what had I been grieving over when the telephone rang? Ah yes. It swept over me again.

The price of burgundy.

A Certain
Strength

*War is the province of physical exertion and suffering. In order not to
be completely overcome by them, a certain strength of body and mind
is required.*

—*Clausewitz*

At seven on the dot, I was pressing the bell marked V. Duff-
Jones. Ginny's flat is on the sharp corner overlooking
South Kensington tube station, with windows on three
sides and odd triangular-shaped rooms; you can see in several directions and look down on the rivers of traffic as they merge and
diverge.

"Yes?" squawked the metal grille beside the bell push.

"It's me," I announced.

"William?"

"Who else are you expecting?" I said, cross at having made
the same mistake twice. If she didn't know my voice after all this
time . . .

The door opened with a click. The geriatric lift groaned its way
up to the top floor. One day soon it isn't going to make it; it must
be well past three score years and ten. Did it have its regular check-
ups, I wondered? I never gave a thought to all that until I was thirty-
five. That's the top of the hill. That's the age when you're suddenly
no longer eligible for ski groups and Club Méditerranée: before
thirty-five, I was immortal. Now it only takes a creaky lift to remind
me of my age.

The sight of Ginny standing in her open doorway acted as instant elixir. We went inside, and she helped me to unload the parcels I was carrying. Then we had a little exploratory hug.

"You look . . ." What to say? Every word overworked. How to describe this object of my desire without blundering into the minefield that has been built around your modern male, including me. Don't want to sound like a man in a pub on the *make*. Mustn't be *crude*. Got to avoid the patronizing compliment. But she wants to hear something, all the same.

"*You* look *dishy*, William darling," she said. (Oh now, look here!) Too late. I settled for some heavy breathing and an extra squeeze.

I had responsibility for the supper, and spent a couple of minutes in the kitchen. Then I joined Ginny in the sitting room where she was throwing things into cupboards and stuffing books back on to shelves. It was a small room, full of friendly objects. A thick Berber carpet, a large squashy sofa heaped with cushions, two shaded lights on low tables. Ginny was drawing the curtains. "Something's wrong with your fire," she said over her shoulder.

My fire! My Magicoal present to Ginny! Its glowing warmth the symbol of our relationship—when it falters, we falter. Or so I feel. Luckily I'm good with electrical things. But this was an emergency: I dropped on my knees to see what was wrong and what could be done. The bars were glowing, but the little fans that make the shimmering effect were not revolving. The coals were lifeless. That was a bad omen; lifelessness is definitely not our style. I twisted the fan blades to a steeper angle, and put them back on their spindles. Gradually, in the rising heat from the red bulbs below, they began to turn. I put the molded plastic simulated coals back on; they shimmered as they should. Ginny had come to watch, kneeling by my side. We both sighed with relief. "You're so *wonderful*, William darling," she murmured, leaning on my shoulder. "It's nothing," I said. Red patterns from the fire swirled across the ceiling. We looked at each other. I got up, and pulled her up after me. I turned out the table lights and threw the cushions down in front of the fire. Ginny put a record on the player, went into the kitchen, came back with the kitchen timer, which she put on the hearth. Tinkling arpeggios filled the room. Indian classical sitar. We stood by the fire again. I looked at Ginny, smiling in her pink track suit. "Like it!" I said. "Easy to step out of," she said, stepping out of it. "I say Ginny, you're starkers!" I said, hurrying to catch up. We fell on to the cushions. The sitar tinkled on. "What's he playing?" I asked. "He's just warming up," she said. Oh yes. Oh yes.

Oh the soft silkiness, the sights, the sounds, the scent of her. Oh the billows, the pillows, hummocks and valleys of her. Oh the exploring, upturning, pillaging and voyaging, the rolling and the moling and the merging.

"He's settled down to a steady rhythm now," said Ginny.

"Has he?"

"Yes," she said definitely. "He's a long way to go," she added.

"*How* long?"

"Twenty-three minutes."

"Dear Ginny . . ."

"On this side. And twenty more on the other."

"What's that thing going glup, glup-a-glup?"

"A long stringed instrument. Sexy, isn't it?"

"And the drums . . ."

"Tabla, William."

"Tabla."

"Ginny?"

"Ummm?"

"Why don't you give up barristers, as Evan was such a flop?"

"Maybe I will, darling."

"Or at least move out of Chancery into, say, Building Disputes. King's Bench Walk. Less of that impossible eloquence."

"That's true. He never stopped declaiming, did he?"

"Never. But he was Welsh. Couldn't help it."

"I'll never marry a Welsh barrister again. Not even in Building Disputes. I think I may stay a Miz."

"That's my advice."

"William?"

"Yes?"

"Just move this leg a little . . . that's better."

"How are we doing for time?"

"About halfway through side one."

"I may have to keep talking. To distract myself."

"I like it darling. Both together . . . delicious."

"For me too. That's the problem."

"Courage, my darling."

"William?"

"Still here."

"The red lights on the ceiling are going round awfully *fast*. It makes me feel quite dizzy to look at them."

"I expect I've bent the little fans too much."

"Will you be able to bend them back again?"

"If you like."

"I *do* feel dizzy."

"Keep your eyes shut."

"But I like to look at you."

"Very understandable."

"How long has Claudine gone away for this time?"

"She hasn't."

"Oh. But you always said . . ."

"This is an exception to the rule."

"Is it serious?"

"Not for Claudine."

"Will you tell me afterward?"

"Afterward."

"Jesus!"

"Sorry darling."

"It went off right in my ear!"

"I *said* sorry."

"It's so *loud*!"

"Wait, I'll turn it off. There."

"What was it for?"

"I set it so that we'd know—"

"Yes?"

"—when there's only three minutes left."

"I *thought* the glup-a-glups were speeding up."

"This is a raga. It speeds up all the way through."

"I'm going almost as fast as I can already."

"You're fantastic, darling."

"I know."

"Ooooh. Oooooooooh!"

"Mmmmmmm."

"Ahhhh."

"Ahhhh."

Iced vodka has to be really icy, and I'd put it in the freezing compartment. I made some thin brown toast, loaded everything on a tray, and took it into the sitting room. "Don't get excited," I warned Ginny, who was lying in front of the fire, "it's not caviar, only lumpfish roe. But the vodka is Stolichnaya, of course." "Oh, of *course*," Ginny said, sniggering. She thinks I'm a wine bore. Well, perhaps I may verge on it at times. But anything's a bore if you just skitter about on the surface of it. And vodka isn't . . . Well, never mind. We settled down to it. I'd bought a lot of roe. It was a little too salty, but the Stolichnaya dealt with that. There you are, you see.

We lay side by side, munching and glowing, content to do without words. But a question was hanging over us. It was Ginny who put an end to the idyll.

"Well?"

I sighed. Well, this was the other thing I was here for.

She was the first person to hear the story, and I told her everything, all the details, right from square one. It was much easier than I expected.

Ginny, who had taken to describing herself as a journalist since she split up with Evan (and who had the contacts to compensate for a rather breathless literary style full of personality but largely free of punctuation) at least knew not to interrupt, and I was grateful for that. I had doubts, of course, about the way I was handling the thing, particularly about not telling the police. A sensible citizen, like Edward, for instance, would have gone to the police automatically, expecting protection and sympathetic treatment, and would have got it. Maybe. But whether he got it or not, he would still have played it that way—no other way would have occurred to him. He always plays by the rules, Edward. But I don't. I'm normal, I don't like the rules. It's not, I hope, a criminal tendency, the need to hit back at society; although Winkelmann, with his Customs and Excise background, doubtless has me filed along with the genuine article in his Suspected Fraud section. He's trained to sniff out crime, but he doesn't realize that after years of doing it, the smell has stuck in his nostrils. No, it's simply that I get irritated by rules, their crudeness, their drift from intention to irrelevance. Winkelmann and his mates from Transylvania should have it explained to them: rules are un-*English*. That's to say that, applied without flexibility or common sense, rules can be downright dangerous. Here lies the body of Michael O'Day, who died defending his right of way. He was right, dead right, as he sailed along, but he's just as dead as if he'd been wrong.

"I didn't think so at first," Ginny said seriously, frowning into the energetic flickering of the fire, "but I think you're right. If the police didn't manage to sort it out—and they often don't—you'd be worse off for having told them. Not knowing what was going to happen next, or when." Intelligent girl, Ginny: well balanced, perceptive . . . and agrees with me. I felt ridiculously relieved. Of course, there was some risk to her in my coming here, I knew that. And she knew it too, now, but all she said was, "There'd better be a good story in this, William. Brr! I'm getting cold. Let's continue this in the bath." And scrambling up, she went to run it.

I collected a bottle from the fridge, and a couple of tall glasses, and joined her. We lay back at opposite ends, legs entwined, swigging sparkling Saumur. Water thundered from the gaping jaws of a golden dolphin flying in over the starboard side.

"Terribly Asset Stripper, this," I said.

"Wouldn't it be Dom Perignon, and three girls instead of just one?" she said.

"True," I said. "What *is* it about Dom Perignon? Onassis too . . ."

"If and when you get to Paradise, William," Ginny said, "and the most beautiful dancing girl of them all tinkles up to you on her tiny feet bearing a golden goblet of wine and displaying her incredible charms for you to enjoy with all imaginable caresses, what will you do?"

"Ask if it's Corton-Charlemagne—Louis Latour, of course," I said, "unless *you* happened to be on duty that day."

"Just in time," she said, dropping the sponge back into the water. I looked down the length of the bath at her. A warrior could do worse, I thought: a small girl, but sleek as a seal; her green eyes studied me from under the tangle of dark hair.

"Well?" she said.

"Well what?" I said.

"Well what's next?" she said.

I told her about my plan. I wasn't going to wait for results from the warehouse trap but, leaving it set, I was going to start on my sales trip, keeping close to London until I was sure I was being followed, which I expected. Then I was going to lead my follower away from London, on to ground which I knew well and where I would have the advantage. There I would take him prisoner. The ground I had chosen was the Milford Haven estuary, in South Wales, where I have a cottage. It was isolated, and on a steep hillside overlooking the water, about halfway up the estuary, ten miles from the sea: the ground was covered with bramble and neglected woodland, and there was a disused quarry just behind the cottage. All this was ideal for a potentially lethal game of hide-and-seek. If you were the one that knew your way about.

"Oh my God," Ginny said. I think she hadn't fully taken in what was happening, until I started talking about the days ahead. Everything that I'd already told her, being in the past, was no longer dangerous, but this . . . "Even if you catch him," she said, "what makes you think he'll talk?"

"I won't just ask politely."

"William, you *can't*. You just can't *do* that. Darling William, you're just not the type. You'd stop at the first ouch, and start apologizing."

"I bloody well won't."

"What are you going to do, exactly? Threaten to tickle him to death?"

I didn't want to go into it. Nor did I want to remind her that one man had already died after trying to kill me, and that I had had a narrow escape after being attacked with a knife, all within the last five days. I wasn't feeling softhearted. But I wasn't going to rub her nose in it.

"Let's just say . . ."

"You have ways of making him talk?"

"Exactly," I said.

She began playing with the sponge, lifting it out of the water, squeezing it slowly, watching the warm rivulets pour over her wrist and down her arm. Then she reached for the tap; the dolphin spluttered and then disgorged hot water over my knee. "Wow!" I shouted, moving it across to avoid the stream, "that's hot!" "Sorry," Ginny said, "I wasn't thinking. Water needs topping up." She sounded subdued. "Don't worry," I said. "You forget I've had two years' training as an assassin." "That was *ages* ago," she said, "and maybe the man on the other side has been in the army too. In the *commandos*. Or *paras*." Good point—I hadn't thought of that. I'd rather *she* hadn't. Most of my training was in tanks, which was not going to help me much. But I *had* done basic infantry training, and that . . . oh forget it. I'd done all right so far. So far so good. As the man said, halfway down, when trying to prove he could free-fall from six thousand feet without a parachute . . .

The sponge hit me on the chest. "All right," Ginny said. "Since you seem determined to go to war, let's talk about what *I* should do while you're at the front."

I had already given her my ideas on who the other side might be. We discussed what might be going on at Porton Down. Ginny said she knew people who would know the state of the art of biological warfare, except for the latest top secret stuff. We were both aware of stirrings in the press on the subject: in particular, a battle had been going on for some years between President Reagan and Congress over expenditure on new types of weapon filled with nerve gas. We agreed that Ginny would look up recent newspaper reports;

maybe we could extrapolate likely developments and see where they fitted in to the hard information that she would collect. I told her what I knew about nerve gas from the course I had been on at Porton; it had been classified information then, but later declassification had not resulted in this horrific means of warfare becoming widely known; I was amazed that it had received so little publicity. As someone who had sat in a classroom attending lectures and watching films on the subject, I was more likely to notice what few press reports *did* appear: I knew from these that in 1980, the then Defense Secretary, Francis Pym, expressed fears in public of a Soviet buildup of weapons; that there was an Anglo-American agreement in the summer of 1980 for the production of a new type of chemical weapon; and that the Pentagon obtained approval in 1980 to build a new chemical weapons factory at Pine Bluff, Arkansas, which was to produce artillery shells designed to be filled with gas. And this wasn't mustard gas, so widely used in the First World War, this was nerve gas, so nearly used in the Second World War.

If ever there was an argument in favor of possessing weapons for deterrent purposes, I have always thought, this was it. Hitler had nerve gas at the outset of the war. He could have used it in bombing raids, causing such appalling civilian casualties that surrender would have followed almost immediately. Or he could have used it to tip the balance against the D-Day landings in 1944—Montgomery decided not to include gas masks in the equipment to be carried by his men, and they would have been practically wiped out. But Hitler didn't use it, because he thought we had it: in fact, the first we knew of nerve gas was when a shell from a captured German ammunition dump was analyzed in April 1945.

"But, darling," Ginny said, "surely everyone was issued with gas masks at the beginning of the war?"

"Oh yes. But, as the gas has hardly any smell, how do you know when you've got to put your mask on? By the time you're feeling the effect—breathing difficulty—it's too late. And in any case, you can absorb it through your skin. For protection, you've got to wear a complete suit. And you've got to put it on *before* the attack—that's the problem, if the stuff arrives in shells or rockets with no warning."

And then there are the biological weapons—anthrax, for instance.

Was there a revival in all this madness?

Isn't there enough madness going on already—the nuclear madness?

But what if the nuclear madness was controlled—suppose that the endless disarmament talks were *in danger of succeeding*?

What would the madmen do then? They weren't going to become sane overnight.

They would need new toys to play with.

And they would resent any attempt to upset the game.

"Try it on me," Ginny offered. I had lapsed into silence.

"Right then. I'll put a series of propositions in the form of What if . . . ?, and you give me the best answers you can think of. Number one: What if disarmament talks succeed in banning, or severely limiting, the stock of nuclear weapons: is it more likely that existing delivery systems—Polaris, Trident, cruise, etc.—will be scrapped, or that they will be converted for use with other types of warhead?"

"Impossible to believe that they'll *all* be scrapped. Likely that some, at least, will be converted."

"Number two: What if some delivery systems are converted: will there be military pressure to use the most deadly alternative warhead available?"

"Difficult to imagine the military accepting anything less effective than the other side are likely to have. But isn't there a treaty banning gas weapons?"

"There was a treaty banning biological weapons signed in 1972. But it doesn't cover *chemical* weapons, such as nerve gas. And since then, stocks of nerve gas have been built up, on both sides of the Iron Curtain."

"All right, then some delivery systems are likely to be reloaded with nerve gas in place of nuclear warheads. Yes, I agree with that."

"Number three: What if there has been a development either in the gas, or in the warhead containing the gas, which puts us ahead of the other side: would this be the type of secret that would be protected at all costs?"

"Both sides must have secrets like that, and would protect them, yes. But how would *you* . . . ?"

"I don't know. But it doesn't matter. What *does* matter is that, if all this theory is correct, the people protecting the secret *think* that I'm a security risk. Perhaps the secret's at a critical stage, and perhaps they're edgy. The most unlikely people . . . Burgess, Maclean, Philby, Anthony Blunt . . ."

"Foreign Office, mostly."

"I go abroad a lot, France, Germany . . ."

"So do lots of people." Ginny wouldn't accept it.

"Well, I don't *know* why they think that. That's what I reckon to find out. What I *do* know is, I've been shot at. And had my house raided. And I'm not going to sit around waiting for next time. I'm going to catch one of these sods and thump the answer out of him."

Ginny shook her head. "Don't try to give me that," she said. "I don't know what else you can do, but this plan of yours isn't about *thumping*. Is it?"

No, it wasn't. But I still didn't want to go into it. Nor did I want to think about what might happen if things went wrong. All that, I decided, was for tomorrow. Tonight still had a long way to go.

We lay for a while in silence, swirling the warm water over each other and finishing up the bubbly. If more people, if world leaders, did this and enjoyed it as much, I mused with vinous solemnity, there might be less chance of universal annihilation. If only it were so simple. Perhaps it was. In the meantime, no time to waste. And with that ancient theme came the realization that my personal Polaris was rising from beneath the waves. Ginny had noticed it too, I saw from the direction of her gaze.

"Don't say it, not again," I warned her.

"Don't say what?"

"All that stuff about men and rockets."

"Me?" Ginny said, giggling. "Never said a thing, did I?"

"No, but you *think* it, don't you?"

"It would be a pity to argue," Ginny said, "at a time like this."

Suddenly, I remembered I'd left pheasant in burgundy sauce from Fortnum's in the oven; philosophy would have to wait. I jumped out of the bath.

To my surprise, Ginny jumped out as well.

"There's pheasant in the oven," I explained. "Oh," she said, not sounding overjoyed. I stared at her for several seconds before I got the message.

"We'll have it for breakfast," I said.

"That's my boy," Ginny said, and headed for the record player, leaving wet footprints across the carpet.

Possibly she cheated and put on a tape instead of the flip side. Certainly the carpet was dry and the footprints vanished by the time I was next up and about. The important thing is that I got myself, wrapped in a rug, to the window of the spare bedroom without turning on the light. From there, I looked down into the street. The entrance to the flats was just below. Opposite, there was an estate car parked on the double yellow lines. As I watched, a woman came out of an antique shop, carrying a picture. I could see that it had a heavy gold frame. The woman propped the picture against the shop window, and went back into the shop. The lights went out, and she reappeared, turning to lock the door. Then she lifted the picture, crossed the pavement, and propped it against the side of the car. She found keys in her handbag, opened the tailgate of the car, lifted the picture again, struggled to hold it horizontally, maneuvered it carefully into the car. When it was in she stood for a moment, looking down at it. I could almost feel her relief at having got it into the car without damage. She shut the tailgate carefully, got into the driver's seat, drove off. All utterly normal. Nothing to concern me there.

I looked farther along the street. The double yellow lines extended about fifty yards from the corner. After that it was residents' parking only. It was now about eleven o'clock, and most residents would be at home. There was a solid line of cars there. The first one was parked half on the double yellow lines, streetlight reflected in the windscreen. Would he get away with it when the traffic wardens came swooping down in the morning? Or would he come out later and move it? The usual problems of a city dweller.

The only shop still operating across the street was a hamburger bar. I hate the things. I hate the whole idea of fast food. But most people seem happy to stuff themselves with tasteless bun and regurgitated meat. Customers were still trickling in and out. I watched them appear and disappear like bees round a hive. Some came out already eating. Others hurried away, each bearing a white paper bag. The bags were bright in the lamplight. I began to watch the bags instead of the carriers. They floated along the pavement; vanished into doorways; crossed the street to the Underground station.

And one bag stopped at the first parked car. The one that was half on the double yellow lines. The bag was passed in through the front window on the pavement side. With the movement, I could now see that someone was sitting in the driving seat. Had been there all the time.

It was too far to make a note of the number, but I could see it was a Ford Cortina, black or dark blue, with two CB radio aerials sprouting from the roof.

The man who had brought the hamburger stayed briefly, talking through the window. Once he looked up, in my direction. Then he nodded, and walked off down the street, shrugging into his bulky jacket. It must be cold out there. I hoped so.

I thought I heard Ginny calling from the sitting room, and padded back there to see what she wanted. It was a mistake. She was still in the nuddy, loitering palely by the record player, *belle dame* without mercy. I knew I shouldn't have put so much twist on those fan blades.

8

VOLUNTARY PROGRESS

The impulse toward a great battle, the voluntary, sure progress to it, must proceed from a feeling of innate power and a clear sense of the necessity.

—Clausewitz

"You aren't serious about eating this, William, are you?"

It was just after half-past seven, A.M. I was sitting opposite Ginny at the little table in her kitchen. Between us, on the table, sat the dish of pheasant in burgundy sauce. As a breakfast dish, it did have a certain air of irrelevance. This became clearer the more I looked at it. It was a wrench, and I meant no disrespect to Fortnum's, but I got up and dumped it into the bin. We decided to have scrambled eggs on toast instead. Another of the world's great dishes, and more appropriate to the time of day.

Basically, Ginny doesn't cook, she opens tins, but she can manage scrambled eggs. While she was managing them, I went to look out of the window. The black Cortina was no longer there, and there was a red Fiesta in its place.

I found I was disappointed. Having made a plan, I now wanted to get on with it, and I had felt sure from last night's observation that I was already being trailed. I couldn't leave for Wales and Quarry Cottage *until* I was sure of this. So it was a setback that the black Cortina had gone. It was also a lesson in not allowing my imagination too free a rein. I should have watched for longer—all night, if necessary. Or got dressed and gone down to take a closer look.

Ginny called from the kitchen that the eggs were ready. There was a smell of burning toast. I will amend the record—she can *almost* manage scrambled eggs. "Shall I make the coffee?" I offered. I was just in time to salvage that.

I took my coffee back to the window. It overlooked the only street where any form of long-term parking was permitted, and the flat's entrance was on that side: the opposition *had* to watch the entrance, and I thought they were most likely to do it from a parked car. But I watched for anybody loitering on foot, as well. There were plants on the windowsill: I sat in a chair brought in from the kitchen, keeping still, and watching through the leaves; the light in the room was dim and I would be almost invisible except through binoculars. Of course, they could be watching from one of the buildings opposite, but that would be more difficult to arrange, and no more effective—they only needed to watch the entrance and that could be done just as well from street level.

I had been watching for some ten minutes when I noticed that the red Fiesta, now parked in place of the black Cortina, carried twin CB aerials on the roof. Could be a coincidence: it's become a status symbol among, how would you describe them, compulsive communicators, to have a car loaded with electronic gadgetry. There's a lot of it about. Personally I can live without it. As I can live without hamburgers.

Which reminded me of last night's closing scene. I looked again at the hamburger bar, now extending a chromium yawn in the low morning sun. Not hamburgers at this hour? No, it looked more like croissants. A trickle of customers, no more, but the white paper bags could be seen, being borne away to bedsits and park benches. There goes one now, along the pavement.

And through the window of the red Fiesta.

And it must still be cold. There's that characteristic shrug of the bulky jacket.

"Ginny."

"Darling?"

"I must be off."

She appeared in the doorway.

"What's happened?"

I put her in the picture. Then I gave her a page from my notebook on which I had written the description and number of the red Fiesta, and the description of the black Cortina. Two men involved.

"Just in case."

"You *will* be careful?"

Idiotic and useless to say that. But I was glad she had.

I had nothing to carry as I had packed all I needed into the Citroën the day before. I went out of the flat entrance feeling, as I pushed through the double doors, as if I was going on stage. Enter Warner, center; with a nonchalant air he strides along. I strode round the corner into the side street where I'd left the Citroën. That was a risk—they might have interfered with it during the night. A car bomb. Homing beacon. Loosened the wheel nuts. I think I'll go back to Ginny.

It didn't explode. The wheels didn't wobble. They wouldn't have bothered to wait for me to come out if that's what they'd planned. No objection to a radio beacon—I *want* them on my track.

I drove to the Cromwell Road and headed for the M4. Knowing where I'd parked they had their route planned, and were round the big South Ken road junction and waiting for me as I turned the first corner: falling in behind, they kept three or four cars between us. I couldn't see if Bulky Jacket was in the car with the driver, or not; so far I hadn't seen the driver, just the outline of him as he leaned across in the dark to take the hamburger.

I could have driven straight to Wales and the cottage, but I thought they would be on their guard if I did this. So I was prepared to spend two days getting there, calling on hotels en route as if this was a normal business trip. They wouldn't know that my hotel customers only extend as far as Bristol: I hoped that, if I continued to call at hotels all through Wales, they would think this was just part of my usual routine. When I arrived at the cottage at the end of the second day, it would seem natural for me to stay there over-

night before making the return journey to London. Of course, they
might be better informed than I thought. But I didn't think they
were all that efficient. They'd been successful in catching up with
me at Ginny's flat. But they hadn't been very clever with the stake-
out. I would feel differently about hamburgers in the future. I might
even try eating one, some day.

So that they didn't lose me, I kept to main roads. This allowed them
to hide in the traffic: if I'd taken one of my country shortcuts, they
might have felt exposed and fallen too far behind, or take the opportunity to make a grab for me—I had to be careful to avoid that
until I was good and ready. I turned off the motorway at Maiden-
head; made quick calls on two hotels there; drove on to Henley-on-
Thames where I have a very good customer, and stayed to drink
some coffee and take down a sizeable order. Then it was on to Reading—calling in at Sonning on the way. The Thames-side hotels are
getting too expense account and standards are slipping while prices
are going up. Reading is a desert, and I spent very little time there.
I got back on to the motorway and was in Newbury by lunchtime.
I stopped at a bistro in the high street, where I was able to park the
car just outside and keep an eye on it. Sitting at a table near the
window, I saw the red Fiesta drive right past, and slow down. He
would park further down the street. He seemed to be having no
trouble keeping up with me. I still hadn't been able to get a good
look at the driver; there had been too much shine on his window as
he passed, but I could see he was on his own.

I ate a piece of quiche with a glass of red house plonk, and was
back on the road in twenty minutes. I took the A4 to Hungerford,
and then continued on to Marlborough, Calne, and Chippenham,
calling at one or more hotels or restaurants in each town. In some
of them I only stayed long enough to leave my card after scribbling
a personal note on it: I hadn't made appointments and it's a mistake
to press to see a customer if he's busy. I got to Bath just after six
o'clock, and struggled in through the rush-hour traffic to my hotel.

It's the Beau Brummel; a small, privately owned hotel a little way
up the hill behind the Royal Crescent. Sue and Johnny are among

my best customers, not because they buy huge quantities—the hotel's too small for that—but because they buy regularly and are
willing to take the *petits châteaux* that I import direct. Johnny does
the cooking, and is the wino: I sometimes wonder how much of it
gets on to the tables; he has a real chef's belly, and can make a bottle
disappear with a wave of his fat fist. When he makes his round of
the tables, doing his bit with his chef's hat on, diners sometimes
make the mistake of asking him to taste their wine. "Ummm, ahhh,
nothing to worry about there. Just a touch of tannin," Johnny beams,
having swallowed the lot in one gulp. And gets away with it. You
can *see* he's enjoyed it. No arguing about that.

I had been given my usual room at the front, with a telephone
and private bath. I started the bath running, and took a look out of
the window. This was becoming a way of life. No sign of the red
Fiesta. My Citroën was in the small forecourt, in clear view. No
doubt he was waiting somewhere along the street: as it was one way,
he only had to cover the exit. He'd have to get his own hamburger
tonight. I would rather be me, looking forward to Johnny's dinner.
I slid into the bath, and was soon feeling warm and drowsy. It had
been a busy and rather frustrating day.

These trips aren't the fun they used to be. More and more hotels
are being taken over by the big combines, and they buy wine by
the label, not the taste. "Hullo," they say, "nice to see you. What
have you got in Boojolly?" They don't mind if it tastes like it's been
squeezed from a squid as long as it says Beaujolais on the label. At
the price they're prepared to pay, they'd be better off with a lesser-
known *vin de pays*, or one of the Bulgarian reds, Merlot, or Cabernet
Sauvignon, but they won't buy them; they haven't got the right label.
Liebfraumilch is another of my problems; German wines are not
suitable partners for many types of food and are usually better drunk
on their own, but ever since intensive advertising persuaded nervous
novices that they would impress both the girlfriend and the wine
waiter by ordering Liebfraumilch to drink all through the meal, our
restaurants have been flooded with the stuff. A semisweet wine with
steak and chips, for heaven's sake! A lake of Liebfraumilch laps at our

hostelries, and seeps into our cellars. But slowly, with the help of our allies the French, the tide is being turned. It must be done. To achieve this, I will even ally myself (for the duration of hostilities) with Boojolly. After all, Churchill had to get on with General de Gaulle.

"That was some dinner, Sue," I called across to her.

She abandoned the cash desk and came over to my table. It was late, and most of the other diners had departed. "Sit down, and have a glass of wine," I offered. "Thanks, William, yes, I could do with one," she said. I reached for a glass from the next table, and filled it for her.

"Cheers."

"Bung ho. Johnny's on form."

"Yes," she said. "But it's hard work. Morning, noon, and night. We're always knackered by bedtime. Then, as soon as you shut your eyes, the alarm goes, and you're off again."

"But it's still going well?"

"Hard to tell. We're busy enough. But the overdraft keeps going up. I think we're just working for the bank."

We exchanged financial horror stories. The remaining diners left in a group, and she went to deal with them. The evening seemed to have gone well for them; compliments were pronounced by the men in those avuncular tones by which a patron indicates the quality of his patronage. Sue took it all gracefully, inclining her head with becoming modesty. The group passed into the hall, spent some time discussing overcoats—"This yours?" "No, it's mine"—and, at last, were gone. Sue came back into the dining room and flopped back into her chair. "Pompous sods," she said. She took a large swig of wine.

"Sue," I said, "can I borrow you for a few minutes?"

She spluttered in her wine. "La, sir," she said, "and my husband in the house!" She looked at me straight, smiling: goodness gracious, I realized, she *would*, too . . . if he wasn't. It's our age: young enough to want to; old enough to feel the press of time. Old friends in a new light. Now, or never?

Well, it obviously couldn't be now. And I hadn't meant *that*, anyway. What do I say?

"Your face is better than a movie, dear William," she said.

Too late.

"Tell me what you saw," I probed, fascinated.

"Surprise, hotly pursued by lust. It was quite flattering."

"You saw right. Now you know."

We smiled at each other. We filed the information. Then she sighed and said, "Well, what *did* you want to borrow me for?"

I told her. Walk up the street. Look for a red Fiesta. Note if there's anyone in it; if so, how many. Don't stop. Don't go close. Don't come back the same way. That's all.

"Who are they?"

I hesitated. I leaned closer. "VAT!" I hissed.

"My God!"

"I think they're following me."

"Can they do that?"

"Yes. They have *powers* . . ."

Brave girl! She would have hidden me from the Gestapo, if I'd parachuted into her farmyard. I could see it all. *Formidable!*

"Have you got a mackintosh? And a beret?"

"What *are* you on about, William?"

"I'm just a bit overexcited. Take care."

She was back in ten minutes. The red Fiesta was parked near the top of the street, with one man in it. He appeared to be asleep.

"I could hardly believe you. But it *is* odd, that, to sleep in a car when there are so many bed-and-breakfast places nearby. In this street, even."

"Can I borrow a torch?" I asked. I didn't want to use the tungsten-halogen monster.

"What're you going to do now?"

"I just want to look under my car. The exhaust pipe."

I'd been wanting to do this, and now, with chummy snoring away up the other end of the street, I could do it unobserved. There was a low wall between the courtyard and the street, and the Citroën was parked with its rear bumper a couple of feet from the wall. I had left just enough room to get down behind it. Once down, I was well hidden.

I shone the torch under the car. Strange how much of this drama had taken place in the dark, in streetlight, or torchlight. The beam was small, and quite feeble. I swept it slowly across the blackened, muddy metal, full of mysterious humps and hollows like a model battlefield upside down. Even after hours of being parked, the car still ticked as it cooled and contracted.

There were so many pipes and lumps of equipment under there that I almost missed what I was looking for. A small black box, already thick with road dust. It could have been an electrical junction box, but Citroën don't fix these on with insulating tape, and there were no wires running to it. It gave me quite a jolt to find it, even though I had thought it possible that there might be something there. Could it be a bomb—ready to be fired by remote control when I got to some lonely place? But they didn't *know* I was going to Wales, and we had already passed dozens of places where they could have exploded it without involving other cars or passersby, if they cared about things like that. It seemed more likely that it was a radio beacon, to make sure they didn't lose me on the road. They didn't know I didn't *want* them to be lost.

It was important that they didn't know I'd found it, otherwise I would have tried to get the cover off. It seemed inadvisable even to touch it, in case some noise was transmitted—a dead giveaway at this time of night. I had to be content with wriggling as close as I could and shining the torch on it: there were some code letters, stamped into the steel cover, and some numbers, mostly obscured by tape.

None of it meant anything to me. I decided I would assume the thing was a radio beacon and leave it alone until I could get a garage to look at it.

"Thanks for the torch, Sue."

"Everything all right?"

"Exhaust pipe just a bit loose, that's all."

"What're you going to do about the VAT snooper?"

"I'll think of something."

Nobody in the hall except us. It was a chaste, good-night sort of a kiss. Well, perhaps a bit more than that. "My compliments to the chef," I said.

Next year, sometime, never.

INTIMATE ALLIANCE

The essence of the defense consists in an intimate alliance of the Army with the ground on which it fights.

—Clausewitz

He wasn't there!

Conspicuous absence of a red Fiesta. An absence legible at twenty-five yards (with spectacles, if worn). Leaving the blackest of black holes, an oblong of black tarmac, shimmering with emptiness, ominous.

Where was he?

Why had he gone?

What were they up to?

They could simply have wanted to see me safely out of the way before making a concerted attack at the London end: now they could be going to raid the shop and the warehouse, taking everything apart to find the "papers." Which, as far as I knew, I didn't have. It was to find the answer to this problem, to find out what the whole thing was all about, that I was leading one of them into the ambush I had planned. And now he'd taken himself off the lead.

I'd made an early start—for me, that is. Breakfast at half-seven. On the road before eight. I had about a hundred miles to go, to Pembroke

Dock where I kept the boat; then I had to motor two miles upriver to the cottage and make my preparations. This had to be done before dark, say by eight this same evening. On the way, I had to call in at a number of hotels to maintain the impression of a business trip. It was going to be a full day. Followed, if all went as planned, by a busy night.

And now, this. Loss of contact with the enemy. And the day had hardly started.

Right Brain was doing the driving, while Left Brain was sorting information and listing hypotheses. I've learned that the process of decision making takes time, and that any attempt to force the decision is liable to result in error. Decide in haste, repent at leisure. (It's amazing how often these old saws get support from biological theory.) So, being anxious to get the right answer, I didn't interrupt. In spite of all this activity, I was still able to notice that the sun was shining for the third day in succession; the stone streets of Bath were glowing in the golden warmth; and the trees in every park and crescent were tinged with bright green. Beautiful day for a battle.

We seemed to be heading out of Bath in the direction of the Severn Bridge and Wales. Right Brain obviously felt this was the thing to do, at least until an alternative plan was adopted. Petrol was getting low, and I stopped at a filling station on the outskirts. It wasn't self-service, and I sat in the car in comfort while the tank was filled. Spring was definitely in the air: even the attendant was feeling it, and hummed to himself over the whining of the pump.

"Flowers'll be out soon," he said.

"The flowers that bloom in the spring," I agreed, taking the change.

"Yes, that's it," he smiled. "Well, tra-la."

"Tra-la."

I had to wait at the edge of the forecourt for a gap in the traffic. It was a long wait. Bath is well supplied with multistory car parks, and this was the time when they were being filled up. A solid line of cars filed slowly past, bearing shoppers to their Saturday spree. On and on, it went. Perhaps I should open a shop in Bath.

Then the alarms went off. *Achtung! Achtung!* I just had time to grab a map and pretend I wasn't looking. Less than five yards away, the red Fiesta was hauled across my bows, a fixed link in the chain of traffic. How he must be hating it! After all that hiding round corners, and behind other cars, to be presented for inspection like that, on parade, marched past my saluting base! I caught a glimpse of his face, fixed straight ahead: no eyes-left from him. He looked younger than I expected: a thin face, not unintelligent, his dark hair cut short-back-and-sides. Not the face of a thug, not one of their heavies like the one who had broken in. I couldn't associate that face with a bayonet, though he could perhaps wield a more impersonal weapon; a shot from a distance. This was good news: for what I had in mind, this sort of opponent would be easier to deal with than a bully boy.

But, at the moment, Thin Face was being borne away, back into Bath. I guessed that he had overshot, or had been waiting for me further along the road and become worried when I didn't appear, not knowing that I'd stopped for petrol. *Too* impatient—he needed a further session at sleuth school. Perhaps he'd relied on the radio beacon, if that's what it was under my car. Surely you need at least *two* monitors, direction finders, to give a fix on a beacon source? Was he relying on his partner to take up the trail? What should I do now?

Well, I couldn't chase after him shouting Here I am. There was no alternative to proceeding as planned.

It's always men who make room for you in traffic, if you manage to catch their eye. Women never do—they're oblivious to everything outside their own car. They're not trained to function cooperatively outside the family circle. I had some time to ponder whose fault that was, before a cheery van driver stopped and let me across. Back on course.

The tollbooths of the Severn Bridge are on the English side. (Of course they are—we don't trust the Welsh with all that money.) I had been watching my mirror closely all the way from Bath, but there was no sign of the red Fiesta. Lost him again. It was very unsettling, not knowing whether this evening's engagement was on or off. I looked at the other booths, then gave a long stare at the central driving mirror, while the queue I was at the tail of moved slowly toward the tollbooth. A car that looked familiar was going round the roundabout behind me. Black with aerials. But it didn't turn up toward the bridge. I watched. It made a second circuit of the roundabout, going slowly. I reached the booth, handed over money and got my ticket, and started off toward the bridge. In the distance, far behind me now, I saw the black car turn off the round-about and head for the line of tollbooths. The black Cortina of the night watch.

It gave me a chilly feeling in the spine.

If, as seemed likely, the pursuit had been taken over by Bulky Jacket, I didn't like it. From what I'd seen from Ginny's window, as he walked along the pavement opposite, Bulky Jacket was a thug, Grade A1. He had walked with that springy step which comes naturally to men who live by their muscles. He, too, had a short-back-and-sides, ginger in his case, and so short as to be a kind of trademark, the trade of grievous bodily harm. It's an ancient tra-dition, the stern warrior with short hair, and the wars are always worst when they're waging it. Think of Cromwell. Or the Teutonic knights. Or Nazis. Short hair, short on chivalry. I *definitely* didn't like it.

"We could turn round and go back to London," quavered Right Brain. Shut up. In evolution, it's subtlety that wins over brute force. "Yes but . . ."

Keep driving.

Chepstow, Usk, and then on to the A40 at Abergavenny. Then the green and lovely valley following the river Usk, and the canal along-side, setting its level datum along the sides of the mountains that it measures. It never stares, the sunlight, into these dark Welsh valleys, but comes soft and shy, no more than is needed for half-truths, myths, and magic. The mountains crowd the road on both sides, threatening the incautious traveler with purple prose. There were no dragon clouds flying above their peaks. But there was a tiger on my tail.

The black Cortina followed as far behind as he dared, occasionally dropping out of sight, then catching up under cover of a faster car.

He did it well, I thought: if I hadn't been watching closely I wouldn't have noticed that I was being followed.

Brecon, Llandovery, Llandeilo—the road led on and then out of the valleys. According to plan, I left my price list at several small hotels on the way. I had lunch at the Picton Arms in Carmarthen— a quick snack at the bar: I chose a town center for this stop so that my follower would not feel exposed, as he would have done if I had made him wait in open country. I saw him park some distance behind me down the street, where he could watch but be almost hidden. My plans required some more shopping, including a visit to a butcher's, but it must have all looked innocent enough. Then we were off again.

St. Clears, Kilgetty—a straight run now. I made no more stops after Carmarthen until I arrived at Pembroke Dock, and pulled up outside the boatyard gates.

It was half-past three. I had to get moving. The boatyard had got my Avon dinghy out, as I had asked them to do by phone before I left my office two days ago, but they hadn't blown it up. They had, however, got the outboard motor in their test tank and had run it up; they said it had needed new plugs but otherwise was fine. Would it be reliable? They smiled Welshly; that is a question, isn't it? Oh yes indeed, it *should* run beauti-ful. I understood that if their wishes would make it so, all would be well. Better make sure to load the tool kit.

I got the dinghy pumped up with the foot pump, and had the usual struggle to get the marine-ply floorboards installed. Jack from the boatyard helped me carry it down the slipway. "Early in the year for you, isn't it?" he asked. It was: the water looked cold. There was a light breeze coming up the estuary, making me shiver even in the bright sunlight. The waves out in midstream were small but choppy, wind against tide, an occasional white horse sparkling where the current was strongest. We slid on the weedy cobbles of the slipway, a massive construction where the Neyland car ferry used to land before the new bridge was built. It was weedy then; now, with much less use and much more weed, it's like an event in the game *Jeux sans frontières*. We arrived at the bottom at speed; the dinghy crashed into the water; we tried to make it look as if we'd meant to do it just like that. "Launching the lifeboat, look you!" someone joked from the quay above our heads. Jack aimed two fingers upward, and I tied the skinny painter to a huge iron mooring ring. The next problem was bringing down the motor and my suitcase; we managed it without more loss of dignity. I parked the car inside the boatyard, which is protected by a high fence with barbed wire on top: it would be locked at sunset, but as a valued customer of many years I had my own key. Then I struggled into my sailor suit: short wellies, thick sweater, yellow overalls. I locked my shore clothes into the car, pulled on my black woolly hat (the plain version with*out* a pompom) and was ready for embarkation. Time: four-fifteen. I was on schedule. Or would be, if the outboard didn't play up.

There's a powerful tide in the estuary, even at that point, where it's a quarter of a mile wide, and the tide was a half-ebb, at its strongest. I suppose the current is running at two to three knots, a fast walking pace: that's not up to Yellow River standards, but you couldn't swim or row against it, and from a small boat you are uncomfortably aware of the weight of water rushing down to join the sea, and trying to take you with it. If the motor conks, all is not lost, of course; you can paddle to the shore *across* the current, though you'll be carried a long way downstream before you make your landing. If that happened to me now, I'd never make it to the cottage, as it was upstream and against the current. The plan would have to be aborted. I don't like being that dependent on machinery, especially two-stroke outboard motors—the most temperamental of all man's inventions— but I could think of no better way to get me to the cottage, the battleground, the necessary hour before the enemy.

But the good wishes of the Welsh were with me, and the motor sounded in good heart: its throaty roar was smooth and unbroken, and the white wash jetted out behind the boat. Once out in the middle of the estuary, I looked back along the shoreline: I soon located the black Cortina, parked on the slip road leading to the bridge. That was a stroke of luck; he could easily have parked it out of sight, but hadn't bothered. Was he overconfident? I hoped so.

What else could be seen? I turned to survey the other side of the estuary, which I always think of as the Nelson side. Further downstream, opposite Pembroke Dock, is the upstart Milford Haven: a new town built to compete with old Pembroke, where wooden warships had been built for hundreds of years. And who more suitable to declare the place open than Horatio? said Sir William Hamilton (who was the local bigwig involved). How exciting to meet the hero! doubtless exclaimed his wife. Who was, of course, Lady Hamilton. And so she did. And so it was. That's one of the things a sailor suit does for a man. The other is to get him shot.

I wasn't alone on the water. From farther downstream, a small powerboat was sending up puffs of white spray as it bucketed in my direction: the sound of its engine was audible even above the din of my own. Beyond it I could see a black figure poised on a monoski, leaning against the pull as he cut back and forth across the powerboat's wash. They were going at twice my speed, and soon were near enough for me to see details: the boat, shaped like a shark, with two towering outboard motors on the stern; and the skier, fair hair tugged by the wind, protected against the chill by a black wetsuit, knees flexing as his ski jolted on the lumpy water. Fifty yards away now and, perhaps because he saw me watching, he took one hand off the tow bar and made a wide sweeping gesture, like an acrobat or ballet dancer, inviting me to applaud his performance. Nearer still, and I saw him dip his free hand into a pouch on his belt. It emerged holding a squarish object. In a moment he would pass within a very few yards. A very few yards. Very close. If he made one of his sideways sweeps he could pass within a few feet. *Could almost touch my boat.* Too close. Too close . . . and what was that object in his hand? Was it a gun? It could be a gun. If it *was* a gun, pulling alongside, slowing a little, at that range, he couldn't miss. Then he'd be off at full speed, the pistol shot sounding like a backfire, if it was heard at all above the combined roar of our motors. My dinghy, out of control, spinning into the bridge pier, capsizing, everything carried away by the current, days before my body would be found.

He was raising the object, in his right hand. *Was pointing it at me!* I put the tiller over sharply. The dinghy spun in a tight half-circle, bouncing violently. Now I was speeding back over my own wash, speeding in the opposite direction to the skier. We were about to pass, now, at about thirty knots instead of ten. His broadside, now, would be difficult to deliver. I hoped Nelson was watching.

The skier was laughing as he passed me, the object held high. It didn't somehow appear to be a threatening gesture.

Then he put it to his lips. I saw his head tilt briefly as he drank from it. His voice floated in the wind.

"Cheers, boyo!"

After that, er, precautionary diversion, I had to turn the dinghy again. I did so rather more slowly, making a wider circle to keep the spray down—there was a bucketful of water sloshing over the floorboards as a result of the first turn. I pushed the paddles under the suitcase to keep it out of the water. The shoreline revolved about me as I came back onto course.

The skier had done me a good turn. There, still parked on the slip road, the Cortina still sat: at this distance, and with its antennae, it looked like a long black beetle. But now a hundred yards further on, and nearer to the bridge, there was a new arrival—the red Fiesta.

A gathering of the clans. Now I knew I would have to deal with an enemy force of at least two. Maybe others had been summoned. I must be careful to provide a line of retreat if the opposing force was too great. My plans already made some provision for this; I'd better make sure of it.

Heading back upstream now, I was closing with the bridge. The river is narrower here, and the water is compressed into a stronger current. The huge gray arch of the roadway was far overhead, the steel showing streaks of yellow rust. I headed for the center span, wide enough for two tankers to pass in comfort; the giant columns rose from the water, corroded by salt water and crusted with barnacles to the high-water mark way up above me. The dinghy pushed against the current, tiny and fragile among all these tons of impassive steel and rushing water. Passing under the bridge, the sound of the motor came echoing back with a fearsome clatter.

Now I could see the cottage just coming into view round the next bend in the river: a triangle of glass, the big upstairs window in the gable end reflecting the early evening light. From up there, you can look out to the west, down the estuary; enjoy the last of the sunset over the shining water; and watch the homecoming yachts motor up to their moorings at Lawrenny, two miles farther upstream.

I wanted to look back at the bridge, to see if I could spot the watchers who must be there, leaning on the parapet probably, staring after me, worried about losing contact. I might be going to disappear upstream, for all they knew. But I was making it easy for them. They would be able to see the dinghy all the way as I motored to the foreshore in front of the cottage: they would see me land; unload; drag the dinghy up the beach. Then they would almost certainly ask at the boatyard; be told that the cottage was mine; set off on the long journey round by road. So they wouldn't be there before six-thirty. The dinghy zipped over the water, and in another ten minutes I was opposite the cottage. I slowed right down, and began to edge into shore between the thick clusters of seaweed. In another moment, the motor spluttered and died. I tilted it: slimy strands of weed had a stranglehold on the propeller. I got out the paddles and rowed the last few yards, until the dinghy grounded on weed: there was a gentle scrunch as the barnacled rock made its presence felt. I winced: that does a rubber dinghy no good at all. It's not the most hospitable of beaches.

I climbed out, managing to keep the tops of my boots above water, and eased the dinghy up onto the seaweed slope. Then I unloaded it, lugging everything, including the motor, to the top of the beach. Then I brought up the dinghy itself, tipping it over to empty out the water that had been collected *en voyage*, and then carried it sideways, slipping on the seaweed, to the shelter of the miniature cliff—more of a high earth bank—at the top of the beach. Tucked in here, it was hardly visible from the water: a necessary precaution to protect it from the local pirates; its outboard motors they prefer to pillage, and I concealed mine on top of the bank, covering it with branches.

The cottage is sheltered from the waterfront by a disused orchard. It's a jungle now: the orchard trees are grown huge, fighting their last battle for survival with monstrous growths of villainous dark green ivy that rises against the sky, blotting out the light like science-fiction horrors. Through this murky scene of vegetable warfare there is a small winding path, almost a tunnel. I made my way up it; slippery ivy tendrils and strands of last year's bramble stroked and clutched at me. The children won't go through here at night.

Light at the end of the tunnel. I emerged into the cottage courtyard cut into the steep hillside. At my back, the estuary. Ahead and on my right, tumbledown sheds—this used to be a tiny farm. And on my left, the cottage: two up and two down, and no mod cons. Stone walls, rendered and covered with peeling whitewash in many colors—white, cream, pink—a record of changing taste over the last hundred and fifty years. A steep slated roof. A blue painted door facing the courtyard. I unlocked it.

Nobody had been here since last summer, and the spiders.were in charge. It didn't seem worth it to disrupt their efforts, as I didn't plan on being here for long. I concentrated on essentials: filling the oil lamps; fitting new candles into candle holders; and some careful preparations for the impending confrontation. It took about half an hour. I looked at my watch. Five-thirty. I decided to risk a cup of tea. While the kettle boiled I unpacked my battle dress from the suitcase and climbed into it. Absorbed in this, the kettle's whistle startled me. I made the tea and drank some; I ate three chocolate digestives; I finished the tea. Then I stood in front of the mirror.

I don't mean *army* battle dress. I mean the dress I'd chosen to fight *this* battle in. Impressive military uniforms went out, of course, when warfare became impersonal, fought at long range; this encounter, however, was going to be close range and personal, and appearance would be half the battle. As I would be outnumbered, I needed all the psychological help I could get.

So, I looked into the mirror.

It was pretty conventional, really. The all-black look. What your well-dressed nightfighter has been wearing ever since commandos, and latterly the SAS, were invented. A suit of shadows. As opposed to the matador's suit of lights. *He* wants to be conspicuous. *I* wanted to be able to disappear. I rubbed the black makeup into my face and hands. It gave my eyes a strange red-rimmed look, like an angry gorilla. Good. The heavy black roll-neck sweater added beef to my chest and shoulders. The black denim trousers were tucked into my short black rubber boots. I had no holster, so I stuck the big black revolver into my trouser pocket. *Ah non—ça tue la ligne!* as Claudine would have cried. Also, I didn't like the direction it was pointing in. I would have to keep it in my hand. I aimed it at the mirror. Everything looked professional enough; I would think twice before tackling me. But it was just a bit too conventional: maybe I have an identity problem, but I do like to be different.

That's why I'd bought the Ronald Reagan masks.

I slipped one on, settling the elastic at the back of my head.

Even in the declining daylight inside the cottage, the mask seemed to float in space. In the dark, by moonlight or candlelight, the effect would be still better. The contrast between the pink plastic face and the black figure wearing it was unnerving. It's the fixed expression that makes a mask so disconcerting: you still expect a human response, even when you *know* you're looking at a piece of molded rubber or plastic, so embedded is the instinct. I believe the first sight babies learn to respond to is a mother's face. Does the mouth curve up, or down? Is she pleased or angry?

This mask was a happy mask. In that the original, which it copied, was no less a happy *mask*, it was true to life. I'd chosen it for that air of uncertainty, the lopsided grin in which good news and bad news are struggling for supremacy.

And it's that unsettling effect I want to have on my visitors. Well, it sure as hell works on me.

Six o'clock now. Or, to get into the mood, eighteen hundred hours.

I hurried to complete my preparations. In the courtyard, I checked the position, just inside the shed door opposite the cottage, which I had chosen as my main defense post. It seemed to have everything I wanted. I ran a length of fishing line from that position to the door of the shed at the top of the courtyard. In that shed, ready to come to my aid, I propped my alter ego, and then pushed the door shut to conceal him until he might be needed. A few final touches indoors, and then I went outside again, to climb the hill to a watching place. I settled down there, hoping I hadn't forgotten anything.

Shouldn't be long now.

10

MUTUAL
CONSENT

No battle can take place unless by mutual consent.

—*Clausewitz*

From my observation post, I watched the gray film of dusk settling over the cottage, the woods, and the distant shore. Sunset was well past; light still glowed in the west where the sky was tinged with yellow, but overhead there was already a sparkling darkness, chill and clear.

I had taken up a position directly above Quarry Cottage, and just below that was the rough track which traverses the hillside above the quarry, and is the only approach route to the cottage from the landward side. Two hundred yards farther down, the track turns a steep hairpin bend and then returns the same distance, at a lower level, to its end in the courtyard, passing the cottage on the estuary side. Four hundred yards in all. But from my post, by cutting straight down the hillside, it was less than a quarter of that distance. I should be able to observe the enemy as he passes, let him go down the track and out of sight, and then nip down the hill and into my final position in the courtyard before he has turned the hairpin. This observation was essential: I had already decided that if the enemy numbered more than two, or if automatic weapons were being carried, I would decline to do battle. In that case, I would wait until he had passed, and then beat it up the track and away. He would be left in possession of the field, but I would live to fight another day. Tactical withdrawal. As the evening chill began to seep into me, tactical withdrawal took on a siren sound: it meant a hot bath and dinner in some cozy pub; I would have seen the enemy close to, a positive gain with almost no risk. I might well have planned to do just that from the start.

But I hadn't. The plan was to make a capture, make someone talk, get some solid information. Crunch point was—should be—coming up. So stiffen the sinews. Hold the line. It's the waiting that's the hardest part. Once the action starts, there won't be time for second thoughts.

The light level was sinking fast. The scene change from day to night would soon be completed. And all done with lighting. Very clever. Now, in place of the spotlit solidity of day, a landscape of shifting shadows, dark, colorless, insubstantial. From my hillside, I looked down on the cottage: the warm light of the oil lamps made the little windows glow with gold, and I could hear the tiny sound of my portable radio chattering and singing to itself. And there I am, innocently preparing a simple supper, a glass of whiskey in one hand and a wooden spoon in the other, a simmering saucepan on the Calorgas stove, just wondering where the garlic crusher is, when with a crash, the door bursts open . . . So they should think. Perhaps I should have left something cooking, to add a garlic smell to the lamplight and music. Smell is the most evocative of the five senses.

Too late now. And anyway, I would be worrying about the saucepan burning. Remember it for next time.

Virtually dark now, and the stars are out. The sky is a luminous, painted ceiling, still reflecting light. There is a pale illumination from the east now, and looking toward the top of the hillside, a little to the right, I see a misshapen moon escaping from the treetops. Looking down again—past the light gray square of the courtyard, beyond the dark gray density of the orchard—the broad band of the estuary shimmers like black silk. The wooded landscape seems to float on it. Far downstream, I can see the regular red flash of the navigation buoy, and beyond that, toytown Pembroke, diminished by distance, the chain of lights marking the bridge, and the quivering beams of car headlamps. Civilization, still within reach. Upstream, the jagged

silhouettes of obsolete warships, stored at anchor, waiting for the
last passage to the breaker's yard.

Important for the night watch to be familiar with every shape,
every rustle. I memorize the outline of the ground, of bushes and
tree trunks. No details visible in the flat, shadowless gloom; outlines
only. Recognition patterns, all friends. Any changed pattern means
danger. Watch for the changes. Listen for new sounds. There are
rustles all round me; the woods have come to life. A patter of mice,
close to. Down in the wood, a sudden sharp yap, repeated—a fox.
A great white owl lives behind the cottage; too early for him yet,
but I've often seen him sliding silently between the trees: sometimes
a young one sits on a tree just outside one of the cottage windows
and keeps us awake with screech practice, until we throw a boot.
Many a good boot has gone that way. As nobody can remember to
throw them in *pairs*, we're always left with odd boots . . .

Dark as it's going to get now. And, with the clear sky and the
faint but noticeable moonlight, you can still see well enough to move
about. To see, but also to be seen. Must remember that.

I'm well tucked in behind an elder bush. Plenty of old bracken
and bramble around me. I've beaten out a path down the hill to the
courtyard. Nothing to do now but wait.

It's cold. I've got a flask of whiskey mac—prepared to my preferred mix of two thirds whiskey, one third Stones ginger wine. Not
too sweet. Umm. That's better.

Watch, listen, and wait.

Two hours later I'm still watching, listening, and waiting. The price
of freedom is eternal vigilance, sure 'nuff. Likewise the problem of
defense. A skillful attacker knows this, of course, and chooses just
that moment when the defense has got bored and is starting to think
that maybe the attack won't come after all. A skillful defense knows
that a skillful attacker knows this, and *expects* to be attacked at such
a time. So, if the attacker knows that the defense is skillful, he will
not attack then, but *as soon as possible*, as he can expect the defense
to be continuously improved, whether he attacks or not. So, what
to do? Do I think the enemy are skillful? No, I think they're in the

pub. Perhaps I should walk up and join them. Then we could have one of those gentlemanly arrangements to do battle at some agreed time and place, which allowed warfare in the Age of Enlightenment to be conducted in the spirit of a mass duel. Shall we say ten o'clock on Thursday morning? By all means, my dear fellow. If it's not raining. And then the night before could be spent as a possible last night on earth *should* be spent, in perfect security, carousing and saying goodbye to the girls.

Now we've given up mass duels, the trial of strength, in favor of mass extermination. And in place of the decisive outcome, we've got terrorism, the toothache of modern civilization, which cannot and never will decide anything.

I'm going to get a toothache if I have to sit up here much longer. Also backache, leg ache, and frozen balls.

If I *had*, in support of a quixotic impulse to restore civilization by proposing former standards of behavior, started walking up to the pub, I would not have got far.

Out in a blaze of glory, I would have gone. Well, not a blaze, more of a blast. And not one, but two. The definitive verdict on my life spoken, *kerblap*, by a double-barreled sawn-off shotgun.

I heard them coming before I saw anything. A faint, rhythmic thumping, transmitted through the ground, *felt* rather than *heard*. Then I saw, up the track to my right, an indistinct wavering shadow, visible only because it was moving relative to the hedge and tree shadows. Approaching, it grew larger and more distinct; assumed the outline of a man. There was another behind.

They passed within ten feet of my burrow in the undergrowth; close enough for me to hear their panting breath and the creak and slither of their leather jackets. They were like a couple of hounds, following my scent down the track. The leader was Bulky Jacket; I recognized his springy muscular step and bulging outline; he carried the sawn-off shotgun on his shoulder, right hand on the grip, ready for action. A few yards behind followed the slighter shadow of Thin Face, his tread less assured, his face white and anxious in the moonlight, his hands empty of weapons. I decided he was probably unarmed because, if he had any sort of weapon, it would be in his hand by now. Was he an observer, a trainee—the murderer's apprentice?

I let them go out of sight down the track, back into the shadows, and then I got to my feet. Christ, I was stiff! I had to risk a quick stretch to get my limbs working again. Then I was off down my path, avoiding the roots and mossy boulders, moving as fast as I could on the steep slope down to the courtyard. I made it without mishap. Then I was in through the half-open door of the long shed opposite the cottage. I moved through the shed to the second door. Beside it was a grimy window that faced the approach track. Here, peering over the sill, I took up my predetermined position.

Twenty yards away, in line with the end of the cottage, was the five-barred wooden gate that marked the end of the track and the entrance to the courtyard. Beyond that was the track itself, tapering away to blackness under the trees that lined it. I watched. Soon they must appear.

I suppose I had less than a minute to wait, but it seemed longer, much longer. Then Bulky Jacket loomed out of the shadows. He was almost up to the gate. He emerged into the moonlight. It glinted on the gun. Thin Face appeared beside him. They had a brief consultation, using gestures. I understood that Bulky Jacket would advance into the courtyard, while Thin Face stayed in reserve, at the end of the cottage. Very wise of him.

You don't have to open the gate, except for cars. There's a gap by the gatepost. I watched as they found it and passed through. Bulky Jacket came on toward me. For a moment I thought he'd decided to start by searching the shed. But it wouldn't have been wise—he might have made a noise and given himself away. Instead, he turned, and moved up into the courtyard. Now I was on his right. Ahead of him was a small stable building. To his left the cottage, still with *son et lumière* in full effect. Me having a quiet evening at home.

He approached the front door.

He didn't try the handle. Instead, he stood back, looked down to where Thin Face was watching. The next thing would be the run up and the boot against the latch side. Kicking it open. Bloody

vandal! I'd hung that door myself, and a lot of hard planing it took
to get it to fit.

"*Hold it right there!*"

I had taken my stance in the shed doorway, legs apart, feet firmly
planted, both hands gripping the Webley, which had Bulky Jacket
in its sights. I hoped the moonlight was giving them the full effect
of the Ronald Reagan mask. I thought I heard Thin Face give a cry
of surprise, I hoped so, but Bulky Jacket was the one to concentrate
on. I watched him through the mask's eyeholes. He had frozen, was
still facing the cottage door with his back to me, just as I'd planned
it. Then—

Blammmmmm!

The hail of shot splintered the shed window, and shook the old
boarded door. I don't remember seeing him turn, but Right Brain
did, and had me take the single step to the shelter of the doorjamb
just in time. This man is as dangerous as a mad bull: fearless and
furious. And *fast*.

Well, I'd play it his way. And as it's played in the bullring. Come
at him from several directions, exhaust his fury.

I bent down, grabbed the fishing line that led to the stable door
at the top of the courtyard, and heaved on it.

I can only guess what happened as it was too risky to look, but
the stable door must have swung open smartly—I heard the crash.
Bulky Jacket must have seen my alter ego, a second figure dressed
in black wearing another Ronald Reagan mask, aiming some kind
of weapon (a piece of driftwood) at him. He must have taken it for
real, because—

Blammmmmm!

He fired the second barrel.

I was out of the door in a flash, and took up my position again
before he had a chance to reload. But none too soon—the gun was
already broken for loading.

"*Now hold it!* Last warning, *last warning*!"

I haven't shouted at anybody for years. But I can still remember
how to do the parade-ground voice. I did it. He froze. He'd better.
I meant it.

"Drop the gun, *drop the gun*!"

The crisis command—say it loud and say it twice.

He heard me. He dropped it. The gun fell out of his fingers with such reluctance it might have been covered with glue. Even in the moonlight, I could see how he was hating it. My problems were only just starting.

"Now get down, *get down*. Flat on your face, arms outstretched. *Move!*"

I was moving toward him now. If I had to fire, I couldn't miss. He could see that, too. He got down, slowly, like a badly trained Alsatian.

Now it was time to bring Thin Face into the family circle. He was still standing at the end of the cottage, had done nothing to excite my peripheral vision. I risked a direct look at him: *any* slackening of concentration on Bulky Jacket was a risk. He looked back at me; his hands were raised to chest height, palms toward me, a gesture of submission. His face was scared, but thoughtful. I shouldn't underestimate him. His threat, if it came, would be the more thinking, deadly kind. Not like the mad bullishness of his partner.

"You. Up here. Face the wall, hands against it, move your feet back. Legs apart." I came up behind him, searched him with my left hand. Nothing, not even a knife. Quite impressive, in a way, to go on a murder mission without a weapon. Like the Queen going shopping without money. He must have something, and it's probably brains. So watch out.

"Keep facing the wall, but stand up. Undo your belt, drop your trousers round your ankles. Do it *now*." He obeyed. His underpants were Marks & Spencers, like my own. "Now put your hands up again, and keep them there. Any move, just one, you get shot. At this range you've had it. Understand?"

He nodded. I left him facing the wall, and went through the same performance with Bulky Jacket. I felt the vibrations as I searched him, the boiling aggression only just held under control, and kept the pistol barrel against the back of his neck to remind him it was there.

Then I picked up the shotgun, and made them shuffle in file into the cottage, Thin Face first, hands clasped on top of their heads. I got them standing side by side in the kitchen, facing the wall. I could see myself as I looked between them at the tall mirror that hung there: they could see it too, their all-black captor with the smiling mask. Now they had to be tied up, made secure. This was a tricky stage.

"You," I prodded Bulky Jacket, "on your knees, hands behind your back. *Move!*"

He didn't.

I had to react instantly, or lose control.

The Webley leaped in my hand as I pulled the trigger. The noise, in the closed space of the cottage, could be *felt*—a blast of sound, falling on the ears like a giant hammer; it filled the room slamming back at us from the walls, making the china on the sideboard tinkle in alarm and dust spurt from startled old boards in the ceiling above our heads. I fired between my captives at my own image: the mirror burst apart, showering us with splinters; all three of us stared at the football sized hole in the center of my reflection. The message could not have been clearer, even to Bulky Jacket. He knelt, as ordered.

I had arranged the nylon cord in six-foot lengths, with loops ready-made at one end. Now I made Thin Face secure his partner's hands. When that was done, I felt a lot safer. Then I made Thin Face kneel, and secured his hands. I had to put the pistol down to do this, but kept it well within reach. At last I had them both secured to my satisfaction. With hands tied, and trousers round their ankles, I reckoned I had things under control. The first part of the plan was complete.

I told Thin Face to get up. He struggled to his feet, and I made him sit on a wooden kitchen chair: I lashed him to it at the waist and round the legs. Then it was Bulky Jacket's turn. He got lashed to a chair in the next room, which has bunks in it (the sitting room is upstairs, overlooking the estuary) and racks for boots, oilskins, lifejackets, and all the heavy equipment needed for boating in the British climate. Bulky Jacket's chair was lashed in position against the bunks—I wanted to be able to find him where I'd put him. Then I went back into the kitchen.

Thin Face's eyes were blue and watchful. They followed me as I moved about the kitchen, collecting equipment for part two of the plan. He saw me take down the white enameled pie dish from the top shelf of the dresser, and put it on the table. He saw me take the remains of an old sheet out of the top left-hand drawer of the dresser and tear part of it into bandage-sized strips. Then he saw me take the big Sabatier cook's knife from the top right-hand drawer of the dresser. And sharpen it on a carborundum stick. He moved uneasily in his chair when I picked up everything off the table and walked across the kitchen. I didn't look at him. I walked past him and out of the door, leaving it open just a crack. I shut it, actually. But I held the handle so that it didn't catch, and let it fall open as if by accident.

I put the equipment—the knife, pie dish, bandages—on a bunk where Bulky Jacket could see it, and turned to face him. I put the oil lamp on a higher bunk where it would light his face, and turned up the wick. I sat in an upright chair by the window, to his side. He had to turn his head to see me. But there wasn't much point. He only saw Ronald Reagan smiling, that uncertain smile; plastic, permanent. What did he think of it? If he thought at all. Perhaps Bulky Jacket was a freak of evolution; perhaps there was nothing in his head but the ancient reptile brain, the R-complex, without any of the later accretions that made us into *Homo sapiens*. He had the killing instincts of a crocodile. How he would like to snap me up. A mad bull, or a sane crocodile? It's a fine distinction, brain-wise.

And it's a problem, interrogation-wise. How do you get a crocodile, or even a mad bull, to talk? Do they have beans to spill? Are they programmed to feel fear? What key will unlock a creature like this?

I sat, silent. I didn't have to worry about my thoughts showing, giving me away. Ronnie kept smiling for me. I saw Bulky Jacket shift in his chair, and I checked the Webley was in easy reach, on the windowsill beside me. He strained to turn his head, glaring toward me, once, then after a pause, twice more. Something was cooking. I said nothing; I figured that waiting would do more than words.

He boiled over suddenly: there was a loud creak as he struggled against his bonds to face me. "All right, Warner, all right," he burst out. "Come out of that kid's mask." His voice was that of a netted wild beast, snarling at captivity. "You're gonna get torn apart, torn apart . . ." He fell silent again, and sat with the breath snorting in his nostrils. If he did get loose now, he'd tear the house down. I knew it. There was no chance of tying him up ever again—he'd die first.

I got up, walked across the little room, stood over him. I held the big knife in front of his face. Lamplight glinted off the newly sharpened blade. He looked at it. He didn't seem much impressed. He knew knives.

"Who, what, why?" I said.

"Fuck off."

"I'm glad you brought that up," I said, "because if you don't answer my questions the next time I ask, fucking off is going to become a subject on which you'll no longer be qualified to pronounce. You've come, if you understand me, to a sharp divide. Get it? You talk, or I cut your balls off. No messing."

His eyes stared at me, dark caverns with fire burning deep inside. *Still* I was failing to impress him. What did I have to say? To do? What *could* I do, worse than that? In his place, I would talk, I knew it; that's why I'd chosen this particular threat. Perhaps he didn't believe I'd do it. But he *should*—after all, he had shown me that he was prepared to remove my guts with a shotgun blast. Gelding seemed a minor operation beside that.

Well, it takes all sorts. And apparently this *is* the reptilian sort, indifferent to the sexual socializing of us mammalians. Reptile sex is all done by remote control: she lays the eggs, he waddles up later and fertilizes them. That's why they've never developed: they've never had to communicate. And that describes this human croc exactly—no feelings, no sympathy, no communication. What am I going to do with him—with *it*?

"Your last chance. Who sent you, what were you sent for, and why?"

No reply.

I tried a new tack.

"If you ever want to go out with the lads again, Sergeant . . ."

He stirred, tried to sit up. "Where did you get that?"

It had been only a guess, but now it was a fact. I knew the type.

That springy walk, an air of discipline about his movements, his speed in turning to crouch and fire . . . Physical training, hand-to-hand combat, sergeant instructor if ever I saw one. About thirty-five now, a loner, certainly; perhaps once he would have passed as one of the boys. But sooner or later the croc would have escaped: he got into a fight, couldn't stop himself from going all the way. Someone would have got snapped—a comrade, probably. Then, court martial, jail, and unemployment—an uncomfortable civilian. Until this job came up . . . How many had there been, before me?

"I know what you did," I said, "but not which lot you were in."

"Who cares? I'm better on my own."

"What about your employers?"

"What about them?"

"They must be worth something to you, if you're prepared to go through this to protect them."

He seemed to smile. That semblance must be as near as he ever got.

"They're nothing to me."

"Then why . . . ?"

"There's nothing matters to *me*," he said, so quietly I could hardly hear him. "Except . . . except from time to time I get a new aim. I got one now. You want to know it? I'll tell you *that*. Yes?"

I knew it already. I was glad I was wearing the mask.

"It's that I'll get to *crunch* you, Warner," he whispered venomously.

"Right!" I shouted at him. "You won't tell me, you know what's going to happen."

I knew what I had to do.

11

A Spirit of Benevolence

In such dangerous things as War, the errors which proceed from a spirit of benevolence are the worst.

—Clausewitz

What I had to do was *scream*.

Well, if *he* wouldn't, *I* had to do it for him, didn't I? But before my turn came to move center stage, I let him curse on for a while, encouraging him with the knife, until I tired of it. He cursed without inspiration, and I was glad when the time came to slap a wide piece of sticking plaster over his mouth and reduce him to silence.

Then it was my turn. "Right then," I shouted again, "you've asked for it!" and I kicked the door shut. A slight pause, and then I let fly with some short screams followed by groans. I kept it all as hoarse and muffled as I could manage, so that my voice wouldn't be obvious, and I tried not to overdo any of it. I thought it was quite a good performance. When I looked up, his eyes were fixed on me, looking startled, as well they might. Then he understood, and started to make warning noises for the benefit of Thin Face next door, but the plaster over his mouth prevented anything intelligible coming out, and the noises did nothing more than take over where mine had left off. Couldn't have been better, in fact.

I collected the tin dish, the knife, and some of the strips of bandage. Then I flung open the kitchen door and passed through, followed by sounds of distress, wordless and urgent; only *I* knew that their cause was spiritual, not physical. I slammed the door, and stood for a moment, holding the dish, knife, and bandages; I didn't have to assume a ferocious expression as my face was still hidden by the mask. Thin Face still sat tied in his chair: his face, as I started across the kitchen, was white and bore all the indications of a man terrified to the point of hysteria. Good. Thin Face appeared to be made of different stuff from his crocodile companion: from the signs, he was a man like myself. He was at a vulnerable age—I guessed twenty-five—and could expect many happy times ahead if he cooperated.

"Well?" I growled as I walked past, "are *you* ready to talk? Or are you going to make the same mistake as your chum in there? That I don't mean what I say?"

I was carrying the tin dish at just below his eye level, and I saw him catch a partial glimpse of the contents. There were bloody smears on the rim, and on my hands. I continued across to the sink and dropped the dish with a crash on to the stainless-steel draining board.

"To do *that* to someone, you must be outa your *mind*," he croaked at last.

I was washing my hands at the sink. "And what," I said, without turning round, "do you have to be to blow someone apart with a twelve-bore shotgun? Or to tag along to watch it?"

I turned round to look at him; I had washed the knife and was drying it on a tea towel with a print of Pembroke Castle. Norman, I believe. This part of Wales is well supplied with Norman castles: it's known as Little England in Wales. Scenes like this must have gone on in countless dungeons in the good old days. I looked round the room. Flickering candles, a black-clad torturer, fire and flame and candlelight. And Christ receive thy Soule.

"*Are* you Warner? Why are you wearing that stupid mask?"

"I ask the questions," I told him. "*You* answer them. Who, what, why?"

"Warner wears glasses," he said.

Quite bright, this lad. But maybe he hasn't heard of contact lenses, more suitable for the active man.

"Warner . . . *does* wear glasses," I said. Then who am I? Obviously—I hope it's obvious—some freak who's into human butchery. In a good cause, if possible.

He said nothing, just sat there, waiting for the next move. Better get on with it before the atmosphere is lost.

I took the tin dish, tipped the contents into another basin, carried the tin dish over to him and slammed it on the tiled floor at his feet. I left him taking in the bloodstained surface while I collected the knife. Then I stood in front of him. I deliberately tilted the big blade to catch the light, just a few inches from his nose.

"Oh Jesus, *no*," he gasped.

"Who, what, why?"

"What d'you mean?"

"Don't give me that. You know as well as I do. This is your last chance. You'd better believe it. For the last time—*who sent you?*"

He gulped. It was coming. I *knew* it was—at last! When he spoke, he sounded like a man murmuring in his sleep.

"Loewenfeld."

"What?"

"Walter Loewenfeld." He spelled it. It had a ring of truth—too unusual a name for him to invent.

"Get on with it."

"He runs the factory."

"*Which* factory?"

"Protoplastics."

"Address?"

"Stanmore—it's in the phone book."

"What street?"

"Christ, I dunno, *I don't* . . . a trading estate. Off Laurel something. P'raps Laurel Lane, I'm not sure . . ."

It was Lauradale Road, I knew that. Good enough. He didn't know I knew that. He wasn't trying to resist.

"What were you sent to do?"

That was a difficult one for him. He licked his lips nervously. "I didn't have to . . ." he began. "I mean, I wasn't going to, you know, really *do* anything. Just watch . . . no, I mean keep an eye on Kevin. Him, in there. He had to actually *do* it."

"Kill me."

"*No!* Ask questions . . ."

"Now tell me *why*."

"Well. He's wild, Kevin. He does things . . ."

"No—I mean, why was I to be questioned?"

"Oh. Well, to find out what you knew, and who you'd told."

"About what?"

He was silent. "Understand this," I said. "When I ask a question, you answer. Got it?" I held the knife in front of his face, emphasizing my words with it. He nodded. I asked him again. "About what?"

"About the factory."

"What about the factory?"

"I don't know. I don't *know* . . ." He almost screamed it.

"Do you expect me to believe that?"

"It's true! I swear it's true! They didn't tell me . . . I was just to listen to what you told Kevin, and remember it. They didn't trust him to do that."

"That's not good enough."

"But it's the truth! I've told you!" His eyes begged me to believe that that was all he knew.

"Was it about something being manufactured in the factory?"

"P'raps . . . yes. I dunno."

"What sort of thing?"

"I dunno, honest."

"Who was it to be manufactured for?"

"I dunno that either."

"Was it a ministry? A government department?"

"Could be. Yes, p'raps it was."

"The Ministry of Defense?"

"MoD? Yeah, well, I've heard talk about that."

"Tell me."

"Well, I know there's lots of stuff they make for the MoD."

"What sort of stuff?"

"Lots. Moldings, bits for vehicles, equipment. All that."

"Torches?"

"Maybe. Look, I don't work there, you know."

"What's your job, then? Apart from Second Assassin?"

"I'm not . . . I *told* you—someone had to look after Kevin."

"Who's Loewenfeld?"

"He owns it, Protoplastics. And some others. Got pots—runs a Roller."

"Tell me more."

"About Loewenfeld? I dunno more. He's often abroad—France, Germany, and that. S'all I know."

"How often does he send you on murder missions?"

"Look, I keep *telling* you, it wasn't *like* that."

"Tell me how it *was*, then."

"Kevin was going to ask you what you knew about the factory, like I told you. Persuade you a bit." I wondered how Kevin's style of persuasion differed from mine—crude but effective, doubtless. "Go on," I said.

"Well, then you jumped outa that shed door. You pointed your gun at him. Kevin doesn't like that."

Too bloody bad.

"Then the other shed door opened . . . how did you *do* that?"

"Get on."

"Then you got to Kevin before he could reload. You *know* all that."

Yes, I knew all that. But what this kid didn't know—but to me was ninety-nine percent certain—was that friend Kevin wouldn't have stopped with answers to my questions. He would have gone on to finish me off. The *café cognac* to complete his meal. Had Loewenfeld told him to kill me? Or had he just reckoned on Kevin's natural instincts to do the job for him?

"This Loewenfeld told Kevin to kill me, didn't he?"

"No! I keep telling you! Kevin had to ask you what you knew about the factory. And Loewenfeld told me to be sure to remember everything you said—he said it was very important, but he couldn't rely on Kevin to do it."

Too right—Kevin wouldn't be interested in that side of things.

"And what would Loewenfeld say if you got back and reported that Kevin had blasted me all over the landscape with his shotgun?"

"But he hasn't . . ."

"Suppose he *had*. As he tried to, and nearly did?"

"Oh. Well, we'd have got it in the neck, all right. Loewenfeld's used to getting what he wants. Known for it."

He was perking up, the little sod. Trying to get a bit of his own back, threatening me with Big Brother Loewenfeld. He'll get you next time, he was implying.

Next time I would deal with Loewenfeld direct, I decided. Now, I had a name; next, I would put a face to it. Then we'd see about putting a dent in the Loewenfeld legend.

There was a lot more I needed to know. Not only *who* was behind the attacks on me, but *why*. But I thought it was time now for a pause and a change of tactics.

I walked away from Thin Face toward the sink with the blood-stained basin.

"Is that it?" he asked hopefully.

"The operation's postponed. What's your name?"

"Trevor."

"You can breathe again, Trevor."

It had been a long time since the tea and biscuits. I decided to rustle up something to eat. I took off the mask and looked about me. Not much in sight. Except . . . well, why not?

I tipped the contents of the basin onto a wooden chopping board, and began slicing. Trevor watched as I reached for a frying pan, lit the gas ring.

"I don't *believe* this," he said, his voice unsteady.

I put the pan on the stove, added sliced tomatoes, garlic, herbs.

"Oh yeah. Yeah. I get it," he sighed.

"Yes? Bright lad."

"What were they?"

No reason not to tell him now. "This'll be *Rognons de Porc Provençale*. Well, not quite, but near enough."

"*What?*"

"Pig's kidneys."

He sighed again. "How did you make Kevin scream like that?"

"I didn't."

"It was *you*? And you *are* Warner?"

"I am. And I have a vivid imagination. Which is more than can be said for Kevin. That's why it didn't work with him."

He was silent for a while. The pan sizzled on the stove. Then he said, "I'm gonna really *get* it from Loewenfeld."

"You expect me to weep for you?"

"No, no. No I don't. But, like I told you, I didn't understand it." He paused, then said, "I *liked* it with the cars—following, and that."

"Then Kevin opens up with the twelve bore, and it's a game no longer."

"Yeah. Yeah. From then on, it's a horror movie. Full color."

Do I believe him? Yes, I think I do. In fact, there's something I quite like about him; he at least has human responses. He's no sort of crocodile. And at present we're sharing a sense of survival. Do I trust him now? I think I do.

"You like something to eat, Trevor?"

"Eugh, no way," he snorted. I approached him with the frying pan. He looked at it. It was smelling good, but not to him.

"A biscuit?" I suggested.

"How'd I eat it?" he asked.

"I'll untie your arms."

"All right. And thanks."

"Don't forget I've still got the pistol. Any tricks, and I'll blast your head off."

"Oh yeah. Sure," he said, and grinned. "Your secret's safe with me," he added with a wink.

"I *mean* it."

I *did*. I think.

My motive wasn't so pure, of course. Are motives ever? No, I reckoned young Trevor had more to give, and that he would be more likely to give it if the tension was relaxed. So I fed him. He began to chat quite happily, even with his legs still tied. Then I gave him a large glass of wine. "What's this?" he asked. "Côtes-du-Rhône," I answered, and that was certainly what it said on the label. But, really, it was *vino veritas*—the original truth drug, as administered in crafty Roman orgies to visiting statesmen to make them reveal their secrets, both of policy and personality. That, of course, is what orgies were for: if you thought that they were a simple frolic with food and females, I'm afraid you're a touch naïve.

The color was coming back into Trevor's cheeks all right. "Have another one, Trevor?" "Well, why not. Glad I came along, now," he chuckled. "Cheers!"

"Sorry I can't untie your feet, yet."

"Never mind, as long as I can lift me elbow!"

I nudged the talk round to Protoplastics. Trevor, it seemed, was hoping to be offered a job as Transport Assistant. "Giving up your life of crime, are you?" I said. "Oh, come on," Trevor said, "I've explained all that. Yeah, well, I thought it'd get a bit rough, maybe, but all in a good cause."

"What cause is that?"

Trevor seemed to be weighing something up. Then he said, "No harm in telling you, I s'pose. That factory—Protoplastics—is gonna show the rest the way. It's so modern, you wouldn't believe it—all done with robots, automatic everything, the lot. It must be making pots. And the best thing is, Loewenfeld's gonna put the work force on shares!"

"A lot of companies do that now."

"Yeah, but listen, with so few workers the shares are really going to be something! There won't be anything else to touch it! It's just how socialism oughter be."

"Socialism?"

"Yeah. You know—returning to the workers by hand and brain the fruits of their toil, and that. Like nationalization oughter do, but doesn't."

"Who told you all this?"

"Loewenfeld, of course. He's the one that's setting it all up. And I'm gonna be in there when he does. Fantastic!"

"He sounds to me like your archetypal capitalist. You believe it?"

"Course! Why not?"

"Too good to be true, for a start. And I mistrust these distant promises, like it'll all be wonderful when the state has withered away. They tend not to happen, you know."

"Oh, I dunno," Trevor said, "there'll always be . . ."

An England? A first time?

I'll never know, because there was a sudden screech from the next
room that sounded like the sash window being flung open. I dived
for the draining board where I had left the pistol, and grabbed it.
I crashed into the next room: the chair was still lashed to the bunks,
but it was empty; pieces of cord lay all about. I knew at once what
had happened: it's that sodding nylon stuff, slippery as knotted eels.
Fuck it! I should have thought of that: should have been in to check.

"What's happened?" Trevor called. He sounded nervous. As well
he might. Crocodile Kevin would have been able to hear us frat-
ernizing, as well as Trevor spilling the beans. Now we were *both* on
his hit list—both due for crunching.

"Sodding nylon cord," I explained. "Worked at it until he got
loose. Then out through the window. He'll be out there somewhere,
waiting." I didn't say for whom, but Trevor didn't need telling. "Oh
my Gawd," he said, the blood draining from his face.

"I've got the shotgun," I said, "but he's still got all the cartridges."
I looked round for a place to hide the gun in case Kevin came back
for it: nowhere secure enough down here, so I ran up the stairs and
hid it behind the bath. When I got down again, Trevor was literally
shivering with terror.

"You shouldn't have left me, he could have got me while you were
up there." He was right: the front door was still unlocked. I locked
it; then I released Trevor from his chair. He bent to rub his ankles.
What to do? What to do?

No choice really. I had to go after him. The crunch would come
sooner or later, and at present I was armed and knew he wasn't.
Meanwhile Trevor would have to stay locked in: he wouldn't be any
help outside. Luckily there was a bolt on the door to the next room:
I slid it. Then I checked the catch on the kitchen window. "What'll
I do if he smashes the window?" Trevor quavered. "Have a go at
him with this," I advised, handing him the Sabatier cook's knife.
He took it reluctantly—it had unpleasant associations for him. "I
don't know if I could . . ." "Don't think about it, just *do* it."

I took the big torch in my left hand, gripped the Webley in my
right, and signed to Trevor to open the front door and stand back.
As it opened I shone the torch at eye level, hoping to blind Kevin
with the beam if he was there.

He wasn't.

I played the torch beam round the courtyard.

Nothing.

I stepped outside, stuck the pistol under the crook of my left arm, ready for use, locked the door from the outside, and thrust the key into my trouser pocket. Then I took the pistol in my right hand again.

Where to start?

I decided to go up my shortcut to the track, to my observation post. It was possible that Kevin might be working his way up the track, heading back up to where they'd parked the cars, somewhere on top of the hillside. He would be doing it in the dark, just as he'd come down: that had taken some minutes, and I might just be in time to catch him as he passed the observation post. I struggled up the slope, switching off the torch once I was safely on the path, so as not to give my position away. It had become wet with dew underfoot: I had a job to stay upright on the slippery leaves and young bracken stalks; once I tripped and fell, but it was only against the hillside, a short fall and a soft landing. It made little noise.

I reached the top. I waited for perhaps a minute, listening in the dark. Nothing. It was darker now than when I had waited here before. I could see the faint line of the track for only a few yards in each direction. I switched on the torch, gripping the Webley, my finger tight on the trigger. I directed the beam up, then down the track.

Nothing.

Looking for Kevin in this concealing darkness was going to be, I realized, the nearest thing to a nightmare that I had ever experienced, or was ever likely to. Even unarmed, he was deadly—a self-automated blunt instrument. He was certainly stronger than me, and if I failed to stop him with a shot, he would be on me like twenty tigers. And that would be that.

A noise broke out behind me, down in the cottage. I swung round and aimed the torch down into the courtyard. It lit up Kevin at the kitchen window. I could hear Trevor yelling inside the cottage. I saw Kevin pick up something, a stone maybe, and start to smash the window. The yelling stopped. I began to career down the path, keeping the torch on the path. If I could just get to Kevin now I knew where he was, keep him in sight . . .

The path dived behind some bushes and a low wall before emerging into the courtyard. I couldn't see the courtyard all the way. When I arrived at the bottom, in seconds it must have been, and shone the torch across the courtyard, Kevin was no longer at the window. I swung the beam. It caught up with him just as he was disappearing into the dark leafy tunnel through the orchard. Damn. Now I'd lost him again.

How about Trevor? I crossed the courtyard to the kitchen window. "All right, it's me!" I called. I looked in. Everything was as it had been, except for the broken glass on the floor from the window. But no Trevor. I unlocked the door and went in, locking it again behind me. There was no need to look upstairs; I could see where he'd gone; through into the other room, leaving the door open, and out through the back door. Into the night. He'd be panting up the track, making for his car. I'd known he could get out, of course, but I hadn't thought he'd *want* to, with Kevin on the loose. But he was lucky: Kevin was down in the orchard now, well away from the track. He'd probably make it to his car, and good luck to him.

That left me and Kevin. And a duel in the dark.

Of course, with Kevin gone, I didn't *have* to stay around the cottage. I could follow Trevor up the track, get him to drive me round to Pembroke, and pick up my car.

But the crunch would come later. Kevin would catch up with me: he'd said that was his aim. Like a guided missile, programmed to destroy me, however much I twisted and turned.

Better get on with it.

I unlocked the front door again, and headed for the black hole into the orchard.

I made slow progress. Every two or three paces I made a complete circuit with the torch beam, checking that Kevin wasn't closing in from behind. I had the pistol cocked: you don't *have* to cock a double-action revolver to fire it, but it means you need less trigger pressure to fire it, and may save a fraction of a second—I felt I needed all the fractions I could get. It was almost pitch dark inside the orchard: the tunnel of growth closed over my head, shutting out even the faint glow of the night sky. The torchlight slid over black tree trunks and green ivy columns: the shapes sprang out at me. I searched among them for a human outline, or part of one—a head, an arm, anything out of place in this vegetable kingdom. It was like traveling through the intestine of some monstrous creature; from the far end came the watery sounds of the estuary, adding to the illusion. I was being swallowed up. Where was Kevin? I saw no sign of him. Perhaps he had already been digested.

Il vaut mieux.

He appeared twenty yards away, stepping out from behind a tree to face me. I stopped, aimed the pistol. Too far for an effective shot with the little .410 cartridges it was loaded with. I held my fire. He stared into the torch beam, blinking, scowling.

I ran at him, hoping to close the range. But he turned instantly and pounded off through the tunnel. I sprinted after him. The sound of water grew louder—we were getting near the end of the tunnel.

Then I saw him fall. He went down heavily. The ground was rough and strewn with moss and rocks. He lay still. I bounded forward, almost bursting with relief: perhaps he could be recaptured.

The tunnel whirled about me as my feet skidded on moss. I crashed against the trunk of an old apple tree, and didn't quite fall.

But the Webley was gone. Not on the track. Somewhere in the undergrowth. I shone the torch. Could be anywhere. No time to search—must find another weapon.

The end of the tunnel was only a few yards away. There, I had hidden all the gear from the boat. Including . . .

The paddles! I staggered past Kevin; saw him stir. There! Under those branches on my right. I seized a paddle. Kevin was already heaving himself up. I took the three paces back to him, lifting the paddle; as he lifted his head I hit him.

The paddle blade took him on the side of the head, and he dropped without a sound. I stood over him, and lifted the paddle again. It was small, but wooden and heavy enough. Now I must finish him off. Break his neck.

I must.

I must.

But I can't. I can't do it. Not in cold blood.

I've been trained to do it. Stick bayonets into sacks. Shoot all kinds of firearms at all kinds of cardboard targets. Fire armor-piercing shells into obsolete tanks.

But not to hit an unconscious homicidal maniac on the back of the head with a wooden paddle. To my obvious benefit. And maybe to his.

Ah shit.

In that case, I'll just get in the boat and fetch the police from Pembroke. Hand it over to them. I can't fight a war if I'm not prepared to do what's necessary. So I'd better get the professionals to take over. I can alert them within half an hour. In time for them to pick him up when he gets up to his car. So I'll just leave him and piss off. Come back and shut up the cottage afterward.

I heaved the gear down the bank. The tide had been out and come in again: I didn't have far to lug the dinghy down the beach. I went back for the outboard motor—a heavy beast. The moon had been hidden in cloud: now it came out again, and lighted my retreat. Feeling subdued, I clamped the motor on the dinghy transom, dropped the paddles in, and pushed off through the weed.

The water shone like black oil in the moonlight. I had plenty of time to admire the effect as the motor refused to start. Apparently the wishes of the Welsh expire at midnight. I tried the choke button in different positions, pulled the starting cord again and again, and swore. I've *had* two-stroke motors. Permanently. Meanwhile I drifted further out.

Oh God, it's starting all over again. I can hear him scrambling down the bank. On to the beach.

Will he *never* give up?

Now he's crunching down the beach, boots clattering on the rocks.

If this bloody motor doesn't start, I'd better paddle farther out.

I can see him now. And he can see me. In the moonlight.

Jesus! Straight into the water, and he's heading this way. Just like a great crocodile! And about as indestructible.

Paddles, quick!

Farther out now. Should be safe here. I can't see him, but he must be some distance away. Time to try the motor again. Pull, splutter. And again—*pull*, splutter. Useless lump. Always chooses the worst possible time to let me down.

The boat rocks. There are hands on the side, scratching for a grip, but it's smooth, rounded rubber. All the same, use the paddle. Wham! That must have hurt. And he's let go. He'll never get in over the side.

One more go at the motor. This is another kind of nightmare—I'm sure I've already dreamed it. Try the choke halfway. *Pull*. No good.

And now he's trying to get in over the stern—he *could*, too. Done it myself; you can get a grip on the wooden transom. His head's coming up over the motor casing. We're glaring at each other. I shall pull the cord once more, then I must grab the paddle again and fight him off.

With a roar, the motor starts! It's started!

Idling in neutral. Now all I have to do is zoom off. Fifteen horse-power taking me away. But he's reaching for the gearshift to stop me. His shoulders are out of the water. He's almost aboard!

There's one way out.

Reverse gear—wind up throttle!

Do it now!

I still have that nightmare sometimes, but I always wake before the end. At the point when he is emerging, dripping, from the black water, his face coming up over the motor casing, his hand reaching for the gearshift lever on the side of the motor. By the light of the silvery moon.

He knew what I was intending, and tried to stop me. Our hands met on the gearshift lever. But mine was underneath, and I had the better purchase from inside the boat. Our hands fought for control of the lever. A simple question of this way or that; of forward or backward. Of him or me. Then his hand, slippery with oily sea water, lost the battle.

The boat charged him in reverse, the motor snarling, the un-weighted bow rearing up as the nine-inch coarse-pitch propeller drove into the obstruction of his body. He was pinned against it by the pressure of water as the boat strove to follow the propeller's urge. I imagine he was disembowelled in seconds. Then his body was drawn under; the boat churned over him to the clear water beyond. I cut the throttle, put the shift into neutral.

I sat in the boat on the shining black water, the motor purring now as tame as a contented pussycat. If there was color in the water, it did not show in the moonlight. The boat was out in the current, and we were already several hundred yards from the cottage beach. Nothing showed on the placid water, except a few ripples; there was no wind. It was as calm as I have ever known.

VICTORIOUS
SUBSTANCE

Then it is mostly, as we have before said, that the trophies which give substance to the victory begin to be gathered up.

—*Clausewitz*

There are still a few English hotels run for the benefit of the guests. The White Hart in Salisbury is one: a motto in the office reminds the staff to "Find out what people want—and *give it to them.*" In the hotel trade, such a statement amounts to heresy. Roger-le-patron must be shortlisted for *auto-da-fé.* The Grand Inquisitor must soon arrive, direct from the offices of the *Hotel and Caterers' Weekly,* to put the question that, according to evidence, he has been heard to answer to guests *in the affirmative*! Said yes to serving afternoon tea at 5:01; yes to taking drinks into the garden; yes to breakfast in bed and meals in rooms. All this in defiance of the first commandment of hotel keeping, viz.: *Thou shalt not inconvenience the staff.*

In fact, the staff don't look inconvenienced; rather, they appear to take pleasure in being obliging: in particular, the smiling girl who brought up a tray heavily weighted with homemade steak and kidney pie and a bottle of burgundy. (Maybe *she* would have said yes. No, no, I'm not a baby snatcher. Anyway, I'm expecting Ginny.) "I hope you enjoy it," she said. "Sure I will," I said; it smelled terrific. "And would you ask them at the desk to be sure to tell Miss Duff-

124

Jones where to find me? She should be here soon." "Certainly," she said, her smile brimful with fellow feeling. I wondered who the lucky lad was.

Ginny was coming down by train and had said she probably wouldn't make it to Salisbury by suppertime—she had an article to finish. It was already eight in the evening, and after the exertions of last night I felt tired; aches and bruises, unrelated to anything I could remember happening, had developed during the day. I started the bath running, drank a glass of burgundy, arranged the tray on the old-fashioned slatted-wood bath bridge, and inserted myself under it, into the swirling waters thundering in separate streams of hot and cold from the bulbous, antiquated taps.

Ah, blissful bath. Ah, blissful burgundy. Vougeot, Clos de la Perrière, '76. I knew it was good stuff—I'd sold it to them. And ah, blissful steak and kidney pie. Definitely one of the world's great dishes. Rich and juicy, the pastry not too flaky, enough body to soak up the juice. And clearly, neither bottled browning nor catastrophe cubes in it; fallacious flavoring is forbidden in Roger-le-patron's kitchen.

Maybe I dozed off. Anyway, I became aware of this person standing over me. I nearly had steak and kidney in the bath as I sat up, startled. The only weapon to hand was the bottle. But of course it was Ginny. "It's all right, darling, it's me!" But I was already out of the bath and wrapping her in a passionate hug. Hadn't I just survived death and disaster? More: hadn't I just won a battle against superior forces? There is a tradition to be kept up: "Returning home, the duke pleasured me twice before removing his boots," reported the Duchess of Marlborough after Blenheim. Got his priorities right. Did she demur? Ginny was thumping my ribs with her fists. I sometimes get the feeling she isn't into history.

"You've soaked me, you swine."

"Hello, Mrs. Marlborough."

I pleasured her on the bath mat. With *her* boots on. History never repeats itself. Afterward we rang for more steak and kidney pie and another bottle. The smiling girl brought it. "All right?" she asked. "Heaven," I said, "especially the pastry."

• • •

Dinner was served in bed. Between mouthfuls, Ginny told me her news. "The word is," she said, "that there's a revival of interest in nerve gas on both sides of the Iron Curtain."

Oh God, I thought, I suppose we *have* to discuss this now.

"Is that because a nuclear arms reduction treaty is now on the cards?"

"Not exactly. Some reduction in nukes seems likely, yes, but that's not the reason, or not the *main* reason."

"Then what is?"

She took a swig of wine, collecting her thoughts.

"Here's the buzz. This is just journalists' gossip, but I've tapped the defense correspondent guys, and they're all saying the same thing.

"Number one: nukes are getting more and more politically un-popular, or at least having more of them is. It's very unlikely that there will ever be a majority in favor of unilateral disarmament in the West, that's to say by NATO, but many Western governments would like to make a reduction in the stock of nukes, particularly the short-range and medium-range types. But the military are mostly against this, because the Russians have superiority in conventional weapons. So there is growing tension between governments, who want to get reelected, and the military, who want a strong defense.

"Number two: there's a growing feeling, except in the military, that short-range battlefield nukes are too dangerous to have around, and far too dangerous to use. They are the most likely spark to start a nuclear war; the risk of escalation is too high; therefore they can't be used against any Russian attack; therefore they're useless. That leaves the West vulnerable to attack by superior conventional forces.

"So the search is on for an alternative tactical weapon. Something more effective against advancing troops than high explosives but less catastrophic than a nuclear explosion."

"And nerve gas is the answer?"

"Well. It has the problems that gas warfare has always had—the dangers of handling the weapons containing the gas; the difficulty of delivering it in sufficient concentration; the risk of the wind blow-ing it in the wrong direction. But many of these problems are solved by using cruise missiles to deliver it: they can be fired from a distance so that there's no risky transportation of weapons; the missiles can be designed to spray the gas over a large area."

"But troops can be equipped for protection against it."

"Yes, but a concentrated attacking force is put at a huge disadvantage: the protective masks and rubberized suits make it difficult for them to use their weapons. And slowed up, they're more vulnerable to conventional shelling from a distance."

"It's always more difficult to attack than defend, anyway."

"That's what I'm told. So the search is on for the modern equivalent of the castle wall. A weapon that will turn a limited zone or strip of territory into a no-go area impassable by advancing troops. Patrolled by cruise missiles spraying deadly droplets that lie around for months. A weapon that is *only* effective in defense. That gets over the political problem; who can object to defensive weapons? And the West could then withdraw all nuclear missiles except long-range ICBMs designed to prevent nuclear blackmail."

"How far has it got?"

'The main problem is still the *quantity* of gas that's needed to create a no-go area. Western scientists have been working for years to improve what's known as VX agent. An East German professor called Frucht has passed information to the West about an improved Warsaw Pact nerve gas agent called VR 55, which is supposed to be more powerful, and more resistant to freezing and sunlight, than VX agent. There's a chemical warfare arms race going on *right now*. And although the 1972 Biological Weapons Treaty still holds good in theory—without agreed verification procedures—there is no treaty to ban *chemical* warfare weapons. Both East and West hold large stocks."

"And Porton Down?"

"It's now officially a Chemical Defense Establishment, run by the Ministry of Defense. Work on germ warfare is said to have been discontinued, although there is still a small unit there doing research into defense against germ attack. But in 1980, a big new battle range was set up, where military units are trained in chemical warfare. It's not a popular course: the antigas suits they have to wear are very uncomfortable—hot, sticky, and cumbersome. Difficult to fight in. And that's how it would be for the Warsaw Pact advancing through a gas defensive screen. They know that they're supposed to have hundreds of gas warfare training grounds, and special antigas equipment; they've got tanks fitted with pressurization and antigas seals, decontamination units, the lot. But, no matter how much antigas equipment they've got, just having to use it must reduce their fighting efficiency, slow up the advance, and make them much more vulnerable to conventional shells and bombs. And if they use gas against the defense, they're poisoning the area that they want to capture—they'd have to advance into their own gas.

"The only answer I got," Ginny said, "in response to a purely hypothetical question, was that people suspected of spying have been known to disappear. Even in dear old England. That's what they say. And you do go abroad a lot."

"So, as you reminded me before, do millions of other people," I said, "without getting put on a ministry hit list. Why *me*? I'm not even interested in politics, except in a remote sort of way. I'm just a self-indulgent sixties person; I want to make love, not war. As often as possible. With pauses for food and drink."

"That's not quite true, darling. Otherwise you would have gone to the police at the start. Instead of taking on the MoD single-handed."

She's right, of course. There must be something in me that responds to the stimulus of competition. If it's small scale, personal. It's a basic human instinct, competition, as everybody knows but not everyone admits. But it has been perverted. An extremist is someone who is only interested in winning. That's perversion. The *cause* is forgotten; nothing matters in the end but *victory*, at all costs, no matter how high the smoking heaps of rubble. That's not competition; that's an identity crisis. Beware the insanely insecure.

Ginny was asking what happened in Wales. I didn't want to tell her all of it: I was afraid of what she'd think. All that theatrical nonsense with the knife. And then the battle with Kevin. But I had to. "Swam after me like a killer crocodile." "He hated you so much by then?" she said, trying to imagine it. I decided to give her the full story of how it had ended then. Kevin, after all, had brought it on himself. I didn't feel responsible.

To my surprise, she didn't draw back in horror. Or anything like
that. Instead she slid her arms round me, and gave me a squeeze.
"Oh William," she said in a voice at once sympathetic and cheerful,
"yuk. Yuk, how horrible. Did you see him . . . it, again?" The fact
is, I decided, women are competitive too. However much they claim
the world would be a safer place if they ran it. They like to be on
the winning side.

I had seen no sign of Kevin's body, I told her, although I had
been back to the cottage to close it up, recovered the pistol, and then
motored the boat back to Pembroke, watching the water all the way.
With the strong current, it could be anywhere in the estuary by
now. It would be found, eventually; then all the members of the
Powerboat and Ski Club would be interviewed, one by one. My
boat had, of course, got a thorough washing on the way to Pembroke.
Only Trevor knew that Kevin had been to the cottage, and I had
seen no sign of him since his flight from the kitchen. Either back in
London, or far away, out of reach of Loewenfeld.

"Oh William," Ginny said again. She began to stroke my chest
hairs. "I'm so glad you didn't get crunched."

War and peace.

Steak and kidney.

First one. Then a bit of the other.

In time, I may achieve perfect balance. If I don't fall off the high
wire.

"Are you there, William darling?"

But not mind and matter. No, no. Definitely not. My mind *is* my
matter, inseparable. Renoir said he painted with his prick. Jokey
image, but true statement.

"William!"

And you can see it in his paintings. How he was feeling. "Dear
old Renoir."

"Renoir??"

"*J'arrive.*"

Monday morning, and we were motoring up the long slope out of
Salisbury, heading for Porton. Weather, clear and bright. Good

visibility; just right for observation. But no sign of anyone observing us.

"What's the plan?" Ginny asked, frowning into the mirror behind the sun visor. "God, I look a wreck. This life isn't good for me. I'm going to find someone rich and settle down in a manor house in Wiltshire with labradors. I need to be cherished."

"That's just Monday morning. I keep telling you," I said, "that your holy quest after barristers and other professional gentlemen of excessive means is based on a misapprehension. They won't cherish *you*. They'll be obsessed with their careers and you'll be expected to cherish *them*."

"Oh yes? So what's your advice?" Ginny said. Her voice had a hard edge to it. I recognized the signs. Last night, my return from the war, had gone too well. Beyond the limits of fun and games. Drama and high tension had begun to melt the frontier between our sovereign states. Was tearing our treaty of independence, maintained and so carefully observed over so many years.

"Are you a Miz, or aren't you, is the question," I said carefully. This was a minefield, I knew. Either, or both, of us could get blown up.

"Which would you prefer?"

Oh no, Ginny. Oh no. A liberated woman should declare herself, not lie in ambush. I said so.

"I think I may be changing," she said. I could feel her, across the car, watching the shell burst on me, her target.

"I thought we had a mutual nonaggression pact," I complained. "And in the land of Warner, there is no wealth. Would invasion be worthwhile?"

"You may not be rich. But you are randy," she explained.

"I'm shocked! This is what happens to girls who are brought up with ponies. I *knew* it!"

She wants me for my body. She doesn't care about my mind. What are things coming to? I shall chain myself to the railing outside the offices of the Virago Press.

Meanwhile, Ginny was smiling again. Our treaty appeared intact, at least for the time being. That's all you can say about any treaty.

"I'll tell you about the plan," I said. "Today's orders are: play it by ear. I'm just going to find a good spot outside the wire, and see what develops. I'd like you to take your cue from me. Have you got your press card?"

She had. I drove on up the A30. Salisbury Plain, its prehistoric slopes scarred by tank tracks, appeared on the right. And on the left, a high steel fence topped with barbed wire and punctuated with notice boards: MINISTRY OF DEFENSE PROPERTY—KEEP OUT. This was it, the core of the mystery, Porton Chemical Defense Establishment.

Right then. I swung the Citroën off the main road, and followed a track that skirted the perimeter fence. It led uphill and, I hoped, to the sort of vantage point I was looking for. On the left, through the wire, I could see distant buildings, white and laboratorial, with strip windows and flat roofs. An improvement on the tatty Nissen huts that I remembered from my course here, all those years ago. I found the best view, and stopped.

"Aren't you going to stay in cover?" Ginny asked, surprised.

"Nope. After last weekend, I've had it hiding behind bushes, up to here. I'm going to play this one in the open."

I got my shooting stick out of the boot, and the binoculars, and walked over to the fence. I planted the stick, opened the leather seat, and sat. I slowly scanned the place through the binoculars. Ginny wandered about, picking wild flowers and grasses.

"Can you see anything?" she called after a while.

"No. Nothing useful."

Then, from behind the group of buildings, a Land-Rover emerged. It stopped, and I got the impression that I, in turn, was being observed. Then it drove on to the grass and headed directly for me. Through the glasses, I could see there were four soldiers in it.

"Put away the floral arrangements, Ginny, and look like a serious journalist. We're about to be interviewed."

I let the glasses hang on my chest, and sat watching as the Land-Rover bumped over the rough grass toward me. It stopped about ten yards away. A young officer got out from the passenger side, and shouted at me through the tall fence that divided us.

"You there! What d'you think you're doing?"

I said nothing, but just sat there on the shooting stick, looking at him. He was tall and thin, and wore the uniform of a well-known infantry regiment. A second lieutenant, and not long commissioned. The driver and two soldiers with FN rifles clasped between their knees stayed in the vehicle, watching. My lack of response infuriated him. Soon the men would start to snigger.

He strode toward me, shouting.

"I asked you what you were doing. Well?"

He arrived at the fence, glaring at me. His face was already red with anger. I looked up at him from my throne.

"It's all right," I assured him quietly. "No cause for alarm."

"That's not the point. I'm asking you for the third time, what are you doing here? You'd better have a good answer."

I sighed. "Look," I said, "I didn't answer you because I wanted you over here; I don't want your men to hear what I've got to say."

"What the hell . . . ?"

"For your own benefit. Fair enough—it takes time to learn these things. Number one: I suggest you don't shout at intruders as you've just done at me. You simply walk up quietly and say something like, 'Good morning, this is a restricted area, and I'll have to ask you to move on.' Most people will, and good public relations will be maintained. Number two: you might bear in mind—"

"Why should I listen to this? Who d'you think you are?" His eyes were popping.

"Warner, Home Office Inspectorate. Bear in mind that while you *inside* the perimeter are on MoD property, an intruder *outside* the fence is not within your jurisdiction, but within that of the Home Office. You must not threaten where you cannot carry out the threat."

I was getting to him. But I wasn't there yet.

"Where's your ID?"

I looked at him with sad eyes, as if he were a stumbling schoolboy. "In my department, ID is *never* carried. For obvious reasons. But it doesn't matter to you. I'm not proposing to come inside today. I'm staying outside, on my territory. While you stay inside, on yours. Have you got *your* ID?"

"It's back in my room."

"Exactly. Now I'll tell you why I'm here, even though you have
no ID." I paused to see how I was doing. He didn't interrupt. OK,
it seemed. "The minister is concerned about the handling of protest
groups by perimeter patrols. Injuries have occurred that could have
been prevented. My department has been asked to prepare a circular
that can be incorporated into regimental standing orders. It is hoped
that this will improve public relations, and I have with me Miss
Duff-Jones who is preparing a press release on the subject. Now,
she *does* have some identification, I expect, ha, ha." Ginny produced
her press card. I waffled on. He began to look bored. Perhaps it
was time to change tack.

"Of course," I said, "it's all very different since I was last here,
and why my old regiment decided I should be the one to be loaded
with all the ghastly secrets I'll never know. Perhaps they just wanted
to get rid of me. The thought certainly occurred, especially when
I had to take my mask off for a few seconds in the gas chamber for,
what d'you call it, effect familiarization. Still have to do that?"

The assault course in full protective gear was, he said, the worst
thing they had to do. Simple necessities like having a pee or eating
your sandwiches become enormously laborious—gas could be absorbed through the skin. We chatted on. He asked my regiment,
and I told him. "Oh," he said, "armored corps. Lazy buggers, riding
everywhere. Never using their feet. Don't envy you now, though,
with the antitank missiles we've got. Wouldn't like to be sitting in
one of your tin cans when one of those hits it."

The chance I'd been working for.

"Oh, missiles," I said, "well, of course, that's why I'm here now.
We don't want any hitches with the cruise adaptation work. We
want to get our circular out and fully understood before the protest
groups arrive. You'll have been warned about that, I expect."

"Cruise adaptation work?" he said. "A chemical warhead? No, I
haven't been warned. But that would be in the workshop and laboratory compound, out of bounds to us simple soldiers. They have
their own permanent security personnel."

And that was that. He stood watching as I got into the car with
Ginny, and we drove off. I wasn't sure that he'd been convinced,

but I'd enjoyed the performance. Maggie was right, of course: I do have a theatrical streak.

I got another reminder of this on the way up to London. We stopped at a garage for petrol, and I saw that it was a Citroën agency. I could get the radio beacon checked out.

"That thing, there," I said to the mechanic.

"This? Junction box," he said impatiently. He'd been pulled off a job to answer my query, and didn't like it.

"Why's it wrapped with insulating tape? And why aren't there any wires going into it?" I persevered.

"Wires are on the top," he said. "As for the tape, I expect it's cracked." From the way he looked at me, so was I. Luckily I hadn't said anything about radio beacons. Well, it might have been.

Ginny was laughing when I got back into the car. Silly moo.

ESPRIT DE CORPS

> *This corporate spirit (esprit de corps) forms the bond of union between the natural forces which are active in that which we have called military virtue.*
>
> *—Clausewitz*

"There's a letter from the VAT," Maggie said, holding it out.

"Oh look, Maggie, what sort of welcome home is that? Try giving me the good news first." Two P.M., just dropped Ginny off at her flat, and just missed lunch. My nerves felt knotted. I used to be able to love 'em and leave 'em without aftereffects. Riding the merry-go-round without slipping in the saddle. Walk on whistling. But right now, I had a feeling I was sickening for something; like flu, but longer lasting. A *meaningful relationship*. A heavy scene. Maybe a bottle of sparkling Saumur would cure it. No— that's what I had with Ginny . . .

"This *is* good news," Maggie said, pushing the letter into my hand. "Are you feeling all right?"

No, I'm not. "Yes, I'm fine, thanks. Just a bit worn. What's this, then?"

I looked at the gruesome object. It had come, doubtless, in a long brown envelope, or LBE. I feel the same about LBEs as I do about adders; they should never be approached lest they bite. "Go on," Maggie encouraged, "read it!"

It had the usual charming, friendly motif at the top; a portcullis draped with chains. I read the message below with pounding heart. "My God!"

"Yes," Maggie said triumphantly, "it's a refund. Well, a credit at least."

Winkelmann had spent his night in the warehouse going through all the filing cabinets. And found, not only that his suspicions were unfounded, but that we had overpaid on the last quarter's assessment. No wonder he had marched out wearing an expression like the north face of the Eiger.

"Wow, Maggie! There's only one thing to do at a time like this. I'll just pop down to the cellar."

"Well, just a small glass," she said. "Some of us have work to do." But her spectacles shone with satisfaction.

I chose a bottle of the Widow Clicquot's best—La Grande Dame. Whether what you need is celebration or consolation, champagne works wonders. A widow would understand that. Maybe for her, as for me at this moment, it was both at once.

What I planned was a direct assault on Protoplastics: I wanted to meet this Loewenfeld, this keeper of psychotic crocodiles. Tackle the problem head on. It would be a tactical reconnaissance, intended to make contact with the enemy and gather information. Dangerous, obviously, but I planned to take all possible precautions, including a backup force.

The operation was planned for Tuesday afternoon, if Loewenfeld would oblige me by being there. I picked up the phone in my office. This should give him something to think about! But I thought I knew how he'd react.

"Protoplastics, good afternoon."

"Ah, good afternoon to you. I'd like to make an appointment to see Mr. Loewenfeld, to discuss a manufacturing project I have in mind. Four o'clock tomorrow afternoon would be ideal, if that would be possible."

"I doubt if Mr. Loewenfeld will be able to manage that, at such short notice," the girl said, "but I'll transfer you to his assistant. What name?"

"Warner," I told her. I imagined my name ringing down the corridors of Protoplastics like an enemy trumpet call. I waited.

I wasn't transferred. The same girl came back on the line to say that Mr. Loewenfeld would be delighted to see me at the time suggested. The tone of her voice was positively apologetic: next time, it suggested, I'd get the full VIP treatment from the start. I rang off, thanking her coolly. Right!

Time to issue the call to arms. I rang Pete at the warehouse, and arranged to meet him there in an hour. Just as I finished, the door opened and Claudine walked in. She'd been out shopping. This was the reunion after my sales trip.

"William, *chéri!*" She dropped her parcels, held out her arms; her perfect teeth flashed me a smile brilliant as a goddess, excellently bright. I bent to plant a marital kiss on her glossy lips. Her arms, sliding from the bulky sleeves of her coney jacket, locked behind my neck. Her eyes, charged with female insight, scanned my face. Hurriedly, I dived for cover, kissing the side of her neck inside her fur collar. "So good to be back." My voice was muffled. How long was it? Four days? Was that *all*?

"'Ave you missed me?" she murmured into my shoulder.

"Of *course* I have." (I 'ave. I '*ave*!). The soft current of Rive Gauche rising from the warmth inside her coat was helping to convince me. I slid my hands down her back. Even through the heavy fur I could feel the swell of her buttocks. So soon? Couldn't I manage a decent pause before the act of treachery? Say, until bedtime? When it would be a marital duty?

She has disengaged, and is slipping the coat off. She has a shining scarf over her hair, tied at the back, sleek as only French girls know how. Her Gucci jeans fit like, like . . .

"I have to go to the warehouse, Claudine, I'm sorry . . ."

"Oh *chéri!* Now? But you 'ave not told me about your sales!"

Commerce was on her mind. Oh why couldn't it be on mine?

"I'm afraid so." Yes, yes. Go now. At once.

Or else I shall be a traitor without a pause.

. . .

I'd decided to take Pete into my confidence, as his help was essential: I needed him and the taxi as my backup force. In the office at the warehouse, with the door closed behind us, I gave him an outline of the war so far. I had to do this to make sure he took the whole thing seriously, but I trusted him to keep it to himself; it would be a disaster, I told him, if the authorities got to hear about my goings-on before I had the explanation ready. I didn't have to labor the point: where he was brought up, you didn't tell Them anything you didn't have to.

"Knew there was sumfink up," he said, "but this sounds really bad, like." His eyes gleamed with excitement. I explained what I wanted him to do, and the only problem was his disappointment at not having a bigger part to play. But that I wasn't having, and didn't need. Or so I thought.

He went out to get on with shifting crates then, and I sat at the desk to telephone Edward. Only two changes of secretary, this time, before I got him.

"William," he said, sounding displeased, "I'll have to ask you not to call me here. I tell the staff not to take personal calls in the office except in emergency, and I can hardly do less myself."

"Sorry."

"Well, what is it? Have you changed your mind about what we were talking about before the weekend?"

"No," I said, "no. I haven't. In fact, I was wondering if *you* had. It really would be an enormous help if you were able to do a little research on my behalf, and I wondered if you would agree to do it on the basis of absolute confidentiality. For my eyes only, you know. Would that make it possible?"

There was silence. I took that as a hopeful sign, waited patiently, crossed my fingers. Then Edward said, "Afraid not."

Just that. I waited a moment for a word of apology, explanation, sympathy—but none came. Dear old Edward, dear old chum. Old chum that was. Don't expect discount on your claret in future. No, I didn't *say* that, just felt it.

"Quite understand. See you sometime." And I rang off, dignified in my disappointment.

• • •

When I got back to Church Street, Claudine was in the kitchen, sounding like a whole clattering of chefs. "What's this?" I asked. You can never have a surprise for your dinner, if you have to choose the wine to go with it. *C'est si tragique*, as Maurice Chevalier used to tell us.

"*Moules à la Normande*, with the cream sauce. Then after we will not want more cream sauce, so I do *Suprême de Volaille à Brun*, sautéed in butter, you know it. Then cheese, of course, and I have bought some little *Tartes aux Fraises*, not too bad they seem. After this trip in *le pays de Galles*, you need a good dinner, no?" She was right of course. There is nothing to eat in Wales.

I'd almost forgotten that this was how I chose to live. But now, the familiar pattern closed around me, as easy and comfortable as a warm bath. I was almost sleepwalking as I descended to the cellar and chose the wine. A good, old-style claret to go with the chicken— a Lynch-Bages '70 would be perfect. Then some Muscadet for the *Moules à la Normande*: often sharp and disappointing, but *sur lie* should be better than average. And finally—as it seems to be that sort of evening—some sweet Vouvray to go with the *Tartes aux Fraises*.

Sweet! Yes, that's what my life had been. Too easy, too sweet. I'd been drowning in a honeypot.

Now I was risking all that, in return for experiences of a more stirring sort.

I shouldn't be doing it, I know I shouldn't. I *will* stop soon, but not just yet. I want to get things to a more conclusive stage.

But I mustn't become an adrenaline addict. I mustn't lose my balance, go too far out on a limb, lose touch with Claudine and the family.

Tonight must be family night. I must eat the delicious dinner, and gratify my beautiful wife. That is my duty.

Only then can I safely indulge in tomorrow's aggro.

"*Chéri!*" calls Claudine. Dinner must be ready.

"Coming!" I call back.

I march resolutely toward the dining room.

• • •

It's a well-known fact that duty, once accepted, is often enjoyable. Once the agonizing is over, there's nothing left to do but get on with it. Become a simple soldier. Leave the politics to tortured chaps with double firsts. Get stuck into the Pathan tribesmen. Or the *Moules à la Normande*.

The cheerful clacking of mussel shells marked the turning point of my evening, when philosophizing gave way to food. What I like best is when you've polished off the mussels and there's a lot of cream sauce left over. I pour in half a glass of Muscadet, swirl it round to achieve a perfect mix, and drink it all out of the bowl. Fantastic!

"*Ah voilà!*" cried Claudine. "*Tu fais la Chabrol!*" It's supposed to be a custom of the country people in southwest France, where we have a house, but *embourgeoisement*, with its stilted manners, has dealt the custom a fatal blow, and only ancient farmers and English tourists preserve it. Sad, because the warm plate does something to the wine which, joining forces with the gravy, is instantly converted into a heady and intensely aromatic liquid capable of sending me into a paroxysm of pleasure.

"Careful, Papa," giggled Nichole, "you're going to have a, you know, *cardiac arrest!*" She specializes in the *mot juste*, that one. A bit *too* sharp for her own good, at times. Can do it in French, too. Both the girls go to the Lycée and speak better French than I do.

"We don't want to lose you!" chipped in Sylvie. They hunt in a pair, and were sitting together, as usual, at one side of the table. Now they were both stricken with giggles, falling about.

"*Ça suffit! Assez!*" rapped Claudine from her end of the table. She bent toward them, putting on her antiriot face. The giggling subsided. "Now," she said, "*soyez sages*. I am going to do it, too." She flashed me a smile of solidarity. I appreciated the gesture. She is of the Bordeaux bourgeoisie, and they do *not* drink out of bowls. But she performed with elegance. "Mmmm," she said, "*dé-li-cieux!*" She dabbed her lips with a color-coordinated paper napkin, pink, to match the pink candles which we all had by our places. Our eyes met across the table, and she gave me the slightest inclination of her head: I know my duty, she was telling me. She didn't have to. She always has.

I nodded back to her, my dutiful, beautiful wife. She had slipped into something different for dinner, and was now wearing a dark red dress with long sleeves and a discreetly plunging neckline, the color of old burgundy; she had changed her lipstick to match. "Now," she said, "a little moment. Then we will have the chicken." She went into the kitchen: there, she would put on her apron *and* scarf over her hair against the cooking smells. Nichole collected the bowls of mussel shells. I finished the Muscadet, and went to the sideboard to deal with the claret.

Julian had supped on a peanut-butter sandwich and gone out to see some friends. He usually opts out of dinner, and lives as a lodger in his room over the garage rather than as one of the family. Strange for him, to find himself caught up in this French-style family, but he bears it bravely. I found myself wishing he'd been there this evening. Why? Because of what might happen tomorrow, I supposed. Oh, come off it. Nothing's going to happen. And anyway, tonight is Family Night, that's what I decided.

The cork left the long neck of the claret bottle with the softest of pops, and Claudine made her reentry, bearing a dish of chicken breasts gleaming with just-made golden brown *Beurre Noisette*. And *Pommes Mousseline* flavored with garlic. Just that. Plain and perfect. With the Lynch-Bages. Oh my, oh my. Claudine served, I poured, and we set to.

My expressions of ecstasy set the girls off again. But in French this time. When they do the rapid schoolgirl jargon I can't even understand it. That's hard for a father to take. But there was no stopping them. It was best to rise above it with adult conversation.

"Seen Tricia?" I asked.

"Oh yes," Claudine said. "I bump into her this morning, quite by chance, when I am doing the shopping. We have coffee together."

"You really like her a lot, don't you?"

"Oh yes. She likes to laugh, she is fun to be with. But, this morning . . ." She shook her head.

"Something wrong?"

"She is a little, what shall I say, *distraite*. Not such fun."

"Why?"

"Oh, I don't know. I don't like to ask, there is nothing positive. I do not want to be indiscreet. But I think, perhaps, it is Edward. Tricia says he is working very hard. Always at the office. Or away on his affairs." (Not *Edward*, surely! Ha, ha! She means on business . . .)

"He'd better watch out, then," I said. Claudine isn't the only one that finds Tricia fun to be with. And some of them are fellers. "Or it could be that his career will muck up their marriage." As Ginny's had been. Ginny. Where was she now? And doing what?

I took a long draft of Lynch-Bages. And concentrated on it.

Claudine gave a rather theatrical light laugh. "Oh, Tricia is *very* happy in her marriage," she announced with the smile and tone of a Good Fairy in a panto, who has only to *say* something to *make* it so. I looked up in surprise. Then I caught her sideways glance at the girls, who were now sitting quiet as mice, their beady little eyes noting every nuance. *Pas devant*. Not in front of the children was her message. I understood, but I decided to overrule.

"I've never been able to see what Tricia saw in Edward," I said, ignoring Claudine's eyebrows that were semaphoring me to stop. "In fact, I decided when I was having lunch with him last week that knowing someone for twenty years or so when you don't actually *like* them is a sign of sentimental weakness. I've decided to stop. I think the search for Edward's hidden depths can be abandoned. I hope Tricia leaves him. She can't do much worse, and she's likely to do much better."

"*Ah, mon Dieu!*" Claudine exclaimed.

"Papa's right!" Nichole was joining in. This meant trouble.

"Edward's *horrible*!" Sylvie this time.

"Yeah. Eleven out of ten for creep appeal!" Nichole, of course.

Claudine exploded. Even *I* was rocked in my chair by the tree-bending force of her fury. I should have known better. If you're going to subject Claudine to outrage, whether it's matters marital or the price of fish, it's wise to choose an open space, well away from fragile plants and small buildings. It was a miracle that the crockery stayed on the table.

In seconds I was alone in the room, the boy on the burning deck. As I relit those candles that had succumbed, I could hear the girls retreating up the stairs with Claudine in hot pursuit. Then wails. Then silence.

Claudine reappeared, looking flushed. "Sorry, darling," I said. She faced me, and I prepared to receive a cannonade. But then, slowly, she bore away; all hands were at work extinguishing the fire on board. Course was resumed. She smoothed down her dress. "Some more wine? You know, I think that's my favorite dress." "I bought it this morning," she said distinctly. "Ah. My favorite *sort* of dress, I mean."

There was a pause. Then, "William?"

"Yes?"

I was standing, the claret bottle in my hand. She approached; stood close, looking up at my face. Her lips formed a word, or words. What were they? It could be *"Je t'aime."* Or *"Merde."* Or a lot of things. There was an M in there somewhere, I was sure of that. But then her lips began to curl. Upward. Then she was smiling. And laughing. Hooting. In an earthy way . . .

"Let's . . ." she got out between hoots.

"Yes?"

It was for me to suggest it, really. My duty.

"Have our Vouvray and *Tartes aux Fraises* in bed?"

"Comme tu es sage, my William."

DOUBTFUL
EXECUTION

No important undertaking was ever yet carried out without the Commander having to subdue new doubts in himself at the time of commencing the execution of his work.

—*Clausewitz*

I got Pete to drive me to Stanmore in the taxi. After delivering me to Protoplastics, he was to hang about until I was ready to be picked up: I had no idea how long I would be in the factory, and he would be much less noticeable in the taxi than in the Citroën. He was to stay out of sight of the factory, but within range of the compact two-way radio I had in my briefcase, bought yesterday in the Tottenham Court Road and said to be effective up to half a mile. We'd only time for a single practice session: I trust electronic gadgets about as much as I trust outboard motors, which is to say not much, but although crackly, we had been able to understand each other. Which mattered: this small plastic box, made in Taiwan, was to be my lifeline as I probed the unknown territory of Loewenfeld.

"'Ere you go," Pete called over his shoulder, "this is it." We had been driving past endless rows of gray-rendered semidetached houses, down a succession of identical tree-lined roads all called Laurel this and Laurel that, built, I guessed, in the thirties or late twenties to house a workforce within easy bike ride of the industrial estate that squatted at the center, the gates of which we were now

approaching. Just inside the entrance, a large painted panel confronted us with a map of the estate. Pete stopped, and we studied
it, puzzling over the maze of roads and factory signs deployed on it
like some mind-bending board game. Protoplastics located, we set
off into the estate, gridded with concrete roads, past an assortment
of buildings ranging from the low-rent red-brick tombs of enterprises
in decline to shining palaces glowing with the white heat of new
technology.

And the greatest of these was Protoplastics. I felt sure we had
arrived, even before I read the discreet sign beside the entrance
because, parked impressively in the best position, was a big black
Rolls-Royce. Trevor had said that Loewenfeld had pots and ran a
Roller. This was surely it.

We drew up at the entrance portico, all black steel and tinted
glass, and I prepared to dismount, feeling a sudden nervous twinge
at the base of my spine. Ridiculous!—nothing could happen to me
on such a public visit at this. The most likely outcome of this reconnaissance was fiasco. There would be a polite, noncommittal
exchange, and then after a very few minutes I might find myself
outside again, having learned little or nothing of value. On the other
hand, I might see enough of the layout of the place to be able to
plan an unofficial return visit. But now, today, there could be no
danger while so many people knew I was here, definitely not.

"Make sure you've got that bloody thing switched on," I told Pete.
I must have sounded edgy, as he gave me a speculative look, and
said, "You could still give it a miss—go off 'ome."

"I'm here now, aren't I? But just stay tuned in—all right?"

He nodded, and I got out, clutching my briefcase. I thought I
saw out of the corner of my eye a watcher at an upstairs window.
We were on stage. I went through the motions of paying for the
taxi; Pete thanked me gravely, and then drove off. I felt very much
alone. Well, let's get on with it.

I strode to the entrance doors and pushed into the reception hall.
The desk was manned by a severe-looking blond girl whose gleam-
ingly groomed perfection was reflected in the polished glass of her
desk top. Not for Loewenfeld the cheerful tinted matron who pre-
sides at most factory reception desks. This incumbent might have

been recruited from IBM, or some upper-crust advertising agency—
she had the translatlantic accent too, I discovered.

"Warner. Mr. Loewenfeld is expecting me," I said in reply to her
look of inquiry.

"Please take a seat, Mr. Warner. Mr. Loewenfeld is taking a call,
but will see you directly. Welcome to Protoplastics." She issued me
with a welcome smile, switched it off abruptly when my two seconds
was up, and returned her attention to her push-button console.

I turned away from the desk, and began to stroll about the hall.
It was about the size of a minor airport lounge: black leather Barcelona chairs were neatly grouped on the studded black rubber Pirelli
floor. Giant rubber plants in self-watering pots added the necessary
touch of green free form. It was all very modern, expensive, stan-
dardized. Except for the blown-up color photographs that hung in
frameless mounts on the white paneled walls. I studied them. They
were, I supposed, of the boss himself. It was the first time I'd been
able to put a face to my presumed opponent. He looked alarmingly
fit and confident. The backgrounds helped, by placing him in a
context of sportive exertion. Here he goes, at the wheel of a Contessa
43, looking aloft to check the trim, close hauled on the starboard
tack with the white spray a-flying. There he goes, on skis this time,
knees together, zipping past a flag on the downhill run. With the
white snow a-flying. And a bloody precipice it looks to be. A bad
omen, Warner-wise. This man is going to have clear blue eyes, a
mind like a computer, and get up at half-past five every morning
for a cold bath and an hour of callisthenics—a winner, if ever I saw
one. *Ouch!*

My enthusiasm for this confrontation was fading rapidly. But,
just as the notion of an orderly retreat followed by some more un-
dercover form of reconnaissance was being forcefully proposed by
Left Brain, the trap closed with a clang.

"Pardon me! Mr. Warner, will you go up please? Mr. Loewenfeld's office is first on the left, at the top of the stairs. Thank you."

"Thank *you*," I said automatically. As I walked past the desk, we
both fired off smiles like air-to-air missiles: she won, I reckoned.

I mounted the slim steel stairs. Perhaps, in spite of all that sporty
stuff, he will be, actually, quite small. Better for skiing—a low center

of gravity. Quite small, preferably dwarfish. A keen-eyed, sporty dwarf. Here's hoping.

He was waiting for me at his open office door. Eyes like lasers, in a deeply tanned face, slightly pockmarked. Some tropical disease? Short, thick black hair. A triangular, athletic frame: mesomorph— man of action, the warrior physique. About my age. And at least six feet two.

Shit!

I inspected him surreptitiously while trying to look bland, polite, just another customer; a necessary farce. He, on the other hand, bowed, beamed, and shook my hand as though he'd been looking forward all day to this meeting.

"So pleased, Mr. Warner! So pleased! Come in, please." He led the way into his office. Thick Berber carpet, chrome and black leather furniture. And more sporting photographs.

Loewenfeld ushered me to a little group of chairs round a low glass table. "So!" he cried enthusiastically, "this is a pleasure! I have heard much of you, of course."

Already he had taken the initiative. "You have?" I said doubtfully.

"But yes! Of course! You are too modest: your firm has a first-class reputation in London, since many years I believe? Especially among men such as myself, who like to drink good wine, only good wine. Not too much, but good. So, your firm was soon told to me." His accent was more Dutch than German, I decided.

"Do you buy from us, Mr. Loewenfeld?" It had never occurred to me to check our files; surely *that* couldn't be the connection?

"Ah, Mr. Warner, unfortunately I live in Hampstead, and I am a too busy man. So I buy from a local merchant. But he is not so good, and if *you* had a branch there!—I am sure you *should* have a branch in Hampstead. You will find there the best clientele. It could not fail. And for myself, it would mean that I could buy good wine— the best!—on the doorstep. Yes, I really think you should do it. What do you think?"

We chose chairs and sat down. Loewenfeld leaned forward confidentially, smiling at me. "What do you think?" he asked again.

"We deliver to Hampstead," I said.

"Ah yes, but Mr. Warner!—excuse me—it is not the same thing

to order from a list. For myself, I must see the bottles; taste some of the wines, perhaps; talk with the merchant. Is that not so?" And he went on about his idea in such persuasive detail that I began to think he might even mean what he was saying.

And, whether he meant it or not, he was right. I'd known for some time that private customers were dropping off because of local competition. Hampstead *was* the obvious place to open a branch.

I went along with the discussion, to see where it led. Loewenfeld was probably using it as a means to cross-examine me about a whole range of subjects, all related more or less to business but, if so, it was done with a light and subtle touch. I had to admit to myself, as the conversation rolled on, that if the views he was putting forward were genuine, as they appeared to be, they made a great deal of sense. In a very short time he had picked up all the essentials of the wine trade, and we were discussing how problems could be eliminated and improvements made. It was very impressive.

We returned to the Hampstead project, and after twenty minutes the talk ran out, but not before Loewenfeld had said he'd keep an eye open for suitable premises. "Why not?" he said firmly. "This I will do. And so, the sooner you will have your shop, the sooner I will have my good wines." And he nodded, and smiled his encouragement. "So, that is settled. Now, let us discuss this idea of yours— a new type of wine box?"

It wasn't entirely bogus—it was an idea that I'd been playing with for a year or two. Wine boxes are much more expensive to produce than traditional bottles, and the wine you get in them is not therefore such good value: the saving comes because you can draw off a glass at a time without letting in air to spoil the wine, and you don't have to drink a drop more than you want. I proposed an alternative in the form of a large cylindrical glass decanter fitted with a float to keep the air off the surface of the wine. This would be easily cleaned and reusable, and would hold three bottles of wine, which should last a week or two before starting to deteriorate. The float would need to be close fitting, and plastic seemed the obvious material for it to be made in. "But, of course, I don't know enough about plastic molding to be able to design the float in detail."

"Then you shall see how it is done," Loewenfeld said at once, "and for this, we shall call upon Philip." He went to the telephone on his desk.

It looked as though I was about to get the tour of the factory that I had been angling for. Loewenfeld could easily have found an excuse to avoid this, and so I must assume that he had prepared for it, or had nothing to hide. Well, I'd never had high hopes of this frontal approach, but at least I'd get to see the public face of his operation, which might suggest some clues to what might be going on underneath. And, much more important, I would get to know the factory layout. If possible, I hoped to make my unofficial return visit this same evening, if the opportunity occurred. The thought of which brought back the tingle at the base of my spine: it wasn't just nerves, I decided, but exhilaration at the thought of action. I've read that burglars—especially the young ones—enjoy the adrenalin surging in the blood as much as the loot. They like to prove they've gotta lotta bottle. And, as I watched Loewenfeld smiling and chatting so smoothly, I was glad to be making plans. It helped me to smile back.

There was a tap at the door, and a face appeared round it: pale, with pale blue eyes behind gold-rimmed glasses, and smooth fair hair cut short. The mouth wide but thin lipped, unsmiling. Mid-thirties, intelligent. "You wanted me?"

"Come in, Philip," Loewenfeld said, and introduced us. Singer, his name was: a science Ph.D. and, according to Loewenfeld, the factory's resident production genius. I could believe it—he looked a calculating man. I didn't think we would hit it off too well, and after I'd explained my project to his barely concealed contempt, I was sure of it.

"How do you expect to get a good seal between this float thing and the walls of your decanter, when the walls are unlikely to be perfectly parallel, being only made of unground, molded glass?" he asked sharply.

"If I knew that, I wouldn't be here asking you, the expert," I told him. I hate his sort of expert, their insolent superiority. They're *expected* to know more of their subject than the rest of us—*paid* for it. They don't have to use their knowledge to belittle people.

"Well," he said reluctantly, "I'm afraid it'll be a waste of time, but if you think it'll help you to see the production process, we'd better do that."

"Yes," Loewenfeld said in his firm voice, "you'd better do that, Philip." Turning to me, he added, "I have to leave now, but I am most glad to have met you, Mr. Warner, and I hope you will take my suggestion to open a branch in Hampstead! Remember, please!—I will be glad to assist you in any way, any way at all. And as for this project, Mr. Singer here will guide you, won't you, Philip? I leave you in very good hands. Goodbye, Mr. Warner, goodbye. I look forward to our next meeting."

He shook my hand, smiled, and bowed his head slightly. Our eyes met. I'm no poker player, but hoped my face was as impenetrable as his. No special interest betrayed, but he gave me a burst of that automatic intensity which many businessmen switch on to impress themselves on a client. *Was* that all? Or had Trevor cheated me, after all, and had pointed me at Loewenfeld in order to point me away from someone else? I was still trying to decide as I followed Philip Singer out of the office.

Loewenfeld's office was the first of a row of offices along the front of the building. The doors of some of these were open as Singer led me down a corridor, away from the stairs which I'd come up from the reception lobby. I noticed several offices that bore the names and titles of senior staff; on the opposite side of the corridor, facing away from the front of the building, were rooms for the secretarial and junior staff, filing, and computer equipment. Through the open door of one of these, I saw that they had windows looking over the factory floor itself; a subdued but busy hum of machinery came from beyond.

Among my numerous disqualifications for industrial detective work, I now realized, was my total ignorance of computers. I've heard of floppy disks, all right, but what you're supposed to do with them I've no idea, nor do I have any wish to be told. There's some sort of computer in our office, in fact, to deal with stock control, but Maggie uses it, and I just ask her when I want to know something. My talents, I say grandly, lie in other directions—and so far, I've got away with it.

But here at Protoplastics, computers winked from every corner. This was bad news: if all the information was stored in their electronic entrails, I had no chance of getting it out. Good old filing cabinets, full of papers—these were what I needed. We passed a room full of girls seated in front of VDUs, typing away at keyboards. Were they programming computers, or were these word processors, the typist's spelling guide, productivity aid, and status symbol? I hoped the latter—producing words, beautiful, readable *words*!

"Are those the latest word processors in there? Very impressive!" I tried on Singer.

He turned his head to remark, "Hardly the latest. They were installed when the factory was opened, four years ago. But still good enough."

Good enough, friend Singer. Words!

We passed on down the corridor. Near the end, a short branch corridor led to the staff washrooms.

"Oh," I said apologetically, "I was hoping we might pass one of these—I wonder if you'd mind . . ."

Singer stopped, turned, looked at his watch with an impatient gesture. "I'll wait for you here," he said.

I went along to a WC, bolted the door, and tore open my briefcase to get at the walkie-talkie. I pulled out the aerial, switched on. There was a sudden roar of interference like Niagara Falls. I wrenched at the WC handle to cover the noise, and switched off. No hope of contact from here; I'd have to get the aerial out of a window, but for the moment it didn't matter. Worth knowing, though. I pushed the aerial back in, stuffed the thing into my case, and rejoined Singer, relieved to find that the background factory noise in the corridor was louder than I remembered. And he'd started to stroll on down the corridor, so had been well away from the WC. I didn't think he could have heard anything—it would have meant disaster if he had, especially at this early stage. I mustn't take any more risks, not yet.

At the end of the corridor, a heavy fire door opened onto a steel gallery overlooking the factory floor. Steel stairs led down to ground level, but Singer stopped, and we leaned on the gallery rail to survey the rows of busy machines below. They seemed almost unattended. In the whole factory, only two or three men were visible, walking along the rows, inspecting as they went. Everything was as clean and bright as in an operating theater. Robot arms swung and dipped into the machines. Lights blinked on indicator panels. Neat files of completed components emerged, marching away toward waiting containers. Every few moments, a full container slid on steel rollers to one of the pickup points, and another instantly rolled into place. I'd never seen this degree of automation before, and marveled at the speed and precision of it all.

Singer looked over his machines with obvious pride. This, I could see, was the key to his soul, and the best chance of persuading him to talk. So far, he'd been the perfect oyster.

"So this is the new industrial revolution!" I called above the machine noise.

Singer's pale eyes turned in my direction. He said nothing, but nodded. Then he said, "We'll go down."

He led the way down the steel stairs. On the factory floor, the noise was no louder, and it was quite possible to converse if you spoke up. I tried again. "Are these machines your own design?"

"Some are," Singer said, "some aren't. There's nothing very new about the machines." He stopped to pick up a yellow cylindrical object from the nearest marching file, inspected it closely, then chucked it into a container.

"What was that?" I asked.

"That? A hydraulic reservoir. Truck braking system."

"What sorts of things do you make most of?"

"All sorts. Plastics are replacing metal in vehicle parts, building components, household goods, you name it."

We moved on along the row. Weapon parts. That's what I wanted to ask him, but couldn't. Maybe I didn't need to—I already knew the MoD torch had been made here, and it was a thousand to one that they did other work for the MoD as well. The question was, what was being made that was so secret? I'd have to wait to get into the files for the answer to that one. If I struck lucky.

I watched the parts emerging from each machine as we passed by, and tried to make a mental note of anything that might have a

military purpose, but it didn't add up to much. These were only
components, destined to be part of larger assemblies, and these
would only take shape within the security of one of the Royal Ord-
nance factories. It seemed hopeless, but I kept looking. Finally, we
reached the control room, a long, narrow affair that took up most
of one side of the factory, with a continuous window overlooking
the machines. Double glazing kept most of the noise out. Control
panels monitored each machine, registering operating data. Four
supervisors wandered about, mugs of tea in hand, watching the control panels and occasionally flicking a switch or reading a printout.

"Is this it?" I asked Singer.

"Is this what?"

"All the staff you need to run the place?"

"Four supervisors, fourteen maintenance staff, and toolmakers
over the other side. That's all. Plus admin, and transport, of course."

A white-coated supervisor called from the far end of the room.
"Mr. Singer! Phone for you."

Singer left me, and another supervisor who was standing nearby
said, "Surprise you, does it, that we can run all this? Tell it to Them
Up There—we like to be appreciated."

"Why aren't all factories run like this?"

"Ah well. Started from scratch, didn't he? No union problems—
in fact, no union. We don't want to be tied to rates and conditions
worked out to suit older factories. And management know what
they're doing. We're at full capacity nearly all the time—don't know
how he does it, but he does."

"Mr. Warner!" Singer was calling me. I joined him at the telephone. "It's for you—your office."

"Thanks," I said, taking the phone from him. "Hello?"

It wasn't the office. It was Ginny, ringing at five as arranged, to
reinforce the message that the world knew I was here. Since nothing
even remotely sinister had happened so far, this now appeared a
quite neurotic precaution, and the agreed message sounded farcical.
But then, so do most code words.

"Thought you'd like to know, the burgundy's arrived at the
docks," she said, sounding just slightly nervous.

"Oh good, I'm glad to know that."

"So, shall we collect it, or leave it?"

"Leave it. I'm sure it'll come to no harm."

"Yes. All right, we'll do that. If you're sure."

"I'm sure. Thanks for ringing."

Well, of course, I wasn't all that sure, but there was nothing she could do about the next stage, if there was one. That would be up to me, and Pete if I could contact him. Meanwhile I had to waste Singer's time until the office staff had all gone home, and then find a way of staying in the building so that I could get at the files.

The first part shouldn't be too difficult. If I could avoid annoying Singer deliberately—a temptation difficult to resist.

"How would you suggest this float should be constructed?" I began.

15

STRATEGIC
RESERVE

A reserve has two objects which are very distinct from each other, namely, first, the prolongation and renewal of the combat, and secondly, for use in case of unforeseen events.

—*Clausewitz*

Singer wasn't happy. I made him go through the injection molding process from A to Z until I knew enough to start my own plastic factory, but he was about as enthusiastic as a performing bear. We stayed in the relative quiet of the control room for some twenty minutes while I got him to draw diagrams and explain the properties of the various types of plastic so that I could see how the principles were translated into practice; then it was back into the control room again for him to explain why none of my suggestions could possibly work. No, he wasn't happy, not at all. But he had to go through with it—Loewenfeld had made that quite clear.

"I'm afraid I'm taking up a lot of your time," I said brightly, "but I never imagined that it would be so complicated. I suppose you and the office people usually go home about now?"

"Offices close at five," he said shortly. "I usually go about six. Do you think you've got enough to be going on with, now?"

The clock on the control room wall said ten past six.

"Good lord, is that the time?" I said. "I *am* sorry. What about these people here? Working through the night, I suppose."

"Came on at four, go off at midnight when the next shift comes on," he said.

"Roll on midnight!" said the supervisor I'd been talking to earlier. He had a round pink face and a small fair moustache. Singer glanced at him sharply: he would jump on insubordination like a U-boat captain, I decided. But he said nothing; the supervisor noted some readings on a pad, and moved on. This place was in fact run, in the well-worn phrase, like a tight ship. Employees often like that, of course, as long as the organization is being a success. They like to feel a part of it. These chaps evidently did.

I realized that Singer was waiting for my answer. "Yes," I said, "I think I've got enough now."

"Right," he said. "Is your car out at the front?"

"I came by taxi."

"You want to ring for one? You can do it from here."

"No thanks, I've arranged to be collected," I said, keeping it vague. The next stage was the tricky one, and I was having to play it by ear. "I'll wait in the lobby, if that's all right with you. Will I be able to get out?"

"Main entrance doors will be on the Yale—you can get out that way. Just push them shut behind you. Security will be round later to bolt up."

How much later? How much time would I have if I managed to dodge up to the offices now? How much time did I need? We walked down the control room into a short passage with a small canteen and washrooms opening off it, and emerged as if from backstage into the gloss and glitter of the entrance lobby. The glass reception desk reflected nobody; the place was occupied only by the images of Loewenfeld, whose narrowed eyes watched us from the big blown-up photographs across snowfield and seascape. These pictures seemed the more impressive, now that I'd met their subject and toured part of his empire. A natural winner, it was hard to deny. Did he cheat as well?—that was the question.

Singer opened one of the main doors, and we looked out. No taxi, surprise, surprise. "He's late," I said, "six o'clock, I told him."

"Traffic's heavy at this time," Singer said, giving some unexpected help.

"I expect that's it. Well, no doubt he'll turn up soon, and I've got plenty to think about while I'm waiting." I put my briefcase down beside one of the Barcelona chairs, and held out my hand. "Can't thank you enough. It's been very interesting, and very helpful."

He clasped my hand briefly; there was no pressure in it.

"I'll be off now," he said, "my car's in the rear park, so I won't see you again." He sounded decidedly cheerful about that.

"I won't get locked in, will I?" I'd had time to work that question out.

"No," Singer said, "Security won't come round until eight."

It worked!

He disappeared up the stairs to the offices. I settled down on a chair after checking the time. Twenty past six. I decided to give him fifteen minutes to collect his things and get clear.

After only five minutes, a white Rover drove past the entrance with Singer at the wheel, going slowly. I could see him looking in, and gave him a wave that he didn't return. Then the car picked up speed, and passed out of sight toward the entrance gates.

Well, I thought, no point in wasting time. I grabbed the briefcase, and headed up the stairs.

Partway along the office corridor, I stopped and listened. I couldn't hear voices, nor any indication that anybody was still about, working late, or engaged in cleaning or maintenance. Many of the doors were open. I walked along the corridor, looking in, and tapping on the closed doors, prepared to say that I'd just thought of a query I wanted to leave for Singer, but got no replies. I reached the end of the corridor. My luck was in—the place was definitely empty.

Which room to tackle first? I thought I'd try the typists' den. The keyboards and screens all had their covers neatly in place. There was a bank of filing cabinets along the rear wall. They weren't locked, and I pulled open drawers at random. All contained correspondence files. I looked through the titles; several government departments were listed, including Edward's. I took out the Trade and Industry file. Yes, there he was. It gave me a curious feeling to see his signature in these circumstances, like meeting a face you know in a crowd of strangers. The letters he'd signed were about an industrial development grant toward setting up the factory;

whoever had drafted them used sentences that were turgid, impersonal, and might have been taken straight from some civil servants'
handbook on official letter writing. It was forgettable stuff, and he
had. Poor old Edward! I moved on to the cabinet labeled M to P,
and immediately found four files of correspondence with the Ministry of Defense.

This was too easy! But, opening the first file, I immediately discovered the snag: the products to be manufactured were referred to
by number only. No descriptions, no drawings. I read two or three
letters, and found one which drew attention to "the revised drawings
enclosed," but they had not been filed with it. I went through the
whole of the cabinet, and found several references to deliveries that
were to be made to Porton Down specifically by Protoplastics's own
transport, but there were no drawings anywhere in it. Evidently
these were stored somewhere else.

I checked the end cabinet to see if the drawings had simply been
extracted and filed separately, but I somehow didn't expect to find
them there, and they weren't.

Where to try next? I went back into the corridor, and looked at
the titles on the doors. Production Director caught my eye. Singer's
office. The door was closed. I knocked as a precaution, and then
tried the handle. The door was not locked. I opened it and looked
in. Singer was favored with wall-to-wall carpet and real leather chairs
similar to those of the big boss himself; his office was far too upmarket to have anything so sordid as a filing cabinet in it.

But there was an inner door. I waded across the carpet, and opened
it. Here were filing cabinets, together with a steel plan chest and a
drawing board on an adjustable stand, fitted with a drafting machine.
This looked hopeful. And it wasn't even a lockable type of plan
chest.

Jackpot! The drawer headings corresponded to those of the files
in the typing pool. I found M in no time. And here the drawings
were! Actual Ministry of Defense dye-line prints! But of God-
knows-what, as they were untitled except for reference numbers.
Somewhere in here would be drawings of the torch body moldings—
I could recognize that. But how was I to tell what the rest of them
were? I pulled a drawing out. It showed some sort of valve, but

whether it was designed to dispense nerve gas or canteen tea could not be deduced from any of the data listed on it, at least not by me. I slid it back into the drawer, cursing under my breath.

Time to call up Pete, I decided. I'd have a few minutes more to look at some of the other drawings while he was on his way, and I didn't want to push my luck; the later it got, the more difficult it would be to explain away my presence in the offices if I ran into a security man. Daylight was beginning to go, and I would soon have to switch on lights or use the pocket torch I'd brought, either of which could land me in trouble.

I got the radio from the briefcase, opened a window ventilator, and stuck the aerial out. This time it worked.

"Come and get me. Main entrance, same as before."

"I'm on me way," said a tinny version of Pete's voice.

I telescoped the aerial, put the radio back in the briefcase, closed the window. Then I went back to the plan chest, and took out another drawing, choosing at random. I spread it on the drawing board, to see better. There was a detailed specification in a panel on the right-hand side, above the job reference number, but again, no title. I read the specification through. Manufacturing tolerances, materials data, testing requirements. Performance specification, British Standards to be complied with, designed impact resistance, pressure capacity, vapor permeability. So many kilo newtons, so many kilograms per square centimeter. All metric stuff. Of course. I was reminded of my physics master going on about the metric system, and how it was going to bring order and simplicity to our lives. Decimals, perhaps. But units of measurement, absolutely not. We used to have units that meant something, were anthropometric— pints, feet, inches. Now length is supposed to relate to a fraction of the earth's circumference, as represented by "a certain bar of platinum kept in Paris." Trust the French to invent a system so theoretically perfect and so perfectly useless. We should never have let them get away with it. No, no. Oh no.

I found myself yawning. This was getting me nowhere. I put the drawing back. Should I try another?

"Found what you're looking for?" said a dry voice from the doorway.

I spun round. Singer stood in the doorway. He held a large and shiny adjustable spanner in his right hand. If he applied it to my head it would be the last adjustment I'd need. I stayed where I was.

"Thought I might find you here," he said. His wide, thin lips were curled up at the sides with satisfaction, pussycat-wise.

I knew what had happened. He'd driven past the entrance lobby so that I'd think he was leaving, but once out of sight, had gone round the other side of the factory and back in. Well calculated.

But what was he going to do now? He could still, just about, be an outraged innocent who'd caught a snooper. In that case, he ought to call in Security, and hand me over. That would be natural, after he'd found me with my nose in his files. If he didn't do that, I could draw the obvious conclusion. And prepare to make a break for freedom. Meanwhile, I just stood there and said nothing. I would keep my excuses for the security officer, if that was the way it went.

Singer moved back from the doorway, into his main office and out of sight, and I heard the ping of the telephone as he started dialing. I advanced to the doorway, collecting my briefcase on the way. He was standing beside his desk, the spanner conveniently to hand; the outer door to the corridor was temptingly close, and I began to weigh up my chances of getting to it before the spanner got to me. Singer glanced up from his dialing.

"Door's locked," he advised me shortly. Never a wasted word. *His* door, of course. Probably left it unlocked on purpose, and been able to lock it with his own key when he came in.

The call was being put through now, and I waited to see who was going to be the first to get the news.

It wasn't Security, it was Loewenfeld.

"Ah, Walter," Singer said. "Yes, I'm still here. So is Mr. Warner. He seems to find our filing cabinets of interest. In my drawing office. Yes."

He listened. I listened too, but from where I stood Loewenfeld's voice was no more than a distant mechanical quacking. It sounded forceful, however. Instructions for my future, I had to assume.

"Right," Singer said, "right. Yes, I'll do that. Good." He put the phone down. "You're to stay here," he announced, "until the police come."

Well, I thought, this whole thing had to be handed over to them sooner or later. At least I ought to get some answers, at last.

Then a less comforting thought struck me. I had to put it to the test at once, although I suspected that I wasn't going to like the answer.

"Well, get on with it then," I suggested. "Ring the police, why don't you?"

Singer looked at me. "Mr. Loewenfeld's dealing with it."

Oh yes. Yes, I was getting the picture, all right.

"Ring Security, then. Or shall I do it for you?"

For answer, Singer bent swiftly, and removed the telephone cable from its plug-in socket. Now I knew where I was with him. War had just been declared, unmistakably. But I said nothing.

"Don't try the windows," he said. "It's a long drop. And I shall be watching."

He backed out of the room, spanner in one hand, key in the other, pushing the disconnected telephone through the doorway with his foot. I should have chanced it and rushed him then, but he moved fast and I was indecisive, left it too late. I heard the key turn in the lock.

Right. Out of the window, then, before he can get down there to stop me. I strode across the room. It wasn't going to be easy, I saw at once. The only part of the windows that opened was a single row of small horizontal ventilators, one of which I'd already used to put the radio aerial through. The rest consisted of large, fixed, double-glazed panels. I'd have to break one, but it would leave a jagged hole. I'd need something to put over the sharp edges. Even then, it wasn't appealing.

I heard the key in the door again, and it was kicked open, revealing Singer standing there warily, gripping his spanner. He saw me standing by the window, and I watched him survey the room with a sweeping glance. What was he looking for?

My briefcase! *No!*

It was still by the inner door where I'd put it down before going to inspect the windows. He grabbed it, and was out of the room before I was halfway across it.

Mr. Cleversticks Singer. I was losing move after move, and I wasn't liking it at all. He didn't know it yet, but he'd just cut my contact with Pete, my strategic reserve. It hadn't been luck, either, knowing him, just a methodical process of eliminating possible dangers, of which my briefcase had been one. What next?

I heard the rattle of a diesel engine outside, and pushed my face against the window, trying to see sideways down to the main entrance. Pete was just pulling up in the taxi. I hurriedly opened a ventilator so that I could shout down to him. But it would be useless unless he got out. I waited, rubbing the window clear as it misted up with my breath.

Singer! He appeared below, talking to Pete through the taxi window. I remembered, just before I began shouting, that to Singer, this was my hired taxi turning up late. Better to keep quiet, and hope that Pete would work things out for himself. It was hard, but I contained myself.

It was harder still to watch the taxi drive away. There had been no delay for discussion or argument. I took this as a good sign, that Pete had understood at once that something was up, and driven off to preserve his anonymity while he worked out what to do.

He'd hardly disappeared from my field of view when a white Ford Granada arrived, sweeping into the forecourt at speed, and pulling up sharply close to the main entrance. It was a good choice of car: maybe the police sometimes use them in this form, without blue stripes and roof lamp. Maybe there are plainclothes police that look just like the two blue-suited characters who now leapt out purposefully, and made for the entrance like hounds on a trail. Maybe.

Feet sounded in the corridor, and the key rattled in the lock. And there they were, the two boys in blue, with Singer close behind. "Police," the leading one announced.

I'd kept my options open and, on seeing their hard eyes and hefty outlines, decided to take the soft option for the present, and join the act. "Right, let's go then," I said, stealing their next line. We pounded down the corridor, myself a liner with tugs to port and starboard. Clattered down the stairs to the entrance hall, with not a word spoken. All action, poor script. Come on then, where's yer powers of invention? Even real police must say more than this.

"You've got my briefcase, Mr. Singer."

He handed it to one of my captors. We went out into the forecourt, and got into the car: I was motioned into the back, and the larger of the pair got in beside me. Singer stayed by the entrance doors, watching. This time I didn't wave goodbye. We took off.

"Where to?" I asked innocently.

"Down to the station. To make a statement," my neighbor said. "Sir," he added.

His acting was appalling. Maybe it didn't have to be up to much. A short performance, one night only. I hoped Pete had more ideas than I did. There was no sign of him.

"Which station's that?" I asked, more for annoyance than information.

"What?"

"Which police station are we going to?"

"It's not far."

I didn't pursue it. The light was going fast, too fast for my liking. It's not far—I didn't like that either. Needn't have said it—must be what's on his mind. Not far. And not much time. Everything now happening so fast there's no time to think, make plans. Come on, Left Brain! Let's have some ideas before it's too late.

We had slowed down and were cruising along a broad suburban road lined with tall detached houses. Their front gardens were of the prewar overgrown wilderness variety, with high privet hedges and close-boarded oak fences. It was quiet.

The car stopped.

"Where's this?"

"Where we get out," my companion of the backseat said.

"What for?"

"You'll see. Out!"

He had got out his side, and was leaning in to pull me after him.

"Hold it!" his partner said urgently from the driving seat. His eyes were fixed on the mirror.

"What?"

"Taxi coming."

I looked through the rear window. There was indeed a taxi coming up behind. And it was Pete.

I grabbed for the door handle. It had been removed. The driver grinned. "Sit tight, why don't you?" he said. But I heaved myself across the car and out of the nearside door, onto the pavement where his partner was waiting. Taken by surprise, he stepped back, reaching inside his jacket. It was going to be a knife job, I had time to note.

And then we all looked round at the sudden crash of tortured suspension and the rattling roar of a diesel engine to see Pete driving the taxi straight onto the pavement and at us. I saw his face over the wheel, mouthing something at me. There was just room for the blundering taxi between the Ford and the fence, and he kept on coming. "Pete!" I shouted, "for Christ's sake . . ." Going to run us down! The man on the pavement thought so too; he dived at the fence, and there was a splintering sound as rotten boards gave way and he fell through into somebody's front garden. I jumped as well— but upward. The bonnet socked me in the stomach, and I fell across the front of the taxi, borne onward, struggling to get my feet down onto the front bumper. I could hear Pete shouting, "'Old on! 'Old on!" There was another crash which nearly lost me as we drove off the pavement, back on to the road. Two hundred yards on, Pete stopped abruptly, and I fell off.

But we were clear. As I picked myself up, I looked back down the road. The driver had got out of the car and was pulling his mate back through the broken fence. Someone was shouting from the house. And Pete was shouting at me.

"'Op in, quick! They'll catch us in a jiffy."

He opened the back door, and I fell in, groaning. I'd never taken a ton of taxi in the solar plexus before, and I can say it's not to be recommended.

"Sorry abaht that," Pete said, accelerating away. "Meant you just to step on the bumper, see. But you 'ad to do a bloody great 'igh jump."

"Please don't apologize."

"Near enough, wannit!"

"That bloke on the pavement was just getting ready with the carver."

"Ah. What d'yer reckon, then?"

"I don't know, maybe never will."

But later on, I worked it out, or thought so. We came on Stanmore Underground at the end of the road, and when I checked on a street plan, we'd been on the direct route from Protoplastics to the Underground. Mugged and knifed while walking to the station was the likely story. Happens all the time. My wallet would have been a bonus.

And it must have been planned in advance. The boys in blue arrived so promptly, they must have been waiting. To be sent into action if events turned out that way. Well, that all helped to put the Loewenfeld charm into perspective. But for this lad here . . .

"You're a genius, Pete." To arrive just at that moment! Nothing like it since Blücher turned up in the nick to save Wellington at Waterloo!

"Oh, I dunno," he said.

16

HONOR AND SAFETY

Those to which in time of War we should prefer to trust the welfare of our women and children, the honor and safety of our fatherland.

—*Clausewitz*

By the time we'd got to the Edgware Road I was sure we weren't being followed. I never saw the white Ford again after we turned out of the road in which Pete had rescued me. Looking out of the taxi's rear window as Pete drove, I saw nothing to make me suspect that any other car was on our trail. We seemed to be in the clear.

It was then that reaction set in. It had been a damned close-run thing, as Wellington said of Waterloo: I never read that the Iron Duke had recourse to a hip flask, but I'm just one of your lesser mortals.

"Stop at the next pub, Pete!"

A double vodka and tonic, with ice and lemon, did a lot to put the world right side up again. Pete had a Guinness.

He drank about half of it thoughtfully, while I looked about me from our corner seat. It was a decidedly down-market pub, dark, with brown tiles halfway up the walls and dingy stained glass in the tiny windows. It stank of cigarettes and stale beer. The clientele were mostly little old men in saggy suits and crumpled pullovers who sat behind their pints, hardly moving, plus a sprinkling of younger, flashier types—motor traders, I decided.

"Well, that's it then, I s'pose," Pete said into his Guinness.

"What's that mean?"

"You gotta 'and it to the Old Bill. No more larkin' abaht."

"Yes." It seemed obvious, after what had happened. Next time, I might not be so lucky. I'd pushed my luck to the limit, I knew that. Almost over the edge, in fact.

And yet.

What was I going to tell them, the police? What did I actually have, in concrete evidence, against Loewenfeld? Where would I begin the tale—on the moor, or could I skip that bit? Would I have to tell them all about Quarry Cottage, and what happened to Kevin? How would I justify all that? How would I explain what I'd been doing at the factory? As far as I knew, no one had seen me being taken off in the Ford, or witnessed what happened afterward. Except for Pete, and he'd had a bit of bother (as he called it) with the police in the past, which wouldn't do much for his credibility or, by association, for mine.

"Of course, I haven't managed to get hold of anything solid to tell them, that's the trouble."

Pete glanced at me, took another mouthful of Guinness, but said nothing.

"Got to do the sensible thing," I said firmly. No doubt about that. Loewenfeld might now field a powerful force against me. On my own, I just wouldn't be able to survive for long.

And yet. And yet.

I would have liked to have got that solid evidence to hand over, instead of a history of amateur bungling that might even land *me* in the dock, in place of Loewenfeld. As things stood, I had a list of activities to explain that needed little misinterpretation to class me as a man with psychotic tendencies and a too-fertile imagination. I didn't want to have to explain all that. I wanted to saunter into a Chief Inspector's office and drop a neat package of evidence on his desk. I think you ought to see this, Chief Inspector. Thank you sir, just a moment while I read it . . . Good God, sir! And under our very noses, too! Quite so, good morning.

"Where's 'e live?" Pete asked.

Even if I handed it over to them now, I still wouldn't be safe.

Unless they put a twenty-four-hour guard on me. Which they couldn't keep up for long.

"Who?"

"The big white chief."

"Why?"

"If it's not far, could take a dekko on the way 'ome."

If only I could get some *proof*!

"Funny you should say that," I said. "The same thought was just bubbling up here. Just a look, of course. Nothing more."

"Oh yeah. Just a look, that's it."

I've never asked what Pete's bit of bother had been, but always assumed it was juvenile housebreaking. Well, not tonight he wouldn't, not even in the best of causes. We'd been in action enough for one day. But just a look—well, that couldn't do any harm.

I asked at the bar if there was a pay phone. It was in the passage that led to the cloakrooms. There were, miraculously in these days of universal vandalism, some tattered directories, and I looked up Loewenfeld. There he was: Loewenfeld, W. S., and an address in Hampstead. I made a note of it, and then rang Claudine to say I'd be late back.

Weird, after all that had happened in our man's world during the last three hours to hear the normal sounds of domesticity coming down the telephone. Claudine was speaking on the wall phone in the kitchen; I could hear the girls in the background going on about homework. "Just a moment," she said to me, and then I heard her shout at them to shut up and get on with it, or else. *"Pardon, chéri?"* she said again. "That's all, really," I said, feeling a sudden revulsion against the whole stupid thing. I wanted to go home, and tell her all about it. But of course I couldn't, because . . . because I'm a male chauvinist idiot. Later, when it's all over. I'll have to play it down, though, which is a pity.

Right, come on, chaps. We left the pub, and Pete drove us down the Edgware Road as far as Cricklewood Lane, where we turned off left. In a few minutes, we were cruising along the edge of West Heath, looking for Loewenfeld's house. I sat well back, trying to keep out of sight: although it was now almost dark, there were frequent streetlamps of the low, ornamental cast-iron sort, which shone their yellow light into the cab. But it was the ideal vehicle for the job—anonymous, ubiquitous, respectable. We could dawdle without attracting attention.

We came on the house before we expected to, and had to drive past: I caught a glimpse of an oak board hanging by little chains from a miniature gallows, with HEATH HOUSE carved on it in barely readable Gothic letters. Behind it, the house stood back at the apex of a short sweep of red tarmac drive, as neat and flat as the surface of a tennis court. It was one of those neo-Queen Anne mansions built about the turn of the century, all red brick with banded corners and white sash windows, part of the heavy-handed gentrification that surrounds Hampstead Village like a herd of elephants round a watering hole. I risked a glance out of the rear window, and saw the Rolls parked precisely before the porch. I also saw Loewenfeld, loading luggage into the boot.

"Pull in round this next corner, Pete."

We stopped round the corner, out of sight. Where was Loewenfeld off to? I told Pete what I'd seen.

"Doin' a bunk, is 'e?"

I didn't think so. Loewenfeld had left the factory early, before my tour with Singer. He hadn't said where he was going, only that he had to leave—obviously some timetable had already been arranged. Suddenly, I very much wanted to know what it was. I wanted to know where he was going, and what he was going to do. I knew now where *I* was going, and it wasn't to the police, not just yet. I was going to follow Loewenfeld.

Pete had turned in his seat, and sat twisted round with his elbow on the partition, watching my face while I decided what to do. I told him my thoughts. "But I can't follow him now. I've got to put in an appearance at home."

"Gotcha," Pete said. "Say no more. Whatcha reckon?"

"Abroad, probably. One of the channel ports, or London airport. He's got factories in France and Germany. Of course, he could be off to see an aunt in the Lake District. Who knows?"

"If 'e 'eads off outside of London, I'll 'ave a job follerin 'im in this. But I'll do me best. 'Ave to see 'ow it goes."

"Worth a try in case it *is* London Airport. If so, try to see which flight he gets on . . . he doesn't know you, you could stay close."

"You're on," Pete said.

"Be careful—you've seen what they're like."

"Oh, I'll look out for meself. There's more risk goin' in the boozer football night."

He looked excited. I got out, and he gave me a thumbs up as he drove away. I hoped I hadn't done something I'd regret.

Things are going to hot up, that's for sure, I decided. Loewenfeld is going to try harder, I have to assume that. I won't be able to go strolling about like this in future. So far, he's paid peanuts and got monkeys, but he won't risk another failure, he'll send a real professional after me. That means I've got to leave home, go to ground. And after tonight, I can't involve Pete or Ginny anymore—too risky. I'm going to be on my own.

I had taken a back way to avoid going past Loewenfeld's house again, and was now walking down the hill to Hampstead Underground. Cars the size of ocean liners purred past, gliding to their berths in the shadows of wide garages, crunching over white gravel, between banks of well-tended shrubs. Curtains were not yet drawn in all the mansions, and I could see polished dining tables being spread with silver. High under the eaves, each house displayed one or more yellow burglar alarms. Which would lose its silver tonight? I wondered. Well, it's one way to keep money in circulation.

I got to the station, bought a ticket to Notting Hill Gate. From there, it was a short walk down Church Street to the shop. It was just after nine when I got in. Claudine was sitting at the kitchen table writing letters in violet biro. She gets in a stock of violet biros whenever we go to France—the French all prefer to communicate in that color, strangely. She got up, gave me a hug, accepted a kiss, smiled, put on her apron, and began to stir pans on the stove. "How was your day—you are hungry?" "Oh, pretty busy—yes, I am," I said, with what I felt was world-class understatement. I went to see the girls while she was getting supper ready: they'd already had theirs and were in the upstairs sitting room watching television—a domestic drama in which a chintz sofa would have got my award for best actor. "Is it good?" "Nope," they replied without moving their eyes from the screen.

I went back to the kitchen, after collecting some wine from my office, and sat down to supper with Claudine. We often eat in the kitchen if we're on our own. I like to have supper with some ceremony, but tonight it was late and I was too tired to care. The thought of having to plan the days ahead was making my head ache. I had to think up what to tell Claudine. Get my things together. Clothes, money, passport. Gun? I couldn't get on a plane with that— it'd be detected, I'd be carted off by airport security. But I'd need it if I was going somewhere in Britain. Wonder when Pete will ring? Jesus, I'm tired.

"You look tired, my William," Claudine said, leaning across the table and putting her hand on mine. Did I look *that* tired?

"Well, I am a bit. Early bed, perhaps."

"I think I put on the electric blanket," Claudine said, getting up.

"Oh, don't bother."

"Yes, I will, it's nice if you're tired." She left the room and I heard her trotting up the stairs. She likes to keep the worker working. No, that's not quite fair. What does it matter? I wish Pete would ring. This probably means Loewenfeld is still on the road to somewhere, and didn't go to London Airport. Must remember to double check the burglar alarms tonight. Wonder where Julian is? I ought to get the garage and his room wired into the system. Claudine returned, sat at the table again. "More soup?"

"Where's Julian this evening?"

"In his room, I think. Why? More soup?"

"Just wondered. Just a spot."

She was ladling it out when the phone rang. "I'll take it in the office," I said, "I'm expecting Pete to ring with some stuff I asked him to check on." I forced myself to move calmly to the door, then took big strides to the office. "Hello?"

It wasn't Pete. It was Edward.

"Can we be overheard?" he asked. His voice had slipped an octave. He sounded like an undertaker who'd missed the hearse.

"I'm in my office," I said. My voice slipped a bit, too. Something was about to happen, my spine was telling me. I'd had *feelings* about Edward lately. Now I was getting them stronger than before, breaking out of the subconscious, shadowy still, but undeniable. *There's something there.*

"Are you alone?" Edward said.

"And feeling blue."

"What?"

"All alone, door closed, Claudine in kitchen, girls glued to telly, nobody else in house, total security in operation. So?"

Here it comes. *Here it comes.*

"I must see you—urgently," Edward said. "Could you find some excuse to slip out for half an hour? I could pick you up on the corner of Church Street and Notting Hill Gardens in fifteen minutes."

"No."

"What?"

"I said no."

There was a heavy silence. In it, my mental cinema ran a short documentary in which a tall man waiting on a street corner watched a car approach, watched a front window roll down, watched flame spurt from a pair of shotgun barrels, watched the man fall and the car take off at speed. No, it wasn't me. It wasn't going to be me, either.

"Very well," Edward said. "What about tomorrow morning? Early."

"Nine o'clock, here," I said. "You'll be coming to choose some wine. And you'll be alone."

"I must say," Edward said, "you sound as though you're holding me to blame for all this. That's a bit much, you know. I'm trying to help you, as you asked."

"All what?"

"We can't discuss it on the telephone. But I'd better tell you that I've been asked to see you urgently and straighten things out. There's been a very serious mistake made, and you're owed an explanation, that's quite clear. You'll get that, in the morning. In the meantime, you should say nothing to anyone, not even Claudine. Is that understood?"

"Suppose I disagree?"

"Do you want my help, or don't you?" Edward said angrily. "If you do, just stop being so bloody minded, and cooperate—at least until tomorrow morning. If you don't, I can't answer for the consequences."

He wasn't persuading, he was commanding. I was confused by his peremptory tone—did this mean he wasn't involved, but could help, as his words suggested? Or did it mean that he *was* involved, but felt his position to be so strong that he could order me about like some out-of-step schoolboy? As he *had*, in fact, all those years ago.

Or was he bluffing? The best method of defense . . .

"Suppose I've already spilled the beans?"

"What?"

"Oh for Christ's sake, Edward! *Told someone . . .*"

Another heavy pause. Then he said, "It would be out of my hands, then."

It was like fencing with pickaxes. We were getting nowhere. I'd just have to live with my curiosity until morning. It looked like being a sleepless night.

"See you in the morning, then, if that's all."

"It is," Edward said. "Good night."

My brain cells were rioting as I put the phone down. It wasn't only wild speculation about Edward. There was also the question of what to do about Ginny. If anything. You can drift along so far—then you realize that things have changed, imperceptibly, all around you. Go on drifting, and things may fall apart, rocks appear through the bottom of the boat. You need to catch up, to act, to take arms against your troubles. But when?—that's the question. *When?* Too soon, a problem manufactured. Too late, a disaster unavoided. Maybe I should be taking action *now*, before the morning meeting? Maybe disaster would strike in the night? Could I trust Edward's assurance that, by agreeing to the meeting, there would be a truce meanwhile? He hadn't actually said that explicitly, just implied it. But what control did he really have over the situation?

I realized that I was sitting in my office, practically spotlit, in front of an uncurtained window. Out there, on the rooftop, in the garden, hidden in the darkness, someone could be taking aim at this very moment. I leaped up and drew the curtains, making sure no chink remained. As I did so, the phone rang. This time, it *was* Pete.

"Pete 'ere," he said, sounding breathless but chirpy.

"Pete—where are you?"

"Like you said, it's London Airport. 'E got on an Air France, flight 739 to Paris. Left the Roller in the multistory. Nearly lost 'im in there, no more places, 'ad ter go right rahnd an' stop outside the terminal. Saw 'im goin' in just as I pulled up. [All right, all right!] I better nap orf—nipped in 'ere in front of a geezer an' 'e's a bit upset. ['Scuse me mate, but you're gettin' on me wick!] That good enough for yer?"

"Terrific—all I need to know. Thanks a lot, Pete. I'll be in touch."

Paris. Trevor had said Loewenfeld had a factory in France, and I ought to be able to find it without too much trouble. Looks as if I'm off to Gay Paree. Could be worse.

I went thoughtfully back to the kitchen to finish my soup. Claudine had put it back into the saucepan to keep warm, and ladled it out again into a clean plate.

"And what did Pete have to tell?"

She'd have heard the phone go twice. No problem—Edward's visit had a good cover story. I told it. "Doing a lot of important entertaining, it seems." A necessary embellishment—Edward doesn't care much about wine for himself.

"Ah, good," Claudine said, looking pleased. And it was some satisfaction to think that Edward would be forced into buying some wine to make his story good. Something expensive, I decided. Schoolboy strikes back.

"Then Pete rang," I said, having swallowed some spoonfuls to give me time to think.

"Ah yes?"

"I asked him to check on our stock of *petits châteaux*. Seems to me we could do more with those, as they're often such good value, but with too small a production to interest the big boys, supermarkets and so on."

"*C'est bien vrai.*"

"So I thought I'd go over and chase up some new ones. They won't be too busy at this time of year."

"When will you go?"

"I thought tomorrow."

"So soon?"

"The sooner the better."

"I suppose so. You are always away, my William."

"Do you miss me?"

"Of course, *ma biche*. I always miss you. But—" she sighed, "if it is good for the business, I must not stop you." She passed behind my chair, leaned over it, and rubbed her cheek against mine.

Very difficult at times, life.

I'm prepared to use every possible ploy to avoid washing up. We have a machine, and it's obvious to me that there isn't room for two people to load it. So I carried a few things through to the scullery to show willing, but not too much, and escaped back to my office. I had to phone Ginny.

"Hello?"

"Hello, Ginny! It's me."

"Oh, William. I thought you'd have rung earlier." Her voice was remote.

"I couldn't. A lot happened. I only just got back."

"Are you all right?"

"Yes. But I nearly wasn't. Listen, I must see you, but I've got to go to France tomorrow night."

"France? What for?"

"I can't tell you now. What about that café at the back of the Victoria and Albert museum, at four tomorrow?"

"It's ghastly. And you have to pay to get in."

"I know, but it's safe."

"Well, all right. Have you had supper?"

"Yes. Why do you ask?"

"Why didn't you ring me *before* supper?"

What's got into the girl?—she's always been so easy.

"I couldn't, you know that. Claudine's here. And listen, Ginny: don't go there direct from your flat; take a tube from South Ken, go one stop, and wait on the platform to see if anyone else from your train waits with you; if not, take a tube back to South Ken and then walk up. If you think you're being followed, go back to the flat and I'll ring you there. And Ginny—bring a weekend bag and plenty of books."

"Oh, William, I don't like it."

"I know, I'm sorry. I know now I shouldn't have got you involved. That's what I've got to see you about, to decide what's the best thing for you to do until it's over. I'm sorry. I don't know what to say."

There was a silence. "Ginny? Are you there?"

"I'll see you tomorrow," she said, sounding as if she was trying not to cry. Would she follow instructions? Women have no feeling for doing things properly.

"Keep your door locked," I said.

"Of course I will, you stupid sod," she said, ringing off.

A quick call to Bolter's Hotel, then—more about that later. After which I sat at my desk, thinking about my problems, until Claudine put her head round the door. "I've made some coffee," she said, and came in with the tray. She put it on the desk and poured us both a cup. I couldn't think while she was there, so I started getting out reference books and maps ready for the expedition. We looked at them together. In fact, finding some new *petits châteaux* was something I'd been meaning to do for some time, so it wasn't difficult to be convincing.

"What about some new whites?" Claudine queried. The balance of sales between red and white wine shifts all the time; lately, it had moved in favor of white.

"Absolutely right, darling," I said. "I thought I'd concentrate on Saint-Emilion—some interesting new blends coming from there. I should be able to get good reds and whites from the same producers."

She picked up the coffee tray, nodding in agreement, and made for the door. Compulsively, I watched her jeans recede. That's how it all started. That's how I know there's no such thing as free will. Or, if there is, I haven't got much of it. At the door, she turned, catching me before I had time to redirect my eyes upward.

"Perhaps you are not *so* tired now, my William," she said softly, smiling.

"Amazing what a good onion soup can do."

"I think I will go up now. An early night—tomorrow will be busy." And tonight as well, unless I've misread the signals. I think she reads in *Elle* about *la libération des femmes*—often takes the initiative these days. Or—a chilling thought—does she suspect outside interests and is making a deliberate effort to keep me at home? I've been less attentive, absentminded. *I wish I hadn't thought of that.*

"I'll be with you in no time—just want a quick word with Julian," I said, blowing her an elaborate kiss. She projected it back to me; she smiled again, nodded twice in recognition of our exchange, and went, leaving me with the image of her red lips, lingering on the air like a promise. Or maybe the seal on a contract.

"Hi, Jules."

"Oh, hello. Hi, Dad."

Julian's studio was papered with drawings that were pinned to every available wall surface.

"My God, it's hot in here," I said. "What's all this?"

"It's a redevelopment project," he said. He showed me round it.

There was a time when redevelopment meant bulldozing a whole area and starting again from scratch. That was in the brave days of confidence in the future, after the war had been won and we were going to rebuild our world just the way we wanted it. Then we discovered we didn't know what we wanted. And couldn't afford it anyway.

"I'm keeping the old infrastructure," Julian said, "but inserting these new transport routes between areas where a clear identity can be established."

"Oh," I said. Most designers that I've come across do this—they decide what would be fun, and then try to justify it with long words.

"It looks like a fun scheme," I suggested sneakily. Julian looked shocked. He has monastic tendencies.

I told him about the projected wine-buying expedition. Then I

gave him an envelope. It contained a single sheet of paper on which
I'd written Ginny's name, address, and telephone number, and a
brief statement to the effect that I was going to France to continue
an investigation into attacks that had been made on me for reasons
which appeared to have something to do with chemical warfare, and
that she knew all that was known at the time of writing. I had felt
unreal writing it, but there it was. "I haven't had time to write a
will," I said, "and I'd just like you to keep this safe in case I have
an accident or something. But don't open it unless you have to. And
don't tell Claudine about it—she'd only worry."

Julian took it, looking puzzled. "Haven't you made a will before?
And shouldn't you leave this with the solicitors?"

"I've made a few changes. And I haven't got time—you look after
it for me, I know I can trust you. Where will you put it?"

Julian indicated his filing cabinet. "This do?" *The* filing cabinet—
they weren't likely to look in that again. "Fine," I agreed. "And
don't you worry about it—your old dad will be back safe and sound.
I just wanted to leave everything neat and tidy, that's all. Must be
getting pedantic in my old age."

If Julian thought I was being odd, he said no more about it, but
put the envelope away in the bottom drawer of the cabinet, and
closed it. I then had to risk being odder still by asking him to make
sure the house was securely locked up at night and the alarm set
while I was away. "Sure, Dad," he said, "don't worry. I'll see to it.
We're bound to get burgled sooner or later, but I'll try not to let it
happen while you're away."

I couldn't have put it better myself. I patted him on the arm, and
left him to his redevelopment.

It would seem different in the morning, I told myself, looking up
in the dim glow of the bedside lamp at Claudine's jiggling breasts
as she rode me firmly toward our mutual satisfaction. In the morning, she would again become the beautiful, hard-edged housekeeper
I was used to, and I would regain the usual feeling of affectionate
detachment toward her that made it possible for me to keep seeing

Ginny. Surely it would be so. That's the good life, and all it needs is a sense of balance.

A good life, and a good deal.

At first, my body responds though my mind does not. But then, as she works away, I get drawn in by her warmth and enthusiasm. I reach up to hold her breasts, running my thumbs lightly over her nipples; she shivers and goes "Mmmm, mmmmm," opening her eyes for a moment to smile down at me. She wriggles as she rides. Whatever she's thinking, it's impossible to believe she's doing this just to keep me happy. All this can't be simulated. She loves me. Or has a strong physical affection for me. Perhaps it's the same thing. Now I'm being drawn into her affection, I feel it myself, a physical bond overflowing into the emotions. Perhaps bed's more important for us because of the language barrier—never quite so comfortable as with someone of your own background—when upright at least. Whatever the reason, I'm feeling . . . but it'll be different in the morning.

"Oooh, ah, *chéri*!" Claudine collapses onto my chest.

"Happy?"

"Mmmmmm, of *course*! You?"

"Mmmmmmmmm."

Of course.

A Doubtful
Character

*[A] great part of the information obtained in War is contradictory, a
still greater part is false, and by far the greatest part is of a doubtful
character.*

—Clausewitz

And, in the morning, it *was* different, though not in the way
I expected. Claudine bustled about with her usual elegant
efficiency; the warmth of the night before hung in the
house like central heating; and I found myself able to enjoy all this
while looking forward to the meeting with Ginny. Perhaps it was
because the war seemed likely to take a new and more positive turn
with the arrival of Edward. Perhaps it was because I'm genuinely
polywhatsit. Anyway, no time for introspection, with Edward due
any minute. I shoveled in some toast and coffee, and scribbled a
note for Maggie asking her to book me on the night ferry from
Southampton to Le Havre, and get me some francs. Then the side
doorbell rang. I took a few seconds to stiffen the sinews, summon
up the blood, etc., and then marched firmly into the fray.

"My goodness, William, you look frightfully stern!" Tricia said,
as I opened the door. No sign of Edward: parking the car, it seemed.
She stepped past me into the hall, and I got a whiff of newly applied
Diorissimo—just been shopping with Claudine, I remembered. I
glanced after her. Reading somewhere about "the small, maneuver-

able body, plump-but-firm, which appeals to the average sensualist"
I had immediately thought of Tricia. That, and the bouncing blond
curls . . .

Claudine arrived at full gallop, having heard Tricia's voice through
several walls, exclaiming in delight, "Didn't know you were coming!" "Brought the old stick over, darling." There was a lot of hugging and kissing. Then it was my turn. "You're definitely slimmer,"
I said, my arms round her waist. "Oh, William, do you think so?"
she cried, "I am trying." "Definitely," I said, "but don't overdo it—
leave enough to get a grip on." "Not a lot of gripping going on these
days," she said. "Poor Edward's up to his ears." "Well," I said, "it's
a shocking waste, and if . . ." "My poor William," Claudine put in,
"Tricia would never have anything to do with *you*! Such a greedy
pig," she said to Tricia. "He thinks of nothing but food." "Well, he
looks all right on it," Tricia said, patting my flattish tum.

Mutual grooming—you know the sort of thing. Written out like
that—well, it looks horribly arch. But it isn't the words that count,
of course; it's the little undercurrents of speculation, the seething of
molecules in the body social. Or something like that. Can go on for
some time. This morning, however, speculation came to an abrupt
stop.

"Here's Teddy," Tricia said, and Edward's bulky shape loomed
in the doorway, a dark gray pinstriped cloud on our horizon, cu-
mulus nimbus rolling up. Nobody but Tricia calls him Teddy. But
he was one once, a cuddly youth with a slow, courtly manner that
appealed to girls who were young and unsure of themselves. Until,
of course, they felt ready for a little action, at which point Edward
. . . went on being slow and courtly. His face, bland and practically
expressionless, would turn to follow them as they deserted him to
be whirled away in other arms, other cars, groped and giggling. His
eyes were teddy eyes, small and dark, trusting and reflective, his
best feature. Tell me a story, his eyes seemed to suggest. And indeed
it was a true impression—he liked to listen, he had few ideas of his
own.

Well, look at him now. Look at us both now, twenty years on. I
think I know what *I* look like. I mean, not what I see in the mirror
every morning, but how I appear to other people. You need lovers

to show you that, not at the early flattering stages, but over time. What does Edward think of himself? Does he look beyond the mirror, see himself as Tricia sees him? She must, originally, have chosen him for his Teddy quality—what else was there? Perhaps it's still there for her. Perhaps when she looks at his face, beside her on the pillow, she still sees something trusting and endearing. Enough, anyway, to keep her from breaking the habit of being with him. At our age, the thought of starting all over again . . . perhaps she's grown independent, and just doesn't care much about their relationship. At least they've got money, and as for the rest, she has outside interests, can or does have flings, though Claudine is always cagey about that. But I'm certainly not the only male to appreciate the small maneuverable body, plump-but-firm . . .

All right, all right. It's Edward we're meant to be studying. Well then, look at him now. I see a bulky bureaucrat, opposite the middle-aged merchant that is me. That's the surface, the public image. I'm not *really* a middle-aged merchant, of course, oh, no—I just look like one to the casual observer; inside is a much younger person, full of youthful energies and aspirations—OK, and somewhat subject to follies and fantasies of sundry sorts, I know all that, it just proves my point. You *are* as old as you feel, in the ways that matter most.

But what's inside this bulky bureaucrat, Edward? I should *know*, after all these years—but I don't. That's why I'm going on about him. That's what's so frustrating. Especially now, when I really *need* to know—my life may depend upon it. He looks just like the cuddly youth, writ larger. Or does he?

"I thought that you and Claudine would have one of your get-togethers, while William and I are in the office," Edward said, swinging his expressionless face from one to the other. He'd brought Tricia, I realized, for just this purpose—to make sure that Claudine wouldn't try to sit in on our meeting. Flat-footed, but effective.

"Come on, then," I said. "Teddy."

He ambled after me, along the corridor to the office. I closed the door, and turned round. He stood there with the window behind him, seeming to fill the room, watching me.

That was the moment I realized what he had become. A slight

shift of character, but significant. Big Bruin against the light—no longer Teddy, but Bear . . .

Ah, come on! These zoological analogies . . .

Have it your own way. But we *are* animals—cat people, doggy people, piggy people. And Richard Coeur de Lion.

Bear people have watchful eyes, and their faces are masks. Impossible to tell what bears are thinking—nothing shows. Bears, it's said, are the most dangerous of animals because of this: they watch, and wait, and strike without warning. Stalin, for instance . . .

"Sit down, Sta . . . I mean, Edward," I said, and he sat.

I faced him across my desk. There's a traditional way to deal with bears—*bait 'em!*

"Before we start," I said, "there's something else. What would you say if I told you I'd been fucking Tricia?"

Nothing like a sharp nip in the ankle to get him going, I thought. He blinked. Then he said, quite calmly, "Well, have you?"

"Maybe."

"Maybe. I see. Well, as a matter of fact, there was a time when I thought you might be. But what's your motive for bringing this up now?"

"I want to know what you think about it."

He paused, his eyes on my face. Then he said, "What I think about it is that if you choose to run round after women like a twenty-year-old, that's your affair, but I'd be surprised if you managed to get Tricia into bed with you. If she was that way inclined, I think she'd prefer a man who had got somewhere in the world. And as for that, I suggest you give some thought to where you're going to be when the music stops—time's running out for your present way of life. Isn't it?"

Wham! Oh, bears are bad, bears are *dangerous*. And this bear can bop when he's had his fur ruffled. That's something learned—plus a few home truths.

"So, what did you think you'd do about it?"

"When I thought that about you and Tricia?"

"Yes."

His eyes were still on my face. He said quietly, "What could I do?"

Well, I thought, you couldn't throw an emotional scene—you
wouldn't know how. You couldn't whirl her away to romantic
places—you're too busy, and wouldn't think of it. You couldn't stop
wearing pajamas and lie skin to skin—it's not in your nature. So
what does a poor tormented Teddy do?

He bops!

"You could hire someone to knock me off," I said. Like a simulated
shooting accident on the moor, far from Teddy territory.

"You're making some kind of joke, I suppose."

"Of course." He couldn't really feel it that strongly. Could he?

"Can we get on," Edward said, "if you've finished being
offensive?"

I wanted to keep the heat on. "Sure," I said. "Let's hear how
you've managed to make a balls-up with your work as well as your
wife. Because when *your* music stops, you look likely to end up
without either. That's not so bloody clever, is it?"

"Leave Tricia out of this," he said loudly.

"Agreed. It's how you managed to get yourself mixed up with
Protoplastics that interests me at this moment. Top civil servant in
criminal cover-up. Gangsters given Development Grant. How are
you going to explain *that* away?"

Edward sat back in his chair. "I can't," he said presently.

"Can't? Jesus, man, you mean you've blown your whole career?"

He shot a glance at me. "That," he said in a flat voice, "depends
on you. Unfortunately."

"On immature, irresponsible me?"

"Yes."

"That must be hard for you to bear?"

"It is."

"Especially if I'm really . . ."

"I told you—leave her out of it."

"Please?"

"Please."

This wasn't what I'd planned, or expected—poor old Bruin with
his tail between his legs. I could try goading him some more, but
it didn't seem likely to succeed. Fact is, I'm not too good at resisting

the soft touch. I sighed. I was going to have to take the edited story after all, give up the angry, testing argument. Godammit.

"All right, then. Let's have it."

"I feel I can trust you," Edward said. "After all, we've known each other a very long time."

. "Man and boy," I said, "yup."

"And there's been no real harm done."

Well, I thought, well. Three attempts on my life, two men dead. Bullets flying, knives brandished, fair quantities of blood, toil, tears, and sweat expended. No real harm? Sure, only those who lived by the sword have perished. Maybe he means they're no great loss.

"Maybe," I said. "In any case, you've got the floor. Proceed."

I won't give what he said verbatim. It was a prepared speech, obviously, though I didn't blame him for that, with his career (as he kept repeating) at stake. There's no need to record every haaa-rumph and pregnant pause of it.

But what it amounted to was this: Protoplastics was way out in front of all the competition with technical innovation. Edward, on behalf of the government, had backed them with public money. Nothing wrong in that—it was what he was expected to do. Back the winners, that was his brief. But then, secrets had leaked. In-dustrial espionage had started—only too common, Edward said, with so much money at stake. Big boss Loewenfeld, furious at the constant nibbling away of his advantage and erosion of his invest-ment prospects, had ordered Singer, director in charge of security, to stop the leaks at all costs.

Singer, overzealous (and overambitious in his own interests) had taken Loewenfeld's words literally and hired heavies. Initially in-structed to carry out surveillance, collect information, and report back, they had (so Singer said) misinterpreted Singer's further in-structions and gone into full attack mode, like dogs unleashed. Where *they* came from, illegal violence and, haarumph, *even worse*, was com-mon. Singer was shocked. Loewenfeld was appalled. Edward was, well, I could imagine Edward's feelings on being told that such people had been employed by a firm he had backed, in *any* capacity. Couldn't I? If *that* news got out, tremendous damage would be done

to this promising firm. The chance of further government backing
would be reduced to zero. Heads would have to roll, including Edward's, although he had of course known nothing of what was going
on, or perhaps because of it. Responsibility rests at the highest level,
ultimately, not with the executives. A ship that runs aground, well,
you may blame the watch, but it's the captain that gets the court
martial, isn't it? Fair or not, that's the rule, and normally, we must
accept it. Normally. But in this case, well, as there's been no real
harm done . . . You see my point, William.

"You want me to forget the whole thing? As though nothing had
happened? Just like that?"

"I'm asking you to," Edward said.

"And you can guarantee that no further attempts will be made?
Peace will reign hereafter?"

"Yes."

I sat thinking. Edward sat silent, waiting. I said, "You haven't
been open with me in the past. Why should I believe you now?"

"You mean, about knowing Protoplastics? I told you, I'm in a
position of trust with the firms I support—it's against policy to give
information to members of the public. Friendship no excuse." Civil
service secrecy. Could be true.

"Why did Singer's dogs pick on me?" I asked.

"You ask me that? After you'd been caught with your nose in the
files?"

"No, I mean *before* that."

"Oh, I don't know about what happened before that," Edward
said, "and if you don't mind, I'd prefer not to know. With those
sort of people, anything can happen. The important thing is that
it's all over now. You leave them alone, and they'll leave you alone.
Just give me your word to say nothing to anyone—*anyone*, mind!—
and that's the end of it. Believe me, it's best."

Thoughts raced through my head. Of course Edward knew more
than he was letting on—bound to. But that didn't mean he was
necessarily a villain. He might be just doing his job, as he saw it.
Keeping Protoplastics on the road, protecting innovation, Keeping
Britain Ahead. Maybe the whole thing had been a ballup from the
start, as he suggested. A photograph handed down the line. Someone

that looked vaguely like me. See this geezer—well, go an' get 'im—
it's worth five grand. That, someone once told me, was the going
rate for the job. Five thousand pounds—the price of a small family
car, a couple of splashy holidays abroad, some new suits, tax free.
All for the minimal effort of pulling a trigger. Easy money. Life is
that cheap.

"I'd like to think about it."

"Surely you don't need to do that," Edward said. "Not after I've
explained my position. Not after I've put my career on the line by
telling you what I have. Surely that's enough for you?"

I looked at his large, bland, expressionless face. Did I believe him?

"All right," I said.

"Good man," Edward said with relief. "I knew I could count on
you."

"Just a minute! There's a condition."

He leaned forward. "I don't think . . ."

"Look, you can't seriously expect me to settle for an outline! It's
full of holes, what you've told me. I've been too caught up in it to
be able to accept that."

"What, then? I can't promise anything . . ."

"I want the full story. Not now, but when we next meet, to give
you time to get it all together. Say, in a week's time. That's my
condition."

Edward considered this. Or appeared to. Then he said, "I'm
bound to tell you, William, that it just is not possible. I'm grateful
for your cooperation, and I hope you will stick to what you promised. But please understand that I have an obligation to my department that limits what I am at liberty to tell you. I simply cannot
tell you more than I have already, even if you should go back on
your word and threaten to make all this public. I . . ."

"Now, hold on! I wasn't threatening . . ."

"I'm very glad to hear it."

That seemed to be that.

No?

You're right, of course. No.

I didn't believe it either. Or, to be exact, I believed some parts of it, and not others. The question was, which parts?

I looked at it this way. Edward could be straight, but misinformed. Or he could be basically straight, but holding back, or misleading me, for departmental reasons. Or—let's face it—he could be bent.

If he was straight, I would be safe in the future *only* if he had the influence to call the dogs off. I couldn't rely on that.

If he was bent, all this could simply be a ploy to make me relax my guard, and then—*blam*!

If I kept quiet, and he was bent, I would be simply laying my head on the block.

If I went public, and he was straight, I would damage his career, maybe beyond repair. And his wife was my wife's best friend.

Not surprising, therefore, that the brain cells were feeling a little jaded. A glass of wine does wonders for that condition, and I had the perfect excuse. At nine-thirty in the morning? Well, not normally, perhaps, but *this* morning, yes.

Yes!

"You'll be having some champagne, of course."

"Will I?" said Edward.

"I'm putting you down for a dozen vintage Bollinger," I told him firmly, "and we'll open one now so that you know what you're getting."

"No, really, William," he said, "I never drink at this hour of the morning."

"Too late," I said, quickly twisting the cork off. He took the glass reluctantly.

"Here's to the future, yours and mine!" I toasted him. We clinked glasses. This, I thought, was a moment to savor. Were we friends? Or mortal enemies? Ah, the irony in those bursting bubbles. "You know," I said, taking a second large mouthful down the hatch, "I thought the MoD were trying to liquidate me."

"Why on earth should they do that?"

"Military secrets. Gas warfare."

"But how . . . ?"

"Protoplastics make all sorts of stuff for the MoD. Including torches with special gas seals."

"But why should you . . . ?"

"The only connection I could think of was that I went on a course at Porton Down when I was in the army."

"My dear William, that was years ago."

"Twenty years. But when you're grasping at straws . . ."

"Yes. Well, of course, strange things do happen in military security. I heard the other day . . ."

I would have liked the rest of this revelation, but the door burst open and Claudine came in, with Tricia on her heels crying, "Thought we heard a cork pop—ah, we *did*! Look at them both! Champagne! And we weren't invited!"

"Edward's taking a case of the vintage Bollinger," I told Claudine, "and he kindly suggested we open a bottle now."

"In that case," Tricia said, "I'll certainly have a glass. How about you, Claudine?"

"Just a small one, my dear, and thank you both," Claudine said.

"And what else has Edward bought?" Tricia asked.

"Comes to about half a dozen cases, assorted, mostly claret," I said. "Don't bother to take it—I'll send it over. Tomorrow afternoon be all right?"

Edward was giving a near-perfect demonstration of stiff upper lip.

"What are you smiling about?" Tricia asked me.

"I was thinking about the small maneuverable body, plump-but-firm," I said in her ear.

"Oh! Whose?"

Edward was watching us, I made sure of that. They need to be slapped down to keep them in line, these bears.

18

DISARMING EVENTS

We have already said that the aim of all action in War is to disarm the enemy . . .

—*Clausewitz*

Ten-thirty already, and I had a day's work to deal with before I could get away to meet Ginny at four. Invoices, letters, instructions—all the boring bumf that fills an office like fly-paper when you're not looking. Plus, more pleasurably, making up the order for Edward. Better not overdo it, I decided regretfully, crossing out some big names and substituting a batch of crus bourgeois. Keep it credible. Better chance of getting paid too.

I'd just finished this act of calculated mercy when the telephone rang—it was himself. He spoke in a low voice.

"What's this?" I said. "Not using the office phone for private purposes, are you?" Tormenting Teddy, my new-found entertainment, was getting to be a habit. Sensibly, he just ignored it.

"About our conversation this morning," he said, "I've spoken to Mr. L. and he is very anxious to see you, to explain the situation to you himself."

"Oh yes?"

"He feels a definite obligation to do so, after what happened yesterday."

"He does?"

"Unfortunately he is at the Paris factory for the rest of this week. But he would be very pleased to see you after the weekend. He suggests Monday evening, at his house. It's in Hampstead."

"Is it?"

"Look here, I wish you would do this for me, William. I feel sure when you've heard him reinforce what I've told you that you'll feel more comfortable about the whole thing."

"Bloody hell, Edward, I *heard* Singer arrange yesterday's little jaunt with solicitous, reassuring Mr. L. Thanks, but no thanks."

"Just see him. He'll explain all that. It was Singer, I told you."

Playing with fire, it would be. But . . . maybe I could save myself a lot of tedious sleuthing. A scouting party, well armed and wary. You're supposed to keep contact with the enemy, I'd been taught.

"I'm going to France myself, as it happens. To Bordeaux, but I could stop off in Paris. If I did, and I mean *if*, where could I contact him?"

"Wait," Edward said. I waited, hearing a slapping of papers. "Here it is—he's staying at La Tour Blanche, rue Washington. 555-1433. Will you ring him there?"

"I might," I said, "or I might not. *Ça dépend.* I'll give it some thought." I would, too. Plenty of thought.

"Well, I hope you will," Edward said earnestly, "but in the meantime . . ."

"You'd like me to be silent as the grave."

"It isn't a joking matter for me, William. Please remember that."

"Oh I will, Edward, I will."

All the way to Paris. And, hopefully, back.

Honest toil held me in thrall until well after three—I hardly had time for lunch. Then I dashed out of the house, telling Maggie I had to make a quick call on our shipping agents, and into the taxi I'd ordered by telephone—as safe a method of transport as I could think of. Minutes later I was at the Queen's Gate entrance of Imperial College.

It's a rambling collection of buildings filling the block between Queen's Gate and Exhibition Road. So rambling that I got lost myself, and twice had to ask the way before I emerged at the far end into Exhibition Road. I felt confident that, if anyone had followed my taxi to the entrance, they'd have been shaken off by the time I got to the exit. The Victoria and Albert Museum was in sight, and by ten to four I was installed in the café with a cup of brown liquid in front of me. It could have been tea, or coffee, but fortunately I was too keyed up to care. And apprehensive—there was going to be trouble, I knew. My relationship with Ginny had always been cheerfully affectionate and superficial, which suited us both, but now the war, with its heightened tensions and real issues, had put a dent in that. I didn't know how we would manage a postwar reconstruction—I only knew that I wanted to, *had* to, somehow.

The place I was sitting in did nothing to inculcate optimism or soothe the nerves—a barnlike hall converted for use as a canteen— all bleak gloss-painted walls, stainless-steel self-service counters, and ancient simmering tea urns like failed steam engine prototypes. Surely I had made a mistake to propose this place. No sympathy between man and woman could survive an encounter in this echoing vault.

There was a large station clock on the wall, and the hands had dragged arthritically round to four-twenty before Ginny suddenly appeared, pushing past the cash desk, looking round anxiously for me. I waved, and stood up. She thrust her way toward me, between the tables. She was breathless, and looked harassed. I pulled out a chair for her, and she plumped herself into it, dumping a bag on the floor beside her. I realized what she was going to say just before she said it.

"I've been followed."

"Where?"

"He followed me to the museum, but I may have lost him on the way through. I rushed through several halls, dodging round the exhibits—nearly knocked one over—an attendant shouted—oh, I'm glad you're here. I didn't like it, William. It's creepy."

"How did he manage to follow you when you changed tubes?"

"You'll be furious, William, but I didn't *do* that. I thought I'd just walk here, but I went all the way to Harrods, walked in one door and out of another to confuse anyone following, and then doubled

back here. It all seemed so melodramatic, jumping in and out of
tube trains. Also I was in a rage with you. I think I still am. Is that
coffee?"

"I'll get you some."

"Let me try it. Ugh, no thanks. Listen, what happened
yesterday?"

I told her, and about Edward. She listened intently, frowning.
"My God," she said, "they were really after you, weren't they?"

"Looks as if they still are. So much for Edward's assurances."

"Oh William!—I'm sorry . . ."

"Maybe he hasn't had time to call them off, yet. Or probably
they're just keeping an eye on me. Don't worry."

"But I've led them straight to you!"

"They won't try anything in here," I said, hoping I was right.

"But what are you going to do?"

"I'll see Loewenfeld in Paris."

"But what do you expect to get from that?"

"I shall play it by ear."

"You mean, you haven't the faintest idea."

"I shall try to find out what he's manufacturing. I still think there's
something they're all trying to conceal. Including, it's still possible,
the MoD."

"And if you can't?"

"I shall go on following him until I do."

"And meanwhile his professional thugs are following you. And
me."

"That's what I wanted to talk to you about. You've got to go
somewhere safe while I'm clearing this up. It's got much too
dangerous."

"It's much too dangerous for you, too. I don't know why I should
have to remind you of it, but you're a married man with kids, unfortunately. You're not a secret service agent, listed by the KGB,
expert in espionage, subversion, and hand-to-hand combat. Your
maximum exertion has been in drawing corks out of bottles."

"I seem to remember, not so long ago . . ."

"Oh for God's sake, William, do try to be serious."

"I'm a trained killer, actually."

"National service? You're a Boy Scout compared to the sort of yobbos they'll put on to you now. Face it, William, you've come to the end of the road. You've got to hand it over."

"But there's still no evidence."

"Fuck the evidence." She gripped my hand over the table, and squeezed it as hard as she could, trying to make me look at her. Then she let go and sat back. "I never thought," she said bitterly, "that you'd get addicted to violence. But you have, haven't you? You still look like an ordinary, decent, friendly, nonviolent civilized bloke. But you've become like your enemies, just as policemen and criminals are the same people with different clothes on. Now you look all mulish—I know I'm right."

"I've never accepted that—about policemen."

"You wouldn't. Well OK, it's an exaggeration for the sake of effect, but there's some truth in it. They're both into crime, that's the point, and they wouldn't be if they weren't both fascinated by it."

"Look, Ginny," I said, reaching for her hand now. "There's something in what you say. Most normal blokes like a bit of excitement, even aggro, from time to time, and I'm no different. But I'm not into violence for its own sake. All I want is one piece of solid evidence, just enough to be able to walk into the CID, slap it on the table, and say, 'There you are, get on with that.' I shan't be satisfied if I give it up now."

"And for that," Ginny said slowly, "you're going to risk your life?"

"Well, that's too dramatic a way to put it."

She sighed, and shook her head. "I'll never understand it."

"I thought," I said, "that you did. When we discussed it in your flat that last time, for instance."

"It didn't seem real, then. Now it does. After being followed."

There was a long silence, during which I watched the entrance over her shoulder. Then I asked, "Were you being followed by a man in a rather baggy grayish suit, stocky, medium height, about thirty-five, long brown hair, carrying a blue coat?"

"He's there now, isn't he? What are we going to do?" Ginny knew she mustn't look round, but could hardly bear it.

"You'll have to rely on your psychotic male chauvinist friend," I said. "Follow me, woman. Don't look at him. Do what I do. Especially if I start running."

I began to walk toward the cash desk with Ginny close behind. Before we arrived, the man had retreated round the corner, out of sight. I paid for the tea or coffee—they were the same price—and we then advanced round the corner. The sleuth had taken up a position at the far end of the next gallery where he was inspecting a pair of life-size bronze Greeks, or maybe Romans, locked in an attitude of frozen aggro. I decided that, whatever Ginny might say about it, I was going to have to follow the classical tradition—on this occasion at least.

"Wait here until I've cleared a path to the exit. If he comes this way, take cover in the loo behind you."

"What are you going to do?" Ginny said anxiously.

"Make like it's goodbye," I said, taking her by the shoulders and kissing her on both cheeks. Her eyes were troubled. "Don't . . ." she started to say, but I was off, walking down the long gallery toward the sleuth.

He watched me as I approached, not moving from his position behind the statue. I didn't walk directly toward him, but more toward the exit; I didn't want him to be sure that I knew he was sleuthing Ginny. However inept a sleuth may be, they must always hope they haven't been spotted. Then, when I reached the end of the gallery, I turned in his direction, and the last five or six paces, taken slowly, brought us nearly face to face.

He was older than I'd thought, probably mid-forties rather than thirties. His hair had misled me: it was a young style, long enough to cover the ears; his face was podgy and lined and seemingly much older than his hair, so that he looked as if he was wearing a wig. He was shorter than me, but more heavily built, with a beer belly pushing out his shirtwaist. Remembering what Ginny had said about criminals and policemen, I had to admit that this character could have been an off-duty or plainclothes arm of the law, in spite of his cold piggy eyes. But I'd already decided to act on the assumption that he wasn't.

"Do you know who I am?" I asked in a low voice.

He inclined his head, his eyes watchful, but said nothing.

"I've got a message for your boss," I said, taking the final step toward him. He didn't back away, but shifted his stance slightly, easing the blue raincoat that hung over his arm. He had several gold rings on his right hand. That tipped the odds against his being the Old Bill.

He moistened his thin lips with his tongue. Then he spoke, in a low voice like my own. We seemed to be conspiring together.

"What is it?" he murmured.

"Well, it's this," I murmured back, bringing up my knee in the style taught to me by Sergeant MacWhirter.

It was effective, I'll say that. The sleuth's mouth opened as if he was about to blow a smoke ring, and the breath left him in a single mighty gasp. He sank to his knees, his eyes focused on some distant horizon. I left him to his thoughts, relieving him of his raincoat as I did so, and signaled to Ginny to follow me to the entrance foyer. She hurried after me, and we met on the steps outside.

"What did you do?" she asked; the statue had blocked her view.

"Let's get out of here," I said. "He'll be back in action before long." Somebody was just getting out of a taxi; I urged Ginny in, and scrambled in after her. "Bolter's Hotel, Redcliffe Gardens."

"Well, what did you *say*?" Ginny persisted once we were safely underway. I was looking out of the rear window. No sign of him. That's twice I owe you, Sergeant.

"Nothing much."

"You *must* have. Well, what did *he* say?" She squeezed my arm impatiently.

"He said oof."

The taxi driver could hear us through the open partition. I leaned forward and closed it.

"My God," Ginny said, "you're making enemies *fast*. You're not going to have a chance once they get organized and all get after you."

"He was after us anyway."

"Yes, but in future he'll be putting in *overtime*. That's if he was, in fact, following me. I wasn't absolutely sure. Did you think of that?"

"It's a bit late to tell me your doubts, now," I complained, "but yes, I did think of that. You wouldn't have had any doubts if you'd seen him close to. And if you're still worried that I've assaulted an innocent stranger, don't. There's the automatic."

"What automatic? William, you're being bloody irritating, you know?"

"The one in his raincoat pocket," I said smugly, patting it. No doubt about it, that had been a pretty smooth piece of action, even if Ginny wasn't in a mood to appreciate it. Smooth and successful. This could get to be a habit.

The feeling was still with me when I ushered Ginny into the reception lobby at Bolter's. There was a carefully made-up woman of about my age behind the desk. "Ah, good afternoon," I said, leaning toward her with a bright professional smile, "Potts and Potts; my name's Warner, I telephoned you last night to make a reservation for my client, Mrs. Duff-Jones. This, indeed, *is* my client. I trust everything is in order?"

"Oh yes, all in order, of *course*," the receptionist said, greeting Ginny with a sideways tilt of the head and an expression of extreme sympathy and compassion. Ginny smiled back uncertainly. I hadn't told her the details, only that I'd got her a room. We'd only been a few minutes in the taxi; anyway, I was enjoying myself.

"I hope I made it quite clear," I said to the receptionist, "that Mrs. Duff-Jones wishes to stay in her room and have absolutely no visitors until the court hearing is over. Once the injunction is granted, she will be adequately protected against her husband, and can return home, but until then there is a risk that he may follow her here and attempt to continue his unreasonable behavior. It is also essential that no one shall know her room number except the staff; do you think you will be able to insure that?"

"I suggest," the receptionist said in a conspiratorial whisper, "that she should be booked in under a *false name*. To guard against one of the cleaners, for instance, giving her room number away by accident." She was eager to help.

"Oh, *excellent!* That is a splendid idea. I should have thought of it myself. Don't you agree, Mrs. Duff-Jones?"

"Mmmm," said Ginny, nodding. Fires were building in the corners of her eyes.

"What name do you suggest?" I asked.

"Smith?"

"Too obvious, if I may say so. Let's make it Struther."

"Without an S on the end?"

"Oh, definitely." I turned to Ginny. "Would you like to go up now, Mrs. Struther, and I'll bring up the affidavit for you to go through in a minute, after I've checked the final arrangements." Ginny nodded again, and started up the stairs. "Now," I said seriously to the receptionist, "this is, you know, a matter that could have the most unfortunate consequences if it is not handled correctly. I hope I can rely on you to make sure, absolutely sure, that all visitors are turned away, without exception. Mrs. Duff-Jones is not here, she has never been here, and you have never heard of her. Are we agreed?"

It was obvious that we were. "What *kind* of man is he, her husband?" asked the receptionist. It was a question that a proper solicitor would have rebuffed, but she had been helpful and should have her human drama, if my invention was up to it. "Well, as a matter of fact, he's a barrister. A *Welsh* barrister. Mrs. Duff-Jones is not able to get a word in edgeways. That is one problem. The other is—" (I leaned across the desk and whispered) "his extraordinary demands. Only too prevalent, I'm afraid, among members of the bar. Disciplinarian in their daily lives, and needing to compensate by indulging in masochistic fantasies at home. I must say no more, but she refused to join in, of course. I'm told the equipment is quite medieval."

I hoped she'd got her money's worth. With luck the rumor would get a mention in *Private Eye*—Ginny's ex-husband was a pompous sod.

Ginny was in room 17 on the second floor; private bath, television, small fridge for drinks, and meals available from the service restaurant on the ground floor. It should be a comfortable prison for a few days. After she'd let me in, Ginny sat on the bed and stared at me. She didn't say anything; I'd expected an earful.

"Is it all right?" I asked, for something to say. I went to the win-

dow and looked out, keeping to the side, behind the yellow velour curtain. Outside, traffic screeched and honked in the street below.
There's something brightly aggressive about springtime London that
makes me wince; what suits Paris has our gray and dusty metropolis
looking like an elderly dowager attempting a knees-up. Which reminds me . . .

"Are you upset about me hitting that creep?" I asked.

Ginny stirred on the bed, smoothing her dungarees along her
thighs. She always wears jokey or sporty casual clothes. I can't imagine her in a formal dress. "Of course not," she said absently.

"You were complaining that I'd become nasty and brutish."

She got up from the bed, came over, and put her arms round my
neck. "You did OK, Ivanhoe," she said.

"*Ivanhoe?* Couldn't you update me a few centuries?"

"When you start looking and acting like a late-twentieth-century
man, I'll think about it," she said. "But maybe I wouldn't like it
anyway. Who knows?"

"What the fuck *is* a late-twentieth-century man, tell me?"

"Someone who plays today's games."

So, I thought, in spite of all the assault course of activity I'd taken
on, all the energy expended, all the dangers confronted and obstacles
(so far, touch wood) overcome, I still come over as yesterday's man.
Do I care?

"You mean, who plays cricket in a crash helmet and body armor?
No thanks. If that's what I've got to do, I'll stick to yesterday. As
long as I've got people to share it with."

"People?"

"You."

Ginny sighed. "You said 'people.' There may come a time, dear
William, when I'm no longer able to be one of a crowd. I may be
going to be difficult."

"Oh no!"

"Oh yes."

"But not yet?"

She tugged my hair at the back. She looked into my eyes, and I
was overcome by desperation at the thought of losing her. "You're
crazy, don't think of it, after all the time we've had together . . ."

She closed her eyes and put her mouth up. It smiled. Then it said, "Not yet."

How long does it take to sign an affidavit? The thought surfaced from time to time as we paused between bouts in the hotel bed. It was a long session. It had to be a long affidavit. I hoped they'd think so, down in reception. Ginny wouldn't let me go, kept pulling me on top of her, encouraging me with little gasps and cries, though I didn't need much encouragement; I thought the bed would break. At last we fell into stillness; panting, exhausted. After some time I looked over the bedclothes.

"It's still daylight, thank God."

I got myself disentangled; struggled up and into the bathroom. It was mind over matter, all the way. I got into my clothes; Ginny lay in the bed looking as girls are meant to look when justice has been done: flushed and smug. I sat on the bed; leaned over her; stroked her cheek; kissed her.

"I've got to go."

Then I remembered the blue raincoat. I collected it from the back of the chair where I'd thrown it. I hadn't even looked at the pistol yet. I reached into the pocket and took it out. It was a small Walther automatic, quite old, but in apparently good condition.

"Look at this!"

Ginny heaved herself up, and lay back against the pillows. She watched as I slid out the magazine, worked the slide to extract the loaded cartridge.

"Just the thing for your handbag."

"Not bloody likely," Ginny said firmly.

"Keep it unloaded. You could give someone a fright if you needed to. Remember to slip off the safety catch—here—to make it convincing."

"I suppose I could do that," she conceded.

Then I had to go. "It was a proper send-off," I said in her ear as we had a final hug. "I can't wait to get back."

"Mmmm," she said, not looking at me. "William . . ."

"What is it?"

"Oh nothing. Just goodbye."

"I'll ring you from France."

"All right."

"I'd better go. Don't forget to lock the door after me."

"Of course. One other thing . . ."

"Yes?"

"Why was it Struther, without a final S? And not Struthers?"

"Ah. Well, you see, there was a young lady called Struther, who was fond of a bit of the . . ."

"You're right. You'd better go."

I remember her face as I left. She wasn't smiling. Odd.

MORAL
SUPERIORITY

If the one side through a general moral superiority can intimidate and outdo the other, then he can make use of the surprise with more success.

—Clausewitz

The car ferry, a stranded whale, disgorged me from its rumbling iron belly at seven-thirty on the Thursday morning at Le Havre. I had the Webley tucked up under the driving seat and was a little nervous in case there should be a spot check but, as usual, French customs waved me through with hardly a glance, and within minutes I had left the smog and stink of Le Havre's oil refineries behind and was on the autoroute, heading southeast for Paris. The toytown farms and villages of Normandy flashed past the windows of the big Citroën and, not much more than an hour later, I was on the outskirts of Paris, dueling with local drivers on the *périphérique*. The women are the worst: sitting poised and motionless behind the wheel of a tiny turbo-charged speed-striped silver Renault or Fiat, elegant as tropical fish in their tinted glass aquaria, enormous sunglasses aimed only at the road ahead, they rocket ruthlessly at their destinations, scattering the males like autumn leaves. Do the men complain? Not much they don't—resigned glances and hardly a toot. *Je vous en prie, madame!* And she sweeps past without a nod, without even the shadow of a smile. Tough as old boots under all that gloss, your belle Parisienne.

I knew the hotel where Loewenfeld was staying—well, I'd heard of it, to be precise. La Tour Blanche, just off the Champs Elysées, famously discreet (or discreetly famous), where VIPs who dislike publicity can disappear when they want to conduct a little private business, or pleasure, or both. Gentlemen of the press know not to waste their time trying to penetrate those portals—the door is guarded by ex-sergeant-major commissionaires without, and a reserve force of hall porters within: the reception desk is a mine of misinformation designed to cause maximum embarrassment and confusion to any newspaper rash enough to rush into print.

The nearest I'd come to patronage of this establishment was to eat at their adjoining restaurant—their *Feuilleté de Foie Gras* is, well, OK. Definitely. I resist the temptation to say more—just try it for yourself. If you have a sympathetic bank manager. But as for staying in the place, no, never. I enjoy marble bathrooms, thick towels, and silent service as much as the next man, but a glance at the Guide Michelin—six thousand francs a night (breakfast extra)—put it promptly out of mind, in spite of *jardin intérieur* (no dogs). Anyway, I've no need for that kind of privacy. When I go to Paris on my own, I tend to slum it in a little hotel in the rue de Seine, down in the Latin quarter where, for once, economic virtue and preference are in harmony—I like the atmosphere.

So that's where I fought my way, edging and barging by turns through the milling murderous traffic. Just round the corner from the hotel there's a small garage with about twenty parking places in the basement, and I got the car in there and out of sight without delay—the English plates were an obvious giveaway, and I intended to use taxis from now on. I reached under the seat for the Webley, slipped it into my overnight case, locked everything else in the boot as your streetwise city dweller had better, and collected my parking ticket from the office. Then I emerged from the gloom of the basement garage into the bright Paris sunlight, pausing in the entrance to let my eyes readjust, and to scan the street.

What did I expect to see? Well, nothing, unless the opposition had got a lot more professional. I had been prepared to be tailed from London, had worked hard to be last across a large number of traffic lights, and had driven through a multistory car park to shake off anyone following, but I never had any hint that anyone was. I thought I was on my own, at least for the moment, though I had to assume that they'd catch up with me sooner or later, if they wanted to. I stepped out into the street, walked briskly to the hotel, and presented myself at reception.

"*Ah, M'sieur Warnair! Il me donne grand plaisir de vous voir! Comment allez-vous?*" cried Madame, a small, sharp-eyed, pigeon-shaped lady of some fifty summers. And, doubtless, winters as well. Though it might suit hoteliers to exist only in summertime.

Civilities exchanged, I took my key and climbed the barely carpeted stairs to the second floor. My room was at the back of the building, with a small window into an internal light well—better, I always think, than a view of the street with its shrieking, sleep-destructive traffic. A thin sliding door opened into a tiny bathroom, windowless and unventilated, unless you count a mysterious round hole in a corner of the ceiling, black inside and jagged round the edges as though gnawed by some giant rodent to whom it was home. The bath was for dwarfs. But the towels were clean. A French bathroom, in short. The room itself was supplied with a brown varnished wardrobe and table, and two upright chairs; the walls were papered with a forceful design of puce and yellow roses arranged in festoons against a black background; the double bed was equipped with a long hard sausage of a pillow and coarse white sheets. I sat on it, resolving not to start counting the roses. Home sweet home. For the next few days, at least.

There was a telephone by the bed. I looked at it, thought for a moment, and then picked it up. Might as well get on—there wasn't likely to be a better time than now.

Madame's voice answered, "*Allo?*"

I asked for an outside line, and dialed the number Edward had given me—555-1433.

"La Tour Blanche." With a voice like that, it was a good thing she couldn't see me, sitting on the bed in these low-rent surroundings. I asked if Loewenfeld was, by any chance, available to speak to me.

"*Un p'tit moment, m'sieur.*" She would inquire. She would be called, I decided, Chantal, and have wrists like wrens' legs.

"M'sieur Warnair?" Ah well, all good things come to an end. This was a male voice, smooth and professional, a member of *La Direction*. Loewenfeld had left a message, it seemed, in case I should telephone today. He would be back at the hotel by five, and would be delighted if I were to join him there, in his suite, for afternoon tea.

Afternoon tea—for God's sake! Were we to discuss attempted murder over the tinkle of teacups? Was the man mad? Or did he calculate that civilities could more easily be maintained in an aroma of orange pekoe? He had a certain style, I had to admit that.

"*Faites-le savoir*," I said, "*que j'accepte. Avec plaisir*," I added clumsily. Puts a strain on the soldierly simplicity, this sort of thing.

"*Entendu. A votre service, m'sieur.*"

There had to be some exclamation that would fit my feelings but, at the moment, I couldn't think of it.

"Mr. Warner! How very kind of you to come. Please!" And Loewenfeld ushered me into his apartment with a graceful sweeping gesture. How very popular I was in Paris! Everyone so pleased to see me!

Or so I was meant to believe. I trekked through the knee-high carpet to a small round marble table, where two chairs awaited our tête-à-tête. Oh no, I wasn't taking any chances. I'd ordered a taxi by telephone, leapt straight into it from my hotel door, and kept a close watch on passing traffic, ready to duck if any suspicious-looking cars drew up alongside, windows sliding open like gun ports. They didn't. At La Tour Blanche, I waited for the commissionaire to open the taxi door, and was in through the entrance with such speed that I was promptly fielded by a pair of hall porters suspecting unauthorized entry. My visit explained to reception, and apologies on behalf of the porters tendered and accepted, I asked that a taxi be ordered for six o'clock as I expected to have finished my meeting by that time. Only then did I allow myself to be led to Loewenfeld.

He was as bronzed and as full of genial intent as I remembered, if not more so. We sat at the marble table in front of French windows which gave onto a balcony overlooking the *jardin intérieur*, in which green shimmering willow trees hung over a circular lily pond. Fountains glittered in the sun. A white-coated waiter brought a silver tray—China tea, with slices of lemon, and Limoges porcelain cups. I thought of my room in the rue de Seine. Well, that's more like real life, I told myself, down there among the students and intellectuals, poor but honest. Whereas all this is the wages of sin . . . Keep talking, Warner. Keep talking . . .

Actually, Loewenfeld was doing the talking.

". . . been taking decisions that should have been referred to me," he said. "With the most unfortunate results. But, of course, I accept full responsibility, and so far as apologies are of any use . . ." He left the sentence there, leaning toward me with an expression that was certainly intended to be apologetic, his eyebrows raised, waiting for my response. A man like him, I thought, a man in his position, moving in a world constructed around his will, that sort of man hardly knows how to be apologetic, has no need of it. In which case, he's doing a good job.

"I heard Singer ask you for instructions, on the telephone, before your two gorillas arrived at the factory to deal with me," I told him bluntly. My words startled the Limoges teacups, which echoed them nervously: such gaucherie belongs in the society of mugs, they seemed to protest.

"But," Loewenfeld said, "but, my dear Mr. Warner, although I quite see how you received that impression, what I actually did was to give instructions for informing the *police*. Because you had, you will agree, been found looking at confidential papers in our office in most suspicious circumstances. That was a quite natural reaction on my part, I think. It was Singer who substituted the two men who, as I understand, may have had the intention to assault you."

"With a knife. A somewhat final kind of assault."

"I am prepared to take your word for it, since I know only what Singer has admitted. In any case, I make no excuses for what was entirely inexcusable. Some more tea?"

"No thanks."

"A biscuit, perhaps? I could send for some cucumber sandwiches?"

I looked at Loewenfeld, who met my look with a slight smile. He could have been enjoying himself. Or simply doing his best to be pleasant. It was impossible to tell.

"What's going to happen to Singer?"

"He has, of course, been removed from any further involvement in security," Loewenfeld said. "But I am reluctant to dispense with him altogether, in spite of what has happened. He is, as I am sure you found for yourself, technically brilliant, and a great asset in that respect. I think, Mr. Warner, that what happens to Singer must ultimately depend on you."

Sack the bastard! "I see," I said, "I'll have to think about that."

"It's in your hands," Loewenfeld said, nodding gravely.

Other questions were rising to the surface, things that Edward had been unprepared to discuss. Details . . .

"You're asking a lot of me, to forget all that's happened," I began.

"I'm afraid so, yes, I know," Loewenfeld said with a sigh.

"If it wasn't for the fact that Edward Dundas is an old friend, and would be seriously embarrassed, his career wrecked . . ."

"Is that what he said?" Loewenfeld leaned toward me, suddenly intent.

"Yes, of course," I said, surprised.

"Yes . . . yes. Yes, I *see* . . ."

"What? Isn't that right?"

Loewenfeld fiddled with his teacup, his first sign of less than perfect assurance. I watched, wondering what had stirred him up and whether he would tell me. I could put the pressure on (he'd more or less admitted that) if I wanted to. He was very anxious to get my cooperation in hushing all this up—that was obvious. Well, he would be, wouldn't he? A valuable technological lead to be preserved, as Edward had said—*if* that were true. If not that, then *something*—there had to be some pressing, logical reason behind the whole thing. *Something big!* Had to be. Was what Edward had told me *big enough*?

Loewenfeld had been watching me, and now he put down his cup, sat back in his chair, put the tips of his fingers together like a lawyer, and said, "I see you are not satisfied."

"Of course I'm not. Neither you nor Dundas have told me anything, in effect. Except in generalities so broad as to be practically meaningless. And in return for that, I'm supposed to take a vow of silence on a whole series of events that ought to be referred to the police. I'm asked to do this by a supposedly responsible company chairman who has a lot of money at stake, and a senior civil servant who has a career at stake. There's some hint of an altruistic or patriotic motive for all this mayhem, which is keeping British industry ahead of the competition and up with the front-runners, but it's all too vague to be convincing, and in any case I don't believe that people do this kind of thing for that kind of reason. It's not that I'm an obsessively law-abiding citizen, or that I can't see the need for cover-ups in some circumstances for some particularly good reason, or I wouldn't be here now—but no such reason has yet been given. So I'll say this. Yes, I'm prepared to cooperate, but only if you're prepared to be open with me, and tell me precisely what's going on. So—*are* you?"

Loewenfeld had begun to nod halfway through this, and continued with increasing frequency to the end. "Quite right," he said, as soon as I'd finished, "quite right. A perfectly reasonable attitude. I have to say that I think Dundas made a mistake in not taking you into his confidence. If I had had the opportunity to discuss this with him first . . . But he came to see you in a great hurry in case, by delaying, he should be too late. You will not hold it against him, I hope."

"What I *hope* is, that you will now . . ." I said impatiently.

"Yes."

Could I have heard him right?

"In strictest confidence," he said.

Loewenfeld rose smoothly to his feet, and his economy of movement reminded me of the photographs in the Protoplastics entrance lobby—skiing, sailing, images of a man in control of himself, accustomed to accomplishment, powerful in the effortless manner of carnivores, mind and body in perfect, purposeful combination. You could not be in the same room without being aware of the force contained in him: it radiated from him, raising the hackles and stifling the will. I don't reckon to be susceptible to that kind of thing, but I had to admit that it was, well, hypnotic. Foxes can make birds fall out of trees by simply sitting down, and staring.

I roused myself—what was he doing now? Closing the windows! A stagy gesture, indicating that secrets were about to be imparted. Oh, come *on*! Take more than that to make *me* fall off *my* perch, Loewenfeld, old fruit.

"The Ministry of Defense . . ." he said, impressively.

Oh no! Not any longer! I'd been through all that—decided it was a dead duck, a dramatic distraction. The stuff of endless paperbacks, television serials, films in which middle-aged ex-public schoolboys searched in upper-class accents for the rotter in their ranks, tossing suspicion back and forth like playing cricket with a live grenade. No, no—I wasn't buying any of that. Real life had a more ordinary, less neurotic explanation. Sex, money, things like that.

". . . could not be discovered by looking at each drawing in isolation but, taken as a whole, a risk of exposure, a security leak, that could not be avoided and so had to be accepted. We were therefore asked to advise them at once of any possible security lapse, so that appropriate action could be taken."

Was it possible? If appropriate action meant what Loewenfeld seemed to imply. In dear old fuddy-duddy, democratic England?

And in any case, did it fit the facts?

"But surely," I said, "it doesn't fit, does it? The *timing* . . ."

"There," Loewenfeld said, "I am afraid I cannot help you. My knowledge is limited to our end of the matter. We did what we were asked to do, and were never told, or expected to be told, of what action was taken, or when. We were simply glad to have the contract."

That rang true, all right.

Loewenfeld had the air of a man who has said his piece. He sat, no longer looking at me, but through the window at the shimmering green trees and the glittering fountains, drumming his fingers and thinking, it was obvious, of the next meeting to come, if there was one, or, if not, perhaps of *Feuilleté de Foie Gras*. I wasn't going to be asked to stay on and have some, that was clear enough. The interview was over. It only remained for me to say yes or no to the request for cooperation.

Even the telephone bells at La Tour Blanche have a subdued, respectful quality. Loewenfeld crossed the room to answer it.

"It is reception," he said over the instrument. "Your taxi has arrived."

"I'll be right down." But I didn't move.

He returned to the table, sat down again, and gave me a questioning look. I ignored it, and said, "Why didn't Dundas tell me this?"

"Oh," Loewenfeld said easily, "against all his instincts, would you not say? Protecting the government, his masters, as a good civil servant should?"

Perhaps. But it didn't matter much, not at present. I'd decided what I'd do for the present.

"All right," I said. Then, realizing it was essential to be convincing, I added, "I appreciate the trouble you've taken, and I'm sorry if I spoke rather abruptly earlier on. But what you've told me has made all the difference. Nothing like hearing it from the top, of course."

Nothing like the best butter, either. Loewenfeld looked pleased with himself, either with pride at a neat piece of storytelling, or from genuine relief at securing my cooperation. I was pleased at having bought some time and (I hoped) safety. Everyone was pleased—for his own covert reasons. If there had been an official communiqué, it would have been described as "a successful meeting." Genial smiles and warm handshakes completed the similarity. Loewenfeld walked me to the door.

Then: "Ah!—I almost forgot," he exclaimed. "Wait one moment, Mr. Warner, please!"—and he disappeared into the adjoining room. I waited, warily. Did he ever, really, forget anything? I opened the door and stood in the opening, in case what he had forgotten was called Kalashnikov; or words to that effect.

Nothing so crude, of course. It was a card, printed with a familiar scene: a long, low Bordeaux mansion, posing behind a perspective of row upon row of staked-out vines. Curling copperplate script informed me that I had been presented with the image of Château Gravillon, Appellation Saint-Estèphe Controlée. An address, telephone number, and a name or names were printed at the bottom of the card, but I didn't want to look. I was afraid of what I might see, and it was too much, too much . . .

"Dundas tells me you are on your way to Bordeaux," I heard
Loewenfeld say, "and as I shall myself be there over the weekend,
I hope you will accept an invitation to visit us. Perhaps we may even
do a little business together, though you may be among those who
find our style of wine a little harsh. But, please, agree to come and
give us the benefit of your expert opinion, at least. Will you come?"

Oh, it couldn't be worse! For this, I myself might commit frightful
crimes!

"Do you own it?" *Just good friends, perhaps . . .*

"We Dutch have had interests in Bordeaux for almost as long as
you English, you know. It is a tradition that I intend to continue,
and so, last year . . ."

I hate his smiling confident face. And his too-perfect, textbook English.

"Shall we say tomorrow evening, at eight? We will have dinner,
of course. Would a plain roast chicken meet with your approval as
a suitable background for our wine tasting?"

Oh, unbearable invasion of my territory . . .

"That," I managed to get out, "sounds perfect. Thank you."

"Not at all. It is *I* who has to thank *you*, Mr. Warner."

And I hate his inevitable courtesies.

I seethed along the corridor, down, down, down in the lift, and
across the entrance lobby, leaving a trail of scorched carpet to mark
my fiery passage. If the taxi had ignited when I got in, it would
have seemed only natural. I seethed all the way back to my hotel,
and up the stairs to my room. My simple honest lodgings. My coarse
white sheets and vociferous wallpaper. And the simple dinner I had
planned—bread and cheese in the room, because of the risk of going
out. There isn't a restaurant in the hotel. This grotty, godawful
hotel that I've stayed in quite contentedly so many times before.

The evening stretched ahead of me, dull and dinnerless.

20

NIGHT ATTACK

It is only seldom that circumstances favor the expectation of a successful result from night attack.

—Clausewitz

B
ut, of course, one should always consider a problem in the round. I thought I'd left Loewenfeld convinced that I'd accepted his story, true or false. Whichever it was, we had arrived at a state of truce. I felt sure that nothing was likely to happen until we met again at Saint-Estèphe, though I intended to take every possible precaution before nibbling at *that* neatly proffered piece of cheese. After what I'd already been through, *il faut bien!*

A state of truce. What made this more than likely was the Loewenfeld psychology, or rather, my reading of it. Maybe what he'd told me was true. But if it wasn't, if he was just feeding me a line to keep me quiet, happy, and contented until I turned up at his version of Dracula's castle to receive the coup de grace along with the *poulet rôti*, and afterward be put through the Mouli grater and poured into the Gironde, so conveniently to hand—if that, or something like it, was his plan, how very pleased with himself he must be. Oh yes, he might well be smiling about it at this very moment. People who are very very clever have this one fatal flaw—they get to be so impressed by their own cleverness that they forget other people are not always very very stupid.

And another thing. If, as was quite possible, he'd had my taxi followed from La Tour Blanche, it wouldn't look right for me to spend the evening crouched in a hotel room when all around were the restaurants and cafés of Paris, that world center of gastronomy, not a man of my known alimentary sensibilities, oh no, of course it wouldn't. I'll go further: by not asking me to stay to dinner he may have been setting up a kind of *test*—to see if I would behave normally and take myself out to dinner, in which case I must have believed his story and felt myself to be at risk no longer, or *not*, in which case get him at once, before he has time to do any damage! Yes, it could be more dangerous *not* to go out to dinner!

So, out I went.

Sitting in the Brasserie Albert, still slightly stunned by the flexibility of facts, I ordered a dozen escargots and a carafe of *rouge maison*. I've been here before, over the years, and it never changes: a big, bustling place, all brown-stained mirrors and paper tablecloths, hot and smoky, but full of life. Commercial travelers with their coats slung over the backs of their chairs, gabbling figures at each other; a sprinkling of tourists and tarts; but mostly students and intellectuals, real or self-styled, arguing or sitting in solitary behind books or folded newspapers.

My carafe and a basket of bread arrived on the table with a thump, delivered in passing by a whirlwind waiter in a striped apron, his balding forehead shiny with sweat. I poured myself a glass of wine and sat back, crumbling bread and surveying the crowd. Never fail to amuse, for a while at least, these scenes of the Latin quarter, so foreign in one way, so familiar in another. Always reminds me of those Simenon novels, of Inspector Maigret waiting patiently, slumped in such a café as this, for a suspect to appear, studying the comings and goings and growling from time to time for another glass of *vin blanc* . . .

"*Pardon, m'sieur?*"

I looked up—the waiter had arrived with my escargots.

"Oh, er, *merci . . . je n'ai rien dit.*"

The sizzling dish with its twelve occupants, the special tongs, the little pools of hot garlic butter to be mopped up with the white crusty bread, and the bitter mouthfuls of red wine . . . Thoughts of Loewenfeld were fading fast.

It was past nine, and the place was practically full. I had chosen to sit under one of the rusting mirrors with my back to the wall, where I could watch the door. It stood open, and occasionally a cooling draft reached me from the street outside, now lit by pale pools of light thrown by antique cast-iron streetlamps, except where a neon sign or shop front cast its glaring brilliance. It was hot, too hot, and the two other occupants of my table mopped their faces frequently and helped themselves from the water jug. A pair of American tourists, middle-aged and gray-haired, he with a resigned expression on his large, amiable face, she with pursed lips and eyes fixed on her plate, round which she slowly pushed a number of pieces of lettuce and salami sausage with her fork.

"Well, don't eat it, dear," he said patiently.

"Oh now, see here, if they expect us to *pay* for this . . ."

He looked across at me, but I kept my eyes fixed on the door, beyond the empty place opposite where I was sitting. Whatever her problem was, I didn't want to hear it. Why do they come to places like this if they hate it so? Why not stay in the good old US of A, home of the hamburger? I wasn't going to arbitrate, no siree. Trouble was, they probably had me identified as English. Any moment now, he's going to lean across and say . . .

All right, then—let's play I'm a Frog, starting . . . *now*!

I'm sitting here, relaxing after another day's intense intellectual activity at the Sorbonne, where I'm professor of, er, the Literature of Existentialism, yes, that's it. I frown at my last existing snail, dip my bread in its essence—come on now, give it the full lines-across-the-brow bit, really *heavy*, that's better. Am I getting it across? Well, give it time. I stare at the door because I am expecting one of my students to appear, she of the swinging blond ponytail and large lunettes, behind which her eyes are, yes, fiercely intelligent. When she arrives, dropping into the chair opposite, we will immediately continue, in low but intense voices, our discussion on the value of Meaningless Action, yes. Later on, lunettes off in my apartment, she will bend her fierce intelligence and supple body to a joint ex-

amination of this thesis. Meanwhile, I'll reinforce my heavy frowns
with a little muttering . . .

"*L'acte gratuit, ah oui, ça y est . . .*"

"*Parlez-vous Ahnglais?*"

Oh shit. But time's still running and I can score points for pre-
varication. (It's against the rules to tell a direct lie.)

"*Comment?*"

"He doesn't speak English," she said wearily, "none of them do."

"I said—*parlez-vous Ahnglais?*"

I sighed. Game over, only four and a quarter minutes, not good.
But wait!

A girl was approaching. Not what I had in mind, no. Definitely
not. A goblin creature, wearing a black T-shirt and jeans that were
so tight they pulled her skinny knees together so that she seemed
to hobble rather than walk. Short black hair, cut like a boy's. Iden-
tifiable as female only by a certain minimal bulge of hip and tapering
thigh. She carried a small blue denim kit bag by its shoulder strap.
And was approaching the vacant seat in front of me. Which she now
indicated with her free hand.

"*C'est libre?*"

Black eyes stared at me out of a white face.

"*Oui—je vous en prie,*" I said, making a welcome gesture. Saved!

"*Bon.*"

She slid her bag under the chair, and sat down, glancing at the
two tourists, who had fallen silent, and then back at me. Aha, I
thought, a few Froggie phrases and we'll keep the game going for
hours yet.

"*Il fait chaud.*"

"*Assez chaud, oui.*"

"*Vous êtes étudiante?*"

"*Oui, c'est ça.*"

"*A la Sorbonne?*"

"*Pas tellement.*"

She turned round to look for the waiter, caught his eye, and called
for an *omelette* with *frites*.

"*Aux fines herbes?*" the waiter called back. She nodded. A regular
customer, *évidemment*. Not exactly chatty, but if I could keep it

going, the Yanks didn't seem prepared to interrupt. Five minutes
now, and counting.

I asked her what she was studying.

"*La sociologie, surtout.*"

"*Et la politique, bien sûr?*"

"*Ooph, oui, un peu, comment tout le monde. Et vous, qu'est-ce que vous
faites à Paris? Les vacances?*"

"*Non, non, je travaille, je suis marchand de vin. En route à Bordeaux.*"

"*Ah bon? Mais vous êtes anglais, si je me trompe pas?*"

She's blown it. Still, with pauses, I'd worked it up to well over
six minutes—not so bad.

"Yes," I admitted.

Out of the corner of my eye, I saw the large American face taking
aim in my direction.

Well, of course, the Americans turned out to need nothing more
than a reassurance that they weren't being swindled and, after I'd
agreed that some of the dishes in this place were somewhat minimal,
but pointed out that, by Parisian standards, so was the price, they
paid their bill and departed to catch Notre Dame by moonlight, or
floodlight, or whatever. And I was left alone with my new ac-
quaintance, the goblin girl.

She accepted a glass of my wine, said that she was called
Dominique, and that her studies had taken her to London among
other places. So she spoke English, then? A leetle. And what were
these studies, exactly? She finished a mouthful of omelette, and
replied briefly that they were to do with the spread of *embourgeoisement* in the present century. Oh wow, I said, or something like that—
sounds fascinating. Her black eyes crackled sardonically at this: she
didn't offer to elaborate or explain, but went on eating—must be
used to that sort of response from all but about one in a million, I
decided. And now, I asked, the research into *embourgeoisement*
continues apace? Yes, she said, it does—even, perhaps, at this very
moment . . .

Ah. Well, she's got the fierce intelligence I specified, if she lacks the swinging blond ponytail. Plus a dry sense of humor. Better than sitting here all by myself.

I decided to grant another dozen snails the gift of immortality, and ordered some more red wine to go with them, plus a slice of chocolate gâteau for Dominique. The evening flowed onward with a spiky but entertaining badinage. She wasn't giving much away, and I soon decided that she wasn't so much a serious student as a girl who liked to give the impression of being one, so as to join in the scene. Perhaps she got part-time research work, something like that, to keep her going, but she didn't say, and I didn't ask—if she liked to keep a little mystery about her life, that was her affair. Girls often do, I've found.

Two lots of coffee followed and, suddenly, it was eleven-thirty. Time, I thought, to go back and get some sleep, and I called for the bill.

Where are you staying, Dominique asked. At a little hotel nearby, I told her.

And you're going to Bordeaux tomorrow? You have a car?

I knew what was coming, then—a lift to Bordeaux. Yes, that was what she would like, she was at a loose end, and she had a friend down there she could stay with, near the sea . . .

Well, why not?

OK, I said, you're on. I'll meet you tomorrow morning at—

Wait, she said, listen!—and came round to sit beside me on the banquette. She took my arm. *What's this?*

Listen, I haven't anywhere to stay tonight, she said.

I know all the evidence is against me, but no, it wasn't what you're probably thinking, it wasn't like that at all. Well, it doesn't *have* to be, does it? It was hot in there, you see, and I'd drunk a fair amount of *rouge maison*, and was simply feeling in favor of humanity or most of it, I mean generally benevolent which, I'd like to point out, is my normal state of mind when not under threat. Not that benevolence is any sort of bar to, prevents one from feeling that, what I mean is . . . Oh, forget it.

The real point is that she wasn't my type, that ought to be clear enough by now. I could see from the startled expression on Madame's face as she let us into the hotel that it was clear enough to her. I imagine she'd always thought of me as one of her more conventional clients, not at all the sort to pick up students, especially skinny ones.

But once over the threshold into the light of the hallway, there was nothing I could do about it. I didn't even attempt to mutter "friend of my daughter's" or anything equally limp and useless. I just gave her a brazen "*Bonsoir*" and marched the goblin up the stairs and into my room. None of her bloody business, anyway, I told myself, since all her rooms have double beds in 'em. And a liter or so of *rouge maison* agreed I had reason.

I sat on the bed, feeling stupid. The goblin ranged about the room, making her tour of inspection. Silently, the question formed in the space between us: how were we to arrange ourselves?

I'd vaguely imagined Dominique sleeping in a chair, or at the foot of the bed in some way, producing a well-worn sleeping bag from her denim sack, perhaps. No, it seemed she didn't have one. And the chairs were quite impossible. Oh what the hell, we'd have to share the bed, then.

A sound of energetic toothbrushing from the tiny bathroom, a flushing of the loo, more ablutionary noises, and she emerged, wearing pants and her black T-shirt, stained, I noticed, from the heat of the day. Was she going to get into bed wearing *that*? Yes, she was . . . into the bed we were to share, a double certainly, but only just . . .

I suddenly felt very bourgeois about the whole thing. I'd become accustomed, over the years, to certain, well, standards—simple things mostly, like clean sheets, good soap, down pillows, and the touch of female skin, smooth and faintly scented. Then, of course, there are other sensual delights I associate with bedrooms—the hiss of champagne bubbles, obviously, the melting mouthful of potted shrimps, the dancing glow of pink candles . . .

I reached for the telephone. Look, I said, this bed is smaller than I remembered, I'll see if Madame has another room available for you. Don't worry, I'll pay, no problem, I've enjoyed talking to you . . .

"*Ah non!*" Dominique exclaimed, "*c'est pas la peine! D'ailleurs, je suis pas fatiguée, moi. Je pensais à . . Tu n'es pas d'accord?*"

No, I wasn't. But she didn't wait for my opinion. She just whipped off the T-shirt and pants, and was in bed, watching me with her sharp black eyes. It was easier to comply than to argue. I padded wearily to the bathroom to prepare myself.

The best example of specious pontification that I know of occurs in a book-made-film called *Zorba the Greek*. It goes something like this:

ZORBA: There is one sin that God will not forgive.

EARNEST STUDENT OF LIFE: What is that? Tell me, Zorba, please.

ZORBA: When a woman calls you to her bed, and [*impressively*] *you . . . will . . . not . . . go!*

It's a perfect cop-out for the macho male, of course. But God can't have said it, or He would have prevented the frustration of his command by equipment failure, *les ennuis mécaniques*.

"*Tu peux pas?*"

"*Trop de vin. Trop de fatigue. Trop de tout.*"

"*Ç'arrive. Bon, alors, c'est à moi, hein?*"

"Don't bother . . ."

Too late—she'd thrown back the sheet and got to work—her small hands and pointed tongue took control of the situation with breath-taking skill and speed.

Nothing I could do, then, but lie back and think of England. More specifically, of Claudine, and Ginny, of Ginny and Claudine—anything but the ghastly reality, the grotty room, the goblin girl . . . oh *God*.

"*Et voilà!*" she said with satisfaction. "*Allez-oop! Sauce caviar.*"

The bedsprings sounded a melancholy discord as she sat back on her haunches to view the conclusion of her work. They sounded as I felt.

Perhaps we could get some sleep now.

• • •

I did ask myself, in the period of calm and returning sobriety that followed, why she was so anxious to please.

There were several possibilities. Perhaps she'd developed her art as a way of competing with more attractive girls and was getting in a bit of practice. Perhaps it was her method of paying her way. Perhaps she *liked* me—that was the most sobering thought of all. I shuddered, and fell asleep.

Some obscure discomfort, some distant alarm bell ringing in my subconscious, woke me some hours later. It was still dark, the only illumination coming from the light well outside the small window, the walls of which reflected some of the glare of the city beyond. It took me a few moments to remember where I was. And with whom. I turned my head to look at the neighboring pillow.

The girl lay facing me, her white face a ghostly oval in the dim light. Her eyes looked back at me, black and watchful. Again I felt a twinge of apprehension. There was a feeling in the room, something slight and undefinable, but it set my nerves on edge.

Too much to drink, of course. Or some edginess to do with this girl: some people have that effect—you can't get really relaxed when they're in the room. Why is she looking at me like that, measuring me up? She seems to record everything I do. Her eyes glittering like black glass, like camera lenses.

There's another possibility that I haven't considered, not seriously, because it's too ridiculous. Still . . .

I got out of bed.

The girl said immediately, "*Qu'est-ce que tu fais?*"

I didn't answer, but crossed to the door and tried the handle. It wasn't locked. I turned the key, and tried the handle again. All secure. I took the key, got back into bed, put the key behind my part of the pillow.

"*Qu'as-tu?*"

"*Rien. Bonne nuit.*"

Two can play at this game, I thought, and lay with my face turned to hers, my eyes open. After a few minutes, she gave a faint smile and turned away from me. I waited until her breathing settled into a regular rhythm. Then I, too, slept.

A PERFECT
EXPLOSION

It is quite possible for such a state of feeling to exist between two states that a very trifling political motive for War may produce an effect quite disproportionate—in fact, a perfect explosion.

—Clausewitz

This is it, then. The end of the road.

And you deserve it, I told myself bitterly. Only an idiot, beset by the perils that had swirled around me like shark soup for the past week, would take himself off for dinner in a public place *and* bring back an unknown girl to share his hotel room. Oh sure, I had risen above my alcoholic stupidity long enough to be aware of a sense of danger and to lock the door. Not much use, that, when the danger was already inside the room. It all seems so obvious, now. *Was* obvious last night, really. But I just couldn't believe that this skinny girl constituted a threat or that, if she did, I wouldn't be able to handle it. I should have remembered that, since the invention of gunpowder, size is no guarantee of security.

What annoys me most is that it's *my* pistol she's aiming at my head. I can see the tips of the big blunt bullets, nestling like silver Easter eggs in their cylindrical steel housing. Those ancient bullets, carried by my father into battle, and back again. Aimed, all those years ago, at German youths now become old men. Waiting, now, their turn to swing into the firing position and, at the snap of the hammer, to be projected at bone-shattering velocity through the rifled barrel and across the length of the bed at me. Me, their lawful owner!

Of course, they may be dud. If, instead of oblivion, I survive to hear a click, I must hurl myself out of bed and at the girl before she overcomes her surprise enough to pull that heavy trigger a second time. It takes some pulling, that trigger: that's why, for a more accurate shot, you're supposed to cock the hammer with your thumb before taking aim. If you do that, the trigger pull is reduced to a slight pressure, just enough to release the hammer, the cylinder having already been revolved to the next chamber in the process of cocking. She hasn't done that, she hasn't cocked the thing. Her index finger is going to have to take the strain of raising the hammer against its spring *and* revolving the cylinder, all while holding her aim. With her small hands, it'll be difficult. The pistol is bound to wobble. Bound to—maybe I'd better rush her now, before she thinks to cock it . . .

"*Tu as peur?*"

She's running her finger down the side of the barrel and licking it, tasting the gun oil. Damn the girl—she's *enjoying* this! The sensation of power . . . Her black eyes are alive with it, her mouth has a suggestion of grim humor at the corners, she's watching me as she did last night, studying me as if I were a laboratory animal . . . Here we have a typical specimen of bourgeois man; see how he reacts to the stimuli we shall provide: first, a *female* . . . ah, curious, that, but interesting; now, we shall induce the sensation of *fear*, and see what . . .

"What the hell are you doing? Put that thing down! Dominique— put it down, be careful, for God's sake—it's loaded!"

The pistol wavers slightly. Her eyes behind the muzzle stay fixed on my face, noting every detail of my expression but, yes, the muzzle itself is moving, has shifted off aim, is no longer the mouth of doom, the black hole to the next world . . .

Phew!

I was out of bed in a flash and had taken the Webley from her: I stood over her, shaking with the anger that was already replacing fear.

"That was a bloody stupid thing to do!"

She shrugged. *"C'était une expérience intéressante, non?"*

"Non. And whatever it is you're studying, I don't want to be any part of it, have you got that? *Tu comprends?"*

"Oh, oui, comme tu veux. Mais, tu es un grand émotif, quoi!"

Easily upset! Well, she didn't know the full situation, or she'd know just why I'd been so upset, but as I couldn't explain it to her, she'd just have to settle for the simple answer to her experiment, which was that people don't like having loaded pistols pointed at them. Which, I added, should have been obvious enough without actually having to go through the motions.

She shrugged again, and said that live experiment was *"plus mémorable"* than theory. I let her have a few home truths about the streak of chilly detachment in French intellectuals. Then, as I was still standing over her, holding the Webley and with no clothes on, it seemed a good idea to get back into bed and ring for some breakfast.

"Je m'excuse, hein?" Dominique said, climbing back in beside me.

"Oh, forget it." Nothing I said would make any real difference: her apology just meant, probably, that she'd remembered I was giving her a lift to Bordeaux today. But she was a tough little thing, all right—I wouldn't forget those gleaming black eyes over the pistol barrel for years, if ever.

Still, there was one good thing to come out of it—she couldn't be working for Loewenfeld. If she had, I wouldn't be sitting here ordering breakfast. I wouldn't have to worry about that anymore.

Breakfast came, brought by a small dark girl not unlike Dominique, who managed to bring the tray in, set it on the brown varnished table, and let herself out again, all without once looking at the ill-assorted twosome in the bed. I was grateful for her professional tact, and also for the croissants that had been provided along with fresh bread and strong coffee. A large gulp of coffee, and I was prepared to like the French again. After all, every nation has its problem citizens—we have football hooligans, they have crackpot intellectuals. Of whom my neighbor here was evidently one. And that reminded me: what was she doing in my suitcase, anyway?

She *always*, she said simply, looked in people's suitcases. Also their desks, cupboards, chests of drawers, and in the pockets of their clothes. Not to steal, of course—just to look. She also read their letters, whenever possible.

"*Mais pourquoi?*" I asked indignantly.

To know all about them, she replied in a bored tone, as though it was the most obvious thing in the world for anyone of inquiring mind to do.

The difference between my own discreet, code-bound Claudine and this strange, direct, disconcerting creature was, I realized, virtually infinite. I was also, I realized, beginning to be fascinated, in spite of myself. What was the purpose of all this invasion of privacy, these rifled desks and searched suitcases? What was she *really* a student of, exactly?

"*Tu veux connaître mes études?*" she said, with her grim little smile. "*Bon, alors. Il y a la philosophie, la physionomie, la physiologie, la phraséologie, la phonologie, la phénoménologie, la phrénologié—*"

"All right, all right—"

"*Peut-être la photographie . . .*"

"All right, *si tu ne veux pas me dire, ça y est!* Couldn't care less, anyway." And I got out of bed, shoving the breakfast tray aside, and stumped off to the bathroom. Never again, I promised myself, never again will I fantasize about French students. I'll dump this one in Bordeaux, and that's it.

In spite of no discernable makeup, she took a long time to get ready— so long that I said I'd go and get the car out of the garage and come back to collect her. She said she'd meet me in the hall. I left my bag with Madame, behind the desk, hoping that the temptation to go through other people's baggage hadn't spread to hoteliers—the gun was back in it—and then made for the front door. Nothing was said apart from Madame's polite expression of hope that I had slept well, but I felt her speculative gaze on my back as I walked away. After last night, she'd have to find some other box to put me in.

I was still feeling sore with Dominique, still hearing her mocking voice in my head, and might have been excused for walking straight out onto the street without remembering my now habitual precautions. But I didn't: as if on autopilot, I paused inside the door to check what I could see of the street, now bright in the morning sun.

Fortunately. Because, moving quietly up to one of the pavement tables under the awning of the little café opposite, I saw a figure I recognized. He was wearing the same crumpled gray suit that he had worn when we last met—if that's the right word for what happened in the Victoria and Albert Museum. As I watched, he spread out a newspaper and disappeared behind it in the best tradition of sleuths and spies, almost invisible in the shade. A few seconds later, and I'd never have seen him. No, I wasn't being dealt all dud cards this morning.

I stepped back a little from the door, hoping that the shine on the glass would be enough to hide me. What was he there for? And what was I going to do about it? There was another door to the hotel, but it also opened onto the street, a few yards further along. While Gray Suit sat there, he commanded the field—I couldn't get to the car without being seen.

And shot at? No, I didn't think so, not here in this busy street. If Loewenfeld had ordered that, it could take place more conveniently later, in the open between here and Bordeaux or, more likely, at his château this evening. Gray Suit was there to watch and follow, to make sure that I arrived at whatever place had been appointed.

And that, no doubt about it, put a huge dent in Loewenfeld's bona fides—irreparable, I'd say. I could think of various reasons for Gray Suit being put on my tail, but they all added up to the same thing: Loewenfeld had decided not to trust me, and the war was on again.

All right. Nothing I could do about it here, in Paris. But I could let Gray Suit follow me, all innocence, to some battlefield of *my* choosing, and there ditch him, leaving me to arrive at Loewenfeld's unaccompanied. For I didn't intend to miss that rendezvous: there were questions to be put, and, deprived of his support force, Loewenfeld was going to find it a lot more difficult to avoid coming up with some genuine answers.

Yes—in spite of a bad beginning, this could turn out to be my lucky day.

First, though, I had to disencumber myself of the girl—this change of plan made it impossible to take her with me to Bordeaux.

She would make a scene, certainly, and, as I couldn't explain my reasons fully, it would be best to cut it as short as possible. I decided to get the car first, and deal with her when I got back to the hotel.

I moved out into the street, not looking across at the café, and walked at an easy, relaxed pace toward the garage where I'd left the car. I imagined Gray Suit's eyes following me over the top of his newspaper; imagined, also, his pleasurable anticipation of the day ahead, culminating in a satisfying settlement of the score between us. I could still see his face as my knee struck him: his memory of the event was no doubt clearer still. Beware, beware, I told myself— this man is mightily motivated . . .

Ten minutes later, I was back outside the hotel, having abandoned the Citroën in honking traffic to dash inside and collect my case. I had hoped the girl might still be upstairs and could be ditched without a confrontation, but no, she was at the desk, talking to Madame. Hurried handshakes and farewells took place, and my case handed over. Then I made for the door again, the girl following with her bag.

At the door, I said my piece. A change of plans, not going direct to Bordeaux after all, sorry, but there it is. Another time, perhaps.

Dominique looked at me, said nothing, and then pushed ahead of me, through the door. Oh good, she's off then—could have been worse. Prefer to have parted on good terms, but if she chooses to take it like that . . .

Godammit, she's getting into the car! By the driver's door that I'd left unlocked for that couple of minutes! Has thrown her bag into the back, and is squirming across into the passenger seat!

"*Ecoute, Dominique* . . ."

"*J'y suis, j'y reste,*" she said firmly.

"*Mais je t'ai dit* . . ."

She didn't care how long I took to get to Bordeaux, she said. She'd nothing else to do, she would accompany me. That was it.

I had to throw her out or drive off. If I threw her out, she would certainly scream, shout, attract crowds, the police . . . I would have trouble explaining the situation, in particular the gun in my suitcase, which she wouldn't fail to tell everyone about. The bitch . . .

I drove off.

• • •

Gray Suit had equipped himself with a white Ford Escort: I thought
I'd caught a glimpse of one parked up a side street as I walked to
the garage, trying to make a mental note of everything I saw in case
it should be relevant. He'd had plenty of time to reach it while I
fetched the Citroën. I watched him in the mirror now as we made
our way out of Paris and on to the autoroute to the southwest. He
had put on dark glasses, but I felt sure I had him identified, the
more so as the kilometers passed and the white Ford stayed in place,
three or four cars behind. He was alone in the car, and this reinforced
my theory that he was there to follow and not to attempt a
confrontation.

The presence of the girl would, in any case, have been an
undesirable complication if a confrontation had been planned. Well,
it would be her own fault if she got mixed up in any trouble—I'd
tried to leave her behind, but she wasn't having it. I hoped she'd
have the sense to run for it if things got tough. Though, on past
showing, she might just choose not to—she's a weird, unpredictable
little thing . . .

Once on the autoroute, speeding smoothly southward at a steady
eighty to ninety mph, she made the first move to restore peaceful
relations.

"*Tu es fâché?*" Her tone was more curious than apologetic.

"*Oui.*" Well, why shouldn't I be annoyed?—she's given me two
headaches already this morning.

She turned her head toward me and, I supposed, was giving me
a long look of inspection, but I didn't glance back, I kept my eyes
ahead, on the road.

No need for supposition about her next move, however, which
was to reach across and unzip me. The Citroën swerved on the road.

"Oh no, *no! Lache-moi, j'en ai assez, tout ça!*"

"*Tu veux pas?*" She sounded astonished. "*Mais, tous les copains . . .*"

I told her I didn't want to know what the chums liked, or when,
or by whom—I *didn't* like, no thanks. And I'll zip *myself* up.

"*Bon, alors, comme tu veux. Mais, c'est pas normal, quoi!*"

She slumped back into her seat, and began to whistle tunelessly,

drumming her fingers on her knees in a syncopated rhythm. Tap
tap-a-tap, tap tap; tap tap-a, tap-a, tap-a-tat; tap, tap, tap-a-tap-a-
tat, tap, tap, tap-a-tat tat . . .

Some minutes of this, and I found myself beginning to wonder
if the other thing might not be preferable, less distracting, at least.
I had to occupy my mind with some subject of compelling interest.
Such as French accident statistics. *Normal!* Jesus!

Or why do villains prefer Fords? This tiny scene in the driving
mirror, the rectangle of white bonnet (last time it had been red)
topped with the dazzling glass of the windscreen, glimpsed only for
a second or two as the car dodged out to pass a slower vehicle and
then disappeared back into the cover of the traffic stream, keeping
the distance—all this had become practically routine for me during
the last couple of weeks. Would I ever see a Ford again without
checking the occupants? So, why Fords? Pete told me once—and
he should know, he sees plenty of them in his local—that your
professional villains, the long-term *real* professionals, that is, choose
to appear unremarkable in all things. They're well dressed, often in
casual style, moderately tanned from holidays in Spain, speak quietly, and don't throw their weight about. Makes sense. Also makes
sense that they should drive the ubiquitous Ford. It's the Flash Harry
big spenders who tend to get caught. Gray Suit, now—nothing flash
about him, no gold chains or Rolex Oysters. A bit scruffy, but the
general impression, solid and professional. I caught him by surprise
last time, but he won't let that happen again. Beware, beware . . .
Must stop saying that. Makes me nervous.

We came off the autoroute at Saint-Jean-d'Angély, having covered
some four hundred kilometers since leaving Paris. It was after half-
past two, and lunch was late: a picnic would have to do. I bought
some bread, a Camembert, and a liter of red ten-degree Jolis Grains
from a minimarket. Dominique stayed in the car, determined not
to take any risk of being left behind. In fact, for the last couple of
hours, she had sat silent and been no trouble at all. I hoped this
state of mind would last a while longer, as I wanted no interference

or distractions while I decided how to deal with Gray Suit. And the time for that must be soon.

He was still in place, parked further along the street, invisible among the other white cars, mostly Renaults and Peugeots, unless you knew where to look for him. Again, I felt lucky. If I hadn't known he was there, I don't think I'd have been aware I was being followed. It was professional enough. Yes, I'd need my luck to hold . . .

We set off down the N50 toward Cognac. An idea had come to me, a way to stop Gray Suit in his tracks before we got any nearer to Bordeaux. And Cognac, in spite of being world famous, is a quiet little place set in the back of beyond. It's the first real isolation you come to when driving down from Paris. And so I made my plan.

It went like this. South of the road to Cognac, there's a wooded region centered round Saint-Bris-des-Bois where I often stop for a picnic lunch and a breather when driving down to Bordeaux. Little farms and hamlets tucked into clearings in a vast area of forest, crisscrossed by little tracks, and nobody about . . . So, I was leading Gray Suit to a place I'd been to several times before, a field with a view across a valley, facing south, ideal for lunchtime picnics. To get to it, you have to drive up a rough farm track, which leads past the field, through a farmyard, and out on to another road. The plan depended on this track being as rough as I remembered.

Which it was. We bumped along for several hundred yards, until I could see the field ahead. In the mirror, I saw movement behind us, where the track turned off the road—Gray Suit, looking cautiously round the corner of the hedge after us, having stopped his car on seeing the roughness of the track.

Would he get back into the car and follow? It would have been unwise: his Ford had a ground clearance of maybe four inches or so, and he would have to cross ground that my Citroën had only just been able to manage, using the adjustable hydraulic suspension set to maximum height. *That* was my secret weapon—Citroën suspension. Superior equipment should, all other things being equal, decide the day, and I'd chosen this venue to take advantage of it.

Gray Suit had two choices open to him. One was to follow by

car, and probably get stuck or lose his exhaust pipe—I thought he'd
be unlikely to risk it, but if he did, I could drive away and leave
him. That might only get me a temporary advantage, if he managed
to get alternative transport or make a lash-up repair. His other choice
was to follow on foot, and I hoped he might do that, as he didn't
know that the track had another exit. Yes, I hoped very much he
would do that . . .

I drove the Citroën on up the track, and stopped by the gate into
the picnic field. A bend in the track hid Gray Suit from my view,
and the Citroën from his. Perfect.

Dominique stretched herself in her seat, and yawned. I jumped
out, taking the car keys with me in case she had any more surprises
for me, like driving off. I told her to start on the cheese and wine—
I'd be right back.

"*Où vas-tu?*" she said sleepily.

"*Je vais faire pipi,*" I said, forgetting the adult version in my haste.
I didn't forget the Webley in my suitcase, but had locked it into the
boot and there wasn't time to get it out—in any case, I didn't expect
to need it.

I set off at speed along the edge of the field, on the opposite side
of the hedge from the track. The hedge was thick, and set on a high
bank; I was invisible from the lane unless Gray Suit had a notion
to climb it and look over; I hoped he'd be too concerned to see where
the Citroën had gone. The fields were small: I had to climb a couple
of gates before I reached the field adjoining the road where the Ford
should be parked.

And there it was, pulled on to the verge, just before the corner
where the track turned off. I could see the whiteness of it through
the hedge as I climbed the bank. Struggling up the bank a little
further, trying to make no noise, I could see that the car was un-
occupied, and that Gray Suit was no longer standing by the corner.
He must have started up the lane—yes!—there he was, almost a
hundred yards up the track now, walking fast, and keeping close to
the hedge. He had to be swearing. All this distance with no trouble
and now, suddenly, he's lost me.

I was glad, now, that I hadn't just driven on down the track and
left it at that. Apart from anything else, it would have been a waste

of the box of matches that I'd bought, along with the crusty bread and Camembert.

I've never tried it before, of course, but I've always thought how simple and effective it sounds. Let's hope it proves to be so, in practice.

Off with the petrol cap. Tuck a corner of handkerchief in, leaving most of it hanging down outside. Light just the tip of the hanging end. And run like hell!

Then . . .

Nothing.

Doesn't work.

Still nothing.

Better get back to the Citroën and take off, in case—

BOOOOOOM!!!

"Qu'est-ce qui se passe, là-bas?" Dominique asked as I got back into the car, sweating and scratched by brambles, but triumphant.

"Cherche-moi," I replied, getting the car into gear, and sending us bouncing and lurching on down the track.

An old woman in a black dress and floral pinny was standing at the open door of the house as we drove through the farmyard, scattering dust and chickens. She stared at us, and then down the lane at the column of smoke that rose from the remains of the enemy transport. How would he explain *that* to the locals who must, even now, be arriving at the scene? To the police, to the hire company? Yes, that'd keep him *hors de combat* for quite some time. Two-nil, me and Gray Suit.

"Dis donc!" Dominique urged, *"Qu'est-ce que tu as fait, là?"* She, too, was looking back at the smoke, clinging to the back of the seat to steady herself against the jolting of the car.

We had been followed, I explained. But not, I believed, any longer.

She whistled, a long, descending, windy note. *"Une vrai james-bonderie! Ça barde, alors!"* She slid back into her seat, looking at me, I imagined, with a new curiosity. But she said nothing, perhaps because I was too busy at the wheel to have replied to questions.

We reached the road at the other end of the track, and I accelerated away, concentrating on putting distance between us and the Ford's funeral pyre, driving fast but quietly—I didn't want to attract attention with howling tires or by rocketing through villages. After five or six kilometers, we were coming to a crossroads, when I saw a police car approach at speed on the far side, heading toward us. Damn! I slowed. But it turned off to our right, down the road that led to the far end of our track. I breathed again, and smiled. Gray Suit's problems were building up nicely.

Exciting life they lead, these wine merchants, Dominique remarked, gripping the door handle as we swept round corners. Revolvers, car chases, explosions . . .

I realized it was the first time she'd commented on the gun. Not her style, asking questions. But I'd have to say something now. Trouble was, I couldn't trust her to keep quiet, not after what I'd just done. In bringing her along, or failing to prevent it, I'd landed myself with a ridiculous and unnecessary problem, but it wouldn't matter after this evening. This evening, Loewenfeld was going to explain all, but *all*. I'd find ways to make him talk, if it took all night. After that, the war would be over.

Meanwhile, Dominique was right—*ça barde*! Things *were* hotting up—and the best thing would be to drop her in Bordeaux as soon as possible, and say nothing, or next to nothing.

I told her I couldn't explain what it was all about, but she'd probably be able to read all about it in the papers in a day or two's time. Sorry, but that was how it was.

She didn't make the fuss I expected, but then the unexpected was, I'd found, a way of life with her. She took her pleasure in perversity, or however it goes. At least it made for peace, of a sort.

We drove to Bordeaux in silence.

We reached Bordeaux at six, and I had two hours left before I was due to meet Loewenfeld. Time enough—Saint-Estèphe was under an hour away, including spare time for finding Château Gravillon—but not too long, I hoped, to maintain the resolution that was building up in me at the thought of this last, definitive encounter. I was working myself up into a mood of tense determination—reckless-ness, almost. I was going to storm in there and sort the whole thing out, or come out feet first. The destruction of the Ford, in that sudden sheet of flame, those furious jets of black, oily smoke, had given me a feeling of savage confidence. This, then, was the meaning of drum beating, of chants and spear shaking, of all the primitive paraphernalia of war fever—to induce the battle mood. To read about it is one thing: to *feel* it now, quite another. In fact I . . .

Dominique was asking why I'd stopped the car.

Because, I said, this is where you're getting out. Railway station here, buses just opposite, all you need. Adieu, Dominique.

But, she said, but—

I turned to her. I was about to speak, but when she saw my face, she shrugged and reached for the door handle.

"*Tu m'emmerdes, toi!*" she told me loudly.

"Don't forget your bag," I said.

She grabbed it off the backseat.

"*Et bonne soirée.*"

She slammed the door violently, and I drove off.

The car felt beautifully, deliciously empty without her. Jesus, what a creature!

Don't relax! Don't relax! What you need is rage! Cold, unstop-pable, relentless rage! That's how wars are won, how I'm going to win this one.

Boot the car through the traffic. Shove the bloody Frogs aside. Out of my way, you bastards. Agincourt, Salamanca, Waterloo—*souviens-toi!*

I aimed for Château Gravillon.

A GENERAL IN
EARNEST

There is no longer anything which stands in the way of a General who is in earnest about a decision by means of battle; he can seek out his enemy, and attack him.

—*Clausewitz*

A long drive past curving lawns leading to a lake, with swans on it, of course. A dense, dark green hedge screening the brilliant blue of a swimming pool, just visible through an open, arched gateway. The château wheeling into view, long and low, pale gold stone in the evening light, with tall French windows open on to a balustraded terrace, each with an oval attic window above, crowned overall with a projecting cornice made of rows of orange undulating Roman tiles, with a low-pitched roof to match. Single story, in the best Bordeaux tradition. You could call it a big bungalow, if you were a bloody fool, or an estate agent. It's simply beautiful.

It's also everything I'd feared, or worse. I drove through the lengthening shadows of stately trees, over the golden gravel, into a huge courtyard—and I was grinding my teeth all the way, I'm not ashamed to admit it. You must pay the peasants their due for the privilege of living in a place like this—pay them in *politesse* and treat them right, if you want to survive. *Noblesse oblige*—or else they'll arrive to break in your door.

As I'm arriving now. No *noblesse* about Loewenfeld, and the sight of this place has hardened my resolution. Shits are not entitled to live in châteaux.

I braked the car sharply, scoring tracks in the gravel. I jumped out, and strode to the great door, the Webley in my back pocket bumping heavily as I moved. I found a bell push, and pressed it. I banged on the door with the side of my fist. The sound echoed sonorously from the hall inside. Come on, Loewenfeld! Open up! Let's get on with it!

A rattle of bolts, and then the door opened. Loewenfeld himself stood there, two steps above me. He looked over my head, seemed to survey the courtyard before he dropped his gaze and took notice of me. A smile of greeting appeared on his face.

"Ah, Mr. Warner! So you have come—as arranged. I am very glad to see you again. Please . . ."

His voice died away, probably because I had taken the Webley out, and had it directed at his stomach. There wasn't going to be any mock-courteous chat, not this time. I wasn't going to be led into discussing the progress of planting and grafting in the vineyards, nor the opinion of the *régisseur* on this year's *égalisage*, not a chance.

Behind him, the hall was empty. I could hear no voices, footsteps, or other signs that we might not be alone.

"Out!" I said.

"Now, Mr. Warner—"

"Out!" I gestured with the pistol barrel.

He came slowly down the stone steps to my level. And on down, to the gravel of the courtyard. "Where," he asked quietly, "do you propose that we go?"

That was more like it! No outraged expostulations, prevarications, or attempted side issues. No bluff. No bullshit. This mood of mine was getting across to him, as it had to the girl.

"The fermentation vats. Lead the way. No tricks. And I mean it."

He looked at me briefly, nodded, and started across the courtyard. I slipped the gun into my jacket pocket in case someone should see us from a window, but I could still neither see nor hear anyone about the place. It was as I had expected, if Loewenfeld had planned this meeting for the purpose assumed. Except, of course, for—

"Are you planning to assist us with the blending, Mr. Warner?" he asked, in a would-be humorous tone. "If so, I might suggest—"

"Shut up, and walk!"

Except, of course, for whoever was going to do the job for him. I had been prepared for trouble at the front door, my hand on the pistol butt. That had been a risk I had to take. But speed and force were the keynotes of this action—I had to keep up the impetus, and not be overcautious. He who hesitates . . .

"Keep going."

We were approaching a vast, low, stone and cement building with a gabled end and Roman tiled roof, in a classical style that echoed that of the house—the *chai*, where the blended wine is kept in casks for maturing. We passed down the side of it, out of sight of the courtyard now—I felt easier for that. Through a gap between the *chai* and some smaller buildings, we came into a small courtyard with large stone buildings on three sides, like a stable yard. Loewenfeld led on to the building on the far side, and pushed open a pass door in a pair of massive oak portals. Inside, it was almost dark, but I could see tall, rectangular concrete tanks reaching almost to the roof, fitted with valves and inspection hatches like those of a submarine. The fermentation vats.

Loewenfeld turned to look at me, attempting an expression of polite inquiry. It almost came off, but for an increased intensity about the eyes which he could not conceal. He was alarmed, all right. He thought that something very unpleasant might be waiting for him on the other side of this doorway, in the sepulchral depths of this building. He was right.

"Inside!"

He turned, and stepped in through the small door. I followed. It was dark and chill inside, in contrast to the sunlit evening we had left behind. On either side were ranged the giant concrete vats, square and solid, like church towers on parade. Dimly visible in the further recesses of the building were relics of an earlier age of wine making: huge oak presses, abandoned wooden vats and troughs.

Coils of translucent plastic pipe lay ready for use, shining faintly in the light from the doorway like snakes about to strike. No windows, no roof lights, nothing but gloom in this cathedral of wine.

"Put the light on."

Loewenfeld moved to the side of the doorway, and found the switch. A row of bare bulbs hanging from the ceiling snapped into life, making the flat faces of the vats glare white against black shadows above and behind, and reflecting harshly from the stainless steel of the inspection hatches set in the lower half of each vat. Some stood open, the vats empty, waiting for their next load of freshly crushed grape juice. Others were tightly closed, and I could see from the glass-tube gauge on the face of the vat that some of last year's was still waiting for the right moment to go into cask. Many and various are the ways of wine makers.

And the purposes to which their equipment may be put. I swung open the hatch of the nearest empty vat.

"Get in!"

Loewenfeld stiffened. "Now, Mr. Warner!" he protested. "Surely these dramatics are not necessary? Tell me what it is you want, and why you are behaving in this extraordinary way. I ask you to dinner, and you—"

"I know why you asked me here. You've had me followed—that's how I know. Get in!"

"But I assure you—"

"Get in!"

I took a step toward him, the pistol held ready, my thumb on the hammer. He made a gesture of incomprehension, his hands spread outward. He moved toward the vat and its open hatch. But slowly, very slowly.

"Don't try to spin it out in the hope of rescue," I told him. "Your man is probably still at the police station trying to explain his burned-out car. As you'll know, they're very long-winded about that sort of thing, French police."

Loewenfeld had reached the vat, but he turned and stared at me for a moment. Yes, it must have been a bitter blow, because he didn't even try to conceal the full depth of his disappointment. He bowed his head, and gave a great sigh of resignation. Then, head and shoulders first, legs and feet pulled in last, he struggled awkwardly into the vat.

I looked in after him. Some light filtered down from the loading hatch on the top of the vat high above him. He stood, his chest level with the opening he'd climbed through, brushing off his English-style twill trousers and lightweight dogtooth sports jacket.

Don't bother, Loewenfeld—worse than dust is to come.

"Listen," I said, through the hatch. "I'm now going to connect this vat up to a full one and start the pump that'll make the transfer. What will it take? An hour? or two?—before you have to start swimming? How long can you swim for, Loewenfeld—round and round this vat? In the dark, because I'll have secured the top hatch, of course. How long, even if you're a good swimmer, before your head comes up against the top of the vat, with the level still rising? Think about it! Because that's how long you've got to tell me the truth, the whole truth, and nothing but. You'd better believe it. I'm going to shut this hatch now, and connect up. Bang on it when you're ready to talk. Until then—goodbye."

"Wait!" Loewenfeld shouted, his voice making the vat boom like thunder. "Wait! I think you ought to know that . . ."

I wasn't going to listen, no, not yet. Give him the treatment, first. Then, maybe, I'd get the truth out of him, with wine up to the neck and lapping at his chin. *In vino veritas*—that seems to have become my speciality, first with Trevor, and now this.

But would he talk? And if not, would I go through with it, right to the end?

Yes, of course I bloody well would. Well, probably. Have to see how it goes. He must think I've gone off my rocker, and that's all to the good. It's going to get very unpleasant in there during the next hour or so, with the rising liquid, and the fumes, and the cold, and the dark. He's got to be some kind of superman if he doesn't crack.

Right then. Up the ladder, secure the top hatch—*clang*—but leave the valve open, otherwise we'll get an air lock and the wine won't flow. Down the ladder, drag over some hose and the portable electric pump—never done this myself, but I've seen it done often enough. Now, which grape variety shall we treat him to? The boards on the vats say Merlot, Cabernet Franc, and . . . ah yes, Cabernet Sauvignon—that's it, of course. Nothing but the best for Monsieur Loewenfeld. Five thousand liters here for him to swim in. *Salut!*

I got busy coupling up the hose. It all went together easily enough: I checked the connections and they looked tight and secure. It only remained to open the valves, and switch on.

Should I give Loewenfeld a last chance to talk before I switched on? No, better to let him have it, up to the knees at least, before asking how he was liking it. The shock treatment.

I opened the last valve, and switched on the pump, which whirred into life. The fat, translucent, reinforced-plastic hose shook itself and turned dull purple as the wine filled it. I crossed to the vat to check the connections again, hearing a muffled shouting from inside above the whine of the pump—Loewenfeld getting his socks wet. I'd give it half an hour, I decided, keeping an eye on the outside gauge to see how far the level got up in that time. Half an hour nearer the truth. Maybe the *last* half hour before the truth.

Then the pump stopped.

Oh, how I hate goddam machinery—just when you want it . . . But maybe the plug's fallen out.

I turn to inspect it.

I see immediately what the trouble is.

Not mechanical. But trouble, sure enough. Big trouble.

A figure stands inside the doorway. An unknown figure, tall, broad shouldered, clad in dark blue cord trousers and jacket. Wavy dark hair almost to his shoulders, making him look, with his strong features and long nose, like the reincarnation of some famous figure—Robespierre? Who might, on occasion, have worn black gloves, but would not, certainly, have manifested himself holding the pump's power plug in one hand and a large automatic pistol in the other.

Where's the Webley? On a ledge by the vat, where I'd put it while I wrestled with hoses. Too far. I think I'll stand very still. Robespierre holds his gun as though he has no doubt which end bullets come out of.

He nods, acknowledging the wisdom of my decision, and moves toward me, away from the door. A second figure appears, silhouetted against the light, a meager outline this time, not so threatening. But more familiar.

Yes. Well, I'd had my suspicions, on and off. Said so, didn't I? But I couldn't believe that Loewenfeld would take the trouble to put *two* separate tails on me. And once I'd detected Gray Suit, I'd assumed that my suspicions were unfounded.

Wrong, my dear sir, wrong.

Also unfair. I had calculated the probability, and acted on it, as one should. Now the improbable had turned up. Next time, next time, I would . . . No. Better not think about that.

So this is why Loewenfeld put on that display of disappointment when I told him Gray Suit wouldn't be turning up. To string me along until his reserves arrived.

As they have now, all two of them, him and her.

"*Re-bonsoir, Dominique!*" I jest.

She takes no notice of me, but moves to her partner's side. From the way she does this—the dancing sway of her hips in the tight jeans, the tilt of her head as she glances at him, a hint of submission in her stance—I perceive that he is her guiding star, her *raison d'être*, the light of her goblin life. Poor sod.

Well, I can see it. Those looks, added to a force of personality that is already apparent, without a word spoken.

He speaks to her now, a short, crisp instruction. She unslings the denim kit bag from her shoulder—that same denim kit bag which traveled with us all the way from Paris. She opens it, and I realize now what it is—would have realized before if I'd had the sense to search it as she searched my case. Her *trousseau professionel*.

Out comes a pair of thin black cotton gloves—like his—which she puts on. Then she takes out a second automatic—also just like his. Making like master, very touching. They could shop wholesale, these two.

And now she points her automatic at me, not forgetting to release the safety catch, while he goes to Loewenfeld's rescue, keeping well out of the line of fire. Again I feel the disconcerting stare of those glittering black eyes, taking my measure like . . . well, let's face it, I could have recognized it before, but failed to make the connection, yes, like an undertaker.

The hatch is open, and out comes Loewenfeld, the bottoms of his trousers stained purple and dripping on to the concrete floor as he stands there for a moment, regaining equilibrium, if not poise exactly. Difficult to be poised with your shoes full of grape juice. He looks at me once, briefly. With a look like that, once is enough. He squelches to the door, which should be funny but, in this particular context, is not. He steps through the door and is gone.

Curious, but I suddenly feel quite lonely without him.

Dominique speaks. Shall I find a place, Jean-Louis? she asks. She likes to say his name. Her voice is intimate, eager to please, the voice of teacher's pet. He doesn't reply, but moves to a position three yards from me, raises his automatic to take over from her, and then nods.

She goes off into the back of the building, and I watch her looking from side to side, checking it out. What's wrong with right here, I wonder. No, I don't ask. I'm not complaining. Anywhere, anytime is better than the here and now as far as I'm concerned.

She's coming back—the place has been chosen. Two automatics suggest that I march. *Allons-y!* Thirty paces into the unknown depths I march. Then I am made to turn left, turn right. A small doorway. Inside, a small room, disused office or storeroom. Entirely empty— no furniture, no windows, bare concrete walls, a single bare bulb hanging. Stand there—face the wall!

Look, what's all this about. I . . .

A pistol jabs me in the back, his by the force of it.

I stand, facing the wall, facing a blankness of old whitewash. Is this, is this, is this it? Without warning, last words?

My back is burning, nerve ends shrieking, anticipating . . .

But it's his voice again, nothing worse. Watch him, he says, while I get the money.

D'accord, she says. And Jean-Louis—

Hein? he says impatiently.

Don't be long.

Relief exploded like a Christmas cracker, with jokes. Very professional, this Jean-Louis: no money, and the job's off, everyone go

home. Perhaps Loewenfeld forgot to get it. Or bank manager said
sorry, no can do, your account already overdrawn. Ha, ha.

Then reality was back in charge again. I had maybe ten minutes
to stop joking, start thinking, and get the hell out of here before
Jean-Louis returned to finish the job. Ten minutes, at the most.

I didn't have a lot going for me. Face to the wall, in a bare room,
with a large automatic pointed at my back by a girl anxious to impress
her homicidal boyfriend. Suppose I simply turned round and walked
up to her, talking softly, to take the gun away as people are sometimes reported as doing—would she shoot? Probably yes, from what
I knew of her. Academic anyway—I knew I couldn't do it. Not a
long drawn-out approach like that. Not brave enough.

But I might just manage a sudden rush. My legs might just get
me that far before going on strike. Especially if I could gain some
advantage, however minute, to increase my chances. It helped that
Jean-Louis didn't want me shot before he'd been paid—or he'd
already have done it. She wouldn't be anxious to shoot unless she
had to.

I must look for that advantage. Starting now.

Maybe whoever handles the laws of probability agrees that I had a
raw deal last time. Because Dominique has just told me to turn
round.

Why? I ask. Not to seem too keen.

She tells me again to turn round. Louder.

I do. I see why. It's like this morning, but with her own gun this
time. As before, she has it gripped in both hands, aimed at my head.
The black eyes gleam at me over the sights.

She doesn't ask if I'm scared. Doesn't need to.

All the same, I'd rather be facing her. It may be illusory, but I
don't feel quite so helpless. I feel I've got a chance, if only . . .

Now you know, she says.

Know what?

What I am studying, she says.

Oh? What, then?

A pause before she says, relishing the word, *La mort* . . .

• • •

She's a self-dramatizing little creep. I don't believe she's ever actually shot anyone, yet, or she wouldn't indulge in all this drama. But she may well have watched Jean-Louis do it. I'm not going to risk rushing her, not yet.

Suppose I try to establish a relationship? That's what the experts recommend in a situation like this. Ask her what it's all about—there's bound to be some rubbish rationalization she'll be delighted to spout at me. A lot of crap about death the ultimate truth, or destabilizing the bourgeoisie. She's that sort.

But no—*there isn't time.*

What else then? There must be something I could do. Something to give me a tiny advantage, a fraction of a second to help me on my way across the floor, to slow her aim. *But what?*

Wait!

Maybe *this* will work . . .

Dominique . . .

Tais-toi, she says.

No, but listen, I don't understand, you're scaring me stiff, you can't mean you're *really* going to shoot me, I've done nothing. It doesn't make sense to me at all. I've never met a girl with a taste for violence, a taste like yours. The girls I've known can't bear to see someone cut their finger, to see a finger bleeding. And, at home, my wife never lets me clean the shotgun in the house. I have to do it in the garage, she says she hates the smell of gun oil. It smells, she says, of death.

It isn't going to work.

I'd got it all in, too—taste, smell, finger, gun oil. And not too obviously, I thought.

Never had much faith in subliminal suggestion, anyway. Too bloody clever by half.

Nothing for it, then, but a straightforward charge, and hope she misses. I look across at her, trying to note vital detail. What was it Sergeant MacWhirter was always going on about? "Try to catch 'em off balance, laddie! That's worth an extra man to ye." What could I do about that, except to let all my fright show on my face, give her what she wants? Ah yes—she likes that: she's giving that grim little smile of hers. And a tiny nod of satisfaction.

And while I watch the satisfaction grow on her face, I also see her left hand leave the pistol.

It *is* going to work . . .

That, too, was just like this morning, just what I'd remembered and was hoping for. Her finger stroked the side of the pistol, and then passed to her mouth—the taste of violence . . .

I had my hands ready against the wall, and launched myself across the room with every muscle contributing its last ounce of thrust. Three strides took me there. My right arm swung upward against hers, knocking the pistol off aim, and my right knee went into her stomach. I saw her face seized with panic, heard the hammer fall with a click. Oh yes, she tried to shoot me, all right. I think she would have missed.

But the point remained academic, because she'd forgotten to work the slide, and there was no cartridge in the breech. Safety catch off, as I'd noted, but nothing up the spout. I'd have a long laugh about that—later.

At the moment, I was occupied with grabbing the gun off the floor, where she'd dropped it in order to clasp her midriff with both hands. My knee had caught her fair and square, and I'd not intended to claim any brownie points for chivalry—it had been the best I could do. She'd fallen against the wall, and then slid down it into a kneeling position. I had time to check the gun, load it, and take a few deep breaths.

What to do next was the question. It felt like much longer, but I guessed that about five minutes had passed since Jean-Louis left. He'd be back soon, and I'd better be ready—*his* automatic would be as loaded as any automatic could be.

Dominique was stirring, and I warned her to stay on her knees, but there was clearly no risk of her doing anything else for some time to come. She lifted her face, and an expression of appalling venom blazed at me.

"*Salaud!*" she gasped, "*Jean-Louis va faire t'affaire à toi, bien sûr!*"

"Well, we'll have to see about that, won't we?" They're catching, these dramatics.

I started for the doorway. Just as I reached it, I heard what sounded like a distant shot. I spun round and looked at Dominique.

"*Comme ça!*" she said, breathless but triumphant.

Jean-Louis would be back any moment, then. Or Loewenfeld, but that seemed a lot less likely. Either way, I'd better get a reception ready.

I glanced once more at Dominique, still on her knees, with both hands clasped to her stomach. *Hors de combat* for the next crucial minute or two, I decided. But in case she was putting it on, I ought to tie her up. But there was no time, and nothing to do it with.

I settled for wedging the door from the outside with a barrel stave, and then looked hurriedly for a place that would give me some cover and a field of fire toward the entrance. I found it almost at once—a small stack of new oak barrels with one standing alone; heaved a foot farther from the stack, there was room for me to crouch behind it, resting my elbows on the top, steadying Dominique's automatic, which I trained on the light rectangle of the pass door. The range was thirty yards—too far for a reliable shot with an unknown pistol. But I was in the shadows, and Jean-Louis or Loewenfeld wouldn't see me at first. Twenty yards, I decided, and I would open fire. Unless I was detected before that. Twenty yards should do it.

I stayed motionless behind the barrel, looking down the wide alley between the towering ranks of the great vats, waiting. No cover there, no escape. As ideal for an ambush as the rocky gulch in a Western. A double thickness of Limousin oak to protect me. Will that, in practice, stop a heavy-caliber pistol bullet? Maybe splinters will fly off, oak splinters, as in wooden warships when cannon balls strike. Most casualties caused that way. Hard stuff, oak—splinters sharp as steel. Hearts of oak are our men. How long have I been here?—thirty seconds, probably. But already my hands are sweating, my grip on the gun getting slippery. Hope he comes soon.

Ah!

Footsteps on the gravel, faint but distinct in the silence. Still daylight out there, through that lighter rectangle of the pass door.

Come on then, Jean-Louis or Loewenfeld, whoever you are! Come on!

The doorway darkens.

He's here . . . and by the outline, it's Jean-Louis.

Hold your fire, hold your fire. Wait for the range to close. Twenty-five yards, and closing. He hasn't seen me. Let him get to fifteen yards, then, and make sure of hitting him if he ignores my warning.

"*JEAN-LOUIS! EN GARDE! IL A PRIS MON TIC-TAC.*"

Shit! Sounds as though she's out of the room and—

A crash of sound, and an oak splinter appears by my elbow. Jean-Louis, alerted, has opened fire.

The pistol jumps in my hands. Missed! Finding no cover, he's dropped to one knee. *Keep firing!*

The place echoes with the din of shots, the whine of flying bullets. Why can't I hit him? At this range, it should be easy. I can't remember how many these things hold, is it seven? Or nine? How many have I got left? Hard pounding, this, gentlemen, but we shall see who—

He's down.

I saw him thrown backward, arms flung out.

Is that it?

He's not moving. I think that's it.

I waited, keeping the pistol trained on him, not daring to come out of cover. The echoes died away, but my head was still full of the terrifying noise, my ears ringing with it. Jean-Louis didn't move.

I heard a sound behind, and turned my head quickly. Nothing was visible at first, but I then became aware of the shape of Dominique's small figure, lying on its back on the concrete floor, feet toward me, a few yards away. A piece of wood—the barrel stave

I'd used to wedge the door—lay near her right hand. Her head moved, and I heard the sound again. It was like a sigh.

Jean-Louis still hadn't moved. Looking more carefully, I saw that his hands were empty. I then saw his automatic lying some feet away where it had fallen as he went down. It was surely safe to stand up now—but I still had to force myself to do it, to get up and out from the protection of the oak barrel. In a nightmare, this was the moment when Jean-Louis would rise swiftly to his feet laughing satanically, and produce a *second* pistol from his pocket.

But it was very clear, as I got near him, that Jean-Louis would be making no miraculous recovery. One eye was still open, but the other, where my bullet had struck, had ceased to exist. The back of his head was a mess. I looked away in a hurry, fighting back nausea, and returned to where Dominique lay.

The black eyes looked up at me from the white face. I took off my jacket, rolled it up, lifted her head, and slipped the jacket under. Her breath was coming in short, painful gasps. One of Jean-Louis's bullets, missing me, had hit her in the chest as she came up behind me. It looked bad.

"Ecoute, ce n'est pas grave, je vais téléphoner à l'hôpital."

She gave a slight shake of her head. *"Pour aller en prison? Non. C'est pas la peine."*

I had to do it anyway, whether she wanted me to or not. I stood up. She moved her right hand from her chest, slowly, and made a beckoning gesture.

"What is it?" I asked, bending to hear her reply.

There was blood on her gloved hand. She moved it to her mouth, licked the index finger with her small sharp tongue, carefully. The black eyes watched me watching her.

"Sauce . . . tomate," she whispered, and made her grim little smile.

I straightened up, irritated by these histrionics. The waste of time—didn't she realize . . . I'm going now, I told her. Won't be long, just hold on.

The mouth continued to smile. The black eyes stayed watchful. But didn't move when I moved.

That's how you know.

• • •

Loewenfeld was lying on his face in the hall, shot through the back of the head. Farther down the hall, I found a small office fitted with a wall safe. It was open, and empty except for a few papers. Everything of realizable value would, of course, be in Jean-Louis's pockets. Incredibly careless of Loewenfeld to open his safe with a man like that waiting in the hall—but even very very clever people get careless when they're beside themselves with rage. Skirting carefully round his body on the way out, I noted that my main emotion was one of annoyance that Loewenfeld had told me nothing before getting himself shot—not one single new piece of information. Perhaps it was because I was in a hurry to get out of there, but that's how it was.

It was different when I got back to the fermentation shed. Stepping in through the pass door again, I seemed to be stepping into the past, into a moment of time that had been frozen. These two creatures, made to move, until minutes ago with the power of motion, now suddenly cut off from it. Silence is often said to be oppressive, but the stillness of death is much more so: your mind tells you that *these* will not suddenly jump up, shout, run about, take up where they left off—but you don't quite believe it.

I made myself touch Jean-Louis, to get the Webley from his jacket pocket. There was a great deal of money in there. I tried to make as little disturbance as possible.

It was worse getting my jacket out from under Dominique's head. After I'd done that, I carefully wiped the automatic I'd taken from her with a piece of cloth I found in her bag, in which it had obviously—from the oil stains—been wrapped. Then, holding it with the rag, I pressed it into her right hand, in its blood-stained glove. I placed it where it might have fallen, and removed the barrel stave. She watched all this, smiling sardonically. Or so it seemed.

Then, carrying the Webley and my jacket, I got back into the Citroën, and drove away. There was no one about—Loewenfeld had seen to that. No one had come to see what the shooting was about—it had all happened indoors, and could hardly have been audible off the estate. I regained the main road, passed a girl on a moped, two old men chatting in a gateway, a carload of dusty laborers. The sun had set, and night was closing in. After three miles, I began to shake, stopped the car, and went to be sick in the hedge. It took that long.

ANXIOUS SAGACITY

Thus even in the midst of the act of War itself, anxious sagacity and the apprehension of too great danger find vantage ground, by means of which they can exert their power, and tame the elementary impetuosity of War.

—*Clausewitz*

So this is how it feels.

Well, I don't think I've ever been so naïve as to imagine a mood of flag-waving triumph. There may be cheering in the streets, but it isn't the weary soldiery who do it. They don't feel like going hoorah—they just want to assure themselves that they're still alive, to check the scratches, drink some coffee, find a soft bed, and sleep, sleep, sleep.

And try to forget the haunting horrors that have been added to their stock of images.

Another hotel room, as small as the last, but plumbing new depths of dreadfulness in the way of wallpaper. No matter—I was interested in nothing but the bed. No, I wasn't dining, but I'd like some coffee in the room, if that was possible? It was.

I absorbed some coffee, and then rang down to reception and gave them Ginny's number. One call home would have to do, and Ginny, imprisoned in her hotel room, was most in need of news. Claudine wouldn't worry if she didn't hear from me for another day or two—I'm normally a bad communicator when I'm away on my travels. And if there was a crisis—if I was picked up by the police, or if Gray Suit caught up with me—Ginny would have to get in touch with Julian, and tell him to open the envelope I'd left with him. That wouldn't give the latest developments, but it listed the people involved, and the CID could take it from there.

While I waited for the call to come through, I finished the coffee and tried to make a cool assessment of the situation. It was difficult. My stomach was knotted, struggling to control emotions that kept trying to break out and swamp me—morbid, useless memories and sensations. Perhaps, in time, with practice, you get hardened? I doubted it.

The bedside telephone chirruped, and I picked it up. Madame Struther was on the line. Madame Struther? Oh yes.

"Hello? Ginny?"

"Oh, I'm so glad you've called," came Ginny's voice. "I've been worried sick. I thought you'd have rung me last night. I can't sleep, and I've read all my books already. Oh, William, this is awful, being shut away like this. Time goes so slowly, you seem to have been away for ages. Where are you? What's happening?"

"I've been to Paris, had a meeting with L., who strung me along and asked me to his place at Bordeaux. There was another meeting this evening, and I'm now in a hotel down here. I'm going to move on tomorrow, when I've got my breath back."

"Oh good, marvelous, so you're on the way home? Can I leave here now? You've no idea how awful it is."

"No, Ginny, no, you mustn't, not quite yet. Listen—"

"Oh shit. What's happening then? Is it all still going on?"

"Listen, Ginny. Just *listen*. There's been a bad scene here. Very bad indeed. I'm all right, but L. and two others are not. When the news gets through, the opposition may make a last attempt to stop me, and that gives me one last chance to wrap the whole thing up, once and for all. So tomorrow, I'm going to go to ground in the little gray home in the west, you know where that is. It'll be all right, don't worry, I'll be on my home ground, and I've got friends there I can call on if necessary. I'll ring you every evening about six-thirty, from the café. But listen—and this is important—if I haven't rung by, say, ten-thirty at the latest, ring Julian, and tell him to *open the envelope*. Got it?"

"William!"

"Did you get that?"

"Julian's to open the envelope, yes, I've got it. But William—"

"If you haven't heard from me by ten-thirty P.M."

"Yes! *I heard you!*" Ginny was screaming down the phone. "But what if you—"

"Ginny, I've got to go, I'm sorry, I can't say any more now. Look, I'll ring you tomorrow morning before I leave here. And don't worry—it'll be all right."

I had to ring off, I just couldn't take any more emotion. I lay back against the pillows, thankful for the sudden silence. Once upon a time, it seemed a long time ago, I'd been a happy optimist. *It'll be all right*. But today, it had so nearly been all wrong. It could so easily have been me, now, lying there, unseeing, inanimate, settling slowly into dust . . .

After eight hours' solid sleep, surprisingly dreamless, I was in better condition, able to think constructively about what would or should happen next. Introspection, that worm in the night, had disappeared at daybreak, and I had no difficulty in munching quantities of bread and apricot jam off the breakfast tray, which lay, loaded with these delights, on my lap. Through the window, I had a prospect of round-tiled red roofs and tall chimney pots splashed with the morning sun; from somewhere down below, cheerful shouting and a warlike clashing of pans indicated that the kitchen was being prepared for the Saturday night siege. Eight o'clock and all's well, was the feeling. That's what sleep and food does for you.

Deceptive, though. Because all was not that well.

Loewenfeld was dead. But that left Singer. And, from what I'd seen of him, there would be no more than a short delay, a brief hiccup, before the Loewenfeld organization got back on its feet and came after me, with Singer in the saddle. It would be the mixture as before, or worse. And, although I'd now collected enough circumstantial data to enable me to put together a theory of sorts, I was still short of the hard fact I'd been trying for. The reasoning that had persuaded me to go it alone still applied. To give in now, after all I'd been through—it was unthinkable. One more effort, I told myself, one last chance to bring the whole thing to a satisfactory and, if possible, creditable conclusion—that was what I wanted. Otherwise, and especially after what happened yesterday, I would be involved in long and embarrassing explanations. Criminal charges even, after the, well, *adjustments* I'd made to the evidence in the hope of keeping the police off my back, at least for the time being. Oh yes, I'd dug myself in deep.

But no point in regrets or self-recrimination, not now. Too late for that. I had to maintain momentum, and finish the job. Plan the last, definitive encounter.

I thought about it until nine. Then I reached for the telephone to bid my trumpeter sound a brazen blast.

It's true, of course. Some people never learn.

"Hello?"

By her voice, Ginny must have had a miserable night, worse than mine. This can't go on. And it won't—not after this last effort.

"I'm alive and well and still in Bordeaux," I said soothingly.

"Oh yes, good, it's marvelous to be able to talk to you again. Thanks for ringing. And William—I want to say I feel very bad about last night. I mean I kept going on about how awful it was for me here, and I must have sounded a proper cow. After you'd rung off I kept thinking how much worse it was for you, I mean *serious*. You sounded dead beat. I just wanted to say I'm sorry. I really am. Are you still there?"

Dear Ginny! "Don't think about it. Waiting is worse than anything, everyone knows that."

"Well, anyway, I won't do it again. So tell me, what's going to happen now? Can I do anything?"

I breathed a silent sigh of relief—had thought it was going to be hard work, but this couldn't be easier. That's women.

"Yes, just one thing, which is to ring Edward Dundas at home—number's in the book. I want you to say that I've got the full story on Loewenfeld, but must talk to him before I take it to the authorities, and would he look through his files so that we can go through the whole thing as soon as I get back. Tell him I'd ring him myself, but I'm spending the weekend at the French house, and there's no telephone there. Got it?"

"Will he help to sort things out?"

"Oh yes," I said. "Yes. I think so."

"I've made a note of all that," Ginny said.

"How efficient you journalists are. Now, about what happens next. I'll get to La Sauvegarde by this evening, and I'm expecting some news, some final details, to arrive there during the next day or two, after which it'll be all clear for me to come home, without bringing a trail of destruction. After tomorrow, I'll ring you every evening, as promised, from the café. OK?"

"What news?"

"I won't know until I get it, will I?"

"I don't like the sound of it. You're into some new crazy scheme. It's going to be risky, isn't it? You've got to tell me—I'm not going to sit here, doing nothing."

I didn't want to get into an argument. So I said nothing.

"William?" Ginny said, insistently.

"Look. Promise me you'll keep everything to yourself until I've got these last details cleared up—it mustn't go off half cock. Promise?"

"No."

"You *must*. I'm going to do this, anyway. If you tell anybody it'll make it more . . . it could make it dangerous."

"Why can't you just come straight back here?"

"I've told you. They'll catch up with me. Anything could happen. I'm now a full-grown disaster area. What I'm planning is the safest thing that *can* be done, believe me."

She didn't reply, but I could hear little sounds of anguish and dissent.

"You must promise me this, Ginny. You just *must*. You don't want to make things more difficult for me, do you?"

There was another silence. "Oh, fuck it," she said. "And fuck *you*. All right, I'll keep it quiet . . . But William—"

"Yes?"

"You're a specious bugger."

"Well, I know that I—"

"Specious. Plausible but insincere. You deceive yourself as much as the rest of us. You say anything, but always do just what you want. I thought you ought to know."

"Thanks."

"You're welcome."

"No, I mean it. I mean, you might not have bothered. To tell me."

"Mmmmm," Ginny said. "Well, I don't know why I do. I often think it would be better if I didn't."

"It's been going on too long to stop now. Hasn't it?"

"I don't know. Anyway, it isn't the time to discuss it. This phone call must be costing a fortune."

"It's worth it to hear your voice. It seems light years since I saw you."

"Does it?"

"Ginny, I can't wait to get back. You *know* that."

"But all the same, you *are* going to wait."

"I've explained that."

"I suppose you have, to *your* satisfaction. Oh I'm sorry, I'm being a cow again. I can't help it, I'm worried. I feel sick with it."

"I'm sorry. I'm sorry I involved you. But you've been so much help—"

"I don't think I have. It doesn't matter. William?"

"Yes?"

"Just get back safely, that's all."

"I will. And you won't splash the story about, for my own good?"

"You have my word on that," Ginny said carefully.

I believed her. And she didn't break her word. Not really.

I was out of the hotel by ten, and wasted no time in getting out of Bordeaux and on to the Libourne road, heading east. I'd had to leave the car in the street as there was no garage near the hotel, but it was a side street and Bordeaux is a big place—I thought there was little chance that the opposition might have located it and be waiting. There were no police waiting, either, for which I was grateful— Bordeaux police are inclined to play safe by firing first and asking questions afterward, and they do it with machine guns. A rough place at times, Bordeaux, in spite of so much wealth and so many elegant buildings. Or because of them. I was glad to clear the bridge over the Garonne, and leave Bordeaux behind.

No great hurry, then. Our home town is Périgueux, and although our farmhouse—La Sauvegarde—is ten miles further to the east, I still only had some eighty miles to do, and all day to do it in. Once through Libourne, I decided to call in on one of my contacts, a little vineyard in the Saint-Emilion district, five miles south of the main road. Although the place has the official title of château, it's more like an overgrown garden shed with house attached.

I got the usual friendly welcome and, in the cool, windowless kitchen, all fluorescent lighting and flowery formica, we discussed last winter's frost damage and this year's prospects over some sample bottles. They asked me to stay for a light lunch—pâté, *jambon de pays*, cheese. No, no, couldn't possibly, I said, but did. We washed it down with their new dry white wine, not Sauvignon sec, but basically Semillon, traditionally a grape for sweet wine.

Normal, that's what it was. Just normal. Yesterday was impossible—it hadn't happened.

I left late in the afternoon, hoping my car would remember the way. Through Périgueux, along the familiar boulevards, over the river by the old stone bridge with the best view of the cathedral with its pineapple domes. Then out on the Hautefort road, along the narrow lanes winding along little valleys and between the chestnut groves; past the tilted pastures, each with its row of old walnut trees; past the tiny farms with their mossy red-tiled roofs, warm, honey-colored walls, and crooked shutters; past courtyards furnished with an old kitchen table for lunch under shady vines, beside the open barn door, surrounded by gaudy strutting chickens and rabbits held captive in stacked wire-netted boxes. A little of everything, that was the motto, but every year the supermarkets spread a little nearer, and homemade goodies are harder to find. So it goes, and its name is progress; probably is progress, on balance, but sad all the same.

It was dusk when I finally drove slowly up the stony track that winds up our own little valley, with the Citroën suspension set in the high position to avoid the flints and potholes. The house looks down from the top of the valley over its own fields, with its own woods at the back and flanking the valley on both sides. Our nearest neighbor is the farmer who uses our land in return for looking after the house; he lives about a mile away, over the top of the valley to the west. I decided to call on him in the morning: tonight, I would install myself and get to bed early. I drove up to the house, and stopped the car in the yard at the back. When the engine stopped, there was a sudden, beautiful silence. The absence of noise is certainly one of the great luxuries. I got out and stood by the front door, listening. There were sounds in the woods—branches tapping, birds settling in for the night with a rustling and a flapping. But no humans were near, I was sure of that. You know the sounds of your own patch as you know the pulsations of your own heartbeat. I was certainly alone.

Taking the huge, rusty key from its hiding place in a rainwater pipe, I fitted it into the front door, turned it, and went in, groping for the light switch. The tiled hall with its blackened beams was clean and tidy. I went through to the kitchen and opened the store cupboard: we keep a stock of tins for emergencies, and I took out some asparagus soup—it was all I needed after that lengthy lunch. While the soup was warming on the Calorgas stove, I went back out to the car and brought in my luggage, and the Webley from under the driving seat. Then I locked the car.

Back in the kitchen, I rescued the soup from burning, and sat at the table to eat it. Supper over, I went into the bedroom, which adjoins the kitchen—it's a single-story farmhouse, like most in this part of France. It was stuffy in there, and I opened the window and fastened back the shutters to let in the cool night air, also as a sign that I was in residence. I found some blankets, and threw them on the bed. No sheets, but there was an eiderdown, and I thought I'd sleep under that—less prickly. I shoved the suitcase under the bed and slid the Webley under the pillow. Rough as it all was, the bed looked inviting, and I was more than ready for it.

But, as I debated whether to sleep in my clothes or not, a better, safer plan occured to me. Much better, I had to admit, though much less comfortable. It was to sleep in the *palombière*.

A *palombe* is a sort of pigeon. A *palombière* is a sort of tree house or hide, in which French farmers and their friends gather to shoot at *palombes* when the flocks are passing during migration. It's always built in the tallest tree at the highest point of the woods. Strings lead out to decoy pigeons in the trees around: the *palombière* is fitted with slit windows concealed by shutters that are thrown open when the flock has been induced to circle or settle: everyone blasts away with shotguns in all directions, inflicting heavy casualties on tree branches, *palombes*, and sometimes each other. There is often a long wait before a flock arrives, and this is made endurable by fitting out the hide in great comfort with carpet and cushioned benches, and by drinking a lot of whiskey. Wives come to the bottom of the tree at mealtimes with cauldrons of soup, which are hauled up on cord. A great sporting and social occasion, you see. For influencing people and getting things done—your plumbing fixed, for instance—it's better than a grouse moor.

My *palombière* is one of the highest in the district; it's in a tall chestnut tree that has been allowed to stand when the other trees around it have been cut. Consequently, it commands impressive views in most directions, including over the house. Yes, that's where I should spend the night. There could be no safer place.

Sighing, but decided, I gathered up a couple of blankets and reached for the Webley. Then I remembered a very superior shotgun that I had inherited, and which lived, almost unused, in the hall cupboard. That would be better: I left the Webley where it was, under the pillow. The shotgun was where I remembered, together with a box of cartridges—number six shot. I dropped a dozen into my coat pockets, and went round turning out the lights. Then I emerged into the darkness, closing the front door behind me.

The night air was scented with damp grass faintly tinged with pine. I crossed the field to the bottom edge of the wood and then began the climb up through the wood, along the track, to the *pal-*

ombière. I hadn't brought the torch—the night was clear enough to see by starlight, and I had enough to carry without it. Besides, this was home ground: the shapes and scents were old friends, familiar. I came into the clearing in which stood the *palombière*, its black silhouette reaching, it seemed, almost to the stars. I looked up. Everything seemed to be in place. I started to climb.

That's the snag with *palombières*. You have to get there by means of a series of worn-out ladders secured to the tree with the maximum of economy and the minimum of security. Mine has a total of three ladders, with heart-stopping athletics required at each change-over point. Total height some fifty or sixty feet, but it feels like a thousand. It was a relief to reach the hatch. You climb into the thing from underneath, like a diving bell. I sat heavily on a side bench, panting. Then I spread the blankets, stood the gun against the wall, and settled down. It wouldn't be a disaster now if I overslept. No one could get up that ladder without waking me.

Yawning, I sat up again to open a shutter. The scent of pine was stronger up here, heady, sleep inducing. My mind slowed. Dreams began to stir, memories float to the surface. A goblin girl, laughing, threatening, dead. Was that only yesterday? How quickly the waters close over our heads. I never take photographs, preferring the firsthand of today to the secondhand of times past. And as memory fades, pictures usurp it—in time, it's only the picture you remember, not the real event, the real person. There would be pictures of her, in a pram, on a beach, in some family album—that's who she was, or would soon become. Better, for her, like that . . .

And for me—sleep.

DESTRUCTIVE MEASURING

Every combat is therefore the bloody and destructive measuring of the strength of forces, physical and moral; whoever at the close has the greatest amount of both left is the conqueror.

—*Clausewitz*

There aren't many birds left in France. Centuries of La Chasse have seen to that; the French have always been mad keen hunters, always ready to clap on their tartan caps and blaze away at anything that moves, edible or not. So I was surprised to be woken in my treetop residence at first light by a fair-sized dawn chorus. Perhaps our English-owned enclave has become known to the feathered fraternity as a safe place, a sanctuary. British civilization has, after all, been a moderating influence throughout the world.

But civilization has its price, I decided, as a woodpecker started up unseen within a few feet of my head. It sounded like roadworks. I groaned: to sleep on was impossible. But, then, I ought to be up and ready. It could be a busy day.

I sat up and rubbed my eyes. Then I polished my glasses, and put them on. I felt sticky and dishevelled—I really hate sleeping in my clothes. Yawning, I peered sleepily from the slit window that gave a view over the trees and down the hill toward the house. I

could see the roof, and part of the courtyard, and the far end of the
terrace where we usually have breakfast. Breakfast! I needed some
coffee badly. My gaze swung round to a gap in the trees through
which was a glimpse of the graveled area known as Le Parking. There
was someone walking across it.

Already?

My still-fuddled brain struggled to clear itself for action. I had
expected a visitor, but not this early. How long had he been there?
What was he doing? Was he alone?

I moved from window to window, scanning the early morning
landscape. Mist had collected lower down the valley, blotting out
the distant woods, and giving the impression that I was marooned
on an island. Nothing moved within my range of vision. The woodpecker went on hammering at the next-door tree; I could see him
now, chiseling his breakfast of wriggling grubs from the pine bark.
If only I had some coffee . . .

My early morning visitor walked to the edge of the gravel, stared
outward across the fields, and then back toward the house. He began
to move to the end of the house, to make his way round to the
courtyard. Still he seemed to be alone. His tiny figure was coming
toward me now, round the corner of the house.

I would risk it, I decided. Even if he was not alone, I had the
shotgun and plenty of cartridges. If I made enough noise, our
friendly neighbor would come to see what was going on from his
farm, half a mile away across the valley.

So I put my head through the slit window and let fly with the
whistle I had learned from Julian: finger and thumb against the back
of the tongue, and then blow. Useful for summoning taxis. It echoed
down the valley like a shriek of alarm, and the woodpecker took off
with a frenzied clapping of wings.

He'd heard it, and stopped, but was turning again, confused by
the echoes. So I cupped my hands to my mouth and shouted down
to him.

"Edward! E-D-W-A-R-D! Over here!"

He stared my way then, and I waved my arm out of the window. He knew about the *palombière*, having stayed with us on holiday

with Tricia; he looked up and saw me. He started trudging up the slope to the wood, and after a bit I lost sight of him behind the trees.

So, he'd come. And to get here so soon, he must have dropped everything and got on the afternoon plane to Bordeaux. Poor Edward! And he's not one given to precipitate action. It must be important to him.

He emerged into the clearing beneath the *palombière*. He was still alone. I stayed out of sight while I broke open the shotgun to check that both barrels were loaded, and stowed it flat on the bench behind me. Then I moved to the trapdoor, and looked down.

Fifty feet below, at the foot of the ladder, Edward had turned into a foreshortened toadlike creature. The pale disk of his face was upturned. He smiled. I didn't—it was my turn to be serious.

"Come up," I invited him.

"Oh," he said. "Is that necessary? Why don't you come down?" He put a hand on the rickety ladder and gave it a tentative shake.

"Come on," I said, "it's quite safe. And so am I, up here. That's if you want to talk, as I suppose you do."

He nodded, and began to climb. I stood back as he struggled through the trapdoor and emerged into the *palombière*. He sat on the cushioned bench opposite and looked about him breathing heavily. "Quite luxurious, isn't it?" he said, taking in the cushions and the carpeted floor. "I never actually climbed up here, you know. Just watched you do it. Have you been here all night?"

I must have looked it, crumpled and unshaven as I was. "Yes," I said, "I've been here. Waiting for you."

"So, now you know the full story," Edward said, nodding gravely.

"Yes, now I know. And I'm not taking any more crap from you, Edward. First you deny any knowledge of Loewenfeld. Then you try to shut me up by offering to take the whole thing over. Then, when I find your letters in Loewenfeld's files and you can't deny your involvement, you feed me a line about supporting Loewenfeld for the benefit of Britain, your duty to Queen and Country, and so forth. Well, all right—just possible, though it was asking a lot to expect me to believe that someone in your position could go on providing official support for an organization that had employed

professional criminals to look after commercial security. Loewenfeld
didn't expect me to believe it—he picked up a hint from what you'd
told him I'd said—about having thought the MoD were involved—
and constructed a new fable for me when I met him in Paris. Also
possible—until I found I was still being followed, on his orders. But
that's another story. The point now is, I sent you a message that
needed no response until I got back to London, *if* what you told me
was true. You took the bait and came galloping out here after me
at full speed. So yes, I know you're in it. Up to the neck, it seems.
The only question is, what happens next? Because, if the rest of the
army turns up now, you're going to be the first to get shot. Sorry,
but you'd better believe it—I'm not playing around anymore."

Edward was smiling. He didn't seem at all put out.

"What's so amusing?" I asked. "This means curtains for you, your
career, everything. You know that, don't you? I don't like being the
one to blow the whistle on you, but it's all gone too far. There's no
chance of hushing it up, now."

Edward stopped smiling, but now looked benign instead, like
somebody's favorite uncle. I didn't get it.

"You've had a rough time," he said gently, "and I'm sorry for
that. I would have let you in on it earlier, but you might have blown
the whole operation before we were ready. But I'm glad to say I've
got permission to put you in the picture now, and that's why I came
as soon as I got your message. It isn't fair for you to be kept in the
dark any longer."

I stared at him. "What d'you mean, permission? And who's 'we'?
What are you talking about?"

Edward leaned forward, hands on his knees, and looked into my
face. "You know about the system Loewenfeld was operating?"

I reckoned I did, at last. "It costs a bomb to set up a fully auto-
mated factory, doesn't it?" I said. "And with all that investment,
you've got to keep the work rolling in, or you can't pay the banks.
And it's got to be the right sort of work, too—large quantities, long
runs. Government contracts, ideally. You need to know the right
people. Like you, for instance."

"That's it, precisely," Edward said calmly. "And it was a winning
formula, you know. He started from scratch in the UK just four

years ago. Came to me over the Development Grant question, and I realized then he was a man in a hurry. Too much of a hurry—some of his proposals would have led me to exceed my authority, and I didn't like the sound of it. He was asking for introductions to all sorts of people who might be useful to him, with *my* recommendation, if you please! I told him quite frankly I couldn't do that sort of thing, and when he persisted, I talked to my boss, Sir Richard Bloom. He suggested that I should appear to go along with it for a while, to keep an eye on Loewenfeld, and report back from time to time. That's what I've been doing."

He looked across at me, smiling again.

I sat stunned. Nobody likes to feel a fool, and I'm no exception. I seemed to have followed one wrong turn after another. Could I believe him? Well, if he'd wanted to silence me, he'd surely have brought some support—that was in his favor. Also, what he'd told me did make better sense than anything else I'd heard or thought of. But, but . . .

"A pity you didn't feel able to trust me before," I said. "I could have got killed—nearly did. How can you possibly justify that?"

"But, my dear William! If only you'd told me the whole story when I first asked, we'd have put a stop to it, shut down the whole thing at once. Good God! I'd never have been able to forgive myself if . . ."

Well, it was true. I hadn't told him.

"I must admit," Edward said, "we seriously underestimated their capacity for solving problems with violence. Loewenfeld convinced me that Singer alone was responsible."

"That's what he claimed when I saw him in Paris."

"Did he? Yes. Well, after Friday, it became quite clear that Loewenfeld himself was the instigator. Though it's of little use to know that now."

"What happened on Friday?" I said carefully.

"Oh, you won't have heard, of course. Loewenfeld's dead!—shot by a pair of known French criminals who, it's assumed, he was interviewing. They emptied his safe, and then fell out over the money they'd taken—a large sum. Both killed. Quite a holocaust. One of them was a girl, too. Extraordinary end to the affair."

So my scenario had been accepted—so far, at least. "Good lord,"
I said. Edward and I nodded together, as people do at the news of
sudden death. Then Edward said something inevitable about poetic
justice. We nodded again. I hoped he wasn't going to ask if I'd been
to Bordeaux as planned, and said, to distract him, "Seems I've been
barking up the wrong tree, then. I don't know what to say, except
that I'm enormously relieved."

"Don't say anything, there's really no need," Edward said. "It's
as much my fault as yours. We've both been excessively secretive,
I'm afraid. But you were right, you know, about Loewenfeld: that
must be some consolation."

I leaned back against the cabin wall, sighing. The cold angularity
of the shotgun prodded the back of my trousers. I reached behind,
lifted it off the bench. Edward watched while I propped it vertically
in the corner beside me, feeling embarrassed. I shrugged, and muttered, "Be prepared."

"Oh quite. Don't blame you, old chap."

He was certainly taking it well. I wondered if I would have been
able to show such tolerance in the face of such an appalling mis-
judgement. I should have known that Edward, for all his monolithic
pomposity (or maybe because of it), was not the sort to risk all for
mere riches, like a common criminal. He had his beliefs, and they
were not so ordinary. He identified with his work, his position,
always had done, since responsibility was first thrust on him at
school. Head of House, that pinnacle of power. Whereas I'd never
sought, never been offered . . . well, I wasn't the type. It'd all been
there, in those skimpy schoolboys, what we would become. And
had.

"Sorry."

"Water under the bridge," Edward said. "Forget it. Have you had
breakfast?"

"No." Coffee, oh how I need some coffee!

"Well, then, let's just finish this off, and then go in and relax. My
boss will want a report. I suggest we put our heads together, and
then I'll write it up. What else can you tell me?"

"You mean, the names of anyone else involved?"

"That will do, for a start."

It was agony. Apart from Singer, I could give no names, tell him nothing of value. All my suspicions had been centered on Edward. And before that, on the MoD. Chemical warfare, secret weapons—the stuff of drama. Also stuff and nonsense.

"Never mind," Edward said. "There'll be more than enough when I add it to mine. You didn't keep a diary, notes, anything like that which might remind you of anything you've forgotten?"

"No, nothing."

"I see. But you kept *someone* informed, surely? The girl who rang me?"

"Ginny?" Well, yes, but I wasn't going to tell Edward that. She wouldn't thank me if he sent the police round to ask her endless questions. "No."

"And that's it?"

"I guess so. Can we go in for coffee now?"

"If you're sure."

"I'm sure."

"Let's go in then."

Edward went first down the ladder. I followed, sliding my right hand down the side of the ladder, the gun gripped vertically in my left. Halfway down, I remembered that I ought to have unloaded the thing: it's the classic French hunting accident, getting shot on a *palombière* ladder. But I wasn't going to attempt it in midclimb; in any case, Edward was safely below me. We set off down the path through the chestnut grove, heading for the house, not talking. No doubt Edward would have some more questions ready to put over the coffee. What was going to happen to me about the rifleman, Kevin, Loewenfeld? Would I have to appear in court to justify all that? *Could* I justify it? How much did Edward know? Suppose I said nothing? If I told Edward, he would be bound to tell his boss, and then justice would have to be seen to be done. It wasn't the court appearance in itself that I minded, but the probability that some unsympathetic silk would try to make an example of me. "You say you decided not to report the matter, but to wait until you had proof? Really! Are you not aware, Mr. Warner, that a large and

highly trained police force is maintained, at the public's expense,
for precisely that purpose? In order that private citizens such as
yourself shall have no need to take the law into their own hands?"
Yes, well, er . . . And I could imagine the headlines: WINE MER-
CHANT GOES TO WAR: DECIDES TO BATTLE CORRUPTION SINGLE-
HANDED. I'd never live it down, even if I was allowed to live it out—
out of prison.

I followed Edward down the path. He was in charge now, back
in his accustomed role. I'd have to take what was coming. We passed
a dense clump of gorse that had grown in the patch of light where
a large pine had been felled some three years before, or maybe four—
wherever the sun can get at it, the stuff grows at alarming speed,
becomes unstoppable. I'd have to get my farmer neighbor with his
tractor to drag it out by the roots before it blocks the path. Some
animal rustled in the leaf mold as we went past. We've got rabbits,
badgers, deer, and even an occasional wild boar, ferocious looking
but very shy and—

"Stop right there!"

—you hardly ever see them.

"What?"

We turned, Edward and I, side by side.

Oh no. Oh no!

He'd stepped out of the cover of the gorse after we'd gone by,
and now stood squarely in the path some thirty feet away, both
hands on the automatic, which was aimed at me. Not Edward—
me!

Gray Suit!

I felt the bottom fall out of my stomach, and knew at once what
had happened. Edward had planned this. Softened me with yet another stream of words. Led me to this spot. Where Gray Suit would
finish the job. And wouldn't he enjoy doing just that?

But why the delay? And why isn't Edward walking off compla-
cently, leaving me to face my fate? I steal a quick sideways glance.
Edward looks as scared as I feel. And is putting his hands up . . .

Wrong again. We're *both* on the spot! Apologies later.

"Loewenfeld's man!" I said to Edward in a gulp or whisper.

"Sure?"

"Yes! Seen him in action."

Gray Suit addressed himself to me, personally.

"Drop the gun, Mr. Warner. Please!" He had, it seemed, a dry sense of humor.

Now I had two reasons for being somewhere else as soon as possible. The second was that nobody *drops* a best Holland & Holland sidelock. It can't be done. I whispered urgently to Edward, "Only chance, got to split! When I say . . ." I began to bend, feigning obedience, the gun in my right hand ". . . SPLIT!"

For all his portly outline, Edward took off as though hoisted by wires. I broke left, diving for the cover of the gorse bush, getting off one shot from the hip in Gray Suit's general direction as I went. I heard him shout, and the report of his gun. I thought the bullet sang somewhere over my head, but I just kept going.

I plunged into the wood. These chestnut groves are a crop, coppiced every twenty years or so, and the wood cut into meter lengths to be collected by the chipboard factory. It's . . . All right, some other time. The important thing is, you've got these solid clumps of tree with clear space in between, ideal for escaping through. I traversed the grove at speed until I reached a boundary ditch, which I fell into, and turned to face the enemy. Who wasn't in sight.

I did the professional thing and reloaded. He still wasn't in sight.

Well, of course, he might choose to go after Edward, who wasn't armed. I felt bad about that. Presumably, though, he wanted us alive, as he could have shot us in the back without warning. That would have been easy enough. Poor old Edward might now be stuck in a gorse bush, being ordered to come out. The thought came not without merriment. I was sick of being the unsuccessful member of our duo.

I worked my way with caution toward the house again, hoping to reach my car, taking up a position just inside the coppice from which I could see the end of the house and the parking area. My Citroën was still the only car in it. Gray Suit must have approached from elsewhere. So, for that matter, must Edward.

And there he was now, coming from the bottom of the track on which we'd been ambushed, going toward the house. He was limping slightly. I emerged from cover, and called to him; he waited while I scrambled under the barbed-wire fence at the edge of our back field, and walked down to join him. My companion in arms! Tried and trusty. At least I could feel secure about that, now.

"Close call!" he said. His face was red, and his clothes muddy. He began to brush himself off with his hands.

"We'd better get into the house," I suggested. The woods, with all they might contain, were much too close for comfort.

"I doubt he'll be back," Edward said. "You fairly peppered him, you know."

"You saw?"

"I fell over. When I looked back, he was hobbling away up the track."

If ever we meet again, I thought, which I hope we won't . . .

We walked down into Le Parking, and into the house by the huge old front door, which is the only opening in the otherwise blank north side except for a tiny kitchen window. In the kitchen, I lit a gas ring and put a kettle on. I got out an earthenware coffee jug, and found some beans—Continental Roast. They'd been there some time, but it would still be the best coffee I'd ever had, I was sure of that. Edward sat at the kitchen table while I ground the beans. At last it was ready. I wished I'd had the sense, or energy, to buy some croissants yesterday, but there was some *pain d'épice*, old but edible, in the biscuit tin.

I collected two cups from the dresser, those thick green ones with gold rims that you're meant to warm in the oven but never do. Then I bore the steaming brown coffee jug to the table. At last!

"Sit down," Edward said.

It was an odd thing for *him* to say, in *my* kitchen. Also, he said it in a rather serious tone of voice, even for him. When I looked up from the coffee jug, I saw why.

We sat opposite each other, then. Me with my dark green coffee cup (still empty). And Edward with his dark blue automatic (presumably full). He was resting it on the edge of the table, but his hand wasn't shaking. At that distance the black O at the end of it looked just as big as they say.

"Oh," I said. It may have been a Freudian slip, but I meant every word of it.

"So, now you know," Edward said, nodding gravely.

This was the point I thought we'd got to an hour ago, in the *palombière*. Except that this time, I thought I *did* know. Not that it was going to do me any good. "He got there in the end." No, as Keynes pointed out, in the long run is too late. You're dead.

I should have trusted my instincts. As I said to Claudine, knowing someone for years when you don't actually like them isn't creditable, it's just sentimental. I'd been wrong about Edward's hidden depths, though. They were there, all right, but murky. Yes, Right Brain had known all along.

"I gave you the benefit of the doubt, you see."

"You weren't convinced?"

"You explained it all, beautifully. Yes, you did a good job. Except for one thing. Which I stupidly decided to ignore. Because I could have been wrong."

"Which was?"

"You—are the only connection. The only point of contact between me and Loewenfeld. At the time of the first attempt on me, the shooting on the moor. I should have held on to that. And I still don't know *why*."

"No," Edward said. A slight smile passed across his face, as creepy and as unexpected as a flash of light in a deserted building. "Security," he said.

"Security?"

"I didn't realize at first how dangerous Loewenfeld was. He enjoyed that side of it, you know."

"I've seen."

"I thought I needed an insurance policy, that it would be safer if someone else besides myself knew about my involvement. Then I realized that it was only necessary that Loewenfeld should *think* so."

"And you chose me?"

"I thought he would believe that. After all, we've known each other a long time."

And believe it Loewenfeld did. With bullets. And that, I could see now, had disturbed Edward's peace of mind hardly at all. For him, self-preservation was a top priority, like nuclear shelters for the government.

"Too long, Edward," I said. "Too long."

The sound of a car engine broke the chilly reverie that followed. I looked round. Through the kitchen window, I could see a small Citroën jeep bumping up the track from the bottom of the valley, like a yellow plastic kangaroo. It would be our farmer neighbor come to pay a welcome call, and check on the sounds of shooting.

Edward looked thoughtful. His car was not outside. Nobody had seen him except Loewenfeld's man and myself. He was still in the clear, and he would want to keep it that way. We sat listening to the sound of the car, which died away as it climbed the track past the end of the house, and then sounded louder again as it arrived behind the house and drove into Le Parking. There was a flash of yellow as it passed the tiny kitchen window, but that was all we could see, and Edward wasn't going to risk looking out. He lifted the automatic slightly.

"Just sit still, and quiet," he said in a low voice.

We heard the car door bang, and footsteps on the gravel. Then a loud knocking on the front door.

"Will he come in?"

"Who knows?" I wasn't giving Edward any help with his plans. A second burst of knocking. *"Quelqu'un?"*

No use calling out—get us all killed. Edward was watching my face. I remembered I still hadn't had any coffee.

Footsteps on the gravel again. Car door again. Revving of engine, scrunch of tires on gravel, and we were alone again. Edward rested his gun hand on the table again.

"Let's have some coffee, for God's sake."

"I'll pour it," Edward said. I hadn't intended to fling the pot in his face, as it happened. The coffee was already too cool to do any damage, and what I wanted was to drink some of it. He poured us each a half cup with his left hand. Oh, it was bliss.

"Where I did go badly wrong," I said, "is that I took you for a man of principle, someone who wanted to make his mark, change the world, all that. I must say you were very good at putting it over."

"What?"

"The patriotic front. Putting industry back on its feet. Very convincing. When all the time you were just Loewenfeld's commercial pimp."

"You don't understand anything, really, do you?" Edward said angrily. He had, I saw, gone quite red with indignation.

"Tell me then."

"Order. It's about order. Can't you see that?" Edward spoke in a low voice, but with furious intensity, his eyes fixed on my face. He really wanted me to understand, futile as it seemed. "It's about doing away with obsolete methods and replacing them with order and efficiency. Unions and weak management have held us back for years. As a country, we've just been wasting time and falling behind. Yes, I want to make my mark, as you put it. I've spent years trying to knock heads together, get things off the ground, but it's all been too slow, far too slow. Until I met Loewenfeld. He knew how to do it, how to cut through all the waste and blather and get things moving. All right, he cut corners, he had to, to start with. But we have to get something concrete to put up against rabble-rousing ideology. We're risking a very messy revolution, the way things have been going. Money is the answer to that—we can buy off trouble-makers with a fat National Wage for not working. But first we have to make the money by turning industry round. You've *seen* it, you *know* it works."

"You're cracked, Edward," I said slowly. So this was how Loewenfeld had caught him! Edward's weakness: not money, but making his mark! Replacing the Age of Keynes with the Age of Dundas! Oh Jesus, it even sounds farcical! Truly, my Satan, thou art but a dunce!

"And that's not how Loewenfeld saw it. He was a money-making animal, if ever I saw one, and he was just *using* you."

"Oh yes? How do you know that it was not *I* who was just using *him*?" Edward leaned back in his chair. I wished that lightning would strike, would burn the smug smile off his face. I'd had enough of him, for this or a dozen lifetimes.

Which reminded me.

"You won't get away with it, of course."

"Why not? You told me yourself, nobody knows but you."

"I kept a diary."

Edward shook his head. "That won't wash. When you told me you hadn't you were confiding in me as a friend. I can believe that."

"*I kept a diary*. I didn't tell you because, as I said, I didn't entirely trust you. I can prove it."

"How?"

"It's on loose sheets. I've been posting them to London as each sheet was completed, but I've kept the rough drafts."

"Don't waste your time, William."

"It's in my suitcase in the bedroom. You can get it, or I will."

My shotgun was leaning against the wall behind the door to the hall. Edward looked round, saw it, and calculated.

"We'll go together."

We went in single file into the bedroom. "Ah! Going to get out of the window, were you?" Edward said, walking over to shut it.

Can I get to the bed, reach under the pillow before he turns round? No, I can't. Shit!

I bent down to drag the suitcase out from under the bed, with Edward watching me closely. Since I lost my briefcase in the Protoplastics foray, I hadn't had time to buy a replacement, and all my wine notes and price lists were stuffed in under my clothes in the suitcase. Edward leaned over, holding the automatic against my back with his right hand, and rummaging among my clothes with his left for concealed weapons. Eventually he was satisfied. "All right," he said. I started getting out sheets of paper, spinning it out. "It's got mixed up with some of my other stuff," I muttered. But Edward made a sudden gesture for silence. He stood, frowning at me, listening intently. "There was a noise in the hall," he whispered. "Bring all that into the kitchen. And keep away from that window. I shall stay where I can see it."

He went back into the kitchen, moving quietly.

I grabbed the Webley from under the pillow. If that was Gray Suit in the hall, and if Edward managed to explain to him that they were on the same side, I was in for a two-to-one shoot-out. Better deal with Edward at once, and reduce the odds.

I stepped silently from the bedside: two, three paces and I was in the doorway. Edward was standing at the hall door, listening, with his back to me. I gripped the old pistol. Right, Edward! This is for you.

But then, I thought, if I *can* take him in alive, I should. This is Edward, old if ex-companion down life's twisted trail etc., husband of Tricia who is Claudine's best friend and confidante. I don't think I can do this.

"Don't move, Edward! I'll kill you if you start to turn."

"What with?" he asked. But stood still.

"With my father's .45 first world war service revolver. I had it under the pillow in there."

"I appreciate the detail," Edward said, "but I still don't believe you." But he still didn't move, either.

"If you hold your gun by the muzzle in your left hand—but be careful to do just that!—you can turn round slowly. See for yourself."

"All right."

He transferred his automatic to his left hand, held it by the muzzle.

"Now turn round. Slowly!"

He did. He looked at my Webley.

"Game's up, Edward. Now drop yours."

He frowned. And didn't.

"You've got to drop it, Edward! Drop it *now!*"

I could see the thoughts reeling through his brain, behind his eyes. "*Drop it!*"

But he didn't. Instead, he snatched the automatic back with his right hand and swung it up, toward me. I was slow—I hadn't thought he'd try it. We pulled our triggers simultaneously.

Mine went *click*.

His went *bang*.

I remember thinking, as I fell, what a futile existence that cartridge had achieved. After waiting sixty years to be fired, it hadn't been able to manage it. A life wasted. Pointless.

After the initial kick in my chest, I felt only a dull pain. But my peripheral vision was blurring rapidly. My field of view narrowed to a small area of intense clarity, like looking through binoculars. I lay against the wall next to the great black hole of the kitchen fireplace, aware of the sulphurous smell of damp, charred logs. My eyes focused on Edward's face. I saw that he was going to shoot me again, to make sure. I hoped he wouldn't do it in my face. Vain to the last. It seemed the only thing that mattered. I tried to ask him. Not to shoot me in the face. Surely he could grant me that?

But I couldn't make myself heard. Someone was screaming. It was just like the scream Sergeant MacWhirter had made us give at bayonet practice. But more convincing.

It wasn't Edward.

It wasn't me. I didn't *think* it was me.

Then I saw Edward fall. My binocular vision zoomed in on the knife handle sticking from his back. Sabatier. It was odd how things kept reoccurring. I heard the scream again. It was like that of a caged eagle; it filled the room with fury.

My eyes drifted from the knife handle, up to the figure beyond Edward. It seemed familiar, but it *couldn't* be her. She was still in London; she knew nothing of all this; she couldn't possibly . . .

She was looking round, her movements wild. She was looking for another knife. She needn't, she mustn't!—Edward's face was turned away from me, but I'd seen his fingers cease their scrabbling on the floor tiles.

"No!" I got out. "No! It's not necessary. *Claudine* . . ."

Then she was beside me, kneeling, her face level with mine, but seemingly enormous; her eyes searched mine; her hand took my wrist.

"William?"

"Look," I murmured, "I'm sorry I didn't . . ."

"Oh my William," she said. "No. Not now. Stay quiet."

"Oh, but I *must*."

But I couldn't.

25

DISTINGUISHED
POWERS

The work of War, although so plain and simple in its effects, can never be conducted with distinguished success by people without distinguished powers of the understanding.

—Clausewitz

If flights of angels had been scrambled to sing me to my rest, then they had to return to base, mission canceled. That's obvious, or I wouldn't have been able to write all this. They wouldn't have been sorry; they've got enough to do, with emergency calls coming in all the time from Arabia, Africa, South America, Ireland, etc. I wasn't sorry either; I feel uncomfortable about the angelic ambivalence, the gray area under their gowns—I wouldn't know how to *be*. It was a relief to be in the care of nurses, instead; nothing ambivalent about them.

Claudine was first in to see me. A dark-skinned nurse (Algerian?) came in and held the door open, smiling at me with a glimmer of white teeth. Behind her, Claudine appeared in the doorway, her arms full of packages; she was smiling too, her lips two shiny red ribbons like gift wrapping of the most expensive sort. I breathed in her scent as the first tendrils of it reached across my bed; it was sexual, yes, but also it evoked home, security, a constant mother presence; it was how all women of all ages *should* smell.

"Grapes," she said, unloading her packages onto my bedside table, "some petit fours, some Armagnac (less violent for you, *chéri*, than cognac), and some good soap. The hospital soap is, as usual, *dé-goû-tant*, quite impossible. This"—she held it to her nose and sniffed it, eyes closed, and then nodded—"this is not too bad." She divested herself of everything except a large bunch of flowers; she bent to smooth my hair and kiss me on the forehead, and then began to look around the room. "I shall ask that nurse for a vase," she announced, and reached for the bell.

"Wait till she comes in again," I said. "She'll be back soon. Sit on the bed and talk to me. I want to know . . ."

"Oh yes," she said, sitting. "You want to know how I arrive at La Sauvegarde?" I nodded. I'd been puzzling myself with it ever since I woke up.

"Well," she said, "it is very simple. Virginia told me you were there."

Virginia? *Ginny?*

Gulp.

At that point the nurse came in with some pills. She produced a vase from the bottom of the bedside cupboard. Then she went out again. I hoped the pills were good and strong; I needed all the medical assistance I could get to help me over this little crisis.

Claudine had filled the vase with water from the basin tap, and was now over by the window, her back to me, arranging the flowers to her satisfaction.

"Yes?" I said. I had to say something. The minimum seemed best.

"I like her *very* much. She is *très, très sympa*," Claudine said, bend-ing to check her arrangement, and push a recalcitrant flower into line. *How did it dare?*

"Did she ring you?" I managed.

"She rings me. Then she comes to see me. Such a pretty girl; so lucky to be small and dark like her, you can wear such wonderful clothes, so casual. But I see at once she is *sérieuse*; we have a good talk."

Oh my God.

"She tells me what has been going on."

Well, that's it.

"My poor William! *Ces gens abominables!* I cannot believe what I hear!"

No it isn't.

"Perhaps I should have told you," I said, "but, well, I decided to deal with it on my own, rightly or wrongly. I had to get some evidence, you see."

"Perhaps you should," she said, "but, of course, I understand it that you did not. To protect the family, yes, that is the best of reasons. But perhaps I would not have been so useless, so *hystérique* as you think. Thank God, I have never suffered from *crises de nerfs*, never."

The eagle screams, the Sabatier knife handle.

"You can say that again," I said. "I believe you, all the way. Wouldn't *be* here, otherwise, would I. Formidable is the word, my darling, in your language or mine. *Formidable.*"

"Oh, William," she said, coming back to sit on the bed. "Oh, I was terrified. Terrified! When I looked in through the little kitchen window and saw you both sitting there, and Edward with that gun— oh, it was frightful! And Edward's face, it was all . . . fixed. Like a mask. Often he has looked a bit like that, but I have thought it was because, you know, because he was English."

"Like me."

"No, of course not. Well, yes—even you, sometimes. But not so much, not as if there was no one there, behind the mask. What did it mean?"

"It's a long story."

"Well, you mustn't tire yourself, *chéri.* Tell me next time. But poor Tricia—what can we do? What can *I* do? Will she ever understand why I had to do that, to stop him? We were very close, you know."

Claudine looked down and picked at the counterpane. I could see that it was all flooding back, the terror and the horror of it all; she began to cry quietly, and I found my handkerchief to push at her; my chest gave a stab of pain as I did so.

"Take this," I said, wincing.

"Lie still, *chéri*," she said quickly, taking the handkerchief and lightly dabbing at her cheeks with it; she studied my face with anxious eyes. "Shall I call the nurse?"

"It's only when I move," I said. "Don't worry. Tell me how you got to the house. Did Jean bring you in the jeep?"

"Oh yes," she said, brightening, "we had a plan, you see, M'sieur Reynaud and me." Reynaud is our farmer neighbor: although we've known him for years, Claudine and he still address each other formally. I can call him Jean because I'm an ignorant foreigner.

"M'sieur Reynaud knew you'd arrived the night before," Claudine said, "because he saw the yard light on when he was shutting up his chickens. I arrive just after, and I explain to him the situation. He is astonished, but he is also excited. He wants to get his gun and stay in the house with you." (He would—the Resistance tradition is strong in that region, and our valley is dotted with white stone memorials to the farm lads who took on the *Das Reich* division punitive expedition in 1944, and didn't make it.) "I say no, he must not, but will he watch to see who comes to the house, and then we will make a plan? He says yes, he will do that. So all night he is watching across the valley."

Reynaud is *sérieux*. Also *brave* and *courageux*. "We must give him a case of Scotch," I said.

Claudine looked shocked. "Oh no, *chéri*," she said. "Two bottles will be *quite* enough. Well then, I sleep on a sofa in their kitchen and, very early in the morning, M'sieur Reynaud wakes me and says he has seen a man come up the valley, walking, and go round behind the house. I jump up, and he takes me to where we can watch, and then we see this man go up the track into the woods. M'sieur Reynaud says he believes you must be in the *palombière*, because that is a good place to hide and watch the house. Well, we wait and wait, but see nothing. I am frightened then, and I think we must do something, and at once M'sieur Reynaud says he will run to the woods with his gun and get you away. I am going to say yes, but then we hear shooting from the woods—oh, that was the worst moment. I think we are too late. M'sieur Reynaud goes to get his gun, but then I see someone coming out of the woods behind the house, and I think it is you! Oh, that was wonderful! And you walk down toward the house, and the first man comes from a different place to meet you, and then you both are gone behind the house."

I could imagine it all; the small, dark farmer, and Claudine, straining to see across the valley in the early morning light.

"Then," Claudine said, "we decide to take the jeep and drive to the house. I am to stay down, out of sight. M'sieur Reynaud is to knock on the door, and while he does that I get out and stand against the wall. We know that you and the other man are in the house, and I hope that you will answer the door and everything will be all right. But if you don't answer . . ."

"You'll know that everything is all wrong."

"Yes. If you don't answer, M'sieur Reynaud is to go to telephone for the police. And I will stay to see what I can see."

I swallowed. Claudine also had been *brave, courageuse*. I said so.

"Oh, there was no time to think about it," she said. "Well, when M'sieur Reynaud has driven away, I hear voices in the kitchen. It is then I look through the little window. Oh, very carefully, I can tell you! You know what I saw. So then, I decide to go into the house, and I creep in through the front door, and through the hall. I hear you and Edward talking, and then I hear you going into the bedroom and I think I must do something. So I start to open the kitchen door, but I make a noise, and I hear Edward coming out of the bedroom, saying he has heard something, and he opens the door, but I have quickly hidden round the corner, and he doesn't see me.

"The next thing, I hear a shot! I didn't know if you or Edward had been shot, but I had to look into the kitchen, then. When I saw that it was you, and that Edward was going to shoot you again, I took the knife from the dresser and . . . stopped him."

That was the word. "He had to be stopped," I said, trying to comfort her.

"I would do it again," she said, thoughtfully, but with a firm voice.

I knew what she felt. I'd felt it too. Dominique's automatic exploding in my hands.

"It's Tricia," she said.

"I know."

We fell silent. Then I yawned. "Sorry."

"Oh, you are tired, I have stayed too long," Claudine said.

"No, no. Don't go yet." There was something I had to ask her, but I didn't know how. I wouldn't be able to sleep, tired as I was, unless I knew the answer. Whichever it was.

"Well, darling," I said eventually, deciding that I had no choice but to grasp the nettle. "What else did you talk to Virginia about? Her friends call her Ginny, you know."

"Ginny? Yes, that suits her," Claudine said, nodding approvingly. She gazed at me for a moment, then raised her eyebrows in a very French expression; quizzical, ironic, something like that. "We talked of nothing *else*, my William. Except, you know, the usual things that women are supposed to talk about. We make a *plaisanterie* or two. Nothing else. It would not have been . . . correct."

She held the gaze for a few seconds longer, and then switched it to the bedside table; she slid her slim fingers into the paper bag of grapes; she popped one into her mouth, and one into mine. "Not too bad," she said critically. She reached for some more.

"I've always loved you, you know," I mumbled through the exploding juices. We swallowed. She helped me dispose of the pips; I thought it would be some time before I could reach the bedside table without my chest hurting.

Claudine rose from the bed. Then she bent over me, and kissed me—on the mouth this time. Long, and warm, and grapy.

"And *we* love *you*, my William," she said. "Now I must go, and you must go to sleep. I will come at the same time tomorrow." She crossed to the door and opened it, turned, and suddenly it was just like that other time, whenever it was; the red lips launching a promise across the room. A dutiful, beautiful wife. Then she was gone, leaving me with my thoughts.

Well, I've been luckier than I deserve, in more ways than one. I should have no complaints about the way things have turned out. The fact is, though, I do feel a distinct sense of anticlimax. I'm lying here in a hospital bed, recovering from a bullet wound, and other people are dead, all the result of no more than a squabble about money. Not affairs of state, matters of life and death, but just money. It doesn't seem important enough. Not to me. But that's my overactive sense of drama at work again, I suppose. Everybody else has known all along the world ends with a whimper. It's basically banal.

So it's all over, I thought, as the day's bustle died away, leaving only the occasional echo of footsteps along distant corridors.

But it wasn't, not quite. There was still the letter from Ginny, and the mystery visitor.

Morning now, bright and sunny. My Algerian nurse has just been in to draw the blinds: she's a bouncy walker, her apple bottom quivering under the institutional apron; I must be feeling better. She takes my temperature and my pulse, her fingers cool and firm on my wrist. She glances at my face; she notes my speculative eyes, and my carefully blank expression, and she knows too, that I am feeling better. *Les hommes . . . ils sont tous comme ça.* She rewards me with a letter that has been in her pocket all this time. She is right not to have given it to me before; my pulse might have gone up because I recognize the large, untidy handwriting. Yes! It is . . . *the letter from Ginny!*

Darling,

I expect by the time you get this you will already have seen Claudine, so I know you will be feeling sore with me, or worse. Please believe me, I did it (as they say) for the best. I was so worried, I *had* to do something, and I thought that going to see C. was the only useful thing I *could* do. I promised you not to publish, and at least I stuck to that. If it's made trouble for you, about us, I'm very sorry, I really am. But I thought you were pushing your luck too far, so I decided to blow the whistle. C. rang me yesterday, and told me what had happened, and I think perhaps I did do the right thing. I do hope so.

I dreaded going to see her, C. I mean, as I thought there might be a really bad scene, and you know I hate that sort of thing, but in fact she was absolutely *sweet*, and we got on really well, in fact in other circumstances I think we'd be really good friends. It was a surprise, I must say, when she opened the

door and I saw how pretty she was, I mean I always thought
she must be quite since you are what you are, but not that
much. It must be really marvelous to be tall like that and wear
those clothes, not smart exactly but stylish. The grass is always
greener, I suppose. Anyway I was there for about two hours
and we had some coffee and then wine and talked about it all
and I showed her the notes I'd made and typed out and it was
really awful, she went absolutely white and started to cry, so
then I did too, and then we both felt so stupid and pulled ourselves together and agreed that she'd go out on the next plane
to Bordeaux while I went to see the CID. I think you'll be
getting a visit from them, they said they'd have to send someone
out when I rang them up yesterday to see what was happening.
They've also asked me not to publish, because they say it will
hinder their investigations, and I suppose it would, so I'm not
going to win any awards for my brilliant investigative journal-
ism this year I'm afraid. In fact I'm afraid I'm somewhat broke
because I had to pay the hotel bill, which was huge but I won't
bother you with that now, perhaps we could get some kind of
compensation.

Now, William darling, you aren't going to like this, but the
fact is Evan rang me up a few days ago and suggested lunch to
sort out some money matters to do with our separation, and I
went and one thing led to another and to cut it short we are
going to give it another try together. I don't know if it will work
or not. I really think, William darling, it's a good thing as I
think things were getting a bit out of hand—yes? And of course
now there's C. who knows about me. I must say she handled
it brilliantly, and whenever I veered toward talking about us
she quickly steered me off it and made it quite clear she would
think anything of that sort an unforgivable indiscretion, and I
soon got the idea and talked as if you know me only as a useful
journalist friend but it wasn't at all what I expected as we're
not as practical as the French, I always thought that was apoc-
ryphal. Anyway it seems that things will be all right for you,
so I don't feel too bad about what has happened, in fact it may
be best for both of us as something had to happen.

I hope you get well really quickly and C. told me that they think you'll be as good as new except for the bullet hole. I wonder what it looks like. Darling William, I'm so glad it's all over at last and normal life can be resumed. Try not to do anything like that again.

Signed in her own fair hand with a careless scattering of Xs at the bottom.

So that's it! I'd got the vibes, of course. I knew something was going on. But Evan Duff-Jones! That pontificating prune! How *could* she? Oh Ginny, Ginny, what a waste!

But then—a few weeks, and she'll be bored out of her mind. Then, yes, then normal life can be resumed. It's a hint, what she says about the bullet hole . . .

Hope she keeps the flat.

The little nurse brought breakfast, and arranged it carefully within my reach. It was all right as long as I didn't have to stretch out my arm, which brought the muscles over my chest into play, and they didn't like that. As she went out, she almost collided with someone coming in. *The mystery visitor!*

"Oh—terribly sorry!" he said.

I looked up from my bowl of hospital muesli. He was a tall man of about my age, or possibly a little younger, in a well-cut suit of rather quiet tweed. He carried a briefcase, an umbrella, and a trilby hat which he'd taken off as he entered the room. I looked at him curiously: my off-duty clothes had been just like that when I'd been in the army all those years ago. It was like meeting someone from my distant past.

"Do I know you?" I asked.

He smiled pleasantly, and advanced toward me with his hand held out.

"I'm afraid I can't," I said. "It hurts my chest. Do I know you?"

"May I sit here?" he said, indicating the visitors' chair. I nodded.

He pulled it closer to the bed, dumped his briefcase by the side of it, dropped his hat and umbrella on the end of my bed, and sat down with a long sigh of relief.

"Took ages to get here," he said. "Plane to Bordeaux—baggage strike on at our end, did you know?—taxi to the station, train from Bordeaux to Périgueux, another taxi to the hospital, phew! It's the sudden plunge, you know, if your French isn't all that marvelous, like mine. You live out here a lot of the time, I understand. Very nice too." He smiled his pleasant smile again.

"I'm sorry—,"

"Oh, of course! *I'm* sorry. Fletcher, I'm from the Home Office."

"Oh yes?" I said.

He blinked. "You were expecting me?"

CID was what Ginny had said in her letter. This visitor, with his smiles and his terribly casual air, seemed much more likely to have come from MI-something. Had I expected that? I didn't think so, though his appearance didn't seem to be causing me much surprise, I noticed. But expecting—that was putting it too strongly.

"Oh no," I said, "not exactly."

He said nothing, but took a folder out of his briefcase, opened it, and scanned the contents, nodding to himself once or twice. Then he looked up.

"Not too tired for a few questions?"

"No, I'm fine."

"They told me you were safely on the mend. Well then, I'll just start by running over the events of the last week or so, and then perhaps you'd be kind enough to fill in a few gaps." And, in a shopping-list tone of voice, he read out a detailed account of my movements from the time when I'd got back to London after the battle of Quarry Cottage. It seemed that the young lieutenant on the other side of the wire at Porton Down had not been as naïve as I had assumed: a report had gone straight up to the Home Office together with my car number, and Major Warner had been put under immediate surveillance.

"Really?" I said. "Well, your people were very good at it, I must say. I never noticed a thing."

"I wouldn't say that, exactly," my visitor said. "You noticed one

of our people in the Victoria and Albert Museum. Took him some
time to catch up with you again, even with the help of the French
police."

Gray Suit? I stared, stuck for words. But surely . . . ?

"He held me up—had an automatic."

"Trying to rescue you from Mr. Dundas. You had a shotgun."

Worse and worse! "Tell him . . . tell him I wish I'd missed."

"You could tell him yourself—he's just along the corridor here.
They've got most of the pellets out now. No? Well, perhaps you're
wise."

Why hadn't he shouted "Police!"? Oh, now I thought about it,
he *had*.

"So you knew about Dundas?"

"Yes," my visitor said cheerfully. "Yes, we were called in by his
boss some time ago to make discreet inquiries. Corruption in high
places suspected. We decided to let it run a while, list his contacts.
Gone off his rocker, in my opinion, but we'll get back to that later.
Tell me, did you get to see inside Loewenfeld's factory near Paris?"

"No. I intended to, originally, but then I thought I might learn
more by talking to Loewenfeld, as he'd suggested. Between the lines,
of course. But it wasn't much use, in fact. He spun me a long tale
about MoD involvement, because he thought that was what I wanted
to hear."

"Uh-huh," he said. "I see. But what would you have been looking
for, if you'd gone to the factory? What were you looking for in the
Stanmore factory?"

I couldn't avoid saying it. "Weapon parts."

"*Weapon parts!* Really?"

"That was the theory I was working on at the time," I explained
wearily. It was inescapable. I had to explain my theory that a new
type of weapon was being produced, that some sort of cover-up was
going on, even that Loewenfeld was perhaps passing information
about it to A Foreign Power. The more I said, the more it sounded
like one of those novels you buy at airports. But my visitor was a
true gent: he never allowed a flicker of amusement to appear on his
face.

"I see," he said again, as I trickled off into silence.

"What made me think that something might be going on," I added defensively, "was that, when I got into the files at Protoplastics, the MoD orders and drawings all had code numbers. No descriptions at all."

"Indicative of secret weaponry?" he said. I winced. But there was no trace of sarcasm in his voice. He was making it easy for me.

"Perhaps it would make you feel better," he said, "if I told you that *all* military production is assumed to carry the risk of exposure to hostile powers. Otherwise all factories producing military equipment would have to be kept under impossibly tight security."

"And the coding?"

"Standard practice. Helps to conceal those items that may carry a security risk. And it's easier to use a short coding than to have to keep typing out impact-resistant screw-top water bottles, officers for the use of."

It was all so obvious, the way he put it.

"When attempts have been made to bump you off, you are rather inclined to jump to conclusions," I said sadly.

"Of course! Of course! In your place, I'm sure I would have thought just the same," he said, managing not to sound patronizing.

I doubted it.

"You may even have been right," he said. "Who knows?"

"About Loewenfeld?"

"About Loewenfeld. As I said, it's an accepted risk that some manufacturers will pass on information. He may have been one of them. If he was able to persuade the Russians to part with good money in exchange for information on British military water bottle manufacture, then good luck to him, we'd say." He gave a brief snort of laughter. "But you never found any proof of that, did you?"

"No."

"Well, it seems unlikely then. Certainly he didn't need the money. That factory of his is quite extraordinary, isn't it! The others are all the same, I suppose. You haven't seen any of the others? No? His wife will take it all over now, and be just as good at it, from what I hear."

"What have you heard?" I asked. I must have sounded anxious: it wouldn't have been surprising—I was. If she was anything like her late husband, the war might not be over yet.

My visitor understood at once.

"I doubt you'll have any more trouble," he said, cutting straight to the core of my question in his economic style. "Not now, with Dundas out of it and the contacts exposed. There'd be no point. She's a businesswoman, first and foremost. That's her passion, and she'll have her hands full now."

It figured. I hoped he was right. I hoped I'd fought my last battle. As the Iron Duke said, 'Tis a bad thing to be always fighting. I knew how he must have felt.

"One or two things here," my visitor said, turning over a sheet in his folder, "which my Section Head told me to ask you. This stuff about nerve gas stocks being held in the UK. Converting cruise missiles to carry it. And so forth. Pretty fanciful, wouldn't you say? Whose idea was that?"

He reached into his briefcase for a propelling pencil and wound the lead out carefully. Then he made some marks on a sheet of notes, as if he was correcting an exam paper.

"You must have been talking to Ginny Duff-Jones," I said stiffly, feeling a stab of resentment. It was too much like a trick question.

"Just before I left London," he confirmed, unabashed.

"You'll know, then, that it's an idea bandied about among defense correspondents and the like," I said. "How fanciful it is, I wouldn't know. But I was looking for a theory to fit the facts I was turning up, many of which seemed to lead to Porton Down, and gas-filled cruise missiles seemed as good as any."

He nodded. "Defense correspondents," he murmured to himself. He made another mark on his piece of paper. "I sometimes think—" He checked himself.

"A source of headaches in the Home Office?"

He looked at me thoughtfully, and then his smile returned. "I sometimes think they do for defense what travel correspondents do for faraway places. If you know what I mean."

"Wreck what they profess to support?"

"In the case of defense, with half-baked theories."

"Oh," I said. "Does it matter much? In this case, for instance?"

He tilted his head on one side and pursed his lips judicially. It did seem to matter. Finally he said, "The Geneva Protocol of 1925 bans the use of germ and chemical weapons, you know. We signed it, of course."

"Of course."

"Theories can grow into rumors, and rumors can have a most damaging effect. The Warsaw Pact are quick to snap up any excuse to build up stocks of these things. We like to be able to say our hands are clean."

"Sure."

"Give a dog a bad name, you know."

"Exactly."

"Knew you'd understand."

"Oh, I do," I said, wondering what we were leading up to.

"So it's best not to talk about such things. However theoretically. Just in case some idiot takes it all seriously."

"No problem."

"That's fine, then. I've already got a similar assurance from Mrs. Duff-Jones, I should tell you. Just to be on the safe side."

"Right."

"Right."

Whatever it was, that seemed to be it. We moved on to the subject of Edward. I gathered that there was extreme distaste in the corridors of power over his defection to the powers of darkness, and in particular to the publicity that might result thereof. Edward's minister had received the news with all the enthusiasm of a diner in an expensive restaurant who finds one of his escargots walking off the plate. More than most ministries, it prided itself on an atmosphere of unshakeable dignity, like the Bank of England.

No, not ministry. Department! The Department of Trade and Industry. And that's another problem explained.

The rifleman had made the same mistake, when he made his last jibe about being the Man from the Ministry. I'd thought he meant the Ministry of Defense, but he didn't at all, he meant Edward's department, a ministry in effect but not in name. He must have known that Edward was a friend of mine, and the evil irony of the situation appealed to his weasel mind: he'd be laughing still to know how much trouble that remark had caused me, how far I'd been misled.

My visitor was still going on about unwelcome publicity, to do with Edward this time. "Fortunately," he said, "as Dundas got himself killed in France, British courts will not be involved. We anticipate a brief hearing here, at which the Police Judiciaire will no doubt put in a report of self-defense—*légitime défense*. The motive for the affray: well, the French always assume sexual jealousy if no other explanation is offered. Mrs. Dundas is an attractive woman?"

"Tricia? Oh yes," I said, "very."

"Well, there you are then. And Mrs. Warner, who will have to give evidence, is herself French, I understand, and will therefore receive maximum sympathy. I can see no problem there, can you?"

I was so dazed by his smooth ability to sweep any embarrassment under the carpet that I was slow to reply, but he took my assent for granted.

"Splendid. I think that about wraps it up."

It can't, I thought, surely it can't! People other than Edward have been killed in this war with Loewenfeld. The rifleman, still floating in his bog. Kevin, cut to pieces in the estuary. And the others . . .

"Something on your mind?" my visitor asked.

I didn't want to tell him. And I was sure he didn't want to know. There was no reason for that bog to be drained, and nothing to connect me with its occupant if it were. Kevin likewise, if anything remained after tides and fish had done their work. And Dominique, Loewenfeld—good God, how could I have become such a disaster area? That scenario would be accepted by the Loewenfeld side because any other would lead to a wider inquiry, which would be like a stick in their ant heap.

"No," I said, "nothing at all."

My visitor was packing up his troubles in his briefcase, collecting his hat and umbrella, and preparing to leave. He came to the bedside and bent to take my hand. I risked a slight squeeze; my chest muscles complained all the same.

"Just a last word," he said smilingly, "on what we've been talking about. It's a fact of life that publicity is *never* welcome in government departments, except when we originate it ourselves. Do, please, remember that. The poor old MoD in particular comes in for enough stick without inventing more. So your cooperation will be much appreciated."

As he spoke, I was aware of a hint of steel in his voice. Perhaps it had been there all the time, but there was no mistaking it now. As if in reply, I felt a strange sensation at the pit of my stomach. However, I nodded.

"Good. For our part, you may be glad of our assistance in connection with matters which, if not carefully handled, could become the subject of criminal prosecution. If you understand me."

He was smiling still, but the steel showed more clearly. I could see the edge of the blade, gleaming bright now, and ready for use. If necessary.

Oh yes.

He was watching my face carefully, and I expect it was quite a sight as, like some flashing fruit machine, it rang up the jackpot. Better late than never. And there was the consolation that I hadn't been such a fool after all.

"Oh yes," I said, "I understand you. I can recognize a stick and carrot when I see one. But it's all right—I think we're on the same side. It *is* essentially a defensive weapon, after all. Isn't it?"

He looked at me thoughtfully.

"After all I've been through . . ." I reminded him.

"No credits in this business."

"I have these nightmares, you see."

"You're not alone in that."

"And so?"

"Let's put it this way," he said. "Nobody wants to be forced into a nuclear war, do they?"

He made for the door, opened it, turned to wave a farewell with his umbrella handle.

"So, get some sleep, old chap," he said. And was gone.

ABOUT THE AUTHOR

MARTIN SYLVESTER was educated at Harrow and, after national service in Germany, became an architect. He ran a successful house and furniture design practice for many years before closing it to take up writing full time. He still, however, retains directorship of a modern furniture store in Oxford, and is a consultant wine buyer to the family-owned delicatessen in Devon. Martin Sylvester currently divides his time between Oxford and his farmhouse near Bordeaux.